DYING SECONDS

DYING SECONDS

NICK RIPPINGTON

Cabrilon Books

Published by Cabrilon Books

ISBN 978-0-9933323-2-6

Typesetting services by BOOKOW.COM

In memory of Nick Machin,
A great friend, a top journalist, a true legend

Acknowledgments

THE further you disappear down the rabbit hole of publishing, the more you realise how much you are indebted to people who give generously of their time and knowledge to help you out.

I would like to thank my editor Emma Mitchell for going through the book meticulously and spotting various inconsistencies and improvements. She made me axe a couple of my favourite chapters but which, in hindsight, were probably slowing down the story. I am grateful, too, that she never attempted to change my author's 'voice' at any stage and If it wasn't for Emma there might have been seven men called Pete in the book, for Pete's sake!

Thanks, too, go to my cover designer Jane Dixon-Smith who has produced another award-winning effort in my biased but humble opinion. I'd go as far as to say it is my favourite cover yet. Thanks Jane for searching through images, suggesting things that probably didn't work and things that do, and always being available to respond to my different whims.

Behind the scenes I got great advice on how police might conduct a murder inquiry from one of the Met's finest - we'll call him Mr G. You know who you are. We were put in touch by a mutual friend, the wonderful Nick Machin, who sadly passed away this year and to whom the book is dedicated. You may notice a Machin cropping up at some stage in the story. Nick, I am one of a great many who miss your upbeat, can-do attitude.

Thanks must also go to my long-time friend Laurie Bruce, who I have known since my family first moved to Bristol when I was seven. She put me right on a few matters about care homes, wheelchairs and South African history and politics.

I lost my dad too while writing this book, sadly. He was my greatest supporter and I still remember the day he read my first novel and rang up enthusiastically to tell me: "It's just like a real book!"

RIP Dad.

Finally, I am forever grateful for the support of my wife Liz and daughters Olivia and Jemma who have to put up with my grumbles and groans as I battle writers' block, computer glitches and the intricacies of marketing while trying also to hold down a taxing day job.

'I'm your biggest fan'

Stan, by Eminem

PROLOGUE

IT lay there, heavy, in the lining of his coat.

Through a forest of facial hair, the tramp's bloodshot eyes scanned the room full of lowlifes, many of whom would mug their mothers for loose change. Was anyone paying him special attention?

Goose bumps tap-danced along his spine like a column of ants seeking shelter beneath his tangled, greying, rock-star curls. Feeling vulnerable and afraid, he rubbed at his forehead, irritated by the prickly sweat forming there and amazed his body could react this way when the temperature barely rose above damn cold.

Eyes settling on a group in the corner playing dominoes, his finely attuned ears picked up laughter, banter and jokes interspersed with the odd argument, just normal guys letting off steam. They were the exception to the rule though. Like the tramp, most of the other customers found their closest companions to be loss, regret, shame or debt.

More self-respecting establishments would have pumped this tide of human flotsam out of the door long ago.

Not The Sheldon.

The landlord turned a blind eye to his customers' shortcomings simply because it gave him an edge in the market, affording him protection against an avalanche of economic pressures. Watching the publican serve the thirsty hordes gathered around the bar, the tramp pulled the donkey jacket closer around him.

The coat itself was the type once worn by Irish navvies on the building sites and had been the tramp's single constant companion for more than twenty years. When he first bought it, the jacket had provided him ample protection from the elements on the market stalls of London. Now it was a worn-out husk, the guts spilled out, the pockets ripped, all manner of things having fallen through the holes over time. It closely mirrored the story of his life.

Still, at least it provided a suitable hiding place for things he didn't want discovered. The padded envelope which nestled there now contained £3,000 in notes, enough cash to get him out of the shit, though, as with anything good, there were strings attached.

Patting the bulge, he allowed himself a moment of melancholy, thinking back to the last time he'd had real money, a time when he meant something to someone.

The teeth-jarring sound of warped wood scraping on uneven tile jump-started him back to the present. Looking in the direction of the noise he saw a tall, bulky figure push his way through the front entrance, watchful dark eyes peering out through skin the shade of mocha, jewellery dripping from throat and wrist, a gold tooth clearly on display.

Damn it!

It was too soon.

He needed time to collect his thoughts before the inevitable confrontation. Abandoning his drink, the tramp levered himself from behind the heavy, wrought-iron table and sank further back into the room, watching as the new arrival pushed his way through the crowded bar.

'Hey!'

The protest came from one of the domino crew, the tramp having nudged their table inadvertently in his haste to escape. Ignoring the complaint, he pushed hard at the rear door and disappeared into the alley beyond.

If it was cold inside The Sheldon, outside the bitter wind hit him full force, icy tentacles shooting through the dark to penetrate his bones. For God's sake, it was almost April. Surely, he had a right to expect it to be warmer. He doubted he would ever acclimatise to the weather in this godforsaken part of the world.

Holding his breath to block out the pungent smell of urine wafting from the outdoor toilet, he bowed his head and pressed on, his arms wrapped tightly around the jacket. Reaching a fork in the alley he turned left and, having escaped the prying glow of the solitary street lamp, stopped to light a rolled-up cigarette. The nicotine spread a welcome sense of calm through his body.

Whomp!

A hand clamped his mouth and a rabbit punch crashed into his kidneys. It knocked the breath from his lungs and he dropped the cigarette, following it to the ground. As the shadow hovered over him, the tramp felt a searing pain at his neck and reached for the affected area, a sticky, oily substance coating his fingers.

Prone on his knees, he looked up in the hope of identifying his assailant, but his vision was blurred, and he was unable to pick out any significant features. A palm pushed against his forehead and he fell backwards, head bouncing off the broken ground, thoughts pinballing around his brain.

The gurgle came from nowhere, the closest he could manage to a chuckle, the memory that flashed through his mind so out of place it was laughable, yet perfectly in keeping with this ludicrous situation. The last time he'd been flat on his back like this, some dirty slapper from Newcastle-under-Lyme had been riding him like a seaside donkey and making braying noises to match.

The flash of absurdity disappeared as quickly as it came, replaced by an involuntary shudder which travelled the length of his body to toes too numb to notice. By contrast, his head was stuck firm, like a fly in a gum-lined trap. In the bewildering moments that followed, there was the rapidly fading sound of gravel being displaced by heavy boots.

'No, please,' he mumbled. 'Don't go … I'm hurt! What am I supposed to have done?'

It was as if his protest was being filtered through cotton wool and he thought there was no chance of grabbing his attacker's attention.

He was wrong.

The footsteps slowed and stopped. The only sound now came from his own ragged breathing.

Then the crunching boots started up again, heading back in his direction until halting abruptly at his side. His assailant cleared his throat, and the tramp peered into the shadows of a hooded top, detecting fury in a pair of piercing eyes. With slowly dawning horror, he realised he was a sitting target for the missile falling out of the darkness. The slimy globule exploded on his cheek before rolling slowly into his beard.

'You know what you did.'

The words were delivered in a low growl. Did he recognise the voice? The tramp probed the depths of his memory and came up blank. The attacker sank down beside him and grabbed his right hand.

'But just in case you need a reminder …'

Hearing his knuckles crack, he prepared for more violence. Instead the other hand withdrew, and the figure stood, looked in both directions and then walked off, footsteps fading into the darkness.

The money!

Summoning his remaining energy, the tramp reached down and patted the lining of the coat, sighing with relief when he realised it was still there. The key was to live long enough to spend it. He couldn't let it end here, his lifeblood draining away in an anonymous alley. Not when he'd been given a second chance to make things right.

'Stabbed.'

A squeak of desperation entered his voice. 'Help! I've been stabbed.'

He listened carefully, but it was no use.

No one came running.

The words to the old Sinatra song passed through his brain, the cliché apt.

'Regrets, I've had a few.'

A damn lot really.

If he'd stayed in London perhaps his kids would still be speaking to him. He might be the proud father of a Premier League football star rather than the estranged parent of a boy crippled as a direct consequence of his selfishness. Now he would never get the chance to say sorry.

Sorry to the boy, his wife, his daughter, the other …

Pulse weakening, the chill air settled on him like a shroud. He closed his eyes, waiting for the end.

Hang on!

The eyes sprang open again as the tramp registered the item in his hand. Unclenching his fist, a scrunched-up piece of card slowly bloomed like a budding flower in a time-lapse film. Fully extended, it was slightly bigger than a beer mat.

The brief message was spelt out in capital letters and as he read it, an anguished protest formed on blood-caked lips.

'No, no, no! You don't understand.' His voice was a weak croak. 'I was trying to do the right thing. It's not what you think.'

A salty residue of tears staining his cheeks, he mustered his remaining reserves of energy and ripped up the card. Then, in a final act of defiance, he opened his fingers and urged the wind to carry the pieces away.

If he was to leave a legacy, it couldn't be this one.

Mission accomplished, the tramp let his head fall back, seeking in death the peace which had eluded him in life.

Part I

Recovery

'I never knew my father neither'

- Stan, by Eminem

ONE

January 2016

'CAREFUL you little twat, you're not driving around in one of your old bangers now!'

Arnold Dolan gripped the armrests of the chair as he bumped through another set of double doors, the wheels rumbling across the polished tiles.

'Sorry, Arnie,' said the younger man. 'Why didn't you get an electric one, though? Me and Mum would have clubbed together and got you one for Christmas.'

'You object to pushing me, Bruce, is that it?' said the man in the wheelchair, brushing his hand over his closely shaved head. 'After all I've done for you an' all.'

'Hey, I'm here aren't I?' said Bruce. 'You're lucky you got anyone left. The rest of the family have washed their hands of you and I can't see your pal Vickers burying the hatchet after what you done to his bird.'

'And what did I do exactly, Bruce? You shouldn't listen to tittle-tattle. It's like that bloody TV soap opera *Eastenders* round our way.'

Arnie, born and bred in Barking, east London, didn't even crack a smile at the irony in his words.

'All I know is you've upset a lot of people,' said Bruce. 'Even our sister's disowned you, and Anj used to be your number one fan.

It's going to take a lot for her to forgive you – you tried to kill her bloke, for fuck's sake.'

'Hey, Anj has to take a large portion of the blame for that. She helped create this bloody monster everyone thinks I am. Bitch!'

'Aww, don't call her names Arnie, you don't mean it,' said Bruce. 'She's our sis, and she's always looked out for you in the past.'

'Yeah, until she chose my "best friend" over me, her own flesh and blood. She sent me down for eight years.'

'She loves Gazza, though, don't she?' said Bruce. 'We all sussed it years ago, but you were too wrapped up in your own stuff to notice.'

'My own stuff? It was called developing the family business, Brucie boy,' said Arnie, warming up for a trademark rant. 'It needed 100 per cent concentration, 24/7 attention to detail. You can't be distracted from the job for a second or, bam! Someone else has stepped in and taken it from you. I didn't hear any of them complaining when I was making 'em all rich fuckers. Fuck 'em! I bet they'll all come around when they realise they can't do it without me, though. Look at our lovely older brothers, Chuck and Sly. How are they gonna keep it going, eh? If you took the best parts from both of them, you could assemble a pretty good idiot. They ain't got the nous – neither of 'em.'

He let out a mirthless laugh. 'Families eh? Can't live with 'em, can't kill 'em. Well, not without spending the rest of your life inside.'

Bruce shook his head, which was also covered in close-cropped stubble. You didn't need a birth certificate to work out the two men were related.

'I hear Anj has shacked up with Gazza down in Wales,' he said, changing the subject. 'She managed to get a hospital transfer. It's for Max's sake, you know?'

'Oh yeah, my nephew.' Arnie thought for a moment. 'Really, those two should be thanking me. It was me that introduced them. Bastards.'

'I doubt Gazza's gonna be sending you a thank-you card,' said Bruce. 'I imagine he don't write so well since you stuck a knife through his hand.'

'Wrong hand,' said Arnie. 'Anyway, I only meant to cut him a bit, teach him a lesson for taking the piss. He couldn't even see the error of his ways; felt he hadn't done anything wrong. I just exploded at that. I mean, if you ain't done something wrong why change your name and disappear? That's an admission of guilt in anyone's book.'

He fell silent again, mind fully immersed in the past.

'It's a horrible thing when it dawns on you there's no one you can trust,' he said, sparking back into life. 'Still, she owes me now, Anj does. She'll be back. I know she loves me whatever and, you're right, she's a good girl deep down. Compassionate. Nothing can change that. When she finally comes around, Gazza will come crawling back, too. What is it they say – time heals?'

Bruce raised his eyebrows, his disbelieving gaze focused on his brother.

'For fuck's sake, what would you have done?' Arnie asked him.

His raised voice attracted strange looks from an elderly group of residents sitting in a side room off the corridor. They were clearly unhappy the loudmouthed newcomer was disturbing their night's entertainment. He saw the opening credits for the *Antiques Roadshow* flash across a small TV screen in the corner, heard the famous theme tune. 'What are you lookin' at, you wrinkly old muppets?' he demanded, wheeling around to face his new audience. 'I may be in a Bader-bus but I can still sort you lot out – isn't that right, little bro? Eh? Still use my head, can't I?'

'What's a soddin' Bader-bus?' whispered Bruce.

'Oh, come on!' said Arnie, raising his voice again as the residents looked away, realising it might be best for their dwindling health not to make eye contact with the troublemaker. 'I know you're a thicko, but I can't believe you ain't heard that one. Think about it. What am I sitting in?'

Bruce went silent. 'A wheelchair?' Then he shook his head. 'Nah, I got nothing.'

'Douglas fuckin' Bader, ain't it?' said Arnie, raising his voice again. 'War hero who fought in the Battle of Britain. Ring any bells? I thought you learnt about the war in that fancy school of yours. I saw a film about this Bader bloke when I was in hospital. If it wasn't for the likes of him we'd all be talking Kraut. He had both his legs lopped off, but still whipped their arses. I've lost the use of mine ... hence calling this chariot of mine a fuckin'—'

'Excuse me! Please could you keep the swearing down?'

The raised voice came from behind them. Arnie looked over his shoulder to see a woman in a white uniform marching in his direction. She was in her mid-30s, black, with red streaks adorning hair cropped closely to her skull, her determined expression indicating you didn't mess with her.

'Oh fuckin' 'ell, here we go!' said Arnie. 'What's the problem, ossifer?'

'Think it's funny, do you?' she demanded, standing in front of him, feet anchored solidly to the ground and arms wrapped around her torso, cushioning an ample chest. He averted his eyes, focusing on a pair of white trainers. He had been caught staring, not that Arnie was usually bashful about anything. He couldn't argue with the fact she was a nice shape, though. She was just the way he liked them. Shame about ...

'Chill, sister,' he said. 'If I wanted to get into an argument with the Muslim Brotherhood I would do it intentionally. Hurt your little sensibilities, have I?'

'I'm Christian, not Muslim, for your information,' she said. 'Methodist. You should try some religion for size. It helps you get rid of any large chips that may be resting on your shoulders.'

'Come on, Bruce, ain't got no time to waste on jigaboos.'

Bruce went to push on, but she reached out and stopped him in his tracks.

'What did you say, mister?' she demanded, squatting and glaring into Arnie's eyes. He gave her his meanest stare, but she wouldn't back down.

'Ah, it's all right for you, picking on a bloody cripple,' he said. The self-pity was out of character, like an admission of defeat.

'For your information, you're not the only person in here confined to a wheelchair,' she said. 'I wouldn't be working here if I didn't care about people and I wouldn't dream of picking on anyone. We have rules against prejudice, though, so let's start again, shall we?'

'Sorry, sister, he's very tired,' Bruce interrupted. 'He's had a long and not particularly comfortable journey down from Cardiff. He's been in a few places since the accident in a bid to help him adjust but it's a slow process. We've brought him to Devon because this place came highly recommended.'

'Bloody expensive, too!' said Arnie.

'Shhhhh!' said Bruce.

'Well, first things first,' said the woman, addressing Bruce. 'I'm not a sister, I'm a care worker. What's his name?'

'I'm sitting right fuckin' here!' said Arnie.

'Don't f'ing swear!' she scolded, but there was a mischievous glint in her eye.

Looking up at her, at first his forehead creased in fury. Then the corners of his mouth turned up, he flopped back in the chair and burst out laughing. People could get the better of him once, but it was unheard of for them to do so twice.

'Funny!' he said. 'I like that. Forget my name. What's yours? You're all right.'

'Jeez mas'er, even though I is black?' she said in a fake African slave accent.

'Well, I'll have to overlook that for the moment, won't I? If you're going to be working here, I mean. Anyway, no need to ask the monkey when you can come straight to the organ grinder – I'm Arnie.'

She took a small pad from her pocket and flipped through it. 'Ah yes, Mr Arnold Dolan. Mas'er I's so grateful to you for letting me wait upon you. Ma name is Abigail,' she said in the mock accent.

'Oh, stop with the silly accent!' he said. 'This ain't *Driving Miss soddin' Daisy*. Come on, Bruce, can we find this bloody room?'

'Down here,' she indicated, a long, slender finger pointing along the corridor. 'We put you in the Presidential suite.'

THE room was OK. A bit small perhaps, but it was an improvement on Wandsworth Prison. He was only here for a few weeks to have some physio, rest and recuperation.

'Help us to the bog would you, Bruce?' he said. 'Reckon that fall has done something to my internal workings. I'm virtually bleedin' incontinent.'

'I'll get the nurse.'

'Fuck off, will you? You'll do it yourself. You're my brother, right? We're supposed to be blood. Least you can do is help me onto the fuckin' karzy. What's the matter with you?'

'I've had enough of your shit to last a lifetime, that's what,' said Bruce.

'Little cunt,' said Arnie, laughing.

'Nurse! Ah, look, there's a buzzer.' Bruce pulled the cord away from the headboard and pressed. They immediately heard a beeping sound in the distance. 'I'm sure they won't be long,' said Bruce. 'Now I've got to go. It's a long way back to Barking from here.'

'You're not staying?'

'I told Mum I'd be home and, anyway, Bernice said she'd come around and keep the bed warm.'

'And there was I thinking you batted for the other side.' Arnie chuckled.

'No, that's you. You keep telling us how well you did to last eight years in Wano – maybe you were the perfect bitch for some of the tough guys in there.'

Without warning Arnie swung at his younger brother, catching him in the stomach but overbalancing and sprawling onto the floor. Bruce fell backwards and, reaching out for something to steady himself, pulled down the curtain used by patients who needed privacy. 'You twat!' said Arnie, flopping around like a fish out of water.

'What on earth is going on here?' Abigail appeared in the doorway. 'Oh great! I can see you're going to be real trouble.'

'I don't need you!' said Arnie, grimacing as a pain shot through his abdomen.

'Yes, he does,' cut in Bruce, emerging from beneath the fallen curtains. 'He needs a bloody shit, sister, which is why I called you.'

'Right, well let me get him up then,' she said, ignoring the fact Bruce had elevated her to a higher rank once again. As she summoned up all her strength and lifted the patient back into the chair she looked over her shoulder at the younger Dolan. 'Now I think it would be best for all concerned if you left us to take care of your brother. You seem to be more of a hindrance than a help.'

Arnie felt satisfaction flood through him to see Bruce looking suitably chastised. He was starting to warm to this Abigail, which might explain why he was so unhappy at the thought of her seeing him at his most vulnerable. Still, at some stage he would have to face facts. He was a cripple, and that wasn't going to change. It didn't mean it was over for him though. He might have lost the use of his legs, but people had written him off before: that bastard Big Mo who called himself a father; his sister, his brothers and that fucking spunk donor Stan Marshall.

Out of all those who had deserted him, his entire sequence of misfortunes since birth could be laid at the doorstep of his biological dad, Stan the Man. Once he got out of here, he would make it his priority to find the man who had disowned him and left him at the mercy of others.

'Stick around until I'm done,' he told Bruce over his shoulder as Abigail pushed him into the large bathroom, the space adapted specifically for the disabled and wheelchair-users. Wheeling over a hoist, she then placed the sling underneath him before pressing a button to lift him out of the wheelchair. She swung him over to the toilet on the hoist, pulled down his designer tracksuit bottoms and lowered him. Gripping her arms, he was surprised at how much muscle she possessed for such a petite character.

'I've done a lot of heavy lifting in my time,' she said, reading his mind. 'I've plenty of experience and operating these things isn't easy. Normally I would call for a bit of assistance but you're pretty lightweight.'

'Yeah, I reckon I've lost at least a stone – most of it muscle,' he said. 'I'm wasting away in these hospitals. I need to get back to my fighting weight.'

'The physios can help with that,' she said. 'You've still got a grip on you, though, that's for sure. You're gonna leave me with bruises.'

'How can you tell?'

She gave him a hard look, raising her hand above her head. He flinched.

'It's OK,' she said, chuckling. 'I'm just getting the circulation flowing again. I don't hit those who are worse off than me. You can talk tough, but you need me, boy. Let's try to get along while we are stuck together.'

'I wasn't thinking. Sorry.'

'That's the problem, isn't it? People just blurt things out, not thinking how it might make the other person feel. I get it a lot, but I've learnt to turn the other cheek. My faith helps.'

A loud fart and an acrid smell interrupted their conversation.

'Oh fuck.'

His face coloured. He couldn't remember a time when he'd felt more embarrassed.

'That's the way I look at it,' she said. 'You can be black, white, yellow, green or even blue, but at some stage we all gotta take a dump.'

She turned and walked out of the door, leaving him alone with his shame.

TWO

'AH, Mr Dolan, isn't it?'

A podgy, colourless face stared down at Arnie, a shock of white hair flopping over wispy, thin eyebrows. The new arrival was practically Albino in appearance. He wore a fixed smile, the kind false service workers displayed when they instructed you to 'Have a nice day'.

'How are you, sir?' said the Albino. 'I hear you've been in the wars.'

Arnie had met plenty of misguided souls in the caring profession over the last few months. It was no secret they were paid a pittance, but their cheery outlook suggested they thought their good deeds would be fully rewarded in heaven.

Suckers.

Still, there was no point in looking a gift horse in the mouth.

'I'm OK … a bit sore,' said Arnie, determined to lay it on thick.

'Yeah, the work with the physio does that to you,' said the Albino. 'I'm sure it must be helping, though. I'm Malcolm, by the way, one of the night staff. I've just come back off two weeks hols. You seem to have settled in OK and my job is to help make you as comfortable as possible. Can I get you a nice cup of hot chocolate? You might appreciate it after your exertions.'

'Thanks. Tell you what I'd really like though. A TV. The Hammers are on tonight, big game against Newcastle.'

'You're a West Ham fan? I don't believe it!' said Malcolm, his face gaining a smidgen of colour. 'I follow the Hammers a bit myself. My granddad was from that neck of the woods.'

'Whereabouts?'

'Upminster. He used to take me to Upton Park as a young 'un. I loved it, that tense, close atmosphere, like everyone was one happy family; the shouting and rivalry with the opponents; the banter; singing the songs ...'

'I'm from Barking,' said Arnie. 'Me and my mates were regulars down there. Got into the odd scrape, you know? Who was your favourite player?'

'Oh, it was a while back now,' said Malcolm.

Bullshitter, thought Arnie. Probably never seen a game in his life.

'Come on, everyone has a favourite.'

'Well ... yeah, I guess it was, um, Paul Hartson.'

'John.'

'Eh?'

'It's John Hartson.'

Malcolm smacked his palm against his head. 'Of course, it is! What an idiot. Don't know where I got Paul from. Like I say, it was a long time ago. I was a nipper. Anyway, look ... I'll go and get that drink for you and see if I can purloin a TV. OK?'

Arnie watched him walk away, the swish of material caused by the care assistant's fatty thighs rubbing together. Bloke had to be 18 stone at least. Still, if he managed to get hold of a TV it didn't matter how unsightly he was, he would have served his purpose.

A SHORT while into the second half Arnie's eyelids felt heavy and he started drifting. The Hammers were getting a shoe-in from the bloody Geordies, 2-0 down at St James' Park. They had begun the season well under their new manager Slaven Bilic, but this was poor. Newcastle were bottom of the Premier League.

'Need some shut-eye?' asked Malcolm, sitting beside him. 'I'd better check on the other patients. Finish your drink, though, it will help you sleep.'

Arnie peered through a fog of semi-consciousness at the cup held out towards him, grabbed it and knocked back the sickly chocolate beverage. It was the second one Malcolm had bought him and though he hadn't really wanted it, there was no harm in keeping the slob onside.

Arnie had felt rough all afternoon and could put it down to a number of things, not least the torture administered by a physio called Dave earlier in the day. By the end of the session he wanted to punch the bloke's lights out. It was as if his tall, dark-haired tormentor didn't realise the extent of the pain he was inflicting on his patient. Either that or he was just a born sadist. Dave had explained in great detail how Arnie's muscles had lain dormant during his extended stay in care institutions and were in need of re-training.

Another reason he felt peaky was the uninspiring dinner they'd plonked in front of him. He'd managed the watery bowl of pea and ham soup but had only picked at the main course, some sort of savoury mince concoction, accompanied by lumpy mashed potato and stringy green beans, all wallowing in a pool of lukewarm sludge they had the cheek to call gravy. It had taken time, but he'd managed to eat most of it, something he was starting to regret.

His eyes sprang open as sharp, uncomfortable cramps launched a full-scale assault on his guts. He looked around for Malcolm, but the carer had long gone, the television turned off and the room cloaked in semi darkness. There was just a dim light escaping from the toilet area. Arnie's head throbbed out of control, his vision strangely blurred.

Clenching his teeth, he vowed to ride out the pain but when another jolt speared through him like an electric shock, he decided enough was enough. Reaching for the chord, he pressed the button, noting the travel clock at his bedside said it was just after 1.00 a.m. Where had the time gone?

When the night staff didn't turn up he began to feel mildly alarmed. So much for Malcolm's assurance he would be there to answer Arnie's every beck and call. He hated relying on people for anything, let alone something as intimate as using the toilet. His doctrine, developed in response to years of disappointment and betrayal, was that the only person you could truly trust was yourself.

Finding the TV control on the nightstand, he pressed the red button, hoping some late-night show might take his mind off his predicament. The screen flickered into life and he was assaulted by a deafening noise, the volume turned to maximum. Adjusting it, he realised it was tuned to a medical drama, a subject hardly likely to improve his mood. Channel-hopping quickly, he came across a group of people with shouty Mancunian accents, gathered around a bar.

'Northern muppets!' he muttered.

In a corner of the screen a woman performed motions with her hands. Sign language for the deaf. He was about to click off when the woman leaned towards him as if she was about to climb out of the set. Pointing a bony finger aggressively in his direction, she said, 'You're the biggest Muppet here.'

He sprang back in shock. Was he going crazy? Pressing the off button, he then threw the remote across the room. He was shaking, losing control.

'Nurse!' he shouted. 'Nurse!'

Vulnerable and paranoid, he watched the door expectantly. Was he being deliberately ignored? At the point of no return, he held his finger down on the buzzer, shouting, 'For fuck's sake! Call this a nursing home? Where is everyone?'

Staring upwards in frustration, he noted the ceiling was spinning, a strange gathering of flies congregating in the centre, a constant buzz drilling into his skull. Stop! He needed to concentrate.

Where was his wheelchair?

There!

If he could just get into it, he might somehow be able to manoeuvre it in the direction of the bathroom. He knew the odds were stacked against him, but never conceded anything without a fight. Sweat beading his brow, he swivelled until his body was facing in the direction of the wheelchair. He leaned out to grab hold of it but hadn't factored in the possibility the handbrake might be off. Making contact, the machine moved forwards and he slid off the bed, falling to the tiled floor.

He lay there trying to get his breath back, the gloomy ceiling swaying in his vision, the flies forming a pattern as he watched, spelling out the word LOSER.

'Nurse!'

The pitiful cry escaped from between cracked, sore lips as the floor began to pitch and toss, the sensation that of riding a giant wave. Slapping his hands against the tiles to slow the movement, his nails produced a scraping sound like chalk on a board. Unable to prevent the inevitable, the next to useless muscles in his midriff finally gave up the fight. Flopping over onto his stomach, he tried to crawl like a baby, stopping when he was overcome by a nauseating smell. Hot tears pricking his eyes, his body shuddered, and a tsunami of vomit projected from his mouth.

'Oh fuck! Look what we 'ave here.'

Out of the corner of his eye, Arnie saw the men in white coats arriving.

'Sozzy,' he said. 'I buzzzzed but you didn't come.'

All the voices, including his, were playing at the wrong speed.

'He buzzed us apparently. He thinks he's a waazzzzp! You believe him? What's hizzz name?'

'Dolan,' said his partner. 'Arnollld Dolan and, no, never heard a theeeng.'

'Dolan,' said the other. 'Ah yezzz. The gaaaangster. Doesn't look so tough to me, lying here in shit and vomit. Disgusting bastard.'

Arnie felt a burst of pain as a boot crashed into his ribs, forcing him to roll up in a ball for protection.

'Maybe we should get him to clean his own mess. Better still, perhaps he should eat it. That's what they do with puppies who aren't house trained, isn't it?'

For a brief moment Arnie was able to focus. This pair of bastards looked like a comedy act: One little, the other large. Shit! It dawned on him the big one was Malcolm, the care assistant who had been so attentive and helpful earlier in the evening. Why was he acting like this now? He tried to call the man's name, but no words came.

'Let him wallow in it, Benji,' Malcolm was saying to his partner-in-crime. 'We'll clean him up later.'

'OK.'

As the man called Benji went to join Malcolm at the exit, Arnie felt an excruciating pain in his hand. For fuck's sake, the bastard had trodden on it!

'Ayy, shoo!'

The smaller man turned back.

'You can't leave me like thish.'

The carer walked back to him, bent over, and lowered his face close to Arnie's, the breath sour and rancid, cheese and onion crisps combined with liberal dollops of garlic. Pulling a latex glove from his pocket, he snapped it on.

'Maybe you're right,' he said, sliding his hand down the back of Arnie's pyjamas then smearing excrement over the patient's cheek and top lip. The action brought Arnie out in a cold sweat, though he was convinced his stomach was already empty. Summoning up the fighting instinct that had served him well all his life, he slammed his teeth shut on the man's fingers.

'Fuck! Fuck! Mal, aaaaargh!' said Benji. 'Fucker's gunna bite my bastard fingers off. Help! Help!'

In the background an alarm went off, screams bouncing around Arnie's confused brain. The only way to stop them was to release his grip. He spat out the carer's damaged hand and the man fell to the floor amid the puke and shit. Through his hazy vision he saw Malcolm return and inspect the damage.

He leaned over Arnie, face like a giant marshmallow. 'Nasty little bastard,' he said. 'I'll make you pay for that.'

Arnie curled up again, waiting for the next assault. To an observer he looked distraught and beaten. He wasn't. He had retreated into his own mind, repeating five words over and over to himself.

Don't get mad, get even.

PEERING painfully through crusted eyelids, Arnie recognised a familiar figure on the periphery of his blurred vision.

'Abi … Abigail,' he muttered.

She paid him no attention and he felt a volcano of frustration build inside him as he realised his voice was imprisoned inside his own head. Another woman appeared, rolled up his sleeve and injected him with a liquid which pulsed through his veins. Almost instantly he felt a bit better.

Abigail was talking to someone just out of his sight.

'The only visitor he had was his brother,' she said. 'I didn't see anything untoward when they arrived and, to be fair, he didn't stay long.'

'Drug takers can be inventive.' A man's deep voice. 'Have we taken his drawers out and had a good old root around?'

'We found nothing that vaguely resembles illegal substances, Dr Snelling,' said Abigail. 'He only brought the bare minimum of things with him in the first place.'

'The night staffers are convinced he was on something,' said the doctor. 'They say Mr Dolan was having a fit on the floor, complaining of weird visions. When they went to assist he tried to bite one of the men's fingers off.'

'Bashtards!'

There was a brief moment's silence.

'What did he say?' the doctor asked, moving closer.

'I didn't catch it,' said Abigail. 'He probably wants some water. I bet he's dehydrated.'

'Keep him on the drip for now. After a while we should see the wood for the trees. I'll hand him over to you … Abigail, isn't it?'

'Yes, doctor.'

'Thank you, Abigail. Come on Dr Feltham, there's other patients more deserving of our attention.'

The two medical professionals left Arnie and his carer alone. Having taken a flannel from the sink, Abigail walked across and placed it on the patient's forehead. Then she filled a plastic cup from the jug of water on the bedside table and held it to his lips. It tasted scarily good, refreshing, helping to dispel the awful taste in his mouth.

For a while Arnie watched Abigail go about her business, tucking in sheets, plumping pillows, turning down blankets then tidying up around the room. She placed a cardboard vessel on the bedside table to use if he felt sick again.

'Abi.' His voice was croaky and thin but this time he was sure she could hear him. He watched her run a mop around the floor then rinse it in the bathroom before returning to his bedside.

'Arnold Dolan, what are we going to do with you?' she said. 'Drugs indeed!'

'Never,' he muttered.

'Why should I believe you?' she said. 'You're hardly a boy scout.'

'You can understand me?'

She nodded, and relief flooded through him.

'Listen,' he said. 'I don't do fuckin' drugs … it's against the rules.'

'Oh? And when did you abide by the rules?'

'I mean my rules … as a businessman.'

Despite herself, she laughed. 'You mean drug dealer?'

'Supplier, I would say, not dealer,' he said, attempting a smile. 'Successful, though. That wouldn't be the case if I used my own product.'

She put her hand to her chin, barely concealing her suspicion.

'Things have changed now, though, haven't they?' she said. 'You're not Mr Big any more. You've lost the use of your legs and are stuck here with us. If you needed a release … well, it's not like you don't know where to lay your hands on the stuff.'

She gave him another sip of water. Heaven.

'Whatever you think of me, I ain't a loser,' he blurted out. 'One of my best friends jumped from a balcony under the influence of pills and I won't ever forget it. Ruined his life. Others may have given up the ghost by the time they get here, but not me. While I've the faintest chance of fighting back, I won't turn to drugs.'

'How do you explain the fact you have a generous amount of phencyclidine inside you? You know what that is?'

'PCP. Angel Dust. Yeah, course,' said Arnie. 'There was a lot of it in Wano when I was locked up there. I never used it though. I'm a control freak. Have to be. If I started taking hallucinogens where the hell would I end up?'

'I don't know,' she said. 'Back in prison?'

He shrugged.

'Twelve years for manslaughter, out after eight wasn't it?' she said. 'Killed some innocent lad with a walking stick.'

'Have you been reading up on me?' he asked.

'It's been all over the news. Some retired rugby player has been telling his story to the papers, the one you had the fight with which led to you ending up here. It was his son you killed. Maybe it's on your conscience and you needed to 'escape' for a while.'

'Not me,' he said. 'I can live with it. You don't know the full story. Look, in prison I had to be on my guard constantly. If I'd been using I would have been an easy target.'

She was silent for a moment.

'Do you have another explanation?'

Arnie opened his mouth then closed it again. Only one scenario seemed likely as to how the powerful drug had got into his system and he wasn't ready to share his theory. Abigail seemed on the level, but how did he know for sure? At the end of the day she was one of them. Anyway, he knew from first-hand experience that opening up to people rarely did any good.

'You're the experts,' he said. 'You figure it out.'

'I'm a real whizz at Sudoku and love a crossword, but I can't do them without clues,' she said.

He attempted another smile, amazed at how this down-to-earth woman had the ability to amuse him.

'Whatever,' he said. 'Get me a phone, would ya? I'd like to speak to my brother.'

THREE

'WHO'S this Arnold fella then?'

The veteran sports editor of Wales' national Sunday newspaper looked over the top of his spectacles, studying his colleague's face with forensic zeal. They were quarantined off in one of the two *Sunday Tribune Despatch* conference rooms, earmarked for story interviews and bollockings.

'He was a mate back in my London days,' said Gareth Prince. 'We were pretty close once.'

'Pretty close on this occasion, too – close enough for you to get bloody stabbed, mun. You're lucky to be sitting here, the way I hear it. Bloke sounds like a ravin' nutter, comes at you with a knife and sticks it through your hand, for God's sake. If The Legend hadn't turned up you'd be mincemeat.'

Gareth prepared himself for fireworks. His boss Hugh Jackson, was becoming animated in that endearing way he did when he thought he was getting to the gist of a story. His eyes were sparkling, his hand scraping furious furrows through his whispy, corn-like hair.

'Time changes people,' said Gareth. 'Arnie spent eight years in Wandsworth Prison.'

'Yeah,' said the sports editor. 'For murder.'

'Manslaughter,' corrected Gareth.

'Whatever … you say potato, I say earthy root vegetable with knobbly bits. From any perspective it doesn't sound as if this Arnold character has been reformed by the system in any way. He was capable of terrible violence then and the same applies now. If I was to make an educated guess I'd say you changed your name from Gary Marshall to Gareth Prince to escape him … it makes more sense than the Hans Christian Andersen fairy story you spouted about a stalker girlfriend. God, how was I so naive? I should be furious at the way you hoodwinked me, boy. If I knew then what I know now, I would have kicked you out of those doors like a JW Owens conversion, butt.'

'But what, Jacko?'

'Eh? Oh, uh, no, I meant butt as in *butty* … friend … you know,' said Jacko. 'It's a Welsh term of endearment, though why I'm calling you a friend after the shit you've put me through I have no idea. The editor was far from impressed with these shenanigans. My head was on the block, too.'

'Sorry.'

The reporter studied the floor sheepishly, wondering when the old Welsh windbag would run out of steam. Gareth had certainly deceived him, but he found it hard to understand how an experienced journo like Jacko had failed to see through his thin tissue of lies. The story Gareth had constructed to land the job had been so flimsy it was deserving of close scrutiny. He had claimed he was an expert on rugby when the truth was he barely knew the basics.

Even after Gareth's appointment there were plenty of clues to his incompetence. Ghost-writing the column of Wales' greatest-living rugby player JW Owens, a man the locals referred to simply as The Legend, had been fraught with problems and it was only down to the help of work experience boy, Jason Shakespeare, that Gareth had muddled through. The teenager's encyclopaedic knowledge of the sport was so valuable to him that Gareth ended up lodging with the boy and his father, Will, in their valleys' cottage. Amazingly, the arrangement helped Gareth fall in love with his new home, an area as far removed as you could get from the edgy east London neighbourhood where he grew up.

Twiddling his thumbs nervously, Gareth wondered whether this private meeting with his boss was the beginning of the end. A reckoning had been looming but had been put on hold so that The Legend could recover from brain surgery and Gareth could write a series of articles about the rugby star's fascinating life, including the incident some headline writer had dramatically labelled, 'High Noon at the Millennium Stadium'.

That was the moment his former life had gatecrashed his new one in spectacular fashion. The Boxer Boys, a gang Gareth had run with in London, had tracked him down to Wales, resulting in a violent showdown.

'Despite your casual acquaintance with the truth, the one thing you have going for you is talent,' said Jacko. 'You did a fine job with The Legend. That series you wrote together after he came out of hospital helped circulation figures rise for the first time in a decade. When something like that happens even our lovely editor, Lana Desmund, isn't going to cut off her nose to spite her face. I understand you're doing a book now, published by us?'

Gareth nodded.

'She's still mad at you, mind, butt,' said Jacko, 'and I doubt she will be awarding you a medal any time soon, but she isn't stupid … which brings me to the real reason for this conversation. I've had a word with her and we've decided we need to make a few, umm, adjustments to the department.'

'Oh?'

Here goes, thought Gareth. What was in store for him? Tiddlywinks correspondent? Netball expert? Births, marriages and deaths reporter with a pay cut to match?

'It's pretty obvious to me you're not a rugby man so I don't see any merit keeping you in that role.'

Gareth couldn't argue. If he'd been in Jacko's position, he would have taken the same view.

'I've decided to take you off rugby and put you onto footie,' the sports editor said. 'Matty Lloyd, our current soccer writer, is off to the nationals. He's been tapped up by *The Sun* to cover Wales in the European Championships. Typical! No one up in that London takes any notice of our bloody football team for 58 years. Then our first bit of success comes along, and the Fleet Street wolves are knocking at our door, chasing after our little piggies.'

Gareth was dumbstruck. He wanted to leap up and punch the air in the way West Ham's Andy Carroll might after scoring a winning goal. Having been derided as a fraud, a cheat and a liar, Gareth's punishment was to be handed the job he'd coveted most since arriving in Wales. Inside he was chuckling, tickled by Jacko's reference to Fleet Street. All the national papers had departed the 'Street of Shame' years ago to make way for insurance companies and investment banks, but this was another sign Jacko's heart lay frozen in the 1970s, an era associated with the golden age of Welsh rugby.

'OK,' Gareth said, trying to keep his emotions in check. 'What about The Legend, though? Will I still be doing the column?'

'Ahhh, I'm afraid not, butt,' said Jacko. 'That's not to say you weren't any good at it mind, you did great, but I believe you had some help. Not from The Legend I hasten to add – he can't remember the last time he had a bath! No, I've taken the plunge, with Lana's seal of approval, to appoint someone new and fresh to the role.'

More good news, thought Gareth. He loved John Wallace Owens like a surrogate father and the fact someone was being appointed to keep an eye on him meant the ex-rugby star's services were being retained. Yet however much Gareth had grown to like The Legend, he couldn't deny the man was a nightmare to work with. He had a love-hate relationship with alcohol and a wardrobe full of clanking, moaning ghosts. Together they presented a big problem. To cap it all, the old rugby star was still recovering from life-saving surgery.

Gareth watched Jacko rise from his chair and cross to the door. Opening it, he shouted into the corridor, 'Come and join us, son.'

Gareth was perplexed when, moments later, a familiar face appeared in the doorway. For a brief moment, he thought the new arrival might be bringing Jacko a cup of tea or a bacon sandwich from the local greasy spoon.

'All right, Gar?' said the tall, muscle-bound youth, trapped in a blue suit a couple of sizes too small for him.

'J-Jason?' he stuttered in response.

'You remember this young man doing work experience with us, don't you, Mr Prince?' said Jacko. 'Of course, you do! You got on so well you moved into his gaff as I recall. Well, I thought with his knowledge of rugby he would be a useful acquisition. He knows all about this new-fangled social medium stuff: Titter, Facepaint —'

'Facebook,' corrected Jason.

'That's it. He's also told me he could launch a rugby vlog on You-whatsamacallit—'

'YouTube?'

'That's the fella. If all this nonsense actually pays the bills I'll be amazed, but the youngsters are into it and the Trib needs to move with the times. We need to give our readers online presents, isn't that what they say, like a gift for logging on to us?'

Gareth shook his head, a grin on his face. 'They actually mean presence, boss, like establishing ourselves on the internet.'

'S'what I said,' Jacko said huffily. 'I don't know, but once Jason is up and running he'll be able to teach us all about the interweb.'

Gareth rose, shaking the young man's hand enthusiastically. He felt the strength of Jason's grip transferred through his wrist. It reminded Gareth of Jason's hobby – partnering his father, Will, in a wrestling tag team called the Bard Guys.

'Steady on, Jase, I can't type with broken fingers,' he said, grimacing.

'Oh, uh, of course, Gar,' said Jason, releasing his grip instantly. 'Sorry, mun, I've been on the weights.'

'Right, I'll leave you boys to it,' said Jacko. 'Gareth, I need to know your ideas on how we cover Chrissy Coleman's Wales team in France. Jason, get up to speed with this whole Lions tour down under. Lana is keen to build on the success of The Legend story, promote the book and such, plus we have had a very good offer to 'share' our star columnist with the BBC. I'd start digging out your surfing gear, Jason, there's a good chance you'll be heading down under this summer.'

FOUR

GARETH clambered off the bus and walked the 100 yards along the narrow pavement to the picturesque cottage, its stone walls covered by clinging ivy. He made a note that he would have to tackle it when the weather warmed up having read about how destructive it could become when left unattended. At the moment it gave his new home a fairy tale quality which would only be enhanced when the pretty yellow and mauve flowers poked their heads out from the borders in late spring.

Pushing open the gate, he heard giggling emerge from behind the house and guessed his son, Max, was taking advantage of the unseasonably mild weather to use the 'practice goal' he'd installed in the back garden. Perhaps the five-year-old was playing football with a new friend from school.

Gareth had been in Wales for almost six months now and was growing used to the slower pace of life. When Max and his mum, Anjelica Dolan, had arrived from London to join him, the reporter had spent little time in snapping up the three-bedroom rental property in the valleys town of Pontyprenis.

Peering in through the bay window, he saw Anjie relaxing in the lounge with a cup of tea, the ironing board out and her nurse's uniform draped across it. Soon she would head off for an evening shift at the Cardiff University Hospital. She caught him looking and waved, making his heart skip a beat. He couldn't believe his luck that the two people he cared most about in the world shared his home, particularly when at one stage he thought they were destined to spend their lives apart.

As the excited voices grew louder, he recognised a deep-throated Welsh growl and smiled again.

'Come on, butty boy, you'll have to do better than that if you're going to be the next Gareth Bale!'

Unhooking the latch on the garden gate, Gareth walked through.

'So, you've already earmarked him for Wales, have you?' he said. 'I'm afraid that isn't going to happen. He's English born and bred and, when he's old enough, I intend to contact the scouts at West Ham and tell them all about him.'

A character with salt and pepper hair, fringe hanging down to his eyebrows like an ageing Beatle, stopped in his tracks, letting the small boy dribble around him and plant the ball in the net.

'Ahh, you'll change your tune, butt,' said JW Owens, the man all Wales knew as The Legend, as the young boy's triumphant shout of *Goal*! went up behind him.

'Should you be doing all this strenuous exercise?' asked Gareth. 'I thought you were meant to take it easy after your time in hospital.'

'What? You think now I've been given a new lease of life I should sit around all day, twiddling my thumbs until old age gets the better of me?' said The Legend. 'Not likely, Geraint, old ...'

'Enough!' shouted Gareth. 'The joke's over now. Ha Ha! Geraint, indeed. Your daughter told me all about your little ruse to wind me up by calling me by the wrong name.'

The Legend had a mischievous look on his face.

'Worked, though, didn't it?'

'Hey, Uncle John! Are you still playing? It's 5-0 to me now and you haven't got a hope of getting ... What are you doing? That's hand ball! You can't do that. Dad, tell him!'

Gareth watched as The Legend tucked the football under his arm and hurtled up the lawn, doing a couple of sidesteps to send the youngster the wrong way, before sliding along the floor on his substantial belly and coming to a stop inches from the flowerbeds, hands outstretched in front of him. He looked up with a smile on his face. The two spectators stared open-mouthed.

Levering himself carefully to his feet, his clothes covered in mud and grass stains, he held the ball out to Max. 'It's 5-5 now!' he said.

Max looked puzzled.

'You get one for a goal, boy, but there are five points for a try,' said The Legend. 'Always said rugby was better value than footie, and you don't have to roll around like those pampered wusses, screaming foul every time you get a little tap on the leg. Real man's game, rugby, and once you fit into the grand scheme of things you'll appreciate why it's the national sport of God's own country. *Wytti'ndeall?*'

'*Is diolch,*' said Max.

'Hang on! What the hell is going on here?' said Gareth.

'Uncle John is teaching me Welsh, Dad,' said Max. 'I'm going to have to learn it at school anyway. It's compatible.'

'Compulsory,' corrected The Legend. 'Quite right, too.'

'On my life, JW, I turn my back for one minute and here you are teaching my boy a language that no one else in the world understands,' said Gareth. 'What's the point?'

'He might want to stay here and work,' said JW, 'you know, get a job at the Welsh Assembly. I reckon he would make a great politician. Clever boy. By the way, 'On my life' is a bit of a Welsh phrase, so you're hardly one to talk. Bet you never used it in that London.'

Gareth had to concede the point. He had noticed himself lapsing into the Welsh way of speaking. Anjie said he had strong traces of a Welsh accent now, though colleagues at work still referred to him as The Cockney and made pitiful attempts at mimicking him.

'What brings you here, JW?'

'A few final preparations for tonight, innit, butt. Your wonderful wife …'

'Still girlfriend, I assure you …'

'OK, well, your wonderful girlfriend said she'd get my tux dry-cleaned so I popped round to pick it up. It should be great fun, don't you think? I've never been to a Welsh Media Awards ceremony before. Very classy.'

'I'm not sure about that,' said Gareth. 'The ceremonies I've been to in the past have been populated by drunken old journos having a go at each other and jeering each other's successes out of pure jealousy.'

'Great,' said JW. 'A bit like one of our rugby dinners back in the day, then. Did I ever tell you about the prop who drank aftershave?'

'Probably.'

'Tell us, please, Uncle John,' said Max.

'Oh, I'm not sure it's …' Gareth knew as soon as he spoke he was on a loser. Max loved JW's stories, and JW embellished them in order to shock the little boy.

'Well, I was at this dinner, see, after we gave your dad's lot a good mullering at Twickers,' said JW.

'You beat the English again?' Max looked at him in wide-eyed wonder.

'Course I did, boy. Never lost to 'em!'

The old man ruffled Max's black hair, something he'd inherited from his mother. It was growing fast, and he would need it cut soon.

'Anyway,' said The Legend, '…We all sat down to dinner and there were these little bottles next to every table setting, left by the sponsors. Very impressive, because in those days we didn't get paid for playing so these little gifts were perks of the job.'

'What happened, Uncle John?' asked the boy.

'Well, it was like this see, butt. I asked which of the English side would take me on in a drinking challenge and there was this one brain-dead prop who always wanted to get the better of me – on and off the field. Sure enough, he volunteered. I explained the rules. He would order a drink and we would knock it back in one, then I would do the same, and it would continue until one of us surrendered. Anyway, he called for port first off and we necked those – horrible stuff if you ask me, but he was obviously used to it from his posh English upbringing ...'

'JW,' Gareth warned.

'Go on, go on,' said Max excitedly, jumping up and down on his tiptoes.

'So next it was my call and I asked for vodkas – my favourite tipple back then, before I stopped the drinking ...'

Yeah, five months ago when you found out about the tumour, thought Gareth.

'So we knocked those back, too, and it was level,' said the old man. 'All eyes were on us now. His next choice was double whiskeys and after firing that back I was feeling a bit wobbly. He looked at me from under his thick, black eyebrows, a big smirk creeping across his face. It was as if he was telling me, "I've got you now. Doesn't matter which tipple you pick, I'm ready to finish you off". I wobbled a bit more for show then made some excuses and headed for the bathroom. When I returned, I grabbed the little gift bottle, which contained a well-known aftershave. Unscrewing the top, I slurred, "I nominate the aftershave" and he watched in amazement as I knocked it back in one. He didn't know what to do, mun, was shaking his head and all sorts, but of course his own side were encouraging him and there was pride at stake. As everyone stood and chanted his name, banging the tables and the like, he tipped his head back and swallowed the whole lot. Seconds later we were on the floor in stitches as he made a sharp exit. He didn't realise that when I'd gone to the toilet, I'd swapped the contents of my bottle for water. When he found out the truth I had to give him a wide berth for years, I can tell you, mun!'

Gareth saw tears of laughter streaming down his son's face. The reporter had heard the story a million times but couldn't help smiling – it was great to see his boy so happy. He was adapting to life in Wales far better than his parents could have anticipated. Max might be away from family and friends, but compensation came in the fact he could play in the open air whenever he wanted without some chancer trying to steal his football. Gareth remembered his own childhood and the moment knife-wielding thugs on the estate tried to rob him of his bike, only for Arnold Dolan to come to the rescue. Max was much better off out of that environment. In The Legend and the Shakespeares he had a whole new family to care for him.

'What's all this laughter about?' Anjie stuck her head through the gap in the patio doors. Max climbed from the floor and ran to her, giving her a hug.

'It's Uncle John,' he said. 'He made a man drink aftershave.'

'Yuck!' said Anjie, screwing up her face. 'Anyway, tea's ready. No aftershave on the menu just orange juice. Are you staying, JW?'

'No thanks, lovely, it's going to take a while to get my suit on, let alone that flamin' bow tie. Never mastered them, mind. I've had to wear loads, too, for my public speaking engagements. In the past I've been able to find someone to help me ...'

'Come back here when you're ready and I'll have a go if you like,' said Anjie, who treated the old man like a second father, not surprising when her real dad, Big Mo Dolan, had been behind bars for most of her formative years.

JW bowed, lifted her hand, and kissed it in the same chivalrous manner he had the first time they met. Gareth smiled again. He'd been doing that a lot lately.

WATCHING his son wolf down a plate of fish fingers, chips, beans and two slices of bread, Gareth wondered where the boy put it all. His bony frame gave no clue to his fast-developing appetite.

Gareth thought back to his own childhood, wondering if he'd been the same. He had faint recollections of meals at home, his baby sister distributing her dinner regally among them from her lofty position in the high chair.

'I'll call you G-Man. The G stands for Gannet not Gary.'

The memory made him flinch, his father's voice sounding clear inside his head. The nickname G-Man had stuck, it was just a shame the same couldn't be said of Stan Marshall, who had traded in his family for a young slapper. The shocking betrayal had a terrible effect on the teenage Gary Marshall. He and his father had only crossed paths once since then and that had ended badly with Gareth throwing a water jug at him during a hospital visit following the 'incident'. He rubbed his crippled leg subconsciously.

'Hey, I've got good news!' he said.

Anjie stacked plates in the dishwasher.

'What's that, love?'

'I told you I was having a meeting with Jacko today …?'

His girlfriend turned in his direction, concern etched on her face. That morning, he'd said he was expecting a tongue-lashing.

'So?'

'He's only gone and bloody promoted me!'

'Promotion? Seriously?'

'Well, kind of,' he said, backtracking. 'Some might say it's a sideways move. I don't suppose there is more money on offer, but he has taken me off rugby and put me onto football! I'm no longer the general dogsbody responsible for looking after JW and ghostwriting his column. Now I'm senior football writer and will be covering Wales at the European Championships in France. That's good, isn't it?'

She walked over to him, draping her arm across his shoulders and giving him a playful squeeze.

'Wonderful, honey,' she said, kissing him on the head. 'As a matter of fact, I've got some good news that might even top that.'

Looking up into sparkling dark eyes bookended by curtains of luxuriant black hair, he knew immediately.

'Oh my God,' he said. 'You're pregnant!'

FIVE

A CRUSTY bread roll bounced off Gareth's shoulder and landed in the dregs of The Legend's soup, causing the watery broth to splatter his shirt. Rising slowly, the ex-rugby player scanned the surrounding tables before his eyes landed on an individual sharing a laugh with his mates.

Studiously, JW Owens retrieved the roll, scraped it around his bowl then threw the perfect touchdown pass. It landed smack in the face of his target, a journalist from a rival Welsh newspaper. Standing, the victim wiped soup from his cheek and stared over, only for his embarrassed colleagues to pull him back into his seat. They had no interest in starting a war with The Legend.

Gareth wasn't surprised by any of it. Childish food fights had been part and parcel of these events for as long as he could remember. Outsiders might expect a gathering of the great and good from the world of journalism to be an austere, adult affair, where rival reporters swapped tales of political intrigue or discussed tough interviews they'd conducted. In truth, they were more like the last day of term at a school with an unruly reputation and unacceptable low exam marks.

At the end of the evening, men who arrived in pristine evening attire were likely to be found in various states of undress while women who had tried their best to outdo each other on the dressing-up front would hold each other's hair back and take turns chundering into the porcelain of a flooded toilet cubicle.

Gareth noted the clock on the wall creeping towards show time, the hubbub of noise rising beneath the high, vaulted ceiling.

'Exciting, isn't it, Gar?'

'Jeez, Jase, you've done it again!' said Gareth, chastising the man-boy sat next to him. 'You're silent for ages then burst into life and scare the shit out of me.'

'Sorry, Gar,' said Jason Shakespeare sheepishly. 'You were in another world there.'

'Sure,' said Gareth, holding a hand up in apology. 'I'm a bit on edge at the moment. Nothing's cut and dried.'

'Oh, come on, mun, there have been plenty of hints. Everyone says you did a brilliant job.'

'I couldn't have done it without you,' said Gareth, putting his hand on the younger man's shoulder. 'I didn't have the chance to say it earlier, but I'm absolutely made up for you about the job. Your dad must be so proud.'

'He didn't like journalists until he met you,' said Jason. 'He thought they spent all their time making up stories.'

'I didn't do much to dissuade him of that idea, did I?' said Gareth.

'He worships the ground you walk on, butt. He'll do anything for you. Claims you saved The Legend's life and gave me a new focus. He'd love to be here to see your moment of triumph.'

Studying Jason now, Gareth thought the boy had scrubbed up well, his thick black hair falling across the shoulders of a smart blue blazer. Shame about the dandruff.

'Let's hope there are many more evenings like this.'

Gareth clinked glasses with the 17-year-old. Although the boy still wasn't legally old enough to drink, no one would challenge him given his size and shape. To his credit, he wasn't knocking back the free wine, but sipping from a pint of bitter.

Opposite, Jacko seemed transfixed by the half-empty soup bowl in front of him. He had been deep in conversation with Lana for most of the afternoon, and Gareth suspected budgets and foreign trips were top of the agenda. It was strange for Jacko to be so quiet. Usually he would be regaling those in earshot with tales of his exploits as a Welsh rugby writer during the glorious 70s. Perhaps the meeting hadn't gone the way he had hoped.

Next to the sports editor, Sunday Trib feature writer, Quinten Tucker-Green, was rocking precariously on his chair, roaring with laughter over a story he'd just told news editor, Monica Matthews. She took a large swig from her tall glass of red wine and managed a demure chuckle.

In the background, the paper's picture editor, Len Frankstone, was bouncing around like a grasshopper with St Vitas Dance, pointing his camera in the direction of various guests and urging them to, 'Say Caerphilly'. Gareth felt sorry for the old boy. There was a time when he would have had one of his minions taking the photos. Now, with the advent of smartphones and selfies, the professional snapper was considered expendable. Anyone capable of taking a picture could find their work on the back pages these days.

At the far end of the room, Gareth could see a gathering of well-dressed people toasting each other with enthusiasm. He leant across to grab Jacko's attention.

'Care to talk us through the top table, boss?' he asked.

The sports editor's face lit up, glad for the chance to demonstrate his knowledge of the industry.

'Well, on the far left is the chairman of the Newspaper Society, Graeme Albrachtson. He was once a big wig on The Times, you know? That little git next to him is Percy Brookes, editor of the Press Pass.'

Gareth had been a subscriber to the industry magazine since college, but now tended to log onto the website when he wished to catch up with the latest gossip. It wasn't as if there were many jobs advertised in the publication these days.

'You don't like him?' asked Gareth.

Jacko peered over his glasses as if having trouble focusing.

'Who y'on about?'

'Brookes, the Press Pass editor.'

'Oh 'im!' said Jacko, as if suddenly re-connecting with his train of thought. 'S'all tittle-tattle, what he prints. That mag's just like one of them tabloids – doesn't care about the truth, just prints salacious gossip.'

Gareth decided it best not to point out that the Trib was a tabloid, too.

'I recognise the next person,' he said. 'That's Ernest Bonmayer the Third, right?'

The media mogul was the most recognisable person in the room due to his high-profile persona. He owned television stations, glossy magazines and newspapers on both sides of the Atlantic.

'Yeah and Lana's his guest,' said Jacko. 'She's got some great contacts, fair play. Never backward in coming forward that one.'

Though it sounded like praise, Gareth suspected Jacko was having a dig at the boss. Their relationship had turned the chilly side of frosty.

'Ha, look at that!' said Jacko too loudly, flapping his arms about as Lana bent forward and revealed her pronounced cleavage. It dawned on Gareth what was wrong; despite the early hour, the sports editor was paralytic drunk. Gareth put a finger to his lips in warning, but Jacko either failed to register the gesture or was choosing to ignore it.

'All over him like a rash, she is,' he said. 'It's like the old Hollywood casting couch. Knickers like a Grand National favourite she has, one shot at the big one and they're off!'

His exaggerated arm movement knocked over a wine glass, staining the table cloth and splashing onto his white ruffled shirt. 'Ah shit!' he shouted, dabbing at it with a napkin. 'She's bloody shot me … no surprise I guess.'

'Let me help you clean up, Jacko.'

The ever-dependable Monica materialised at his side, grabbing his arm and lifting him to his feet. Gareth was about to move around the table to give her a hand when she hissed, 'Stay there. You're the one likely to get an award. You'll have to make some excuses for him, say he was under the weather. I'm going to put him in a taxi.'

PLAQUES had been handed out for best news reporter, best photographer and best magazine supplement. They all went to newspapers on the English side of the Severn Bridge.

'Now we come to Scoop of the Year,' Albrachtson announced, pausing to afford the moment sufficient gravitas. Sadly, he let the anticipation last slightly too long.

'Get on with it!' shouted a heckler at the back of the room as others slowly banged the table with their cutlery.

'To announce this award, let me introduce a man I'm sure you all recognise,' said the embarrassed host. 'Please welcome Mr Ernest Bonmayer the Third.'

There was a smattering of applause, punctuated with the occasional offensive word. As the big man stood up, the room fell silent.

'I've read a lot of good stories in my time – and made the news often, too,' the guest of honour said in a voice straight out of America's deep south. 'I have to say, though, this tale captivated me. You've got a famous sportsman going through a traumatic time, a murder, retribution and an illness that lay dormant for years. It was excellent journalism, unrivalled.'

He let the words sink in.

'Of course, I'm talking about the Sunday Tribune Despatch's three-part series The Legend Fights Back. Without further ado, the award – to be presented by the Wales rugby coach Mr Martin Misry here,' he pointed to a man standing to the other side of Lana, '...goes to sports writer Gareth Prince of the Sunday Tribune Despatch and The Legend in question, Mr JW Owens.'

Gareth got to his feet amid a cacophony of cheers, stamping, banging of tables and clapping. Pride swelling in his chest, his heart thumped a tattoo as he scanned the faces he'd grown to know and love: Quinten giving him the big thumbs up, Monica blowing an exaggerated kiss, Jason with fingers pressed into the corners of his mouth to squeeze out a wolf whistle. The Legend? Shit, of course! He walked back a few steps and grabbed JW Owens, hugging him and lifting him to his feet.

'You're coming with me,' he whispered into the old man's ear. 'This is our award, not just mine.'

JW Owens looked at him, his eyes watering. He shook his head slowly. 'I've had plenty of these moments, son,' he said. 'This is yours. I don't want to do a John Terry on you.'

'Come on!' said Gareth, tugging at his arm. 'The reason people took the Mickey out of Terry was he turned up in full kit to celebrate Chelsea winning the Champions League when he wasn't even playing, having been sent off in the previous round. You've been with me all the way. Without you I might not be here at all. So, no arguments. If we stand here much longer, they'll give the award to someone else!'

Reluctantly the old man walked beside him through the labyrinth of tables. People shook hands with the former Welsh rugby star as they went, whispering, 'Well done,' or giving him a pat on the back. Gareth thought of his mother and how proud she would be of his achievement. He wished she was there. He walked along the top table shaking hands with everyone – just like a cup final winner. When he got to Lana her fingers were cold and her handshake limp.

'Well done, young man,' she whispered. 'You're a very lucky person to be standing there right now.'

Slightly taken aback, Gareth moved on. In contrast to Lana, the Wales rugby coach Martin Misry, shook his hand vigorously and said he looked forward to working with Gareth in the future, unaware their paths were unlikely to cross now the department was being restructured.

Taking the offered trophy, Gareth was distracted by a female shriek followed by a spontaneous outburst of applause and laughter. The Legend had attempted to hurdle the top table and was in the process of planting a slobbering kiss on the lips of Lana. The editor pulled away sharply, disgust etched on her face.

'Mr Owens, what the hell do you think you're doing?' she demanded.

'Just showing my adoration for the fairer sex,' he said, grinning.

It was a private joke and only three of them knew the punchline. Gareth recalled the moment he and The Legend had been caught in what appeared to be a compromising position by Lana. The truth was the reporter was merely helping a hungover JW put his pants on after he'd slept overnight in the office following a massive bender.

'That showed her,' he whispered on joining Gareth.

'Yeah,' Gareth said. 'I think HR call it sexual harassment and it carries a penalty of instant dismissal.'

'Ahh well, at least if she gets rid of me I'll have something to remember.'

The Legend's booming laugh accompanied them back to the Despatch table. Gareth had the feeling the continued applause owed much to The Legend's little display. Typical, he thought. The old man didn't want to steal the limelight but had managed it all the same.

LATER in the evening Gareth grabbed Jason and the two of them went in search of JW Owens to impart more good news. They found him at the bar, sipping coke and regaling Martin Misry with some of his old tales. The Kiwi, a man of few words, was nodding politely. Gareth asked if it was OK to intervene and the rugby coach agreed.

'Gareth, mun, what an evening,' said The Legend. 'Are you enjoying it?'

'Just fine, JW. You?'

'Fantastic,' he said. 'I was just putting Mr Misry right on a few things. I suspect the offer of a coaching role is in the post as we speak.'

Gareth nodded slowly. 'They probably do it by email these days,' he said.

'Not another new skill I have to learn.'

Gareth smiled. He knew the old man wasn't as old in the tooth as he pretended to be. He was a dab hand on Skype, which enabled him to talk face-to-face with his daughter and grandson in Australia.

'How would you like to see Ellie and John again soon?' asked Gareth.

'Would I!' said The Legend. 'Are they coming over?'

'No,' said Gareth. 'This time you're going to visit them.'

The Legend looked perplexed, so Gareth filled in the blanks. 'Lana has struck a deal to share you with the Beeb on the Lions' tour. Fantastic, isn't it? You get a free flight to see your family and we get to use your expert analysis throughout the Test series. It's a win-win. You'll stay for a month. What do you think of that?'

The Legend said nothing.

'JW?'

'Did anyone consider asking my thoughts on the subject?'

His stern expression told Gareth it was the prelude to a wind-up. The old man could be a master of deception.

'Come on, JW,' said Gareth, stifling a laugh. 'I assumed you would be over the moon. Don't mess ...'

'We all know what assume did, don't we?' said The Legend angrily. 'It made an ass out of you and I.'

'Um, I think that's supposed to be out of u and me,' said Gareth. 'That's what I said.'

The Legend began muttering through clenched teeth, eager that others didn't pick up on their disagreement. 'Hell, I can't just up sticks and leave? I've got responsibilities. I've said I'll feed next door's cat and ...'

'JW, it's Australia, mate,' said Gareth. 'A Lions tour there must be closer to your heart than any other rugby series. It's where you made your name and achieved your legendary status … and it should amount to a tidy little earner.'

The Legend let out a loud 'Hmmmph!' and started to walk away.

'JW! Hey! What's the matter? Are you OK? It's not …'

The old man turned back, his eyes burning with anger. 'It's nothing to do with my bloody tumour if that's what you're thinking, Gareth, mun! I just hate people making plans for me without asking … that's all. I'm a grown man, so why do people insist on treating me like a little kid?'

He turned and marched away, pushing through the crowd surrounding the bar. Gareth looked at Jason.

'Well that went well,' he said.

The younger man shrugged his shoulders. 'Give him a chance, Gareth, mun. He's probably tired. It's been quite a night and it was just a few months ago he was in a coma and no one was sure if he would live or die. Perhaps he doesn't get on with someone at the BBC. I'm sure he'll come around, given time.'

'Maybe,' said Gareth. He wasn't so sure. From the one occasion he had been on the wrong end of JW Owens's wrath previously, he knew how much provocation it took for the former rugby star to lose his temper.

SIX

'MY God, what happened to you, Pete?' The man with the prematurely greying hair stared at his friend's face. 'Are you OK to play? We can do this another time. Just say the word.'

Pete Vickers picked up his squash racket. 'I'm fine,' he said. 'I got mugged on my way home the other night. No big deal.' He put his hand to the swollen eye, willing the bruises to fade before the entire Romford Squash Club got on his case.

'Speak to the police?' asked Rupert, a 6ft 2in investment banker who belonged to the same squash ladder. Vickers had joined the club at Christmas to improve his fitness levels having continually asked himself whether things might have been different had he been in better shape. All the business lunches, meetings in pubs and clubs and living the high life had taken their toll as Vickers introduced the Boxer Boys to circles of power, influence and money. He had achieved many of his targets only to be treated like a mug by Arnie Dolan, who had paid him back by raping his wife.

'Little scrotes wore hoodies,' he said. 'You know what the cops are like. If they can't identify the culprits from CCTV, they'll send some gimp around to tell you about the criminal compensation board and advise you how better to protect yourself in future – you know, carry a flashlight and avoid dark corners – easy work if you can get it. They didn't take much, a mobile phone and a couple of credit cards. I cancelled them immediately.'

Rupert nodded.

'They'll be well into the wind by now, I guess. Why don't we reschedule?'

'Honestly, it looks worse than it is,' said Vickers. 'Come on, let's get it done.'

'If you're sure,' said Rupert. 'How is that lovely wife of yours, by the way, and the kids?'

Vickers felt the silence crowd in around him. What to say? He had no wish to discuss his private life with a bloody investment banker, but to avoid the question might make him the target for gossip in squash circles, something he could ill afford.

'Same old, same old …' he said.

'Right.' Rupert looked at him expectantly.

'To be honest, Janie's not been up to much lately,' Vickers revealed. 'Her mother's in a bad way. Cancer.'

Stop now, he told himself. There were a couple of other blokes in the dressing room preparing for a game and he knew Janie wouldn't like him giving away personal secrets. Not that she would know. This was strictly his domain.

'Our marriage is on the rocks.'

There. He'd said it. The two guys on the bench wandered over, radars alerted.

'Shit, mate, sorry to hear that,' said Rupert. 'Beaten up, shit going on at home … Having an affair, is she?'

'What?' Frustration got the better of him. 'No! Why would you say that?'

'It's not uncommon is it? You two married young, maybe—'

'Janie wouldn't do that,' Vickers said. 'There are the kids.'

'Course.'

'She being out of order?' said a rough-looking bloke called Barry who had made his money from selling electronic gadgets. He was from south of the river which made him instantly dislikeable to Pete. 'If she's a bit lippy just give her a slap. Only thing my Mrs understands.'

Vickers thought there must have been something wrong with his hearing. This bloke had never met Janie and he was advocating violence against her. Vickers felt an overwhelming urge to slap gadget man himself.

'You want to get away for a bit, mate,' Barry was saying, oblivious to the disgusted look on Vickers' face. 'Why not come with us to Euro 2016? It'll be full of the five F's: France, Football, Fighting, Fucking and Fun... not to mention plenty of sherbets. It's gonna be great and will take your mind off the trouble and strife.'

Vickers deciphered the cockney slang: sherbets was a term used for beer while trouble and strife meant wife. He ignored Barry and turned back to his playing partner.

'You're right, Rupe, this is probably a mistake,' he said. 'I can't handle 20 questions right now.'

Disappointed, the other two squash players drifted back to their bench, putting clothes in lockers and collecting their rackets. Vickers watched, amazed that anyone could think he was capable of hitting his wife. People like Barry might live in decent houses with a nice car and all mod cons, but who knew what went on behind the curtains?

He picked up his bag then shook Rupert's hand. 'Thanks, mate. We need to have a chat about those private family investments when you get a mo. I may be in need of them before long with home life the way it is.'

'Sure,' said the banker.

As he was leaving Vickers heard Rupert call his name again. He turned.

'Hope it sorts itself out, you and Janie,' he said. 'If you need anyone to talk to...'

I won't pick any of you bastards, Vickers thought, waving a hand over his shoulder as he headed for the exit.

OUTSIDE, the rain was lashing down. He pulled up the collar of his knee-length designer coat and headed for the car, his mind anticipating the frosty reception he could expect at home. It made him want to cry.

Until the day of Arnie's release, life had been drifting along flaw-lessly. Vickers was a practical guy, not prone to fairy tales, but for him it was the perfect dream. Janie had always been his shining light in a sea of ordinary local girls and no man in the world could have been happier when he finally won her over. After a string of fantastic dates, he summoned up the courage to ask for her hand in marriage and without the slightest hesitation she said, 'Yes.' Break-ing the news to Arnie, who had shared an on-off relationship with Janie during their teens, Vickers was relieved to find his best mate didn't seem too concerned, his attention fully focused on life be-hind bars.

Janie was four months gone with their first child, Simon, when Vickers dragged her up the aisle and, a couple of years later, daugh-ter Diane completed the family unit. Things couldn't have been better, but Vickers was well aware that best-laid plans could be destroyed in the blink of an eye in his line of business. Even so, the murky world of drug dealing and extortion began to seem more secure as the money rolled in. He played his part, making sure the operation ran smoothly and building in safeguards. It helped that a few of the Met's finest were on the Boxer Boys' payroll.

Only occasionally did he get his hands dirty. Normally Chuck, Sly, Fancy Man and their little crew of toughs sorted out the murky side of the business and, as the acceptable face of the enterprise, Vickers lived accordingly, sending his kids to the best schools and keeping Janie in the lifestyle to which she'd become accustomed. Then Arnie got out and everything turned to shit.

In the multi-storey car park next to the squash club, Vickers became aware of a figure leaning against his top-of-the-range BMW2 Series Gran Tourer. The seven-seater people carrier in metallic blue was his reward to himself for standing up to Arnie and telling him that he was being deposed as leader of the Boxer Boys. That had taken guts, knowing the way Arnie's mind worked and that his mantra was, 'Don't get mad, get even'.

'Get your filthy mitts off my wheels!' he shouted.

A man with long, unkempt, light-brown hair pushed himself away from the vehicle and walked towards him. Mitchell Tiggs had never been a slave to fashion. Today he was wearing matching jacket and pants, the double-denim combination considered a definite no-no with fashionistas. Rolling up his sleeve, he scratched at a new tattoo adorning his arm.

'All right, Pete?' he said as he approached. 'Oww! That looks painful.'

'It's nothing,' Vickers said, again touching his bad eye. 'I had an argument with the garage door. More to the point, why are you leaning on my soddin' car? Cost an arm and a leg that did, Tigger. You want a bruise like this?'

'Sorry.'

Tigger had a desperate look about him, eyes always on the move, darting to and fro as if he was expecting a SWAT team to appear any second and throw him to the ground, like in those American cop shows he loved.

'So how's my favourite drug dealer, eh?' asked Vickers. 'I thought I told you to contact me directly only in a real emergency.'

'Right,' said Tiggs.

Vickers felt uneasy.

'Let's talk in the car,' he said. 'I'll have to put a rug on the seat, though. Those fuckin' kecks don't look like they've been washed in ages, and I've just had the thing valeted.'

If the other man was offended, he didn't show it. He was used to being on the receiving end of this sort of treatment. He fell into step behind Vickers as they walked to the car.

'MISSING? What do you mean, missing?' Vickers leaned across the table of the greasy spoon cafe halfway along the A127 dual carriageway between London and Southend.

'They didn't report in,' said Tigger. 'Two of my best street men. They were doing a roaring trade around the housing estates of Leyton and Walthamstow … then nothing.'

'I hope they're not ripping us off,' said Vickers.

'They wouldn't do that,' said Tigger. 'I know them. Loyal to a fault and, to be honest, they ain't got the brains.'

Falling silent, Tigger studied another scar on his arm, a permanent reminder of what could happen if someone suspected you of turning over your own crew.

'Old Bill?'

'Neither of them has come across the coppers' radar,' said Tigger. 'I suppose it could be an ultra-secret drug squad operation.'

'You were right to come to me,' said Vickers. 'News travels fast. Perhaps the Leyton Albanians have heard about all the shit concerning Arnie and decided to strike while we're looking the other way. I'll mention it to Chuck, see what he thinks.'

His phone chirped. Vickers looked at the number, sighed and put it to his ear. 'Yeah?' He listened for a second. 'Oh God, OK, love, I clean forgot … I know. Something came up.' He paused, trying to think of a way to shut the conversation down quickly before Mitchell Tiggs registered the loud voice on the other end of the line and put two and two together. The drug pusher was the last person he wanted to have a peephole into his private life.

'OK, I'll be home now.' He went quiet again and listened. 'No, I didn't get around to having a game today. This was more important. Be there as soon as I can.'

He closed the phone.

'Trouble?'

Vickers ignored the question. 'I've got to head off,' he said. 'I'll get in touch with Chuck and we'll put out feelers about your missing boys.'

'Thanks, Pete.'

Vickers levered himself out of the booth and headed for the door.

'Hey! You ain't gonna leave me here are you?' Tigger protested. 'I ain't had my fry up yet. How the fuck do I get back?'

'You're a man of many resources,' said Vickers, without changing his stride. 'You'll figure it out.'

SEVEN

'YOU believe the little fucker?' Chuck Dolan sat opposite Pete Vickers in the Hope and Anchor pub on the Boxers' Estate, Barking.

'No reason to doubt him,' said Vickers. 'He isn't clever or devious enough to make something like this up. How long has he been doing this for? He was with us from the start and has never done anything to rock the boat. If he was going to pull a fast one he would have done it when Arnie was banged up. I honestly don't think he would skim off the top.'

'He was scared shitless of Arnie,' said Chuck. 'My bastard brother knew exactly which buttons to press. Tigger might feel a bit more adventurous given the change in circumstances.'

'He wouldn't take you lightly, Chuck,' said Vickers.

'Wow, who clocked you, Vickers?'

Sylvester, the second eldest of the Dolan clan, placed a tray of drinks on the table.

'Accident at home,' said Vickers.

'Ain't seen the Raspberry, have you?' asked the man known as Sly to his friends.

Vickers looked confused.

'Oh sorry, Pete, I keep forgetting you're a bit posher than the rest of us. Cockney rhyming slang, ain't it – Raspberry Ripple? Cripple!'

The two Dolan brothers burst out laughing. They spent so long in each other's company they shared everything, including a warped sense of humour.

'This has nothing to do with Arnie,' said Chuck when the laughter died down. 'Pete says a couple of street kids have gone AWOL; Mick Fuzz and Tommy Weddle.'

'Shit. Anyone spoken to the Turk?'

Sly was referring to Ishmal Durak, the man at the very top of the drug pyramid north of the river. Well connected, the Turkish 'businessman' was a major cog in an illegal import business worth billions of pounds. The Boxer Boys were one of Durak's 'branches' and had done a top job distributing his product throughout the East End, feeding back a generous percentage to keep him sweet. The relationship had thrived over many years.

'As far as I'm concerned, he doesn't need to know,' said Chuck.

'I guess he'd only tell us to clean up our own mess,' said Sly. 'He won't be that bothered.'

'Wrong,' said Vickers. 'If there's one thing I've learnt about Mr Durak it's that he doesn't like bumps in the road. He runs a smooth operation, and nothing can lead back to him. People go missing, the Old Bill come calling. If his supply chain is threatened, he'll burn his bridges. There's always someone willing to do what we do. We're expendable.'

'He'll be happy as long as he gets what he wants,' said Chuck. 'We've just got to make sure that's the case.'

'And therein lies a problem,' said Vickers.

'Oh?'

Vickers finished his drink and started on the next, the alcohol soothing his anxiety.

'These two missing boys weren't just members of Tigger's street teams – they each led 10-man operations. They had just made their weekly collections and were carrying plenty of cash when they did their vanishing act. Their mobile numbers are unobtainable, and no one has seen them for two days.'

'We'll monitor the Eurostar and the airports,' said Chuck. 'Sounds like they did a bunk. Classic behaviour.'

'It is,' Vickers agreed. 'Except Tigger checked with their families: no clothes packed, no suitcases taken and they didn't even have their passports.'

Falling silent, they considered the implications.

'There are a lot of nasty new firms sprouting up in this neck of the woods,' Vickers said eventually. 'They come from Lithuania, Bulgaria, Albania, Russia … and they all want a slice of the pie. Maybe they're challenging us.'

'Fuck.'

Chuck's phone buzzed, and he glanced at the number. 'I've got to take this … I'll make inquiries. How do we deal with the Turk?'

'Mad money,' said Vickers.

'What?'

'You know the stuff your mum gives you when you're a kid in case you got stranded somewhere and need a taxi home?'

The Dolan brothers looked perplexed.

'Never mind. What I mean is I made sure we had some "insurance" to protect us against something like this. Other than that, who fancies organising a whip round?'

CHUCK held the handset to one ear and blocked the other, the traffic on the main road making it difficult to translate the West Country accent on the end of the line.

'He was in a right state, lying on the floor covered in his own shit,' the voice said. 'Those drugs worked a treat. What were they?'

'PCP cut with a healthy dose of laxative. My friendly neighbourhood chemist obliged.' Chuck laughed.

'Any more you can get your hands on would be gratefully received. He's a nasty little fucker, though, nearly bit Benji's finger off. Danger money wouldn't go amiss.'

'You're being paid well enough and you can't say I didn't warn you about him,' said Chuck.

'Fortunately, your man's memory is shot,' said the caller, 'and I don't think them bigwigs will believe his story, especially with his past reputation.'

Good, thought Chuck. He intended to destroy every ounce of self-respect his brother Arnold had.

EIGHT

ABIGAIL peered at the screen. The picture wasn't crystal clear, but she could make out the staff kitchen area. Out-of-bounds to the residents, only those employed there were allowed to enter. She identified the familiar white counters where the meals were prepared, the stainless-steel sink unit and the giant fridge-freezer. In the corner, an industrial-sized hob/oven stood.

The top of a head came into view. The figure was blurry but, as the person moved further into shot, she could make out the white overalls worn by members of the care team. She watched the blurry figure remove a large plastic tub from the fridge. She was unable to make out the label but could hazard a good guess as to what it contained. 'Pea and ham soup,' she muttered under her breath.

Abigail Winstone had used her charm to get access to the CCTV footage. Bernie, the security guard, had made no secret of his desire for her and was hoping the favour might put him on the road to getting lucky. No chance. The old lech might think he'd stored one in the bank, but Abi wasn't that stupid. She had simply used her feminine wiles to get what she wanted.

Leaning closer to the screen, she asked herself for the umpteenth time why she was taking the risk. Her patient, Arnold Dolan, had done nothing to merit her help and what she was doing was a sackable offence. She guessed her in-built sense of justice and fair play had overpowered her common sense.

It had been obvious from their first meeting that Arnie was a bigot and a racist and since then she'd discovered he was also a drug dealer and all-round bad boy. Her mum would never have approved of these 'attributes' when insisting her only daughter looked for the inherent goodness in people. Abi was pretty sure there were other skeletons in Arnie's cupboard, too. An aura of danger radiated from him like heat from tarmac on a sweltering day.

For all his faults, though, she didn't believe dishonesty to be one of them. His opinions might be abhorrent, but they were honestly held, and he didn't attempt to disguise them. She suspected they were born of ignorance, based on the fact the only people he'd encountered of different ethnic origins had probably been out to do him harm. There was bad and good in all shades of humanity.

Over the last few days Abi felt she'd been breaking down the barriers between them. Her grandfather, bless him, had always insisted it would be a huge job to wipe out prejudice, but you had to work on 'one person at a time'.

Of course, Arnie might be a consummate liar, in which case he'd done a masterful job in pulling the wool over her eyes. He'd insisted he hadn't taken any illegal substances on the ward, the inference being that someone on the night staff had tampered with his food or medicine. Though she questioned why that might happen when it was highly unlikely anyone on the staff knew who he was, she felt it her duty to investigate. At least by doing so she could erase any question of doubt she might have about her colleagues.

She redirected her wandering thoughts to the screen. Freezing the frame, she enlarged the picture in the way Bernie had shown her. The figure was grainy, the definition adversely affected by the alteration. She couldn't make out who it was, though she had her suspicions. He was now heating milk on the hob, but the thing that had caught her attention was something he was removing from his right-hand pocket.

A ziplock freezer bag.

Holding her breath, she returned the picture to normal size and let the video run on.

The character pulled down a tin, then opened it and spooned a brown substance into a cup. Hot Chocolate. For a moment he disappeared from view then returned moments later with the polythene baggy open in his hand. As she watched, he sprinkled a small amount into the cup, added the milk and stirred.

'Gotcha!' she said excitedly.

'WILL you tell your bosses?'

Arnie was animated, looking her directly in the eye.

'I can't.'

'Oh?'

'I shouldn't have been in there. It's out-of-bounds to the staff. Imagine if a patient complained that a member of staff was badly treating them?'

'Like me, you mean?'

'Why, are you going to complain?'

'No, because no one will believe me without the evidence and they won't look for it because they don't believe me. You see, we ex-cons are discriminated against, too. I'm in – what's it called – oh yeah, Catch-22.'

He had a point.

'Anyway,' she said, 'if everyone was allowed in there it's feasible security footage could go missing that was needed to investigate a complaint.'

Arnie fell silent, his brain churning.

'What about the security guard?'

'He isn't the sharpest tool in the box.'

'OK. You could brief him, though?'

'Not without …' She went silent, letting him read between the lines. 'Anyway, it isn't clear who did it.'

'Oh, I know who bloody did it.'

'You're sure? Who?'

He put his finger to his nose. 'Need-to-know basis,' he said.

'For God's sake!' She finally lost her temper. 'Here I am trying to help you and…'

'Shhhh!' he said. 'You'll get yourself in trouble, darlin'. Look, you've been a great help. I can wipe him off my Christmas card list now. I'm getting out of this dump today anyway, no one wants me here. My brother's coming to get me.'

'But what about your physio?' she said.

'I ain't a pauper. I'll continue my rehab at home. This place was costing me an arm and a leg as it is,' he smirked. 'An arm and a leg. Getit?'

She shook her head, smiling at his ability to poke fun at his serious injuries.

'Look, there will be loads of physios prepared to rob me blind in the smoke,' he said in an effort to ease her concerns. 'I need to be there, anyway. For business.'

'Drug business.'

'There are quite a few things I could turn my hand to if I wanted to,' he said.

'Wheelchair basketball?' she said, a mischievous glint in her eye.

'Ha bloody ha,' he said. 'Look, our Bruce is a dab hand on the Internet, which offers up all kinds of possibilities. We could design our own computer games. People have made a fortune out of those.'

'Won't the temptation be to lapse back into your old ways?'

'I'm a London boy,' he said. 'Got the Smoke in my veins. I know they say a leopard can't change its spots but when you spend hour after hour in a hospital bed it makes you reflect on your life. Mine don't add up to much – eight years in prison, a long time in hospital, what else is there?'

She shrugged.

'Family?'

He let out a sarcastic cackle. 'Give me a break!' he said. 'Bruce and Mum are the only ones I give two shits about. And you won't miss me … I ain't your type.'

'Racist bigot? No, I guess that's true.'

'Sorry,' he said with sincerity.

'What for?'

'The things I said when I met you,' said Arnie. 'I was out of order.'

'It's OK. It's the scorpion and the frog,' she said.

'What you on about?'

'It's one of *Aesop's Fables*,' she said. 'My granddad told my dad, and he told me. A scorpion decides to change his way of life and asks a frog to take him across the river. The frog is reluctant, fearing the scorpion will sting him, but the scorpion points out that if that happened they would both drown. Convinced he's on safe territory, the frog lets the scorpion climb on his back. Halfway to the other side the frog feels a sharp pain in his back, like a needle. Realising he won't make the other side he says to the scorpion, "Why did you sting me? Now we'll both die". The scorpion says, "I couldn't help it, it's in my nature".'

'You think I'm a scorpion,' he said.

'I think you're over 30 years old and most people are set in their ways by then. OK, maybe your circumstances have changed dramatically – and I'm not saying people can't overhaul their lives completely – but I'm unsure you can override who you are deep inside. All those different influences growing up, your father …'

'Hold on,' he said. 'You know nothing about me. Things I've told you just scratch the surface. Many stories I was told as a kid turned out to be lies. It's only in getting older that I've managed to piece some of it together.'

'What do you mean?'

'Look, I won't tell you the whole story now. Maybe further down the line we can meet for a drink or something. Tell me, where are you from originally?'

'Plymouth.'

There was silence before they both burst out laughing.

'You thought I was going to say Botswana or something, didn't you?' she said. 'The truth is I was born and bred here and have spent my entire life in the West Country.'

'Fair play.' He chuckled. 'What about your parents?'

'My mum came over from South Africa when she was young. My granddad was mixed-race – his father Dutch and his mother

West African. He owned a farm out there but feared that at any moment it would be attacked by nearby black tribesmen believing the land to have been 'stolen' from them at some stage in history. For years, he would sit bolt upright in this hard armchair all night, a gun at his side, determined to protect his family and his liveli-hood. Inevitably, I guess, he developed terrible arthritis but stuck to the routine because he feared that if he went to bed he might not be able to get up for work the next day and tend the crops. My grandmother eventually persuaded him to sell the farm and move over here. With the political situation getting worse, stories of land grabs intensified and she feared for the safety of my mother and the rest of the family.'

'Woah, back up!' said Arnie. 'Your granddad was half Dutch?'

'Yeah, on my Great Grandmother's side. I've seen pictures of her – white as chalk. It's hard to imagine we are related.'

'I didn't mean to be rude, Abi,' he said. 'I'm just shocked. Still, it must have been tough for your granddad to get work over here ... considering his health, I mean.'

'That's why my Grandma took responsibility. She was a great cook and landed a job in a cafe while he stayed home with my mum and the other kids. He wasn't alone, though. A lot of families came over here at the same time having been roughly in the same situation. They helped each other out. There was another South African family who rented the rooms upstairs. My mum's family socialised with them regularly and she got on particularly well with the son, who was a couple of years older. They were married when they were 18 – my mum and dad – and have been together ever since. I came along later, the only girl of five children.'

'Four boys and one girl? Snap!' he said.

'Oh?'

'Bruce, who you know, is the youngest. My sister Anjelica is next, then me and finally my older brothers Sly and Chuck.'

'Sly, Bruce and Arnie? You have to be kidding!'

'Don't forget Chuck.'

'Sorry?'

Arnie laughed. 'No one makes the link. Everyone knows that Sly, Bruce and Arnie star in action movies but Chuck was named after Chuck Norris, another tough guy actor from back in the day. Even Anjelica is linked to films. She was named after Anjelica Huston, the Hollywood actress.'

'I see.' She smiled.

'Abigail?' He sounded earnest.

'Yes, Arnold?'

'You're OK. I mean that. You're the nicest person I've met since the accident, and I ain't got many friends left … I feel foolish for the way I spoke to you when I got here.'

'What is it you gangsters say?'

She looked into his eyes and he shrugged his shoulders.

'Forgedaboutit.'

Nine

IT WAS three short paragraphs on the outside column of page 15 sitting under the headline, *'Two bodies found in wildlife beauty spot'*.

Arnie read on:

Two naked bodies were discovered by dog walkers yesterday on Rainham Marshes, a wildlife area popular with birdwatchers on the Thames Estuary on the outskirts of London.

'The male bodies, which both had bullet wounds, were found in a secluded spot, and police say the scene had all the hallmarks of a gangland execution. Det Chief Inspector Robert Frost, of the Homicide and Serious Crime Command, said, "Both victims had been beaten until their faces were unrecognisable and their hands had been removed so that they couldn't be identified through their fingerprints. This could mark the start of a new gangland war".'

'Interesting,' said Arnie. 'So, what's it got to do with me?'

'They're members of Tigger's crew,' said Bruce. 'I thought you might want to know. Looks like someone's got it in for the Boxer Boys.'

'Give 'em my best,' said Arnie grumpily. 'I knew it wouldn't take long for that lot to destroy something it took me 15 years to build. Chuck always thought he had the divine right to be in charge because he was the oldest, but it was my hard work, planning and brainpower that got him where he is today. The boy's just muscle. You seen him, Bruce?'

'Chuck?' said Bruce. 'Last time I ran into him he was off to visit the old man on the Isle of Wight.'

Arnie looked confused. 'I thought the bastard was banged up south of the river.'

'They moved him. He got a pasting from some Jihadi Johns in Belmarsh, so they put him on the island. Chuck visits regularly but I can tell the journey pisses him off. I don't have a lot to do with him, to be honest. Our mum didn't want me involved, remember?'

'And I kept you out of it,' said Arnie. 'She asked me to. Just one of the many favours I done you, Brucie.'

He grabbed the younger man's cheek with force, pulling him to and fro.

'Owwwww! Leave it out, Arnie!' he protested.

Arnie let go.

'That's peanuts compared with the kind of treatment you'd get behind bars,' he said. 'I remember catching you with drugs that time. You thought you were the Barking equivalent of that gangster who put all that coke up his nose in the film.' He adopted an Hispanic accent. 'Say hello to my li'l friend.'

'Scarface.'

Bruce turned at the sound of the woman's voice and Arnie smiled.

'Good film knowledge, Abi,' he said. 'Maybe you can join my quiz team when I'm on the outside.'

'You have a quiz team?' said the care worker. 'Or are you asking me on a date?'

'Maybe.'

Arnie felt immense satisfaction watching Bruce's mouth fall open at the sight of his big brother flirting with a black woman.

'Abi has been super helpful to me,' he said.

'Are you leaving us now?' she asked.

'You bet.'

'I wish you all the best, Arnold Dolan, I really do,' she said. 'You may be a racist but at least you're *my* racist.'

The two laughed while Bruce sulked, feeling excluded from the joke.

'Nurse, can you help me get him into the chair,' he asked in a deliberate ploy to interrupt the verbal head tennis.

'Of course,' said Abi. She looked at Arnie. 'You've got your West Ham shirt on, I see. I prefer Argyle to be honest.'

'Who?' said Bruce.

'Plymouth Argyle,' said Arnie, chuckling. 'They're in the bottom division, even lower than bleedin' Millwall. Do you remember that car insurance advert in which their fans travelled up and down the motorway? Called 'emselves "Janners".'

Bruce shook his head.

'Never mind, just get me out of here would ya, as they say on that stupid programme Anj watches.'

'*I'm A Celebrity*,' said Abi. 'Love that show.'

'No accounting for taste,' said Arnie. 'You'll have to get together with my sister. You sound like you'd have a lot in common.'

ARNIE could still hear Abigail's cheery goodbye as they sailed through the double doors and out into the reception area. He really did hope to see her again and imagined what that reunion would be like. Preoccupied, he almost missed the overweight figure wobbling through the entrance doors.

'Stop!' he hissed to his brother.

'What?' asked Bruce. 'Not the bloody loo again!'

Arnie shook his head and nodded in the direction of the reception desk. The man he knew as Malcolm was signing in for his late shift.

'That's him,' he said.

'The Albino?'

'Yeah, give it here now!'

'What?'

'You know.'

Bruce fiddled with a plastic carrier bag on the arm of the wheelchair before handing a box to Arnie. Ripping the packaging aside, he inspected his purchase.

'Perfect,' he said. 'Always wanted one of them smart phones. You did charge it? I got to make a call. I don't care how you do it, just get that bastard over here.'

Bruce strolled over and spoke to the fat man, who had been chatting up the woman on the front desk. He looked over at Arnie and his smile instantly disappeared. Sensing the carer's fear, a warm feeling flooded through the man in the wheelchair. 'Yes,' he muttered. 'You should be shitting yourself.'

Malcolm walked in his direction, Bruce following close behind. Stopping 10 yards away, the care worker asked, 'What can I do for you, Mr Dolan?'

'No *Arnie* today, Malcy?' said the man in the wheelchair. 'Still friends, aren't we? I just wanted to thank you for my special treatment, my old Hammers' chum. I'm not going to be around anymore, so I've brought you something to remind you of our quality time together.'

The care worker's big head wobbled on his shoulders, the apprehension flooding his tiny eyes.

'I'm a bit busy to be honest, mate,' he said. 'We're not allowed to accept gifts.'

'Oh, you'll take this one,' growled Arnie. 'Bruce!'

Before Malcolm could react, he was pushed in the back and tottered forwards, his weight fighting a losing battle with gravity as he fell to his knees in front of Arnie. The former gang leader summoned all his strength and propelled himself forwards, colliding with the care worker.

Malcolm's eyes looked like they would pop right out of his head, his body convulsing uncontrollably. Bruce pulled the wheelchair out of the way and the heavy man crashed face first to the ground, foam bubbling from his mouth.

'Help! Help!' Arnie shouted. 'This man's having a bleedin' fit, a heart attack or something.'

People rushed from all directions. Leaning forward until he almost fell on top of his victim, Arnie whispered, 'Think you can fuck with Arnie Dolan? Think again, scum!'

Settling back in the chair, he then pointed to the exit. 'Let's go home, Bruce... this place is an absolute shit-hole!'

Once in the car park, Arnie peered back through the windows in time to see Abigail race to the injured man's side. Looking up briefly, their eyes met for a second and he thought he detected a faint nod, but as soon as it appeared it was gone. He made the universal sign for making a call but wasn't sure if she saw it before attending her stricken colleague.

Bruce chuckled.

'I wouldn't call her on that,' he said, indicating the gadget in Arnie's hand. 'Not unless you want two million volts passing through you.'

TEN

VICKERS sat in the SUV with the engine idling, staring at his phone, his free hand shaking as he guided the cigarette to his lips. *Stupid*, he thought. He had kicked the habit four years ago, but recent events had turned him back to the evil weed. He'd considered getting one of those artificial vape gadgets but there were times when only a full-blown hit of poisonous chemicals would do.

She'd rung four times and he'd missed every call, unable to face another row. A nerve below his eye twitched out of control and he stubbed out the butt in the overflowing ashtray. The smell of stale tobacco made him nauseous, and he pressed a button to let in the cool evening breeze.

Bringing his emotions under control wasn't so easy. This mental fragility was a side of Pete Vickers he couldn't afford to show the outside world. To his close associates he was cool and composed, always using brains and logic to think his way out of trouble. If they scraped away that smooth veneer, though, they would find something rotting beneath, a debilitating layer of self-doubt he thought he'd banished forever.

The semi-detached, three-bedroom former council house where he lived nestled among a collection of similar red-brick homes in one of the up-and-coming areas of Barking. Lifting his foot from the clutch, he released the handbrake, the car moving slowly down the street.

Either side of him curtains had been drawn against the harsh realities of the outside world. The cars in the driveways suggested a middle-class haven, not opulent but expensive enough to give their owners a leg-up on the social ladder, while the neatly trimmed lawns and patio extensions hinted at happy, contented families behind every front door.

He abhorred the falseness of it all. In the old days you had to fight on the streets for everything and treasured any small luxury that came your way. Here it was all smoke and mirrors, people equating happiness with things they owned, even though many of those possessions were on hire purchase or paid for by hugely overloaded credit cards.

The people here believed in a state of conformity rather than a state of mind, and the endless competition to prove worthy of acceptance among such exulted neighbours was tiring. Everyone played the game, conveniently ignoring the mountain of bank statements and bills gathering on the welcome mat.

That Janie had fitted in so well was not her fault. It was his. So keen was he to please her that he provided her with everything she demanded. When they first got together she'd been overjoyed with any little gift he bestowed on her, trinkets of affection which didn't need to break the bank. Now she lived barely half a mile from the humble area where she grew up, but light years from reality. She'd been born to a mother on the Boxers estate who had entertained a succession of untrustworthy boyfriends, enlisted to play the father role in the absence of a real dad Janie had never known. Her mother eventually married when Janie was 10, but the new man in her life was a strict disciplinarian who caused her to rebel.

Vickers had been the knight in shining armour and seemed to provide her with exactly what she needed and, to him, the fairy tale was real. He should have known better. Happy endings rarely came true for those brought up in deprived neighbourhoods like the Boxers, even though he thought he'd found the ideal solution by moving away.

Janie had loved her new home, befriending the neighbours and holding coffee mornings to show off her latest purchases from Next or John Lewis. She indulged herself in expensive hairdos and designer clothes and gave every indication she'd drawn a barrier between now and what had gone before. Yet behind the cloak of normality, Vickers could sense something lurking in the dark recesses of their past, just waiting to shatter their idyllic family life.

When it struck, the human hurricane that was Arnold Dolan unleashed all its pent-up fury on them, smashing their relationship like a fragile ornament shaken from a sideboard. Now Vickers questioned whether things between him and his wife could ever be the same again.

Through the windscreen he could see her now, standing still as a stone sculpture under the porch light. Since their return from that fateful trip to Wales, he'd tried to give her space, hoping the memory would fade and things would improve. He did his best to ignore the nagging voice in his head telling him that she and Arnie had shared intimate moments before, but images of them together flashed through his mind at the most inconvenient of times.

Drawing up to the garage doors, he cringed at the sight of them, the peeling yellow paint representing another 'failure' on his part. How many times had she nagged him to retouch them only to find him too busy to oblige? Absent-mindedly he prodded the tender skin around his eye and winced.

Recently, for the first time, he'd allowed others to peek into the solitary confinement of his marriage. Though seeking out male support had made him feel better and more empowered, he knew he wasn't in charge of his own destiny. There were the kids to consider.

He could still remember the impact on the Marshall family when dad Stan walked away all those years ago, the relationship between father and children never repaired. Pete doted on Si and Di and couldn't imagine a time when he was denied contact with them. Turning the ignition off, he picked up his expensive brown leather briefcase and stepped out of the car, pasting on a smile to indicate a joy he didn't feel.

She flew at him like a tornado, a flurry of indisciplined punches impacting like tiny, sharp hailstones on his skin. He knew she could pack a punch if she wanted to, but there was no real weight behind these. Something was wrong. Holding her at arms' length, he noted the rivers of mascara smudging and staining her cheeks. Her black, knee-length skirt was creased, her tights wrinkled and scruffy. This was not the Janie he knew.

Feeling the fight drain from her, he released his grip.

'Where have you been, you bastard,' she shouted, spittle spraying his cheek. 'It's nearly eight o'clock and I've called a number of times but, oh no, unavailable. I really don't know why you have a fuckin' mobile phone. You …'

Lunging at him again, her actions uncoordinated and desperate, he took a firm grip of her wrists this time.

'Hang on!' he said.

'Don't you "Hang on" me, you arsehole!'

With expert timing, her knee impacted with his groin. Doubling up, he gasped for breath, his head full of stars and his stomach churning. Expecting her to finish the job, he was surprised when he looked up to see her resuming the statue pose, her hands to her face and her shoulders heaving.

Rising gingerly, he put his arm around her and guided her into the house.

HE left her on the sofa staring at the carpet, her hands playing nervously with each other, while he went to fix a drink at the sideboard. Putting the top back on the decanter he had second thoughts and poured a brandy for himself, too.

Whatever this was, it had nothing to do with his failures as a husband. Dropping to his haunches, he prised her fingers apart and slipped the glass into them, then lifted it to her lips. She took a sip and cringed.

'Now then,' he said gently. 'Are you going to tell me what this is all about?'

She began sobbing, punctuating her despair with high-pitched squeaking noises, as if trying to speak but unable to form words.

'Slowly now,' he coaxed. 'Think it over and let it all come out together.'

She took another drink, then a deep breath, before lifting her head so that her eyes focused on his.

'It's Mum,' she said. 'She's gone.'

11

EVERY time he heard the rattle of keys, clunk of tumblers and creak of rust-infected hinges, Chuck Dolan feared he might never emerge into sunlight again. Down the years there had been plenty of reasons for the powers that be to incarcerate Chuck: murder, assault, robbery, aggravated burglary, arson and living off the proceeds of crime to name just a few. He could only think there was a lucky sign hanging over him, some kind of karma kicking into effect.

He didn't believe in that mumbo jumbo, but with no other plausible explanation it made him wonder. Maybe something he'd done on the plus side had balanced out the negatives. It would have to be something massive, though, to erase his extensive roll of dishonour.

'You know the drill, sir, straight down there and to the left … he's waiting for you.'

Chuck inclined his head, what was once dark hair turned to silver, betraying the fact he was now the wrong side of 40, his face showcasing a patchwork of scars, some faded, some recent. His on-off, live-in lover Becca said they added character. He just thought they spoilt the good looks he possessed in his youth.

'How's he getting on?' asked Chuck.

'You'll have to ask him that,' said the prison guard, non-committal.

The old man had been transferred to HMP *Isle of Wight*, a 'super prison' amalgamating the notorious high-security lock-up known as Parkhurst with the island's other offender institutions, Albany and Camp Hill. It didn't look that super to Chuck. Camp Hill had closed already, and Parkhurst reminded him of a prisoner-of-war camp like those you saw in films, a barracks of seven Victorian-style units where society's unwanted could be hidden away and forgotten.

Still, once you got past the giant grey walls, barbed wire draped across the top like tinsel on a Christmas tree, there were at least some splashes of colour and decoration to lighten the gloom. The corridor walls on the approach to the visitors' centre reminded him of those student art projects that sprang up in Shoreditch, an attempt by hipster insurgents to take over the East End.

Yet the makeover couldn't quite disguise the macabre essence of the place, as if the inmates of its past had dripped their DNA into the walls. Notorious gangster Reggie Kray had been housed here, as had his south London rivals The Richardsons, Yorkshire Ripper Peter Sutcliffe and fellow serial killer Dennis Nilsen. Chuck didn't spook easily, but the thought made him shiver.

Since 1990 both Parkhurst and Albany had been downgraded to Category B prisons and, had his dad been fully aware of this, he would have felt slightly insulted. Chuck was now in the Albany part of the prison, housing the health wing, and had stopped outside the visitors' centre to take a deep breath and gather his thoughts.

As he reached for the door a tall, red-haired elderly woman in a flowery dress, flesh-coloured tights, white pumps and some garishly applied make-up flounced through in the opposite direction. Mutton dressed as lamb, Chuck's dad would have said. A sickly scent of cheap lavender perfume assaulted his nostrils and made him feel queasy.

He'd had a similar attack of nausea on the ferry as he left Portsmouth and bounced across the stretch of water known as The Solent. Once on dry land it wasn't plain sailing in the taxi either. It got stuck for over an hour in traffic-saturated Newport, the commercial and administrative hub of the island. Arriving 20 minutes late, Chuck feared his visitor pass might have expired. He was lucky the authorities were feeling lenient today.

As the woman disappeared around a bend accompanied by a prison guard, he pushed on through into a room set out like a school dining hall. He spotted the old man at a table in the far corner, Maurice Dolan's smooth, hairless dome reflecting the glare from the overhead strip lights. A big man, in comparison to his bulk the table resembled a child's outdoor play set.

'Dad!' Chuck greeted him with a display of enthusiasm he didn't feel. The dome revolved, hard eyes and a wrinkled brow emerging, the face frozen in confusion.

'It's me, Dad … Chuck!'

There was a moment's silence before the light of recognition flickered behind Big Mo Dolan's eyes.

'All right?'

'I'm fine,' said Chuck, the chair scraping the floor as he pulled it out. 'How are you?'

Big Mo adopted the grumpy old man expression Chuck had become familiar with over the years: eyebrows creased, lips turned down, jaw protruding.

'It's all shit,' he said. 'Food's shit, neighbours are shit, screws are shit and cell is shit. Why am I here?'

That accusatory look as if Chuck had the power to authorise prisoner movement inside UK borders.

'It's been explained to you, Dad. It's for your own good.'

'Always thinking of me, aren't they, the law? I forget that some-times. Anyway, never mind this hole. What's happenin'?'

Chuck took a deep breath, looking around at the other prison visitors. He reduced his voice to a loud hiss.

'Remember I told you about young Arnie's terrible accident?' said Chuck.

Mo looked blank.

Chuck persevered. 'You know, he fell down a steep flight of steps and ended up a fuckin' raspberry.'

The news brought a couple of blinks.

Chuck forged on. 'Well, a couple of my pals are giving him a hard time in rehab. You couldn't have done better yourself, Dad.'

Chuck felt a pang of sadness as he watched Big Mo delving into the depths of his memory. Hardened gangsters used to tremble at the sight of this phenomenally tough character. If they saw him now, they would laugh in his face. After what seemed like forever, the older man opened his eyes, a smile illuminating the craggy features.

'Raspberry ripple means cripple!' he said with a chuckle. 'I love the old phrases; those were the fackin' days. Not many would cotton on in here, mind. They're all thick as mince or have had themselves a sense of humour bypass. I bet it's tough for you, though, fucking over your little brother.'

Big Mo was testing him.

'He always thought he was better than the rest of us,' said Chuck.

'And now you're in charge, like I told you?' asked Big Mo.

'Yeah,' said Chuck. 'Vickers is helping me. We're a good team.'

Chuck decided against mentioning the missing dealers. He didn't need the old man ranting on at him about being tougher. He would sort the problem when he got back.

'What was he doing there, anyway?'

Chuck took a moment to figure out what the old man meant. Then he twigged.

'What was Arnie doing in Wales? He was looking for the Marshall kid …'

Suddenly, the old man sprang to life, the light dancing like fire on his pupils.

'Don't mention that fackin' name!'

'What have you got against Gary, Dad? You barely know him.'

'Not the boy!' stormed Big Mo. 'His father. That bloody Stan Marshall.'

He spat the words out one by one, gnarled fingers wrapping themselves around the sides of the table as he levered himself to his feet. Chuck gently leaned forwards and pushed him down.

'Calm down, Dad,' he hissed. 'You know what the docs say … it will make you ill.'

'Bit late for that, son,' said Mo.

It was Chuck's turn to look perplexed.

'What do you mean? Have you seen the medical staff?'

'They're doing tests,' said Mo. 'That's why I've been here in Albany. They want me to have a biopsy for … you know, the Big C. Been taking somethin' for the pain. It's kidneys … or maybe bowel, I forget.'

They both fell silent, stewing over the implications.

'I'm sorry, Dad,' said Chuck. 'You know I love you, don't you? I'd do anything for you.'

The question went unanswered. Big Mo was uncomfortable with public displays of affection.

'Ain't your fault,' he said. 'These things happen. Someone's evenin' up the score. Best you can do for me is sort out my move.'

'It ain't that bad, Dad,' said Chuck, looking around. 'It's gotta be better than Belmarsh. That Muslim Brotherhood took over there. They gave you a right kick-in which is why you ended up here.'

'All my mates were there.'

'Couldn't help you when you needed them, though, could they?'

Big Mo stared into the distance, recalling a time when all the London hard nuts were gathered under one roof.

'You only have a short while to go, anyway,' said Chuck, 'and it's a bit like being abroad here, on your own little holiday island.'

'Yeah?' A big smile illuminated Big Mo's face. 'You're right! That bird you passed on the way in … is she the sort of local totty I can expect? Perhaps she's an exotic dancer or a thousand-pound-a-night hooker.'

Chuck's eyebrows creased in confusion. 'I doubt …'

'Muppet!' The older Dolan exploded. 'That was a bleedin' bloke in a wig and a dress. There are about 11 or 12 of them in here prancing around like Dorises. D'you know, some of them are in the process of having their dicks chopped off, courtesy of the taxpayer? It's disgusting! This place is crawling wall-to-wall with trannies and nonces. I'm about the only straight one in here, and, if I stay too long, people will start saying I'm queer, too, or worse … a bloody paedo. Holiday, he says. What shall we call this delightful, fun-packed resort then? Kiddy Fiddlers Sur Le Plage?'

Life in the old dog yet, thought Chuck. It was a typical Big Mo rant. Old School. He particularly liked the reference to the taxpayer as if he'd regularly contributed to the UK treasury. For more than 25 years it had been the opposite way around, in fact, the taxpayer paying to keep Big Mo in the lifestyle to which he'd become accustomed.

Though the former armed robber was becoming more bullish, Chuck couldn't help thinking he was a shadow of the figure he had once been. The way the grey-suited mandarin from the Ministry of Justice had explained it to them, the old man had come off a clear second best in the battle of Belmarsh, being jumped on his way to the showers.

Refocusing on the present, Chuck realised his father had something concealed within his hands.

'Dad, come on, I'm talking to you here.'

Watery brown eyes came up to meet his. Once they'd instilled panic into almost everyone with a single, steely glare. Now their owner blinked rapidly, unable to focus, like a junkie on the way down. Was his dad on drugs? It made sense.

'I want the loose ends tied up in case I die here,' said Mo, his gaze intense, a bronchial clicking coming from somewhere inside his chest as his breathing quickened. Grabbing Chuck's hands, he applied far more pressure than was necessary, fingers turning white with the effort.

'Track down that slag who fitted me up that time,' he growled. 'I know I had plenty of enemies back then, but I reckon it was that Stan Marshall who did for me and got your uncle Clive killed, too.'

Chuck couldn't hold back.

'Christ, why always this?' he said, jumping to his feet, others around the room halting their discussions to watch the show. Two guards stood on opposite sides of the hall, poised for action. 'It was 34 years ago, Dad! Some of the people around back in the day are dead. Remember that Terry Wogan you listened to on the radio?'

A hint of recognition played across the old man's eyes.

'Brown bread,' said Chuck, using the cockney slang for dead. 'He was 77. And that pop star you always took the mick out of because he wore make-up. David Bowie? Popped his clogs, too.'

'It was that Boy George I didn't like, not Bowie,' said Big Mo. 'Faggot.'

'What the hell does it matter?' said Chuck. 'I'm just telling you the world's changing and you ain't the only one who got older. You've been in and out a few times since Uncle Clive died. Why bring it up now? No wonder you're ill if it's been eatin' away at you all this time. I wouldn't be surprised if that Stan geezer was dead, too. He left our neighbourhood years ago ... walked out on his wife and kids.'

Big Mo pointed a shaky finger at his eldest boy.

'Sit down!'

Even at his age, Chuck couldn't disobey the parental command. The response was ingrained in him from before he could walk. Leaning forwards, the old man pushed the item he'd been coveting across the table. It was a photograph, taken on one of those old instamatic cameras. Chuck grabbed it and held it to the light.

Two men were standing arm in arm. One of them had an ugly shaped scar meandering down the side of his face, from his right eye to his chin. The other was a younger version of the man sat opposite. In the picture Big Mo wore a sheepskin coat and pointed a large wooden club in the direction of the camera. Memories flooded back for Chuck, some good, some best forgotten.

'Know where this was taken?'

'Yeah,' said Chuck. 'Hastings.'

'Frank and Reg,' said Big Mo. 'God I miss 'em … those Jihadi jokers wouldn't have been so larey if I'd had those two with me. What happened to them, eh, boy?'

'Frank died some time ago,' said Chuck. 'As for Reg, who knows?'

'Poor Reg,' said Big Mo, his eyes focusing on the whitewashed ceiling. If Chuck didn't know better, he'd suspect his dad was fighting back tears.

'Dad, Reg was just a curtain pole … a lump of wood.'

'Never let me down,' said Big Mo.

They sat like that for minutes, their minds locked in memories. Eventually the old man said, 'Good days all ruined by one person … Stan fucking Marshall. Cunt took everything from me: my freedom, my wife, my pride and my family. It's time the debt was paid.'

Chuck was about to argue, but Mo reached across and put his finger to his eldest son's lips. Chuck couldn't recall the old man making a more tender gesture.

'You're a good boy, Chuck,' he said. 'My favourite. Always have been. Sort this out and I won't ask anything of you again.'

How could Chuck say 'no'? It sounded like a father's dying wish.

12

March 2016

THE woman shrieked as the coffin disappeared behind the curtains. Gareth watched Janie Vickers consumed by grief and could understand her pain. He had known Janie since they were teenagers and could still see the girl in the woman standing before him. Dressed immaculately as always in the best designer gear money could buy, the difference today was that she'd traded the flamboyant colours for black, an outfit bought especially for the funeral of her mother, Irene.

There was a 'whumpff' from behind the curtain as the burners fired up. Janie fell to her right, burying her face in the lapel of Pete's charcoal suit. She was in safe hands. The man Gareth had known as Vickers since the day they first met as teenagers had always been the calming influence in their little group. Often in the past he'd reined in Arnie Dolan's worst excesses, talking him out of things he might later regret.

Not always, but often.

Standing on either side of the grieving couple were their children. Diane, who was five, clung tightly to her father's waist with both arms while the eldest child Simon stood stoically to attention next to his mother. Janie's stepfather, Paul, was on the end of the row. The former soldier stood stock still, eyes front, as if on parade.

Scanning the mourners, Gareth spotted the two older Dolan boys, Chuck and Sly, whispering to each other at the back of the crematorium. He had avoided them thus far, but knew a reunion was inevitable, probably back at the Hope and Anchor later. They both had girlfriends with them though neither was married. The truth was it would take a very brave woman to drive a wedge between them.

Next to her sons stood Beryl, the Dolan matriarch, with whom Gareth had got on so well in the past. This was the first time he'd seen her since learning of her long and intense affair with his father and he wondered whether she'd stayed in touch with Stan Marshall down the years. He would love to challenge her about the relationship but didn't have the guts. She'd become feistier with age and looked more intimidating than the waif-like woman he'd first encountered in his youth. Of course, she was Anjelica's mum too and any confrontation was guaranteed to upset his girlfriend. It was easier to let sleeping dogs lie.

Beryl Dolan had enough stress in her life already, her story like the plot of a long-running soap opera. Husband Maurice, the career criminal they called Big Mo, had spent the majority of married life behind bars and her son Arnie had followed in his footsteps. Could Gareth really blame the woman for finding solace in the company of his happy-go-lucky father?

Well, yes, he could, because his mum, Sheila, had been pregnant when the affair started. With him. If anything, though, his dad was the real culprit. Stan had the gift of the gab – they'd called him Stan the Man at Walthamstow market – and Gareth could only guess at the lies he'd told Beryl to get her into bed.

Casting his eyes across the sea of faces, he was relieved there was no sign of Arnie. He had convinced himself his former best friend wouldn't be callous enough to make an appearance, but a nagging voice in his head reminded him Arnie never had been shy of causing a scene.

Music – 'The Long and Winding Road' by the Beatles – flowed out across the congregation from wall-mounted speakers as Janie,

Vickers and their children led the way towards the exit, followed by Janie's stepfather. Gareth and Anjie joined the trail of mourners walking out into the gentle breeze.

People gathered in small groups, talking, smoking and recalling their own memories of Irene Marsh nee Sullivan while Gareth took in the view. The City of London Cemetery and Crematorium at Manor Park was a stunning Grade I listed landscape in the heart of the East End. The gentle scent of flowers wafted across from the beautiful formal gardens, which stretched as far as the eye could see, while well-maintained roadways meandered through avenues of trees.

Gareth had picked up some literature on leaving which informed him it was one of the largest municipal burial places in Europe, the cemetery itself being the first to be awarded the prestigious Green Flag, the national standard for parks and green spaces in England and Wales.

Should her ashes be interred here, Irene would be in good company. Many famous people were buried in the grounds, one name in particular standing out for Gareth: Bobby Moore, the former West Ham and England captain who lifted the World Cup in 1966. On a more macabre note, two of Jack the Ripper's victims from his Whitechapel reign of terror at the start of the 20th century were buried in the vicinity.

Taken by surprise as a large hand slapped his back, Gareth was propelled forwards. Turning to complain, his eyes met those of Chuck Dolan, flicking ash from a cigarette, his ever-present sidekick Sly in attendance.

'All right, Gazza?' he asked with a smirk.

'Chuck,' Gareth nodded in greeting. 'Sly.'

'Hope you're looking after our little sis,' said Chuck.

'Of course.'

Gareth put his arm out, intending to pull Anjie towards him before realising she'd headed off to speak to her best friend, Janie.

'I don't know about you, Sly, but it seems a bit obscene to me,' Chuck said, turning to his shadow. 'Almost like incest.'

Gareth felt a prickle under his skin, the old anger issues resurfacing. A few hours back in London and all the happiness he'd banked over nearly eight months living in Wales was threatening to disintegrate.

'What exactly do you mean, Chuck?' he demanded, his face hardening. He knew he would stand little chance if the Dolan boys started something, his damaged knee a severe handicap.

'Well, the way I see it you're Arnie's brother and Anjie over there is Arnie's sister,' said Chuck. 'There should be a law against it.'

'Two different fathers, two different mothers,' said Gareth. 'I don't see how you get incest from that.'

Chuck grunted, neither accepting nor rejecting the point.

'Seen him, have you, your "bro"?'

The term was delivered with maximum sarcasm.

'Not since you paid me that visit in Wales,' said Gareth.

'I hate it when families fall out,' said Chuck. 'Poor old Arnie! He's not a real Dolan, but he wasn't good enough to be a Marshall. Little fucker. He discharged himself from a nursing home in Devon, I hear. Understandable I guess. Couldn't take the shame. I heard he humiliated himself, shit his pants … hard life being a raspberry, ain't it?'

The subtext was clear, the jibe aimed at Gareth and his dodgy leg. He refused to rise to the bait. It was a funeral. The deceased deserved respect.

'Look after yourselves, boys,' he said, turning and hobbling off in Anjie's direction. Moments later he turned back. 'If I see Arnie I'll pass on your regards.'

'Don't bother,' said Chuck. 'Just tell him he ain't wanted around here. Any idea where he's staying?'

Gareth shook his head. 'Like I said, I haven't seen him.'

'Hmmm.'

'See you in the pub later?' asked Gareth, changing the subject.

'Not if we see you first,' said Chuck with a smile.

Gareth didn't know whether to take it as a joke or a threat.

13

PETE Vickers watched his wife talking to her best friend and felt a sense of loss. It wasn't so much that he was grieving his mother-in-law's passing – the woman had never liked him much. It was more a reminder of things he held dear when he was growing up. The sight of Janie and Anjie together transported him back to happier times.

Anjie might have been Arnie's little sister, but she'd never resented Vickers for moving in on Janie after her brother had been jailed. In fact, she'd positively encouraged their relationship, giving them the support they needed on their slow and steady journey from friends, to lovers, to married couple and, finally, to parents.

Would Janie tell Anjie about the rape? The Dolan sister was closer to Arnie than any other member of his family. Even so, Vickers couldn't imagine she would condone such a brutal attack on her best friend. He suspected Janie would keep it quiet to spare Anjie's feelings. Anjie's bloke, Gazza, knew, of course, but maybe he felt it wasn't his place to reveal such a sordid secret.

'How are you holding up, Pete?'

Speak of the Devil. Gazza was standing next to him now, waving a tenner in the direction of Irish Phil, the son of the ageing landlady. The only other person serving was an inexperienced barmaid in her early 20s who had been taken on just for the day. The queue for service was reaching epic proportions. Vickers wondered how long it would be before tempers flared and the wake ended like many others he'd attended – in a bar room free-for-all.

'Not bad, Gaz, or do we call you Gareth now?' he said.

'You can call me whatever you want, Pete,' said the journalist. 'We go back a long way. This has hit Janie hard, yeah?'

'Knocked the stuffing out of her.'

'She and her mum were pretty close.'

'Maybe,' said Vickers. 'They went at it hammer and tongs sometimes. On occasion, I wondered whether Janie did stuff deliberately to upset her mum. I don't think she forgave Irene for the fact she grew up without knowing her real father.'

'She got on with him, OK, though, didn't she?' Gareth said, nodding towards the stepdad.

'Nah, not really,' said Vickers. 'Paul was pretty strict. You know his military background? Because he wasn't her real dad, she felt Paul had no right to be so tough on her. That's why she hung around with us and did a few things I imagine she now regrets.'

They both knew the history Vickers was talking about. It was an open secret Janie had been with plenty of men besides Arnie before she settled down. Even so, Vickers had always suspected that what she really wanted was stability in her life, which he'd provided. Right up until …

'You seen him?' Vickers asked.

'Arnie? I'm getting asked that a lot today,' said Gareth. 'No, and I don't particularly want to.'

He held his hand up. Vickers couldn't miss the ugly scar where the knife had entered.

'I'm sorry,' he said. 'I was there too. I could have stopped him.'

'No, you couldn't,' said Gareth. 'No one could. He is unstoppable when he is in that sort of mood and you know it. Drink?'

'Double vodka with coke,' said Vickers, putting his pint down on the bar. 'I can't drink any more of this gnat's piss.'

'As I live and breathe!' Irish Phil said as he materialised in front of them. 'Gary bloody Marshall. Well, well! Good to see you. You ain't graced our establishment in, ooh, five years I'd say. I asked your stepdad about you a little while back, before the trouble.'

Vickers jumped in.

'Irish, no need, eh? Water under the bridge.'

The barman looked warily at Vickers.

'Sure. What can I get you guys, anyway?'

Gareth gave him the order and he walked off in search of vodka.

'What does he mean?' asked Gareth. 'What trouble?'

Vickers sighed.

'Your stepdad, Reg, had a bit of a row with Arnie,' he said. 'Came off second best. Arnie was trying to find out where you were and Reg insisted he didn't know—'

'…And Arnie wouldn't take no for an answer. Anjie told me the last time she saw Reg he was battered and bruised and avoided her in the street. I can't imagine he put up much resistance. He's an old man.'

Vickers shrugged. 'I should have stood up to Arnie. It's my fault—'

When his drink arrived, he knocked it back in one. 'Get us another would you, mate?' he said. 'I'll give you the money. Double voddy this time, I've still got the coke. I need to take a leak then pop out for a ciggy. It's a bit stuffy in here.'

'Sure thing.'

Vickers handed over some money, slipped from his bar stool and made his way past the pool table, the memories flooding back. Reg Philpott pinned to the baize, Arnie Dolan shooting pool balls at his head. It was swiftly followed by another flashback, Arnie standing on the pool table, singing the West Ham tune 'I'm Forever Blowing Bubbles', a bloodstained scarf tied to his wrist.

It was the evening everything changed forever; for all of them.

He shuddered and pushed open the door to the toilets.

'THERE he is … Pete fuckin' Vickers.'

'What are you gonna do, Arnie?' Bruce leaned from the driving seat into the back of the especially fitted-out van, the 'flid' mobile as Arnie called it.

'Take him for a pint, perhaps? Show there are no hard feelings. Apologise to him for the fact his bird still has the hots for me. Perhaps then we could go into the pub and have a good old catch up … just like the old days. Then, to round it off lovely, I'll kick his sorry ass.'

'Not a good idea,' said Bruce. 'Causing trouble at a funeral ain't right, Arnie. It wouldn't be fair on the mourners. You wouldn't like it if the same happened—'

Bruce stopped abruptly, wary of triggering one of his brother's legendary explosions.

'To who?' asked Arnie. 'Apart from you, little bro, and our mum, of course, there ain't anyone left for me to grieve over. Maybe Anjie —'

'What about Gazza? He's your brother, too, remember?'

'Cunt,' said Arnie, raising his voice. 'How can I be close to a chicken-hearted fucker who ran away and changed his soddin' name? He was my best friend and he deserted me. He never visited me in prison even though I was there because I saved his sorry ass. Then, to top it all, he knocked up our sis. How disrespectful is that? Sure, I'll be crying at his funeral … tears of bleedin' laughter.'

The two men watched as Vickers lit a cigarette and leant against the wall, letting a stream of smoke dance in the lights illuminating the pub sign.

'Why are we here, Arnie?' asked Bruce.

His older brother removed a cigar from his pocket and rolled it between his fingers. He was partial to the finer things in life. This was a Cuban special, all the way from Havana, a get well present from his mother. The irony wasn't lost on him. He'd cheated death and there she was giving him something that was bad for his health.

'I used to love this place,' he said. 'Me and the lads played pool here every chance we got, from back when we were 14 or 15. We'd dress up to the nines and slip on a tie or cravat because we thought they made us look more sophisticated. What twats we must have looked! Siobhan knew exactly how old we were but realised we were her customers of tomorrow and wanted to keep us onside. Even back then we had money burning a hole in our pockets after the business took off.'

'Mum wasn't happy with you coming down here when you were under age,' said Bruce.

'Yeah, but when we were older she came down with us. Christmas Day while the dinner was cooking she'd pop in for a Barley wine. Me, Chuck and Sly would have a pint and you would play with your toys at home with Anjie keeping an eye on you, or Auntie Beatrice from over the river in Peckham.'

'I didn't know about the pub but I guessed it wasn't just a Christmas Day walk, like Mum called it. She would ask me if I wanted to come but I'd always say no. You would roll back in good spirits and I knew you'd had a sherbet or two. Mum's in there now, you know?'

Arnie's expression changed. Suddenly he didn't look so cocksure of himself.

'Really?'

'Yeah,' said Bruce. 'She and Irene got on pretty well. That's probably how Anjie became such good pals with Janie. Apparently, they were in the same hospital at the same time the girls were born. Mum told me the other day she was going to pay her respects. What's up?'

'I ain't seen her since that brief visit when I was in the hospital,' said Arnie. 'I miss her. I worry how she's gonna react to me now. Chuck and Sly might have filled her head with poison.'

'She wouldn't listen,' said Bruce. 'Not where you're concerned. You were always her favourite. I think she felt she owed you a bit of extra love, seeing how our dad was so tough on you.'

'She never stopped him, though, did she?'

Arnie was referring to the beatings he received as a kid, always disguised as self-defence lessons by Big Mo. Bruce gave him a concerned look.

'How do you stop a man like that?' he said. 'It's not as if our mum was built like a Russian shot putter, is it? Look at the size of him! They didn't call him Big Mo for nothing.'

Bruce paused for a second, an internal wrestling contest going on in his mind.

'The other day she asked me if you were around and when you were going to visit. I told her it was difficult. She knows there's been some sort of falling out between you and the older boys, but not the details. Probably best if she doesn't.'

Arnie sank into his own thoughts again, snapping forwards once he'd made a decision.

'I need to see her,' he said. "Go get her now, Bruce, it's important.'

'You think she'll come?'

'For her favourite son? Sure. Spin her a yarn. Say it's a matter of life or death and if she doesn't come out, I'll come in.'

Left with no alternative, Bruce reached for the handle of the van.

VICKERS was about to put out his cigarette when he heard familiar voices. They belonged to Sharon and Fenella, two of Janie's mates who had stayed in touch since school. The three of them made a bit of extra cash holding sexy lingerie parties around the neighbourhood. It wasn't as if Janie needed the money, but Vickers suspected the parties were her release valve for the stress building inside her.

'Devastated she is, poor girl,' Sharon was saying. 'Losing her mum like that. They were so close, not like me and my old bag. Who does she lean on now?'

'I've told her I'll be there for her,' said Fenella.

'Sure, but you got your own responsibilities darlin', ain't ya? Four kids don't look after themselves, especially when your old man smokes enough puff to send him away with the fairies for an eternity.'

'Leave him!' said Fenella. 'Anyway, what about her old man? He's always done right by her.'

Vickers felt pride swell in his chest, pleased that Janie had spoken well of him to her friends. He moved closer, listening intently to the conversation taking place around the corner.

'He's never there though, is he?' said Sharon. 'Always out with that gang, getting up to no good.'

'That 'gang', as you put it, paid for that house of theirs.'

'I guess. She hasn't been herself for a while, though, has she? She's been an empty shell since that Arnold bloody Dolan arrived back on the scene.'

'You think she still has feelings for him?' asked Fenella.

'Hard to tell,' replied Sharon. 'There's a rumour he took advantage of her after he got out. Went straight around there and banged her brains out.'

She lowered her voice.

'Our Coleen thinks it was r-a-p-e, but I don't know. She was pretty besotted with him when they were at school. His name was plastered all over her books, remember?'

'She wouldn't do that to Pete and the kids, surely,' said Fenella. 'He's a bad 'un, that Arnie ... hell, what am I talking about, you should know.'

'Only the once it was!' said Sharon. 'Good, mind.'

The two girls guffawed. Vickers thought about sneaking back into the pub before his eavesdropping was discovered but couldn't pull himself away.

Fenella spoke again. 'I don't suppose that stepdad of hers has helped any ... he must have been so strict for her to call him the Sergeant Major.'

'What happened to her real dad?'

'Pushed off when she was tiny.'

'Pete will have to be the shoulder to cry on, then,' said Sharon. 'Even so, she wouldn't want him to know everything. You know, like that—'

'Shhhh!' said Fenella too loudly.

'Married, wasn't he?'

'I know what you're talking about … that skeleton should remain at the bottom of a very grubby cupboard.'

There were a couple of clicks as the girls stamped on their cigarettes, then the tappety-tap of heels heading in his direction. Vickers quickly slipped into the bar, keen they didn't know he'd overheard their conversation.

ARNIE watched his sister, Anjie, and brother, Gary, leave the pub and cross the car park. Hunkering down in the van, he had no wish to alert them to his presence. He had unfinished business with them both, but it could wait. There were more important issues right now.

With his strength returning daily, Arnie had bridges to build and some to burn. He might be confined to a wheelchair for the rest of his life, but the hallmarks of a fighter were still deeply ingrained in his psyche. Continuing his surveillance, he watched the couple climb into a white Corsa, his former best mate behind the wheel. Moments later the car headed off down the street.

Returning his attention to the pub, Arnie saw Bruce advancing towards him, arm interlinked with a stocky, dark-haired woman. He reflected on how his mum had let herself go. Once slim and attractive, she'd put on a ton of weight during the time he was inside.

When she saw him, her eyes sparkled, and her face broke into a big smile. Though he was an expert at keeping his emotions in check, he was unable to suppress his own grin. This was his mum, and every boy needed their mum at some stage.

She slid in alongside Arnie. 'Well, look at you,' she said, beaming as she placed her hands either side of his face. 'You all right, luv? I mean … considering.' She indicated the wheelchair with a nod of her head.

'Yeah, course,' he said, leaning over to kiss her on the cheek. 'Thanks for this, by the way. This electric wheelchair is great.'

Before he could pull away, she wrapped him in a stifling embrace that almost made him topple over.

'Steady on, Mum!' he said. 'I've still got bruises, you know?'

'Sorry, love,' she said. 'It's just so great to see you. Are you coming in to pay your respects?'

'Nah,' he said. 'I'm not ready for that. I'm lucky to have Brucie running errands for me, but I don't feel right in crowds. Anyway, Janie and I had a bit of a falling out.'

'What a shame. I always thought ...' She cut short the sentence, knowing Arnie didn't like speculation about his private life.

'Me and Vickers had a disagreement, too,' he said. 'It's all a bit silly but, look, things have changed. I'll tell you about it in good time. I think you should know though, Mum, I know who I am now.'

'Sorry, dear?' she said.

'Look, I ain't going to beat around the bush,' said Arnie. 'I know Stan Marshall is my dad.'

Her face coloured.

'Oh no, love, you ...Maurice is your dad.'

'Come on, Mum, it's time for honesty,' he said, raising his voice. 'Look at me! Don't I deserve the truth? I've known since I was 12 or 13. I heard you and him, Big Mo, in the kitchen, arguing about it years ago. It feels like only yesterday to me. Later I found that love letter in the bin ... the one written to you by that market-trader scumbag.'

'Sometimes your dad got the wrong end of the stick, Arnold,' she said uncertainly. 'You know what he's like.'

'Please!' Anger burnt inside Arnie. 'A bloke has a right to know who his fuckin' dad is and it ain't that cunt who beat the shit out of me when I was a kid.'

They fell silent, the atmosphere in the van crackling with tension. Without warning it was broken by a screech of brakes. Looking out of the window they saw two black BMW's shoot into the pub car park. A group of men jumped out, ski masks conceal-ing their identity, as the cars pulled up outside the pub's big front windows.

'What the fuck?' said Bruce.

As they watched, the men passed glass bottles around, rags pro-truding from the top. Each man lit the rag and spread out. One of the gang ran from one end of the Hope to the other, shoot-ing out the windows with an automatic weapon. The sound of shattering glass ripped through the air then those with the bottles hurled them forwards, their movements timed with precision like a military operation.

Through the smashed windows of the Hope and Anchor, Arnie, his mum and brother watched the flames dance.

14

'RIGHT, there was this Irish bloke, bit brain-dead like our Phil he was, and he went for this job on a building site.'

Sly Dolan loved telling a story. He reckoned if he'd taken it seriously he might have given that cockney comic Micky Flanagan a run for his money. At that moment, he was performing for a captive audience of female mourners sat in one of the large bay windows of the Hope: his own girl, a mousy haired bird called Millie, her friends, Fenella and Sharon, and Chuck's piece Becca. Truth be told, he would shag any of them given half the chance, and he was convinced the way into their knickers was to make them laugh. It had certainly worked with Millie.

Irish Phil had just arrived to clear the table which was rammed full of glasses, crisp bags and empty cigarette packets. A suitable period of mourning deemed to have passed, it was time to celebrate the life of the departed. Chuck was at the bar persuading the landlady to turn the jukebox back on and a loud cheer went up when the first few bars of 'Achy Breaky Heart' by Billy Ray Cyrus rang out, a reminder that Janie's mum had been a regular at the formation dance classes held in a school down the road.

'Oh no!' protested Sly, 'Who put this shit on?'

'Shhhh!' said Millie. 'It was Janie, I imagine. Don't go upsetting her now.'

'Right,' said Sly, taking a pint of lager from his older brother, who had returned from the bar with refills. 'So anyway, this Irishman … What the fuck? Get down!'

'Eh?'

Irish Phil thought it was part of the joke until he felt Sly's full weight on his back and tumbled to the floor, glasses shattering and people diving out of the way. The girls, having registered the look of stunned disbelief on Sly's face, instinctively threw themselves across the couch. Immediately, they were showered with glass as the window shattered.

'Christ!' said Chuck. 'Move!'

Sly saw his brother turn and grab a table, the old couple sitting at it looking up with surprise and consternation. Holding it in front of him like a knight with a shield, the oldest Dolan boy batted away the first Molotov Cocktail that flew through the open space but could do nothing about the one that fell next to Becca, flames leaping up the heavy, auburn drapes. Black, acrid smoke began filling the room, a dark cloud forming and spreading across the high ceiling.

Acting on instinct, Sly reached over and grabbed Becca's wrist, pulling her away from danger.

'Go back there, now, and take your friends with you,' he ordered, pointing further inside the pub. She was petrified, and he feared she might freeze, but when she put her arms around Fenella and Sharon and stumbled off in the direction of the bar, he felt relief course through him. A screaming Millie arrived, burying herself into his shoulder, but he shrugged her off and pointed her in the same direction as the others.

Billy Ray's best efforts were being drowned out by screams and shouts as the banks of black smoke multiplied, stealing the oxygen from the room. Coughing and spluttering, his eyes stinging, Sly turned to see Chuck holding a wet beer towel out to him, another pressed against his own face.

'I'll get some lads to barricade the doors so the bastards can't get in!' Chuck mumbled through his customised mask. 'You create a route to the back door and take people out that way.'

Turning, Sly saw Pete Vickers holding the arm of a grey-haired woman who was stumbling around in a daze, blood pouring from a nasty cut above her eyebrow; one of Janie's mum's best friends, Doreen something? They had to take control before there were more casualties.

Looking in the direction of the front door, he could see a couple of bodies prone on the floor and wondered whether they were injured, dead or just intent on self-preservation. The scene reminded him of an incident in his early 20s, just before the Boxer Boys went from bit-part players to leading lights on the east London crime scene, when a younger and more reckless Chuck had casually tossed a grenade into a Hackney nightclub heaving with teenagers. On that occasion they'd beaten a hasty retreat, watching from a side road as the fire took hold and panic ensued, people battering each other to the floor in their determination to survive. Four died in the ensuing mayhem and that alone told him the best way to handle this crisis was to remain cool under pressure. He took a moment to weigh up the scene and get a list of priorities straight in his head.

Fortunately, there were no kids in the vicinity and when he continued to scan the crowd he saw a couple of Boxer Boys turning this way and that, unsure what to do.

'Hey, Fancy Man! Over here and bring your mate!'

Despite the cacophony of competing noise, they spotted his waving hands and clambered towards him. All around him people were screaming, shouting, crying, the sounds accompanied by the crackle of wood and the plink-plunk of masonry falling all around.

'Right, get some of these old bastards out,' said Sly, shouting to be heard above the symphony from hell. 'Form an escape route with the furniture, funnelling people out through the back exit. Get them to be as orderly as possible – use force if necessary – and make sure anyone who needs help gets it. With any luck we can limit the damage.'

The two men raced off to do his bidding and for a minute he stood motionless, watching to make sure his instructions were followed. Then a thought struck him. What if the attackers were lying in ambush, just waiting for the pub to empty so that they could prey on those leaving when they were in no position to protect themselves? He had to ensure the escape route was clear and needed to cause a distraction even if it meant tackling the fire bombers head on. Seeing a discarded cue by the pool table, he went across and picked it up before pushing his way through confused bodies.

'Sly! Sylvester! Don't be an idiot!'

It was Chuck, but he had no time to reconsider. A creaking, crashing sound behind him made him pause briefly, and he turned to see part of a wooden beam detach itself from the ceiling and fall towards the crowd queuing to escape.

'Watch out!' he shouted. Too late. A familiar figure took the impact full-on: Chuck's best mate, Fancy Man. He fell in a heap, his face covered in blood, setting off another bout of screaming as those still inside stampeded for the exits.

Chuck appeared at Sly's shoulder. 'What happened? I heard a crash.'

Sly indicated with his head.

'Your boy Fancy Man's buried under there, Chuck.'

A slurry of human bodies moved towards the door, shoving and pushing, shouting and punching, gripped in the thrall of mass panic.

'OK, I'll sort it,' said Chuck. 'You do what you have to do.'

Sly nodded briefly then turned and vaulted a makeshift barricade of tables before charging out through the double swing doors. He was just in time to see two large BMW's with blackened windows tearing out of the car park with throaty roars and a tooth-jarring squeal of tyres.

'Fuckers!' he cursed, mentally grasping for clues as to who would feel the need to turn Irene Sullivan's wake into unholy carnage.

BACK inside the pub, Vickers felt tears streaming down his face. Holding his sleeve to his nose he desperately searched for his wife and children. What unfeeling bastard would launch an attack on a pub full of mourners? Didn't they have enough to cope with after the loss of a loved one?

Having heard a scream, Vickers saw Chuck wading through people blinded by confusion and made his way across to help. He arrived to find the eldest Dolan boy leaning over, attending to someone on the floor.

'Chuck!' he shouted.

'Vickers, son, you OK?'

'I can't find the family. They're—'

'They're all right. Fancy Man took them out the back door and shepherded into a waiting car. They're on the way back to your house as we speak. The trouble is Fancy came back in to help others—' He nodded in the direction of the prostrate figure, the face covered in blood.

'Shit!'

'See if Phil or Siobhan have got some tea towels, would you? I have to staunch the blood.'

Vickers disappeared and came back a short while later with a handful of towels. Without speaking, Chuck grabbed them and lifted the injured man's head, wrapping towel after towel around it. The prone man's eyes were shut.

'Is he going to be all right?' asked Vickers.

Chuck shrugged his shoulders.

From behind, someone pushed Vickers so that he nearly stumbled over on top of Chuck and the patient. He turned angrily, shouting to the crowd to get back.

'You can't come through here, there's a man badly injured. Go around!'

His menacing face and raised fist had the desired effect, and the crowd surged in another direction. A short distance away he saw Irish Phil and his mother, the elderly landlady, Siobhan, fighting the flames with fire extinguishers.

'That was a message, son,' Chuck said.

'Pretty strong one if you ask me,' said Vickers. 'Someone could have been killed.'

'Well, we don't know they haven't been,' said Chuck, indicating the casualty at his feet. 'Bastards! Let's get Fancy outside. Once we've done what we can here, we need a proper chat. First two of our lads are executed in Essex, now this. Someone's decided it's open season on the Boxer Boys. We have to find out who they are and strike back hard.'

ARNIE saw the familiar face charge out through the doors, smacking a pool cue against his hand. Though he was covered in dust and filth, he recognised his brother, Sly. He was too late, the perpetrators having gone.

People were streaming from the back exit of the pub and Arnie caught sight of his eldest brother Chuck and former friend Pete Vickers dragging something between them. The purple and green tonic trousers and expensive loafers gave the casualty away. It was Fancy Man.

Once clear of the burning building they placed the body on the floor and Chuck took a mobile phone from his pocket, quickly tapping in numbers. As he spoke into it, the shriek of approaching sirens ripped through the evening air.

'How awful!' said Beryl Dolan, surveying the scene from the SUV. 'A lot of our friends and neighbours are in there, plus all those lads who used to hang around with you, Arnie. Shouldn't we be doing something?'

'What do you recommend, Mum? Attach a garden hose to my head and send me in like a makeshift fire engine?'

She gave him a dark look. 'It's no time for jokes, Arnold. Really! I'm just thanking God the other boys are all right. I hope no one's seriously injured. Look at that poor lad on the ground. Gosh, it's John Fallon, isn't it? Chuck's friend. He needs help.'

She went to open the door, but Arnie tugged her back.

'Leave it to the experts, Mum, eh? They're on their way. I can't get involved.'

'But they're family.'

'Sure. And how often did they come to see me when I was in hospital? Or at the home? Or in prison? Bruce is the only one I can rely on. I'm sorry, Mum, but look, you can see they're all right and Anjie left ages ago.'

Bruce gave his brother a considered look.

'What?' said Arnie.

The younger Dolan shook his head. He wasn't convinced the attack had been a complete surprise to Arnie. All his new enemies in one place, the gang trying to forge their way without their leader? The cynic might say it was an opportunity to strike back. Were they here because Arnie knew what was going to happen and wanted ringside seats?

As the two older Dolan boys sped off in a waiting Land Rover, three fire engines, two ambulances and a police car arrived in the car park of the smoking pub, medics quickly attending the prone figure of Fancy Man.

'Time we left, too, Bruce,' said Arnie. 'We don't want to have to answer any annoying questions, do we? You know what will happen. They'll search my name on their bloody database, find out I've been inside, and the next thing I'll be getting the full interrogation malarkey. Put your foot down, there's a good lad.'

Bruce did as he was told, the SUV pulling away from the kerb. Arnie watched the wrecked pub disappearing into the distance. The flames were under control now, a black cloud hanging over the building as fire crews went to work with their water cannons.

'Look on the bright side,' said Arnie. 'That place has been crying out for refurbishment.'

15

GARETH stared out of the panoramic window, reflecting on the latest news report on the fire at the Hope and Anchor. The attack had taken place almost a month ago and that morning it had been announced an elderly woman had died in hospital from her injuries. It was now a murder inquiry, and police had revealed they were linking the fire with the two dead bodies found at Rainham Marshes.

Gareth couldn't help reflecting on his lucky break. If Anjie hadn't been working that night, they would have been caught up in the carnage. They had been halfway back to Wales when a news bulletin interrupted the music playing on the radio. Gareth had almost swerved into the central reservation of the M4 as a reporter described the scene. They had discussed going back, but Anjie had been assured there was nothing they could do in a phone call with Janie. As yet, no one had provided a reason for the attack, but Janie was convinced it had something to do with 'his business' – his meaning Vickers.

Two words, spoken completely out of context, jerked Gareth back to reality.

'Sausage rolls!'

A chubby bloke with a mass of black curls on his head leant forward from the other side of the conference table. Jonah Quinn, the media group's chief marketing strategist, was awaiting a response to his rousing declaration. Gareth's brain tried to unlock the clever strategy behind the mention of savoury treats and came up blank.

Was this one of those tricks marketing people had a tendency to use in order to grab your attention?

The room was silent for seconds, Jonah wallowing in the sense of anticipation he'd created. Slowly, gorging on every word as if it was the sweetest, juiciest pastry ever to have seduced his taste buds, he embellished his idea.

'A free sausage roll for every reader!'

Standing back from the table, he awaited an applause that never came. Instead, the suggestion was greeted by a single chuckle. Gareth tried to disguise his impromptu outburst by clearing his throat but the more he sought to contain his amusement, the more apparent it became. He coughed, spluttered, wiped his eyes and squeaked an apology, sounding as if he'd inhaled the contents of a helium balloon.

The previous night he'd been roped into attending a rugby match with the Shakespeares and had drunk far more than was appropriate for a 'school night'. The alcohol was still sloshing around in his system and for a moment he thought this might be to blame for his confusion. Aware he was struggling, Jacko jumped in to draw attention away from the man he'd just promoted to chief football writer.

'Ummm, interesting,' he said. 'Perhaps you could elaborate on this plan of yours, Jonah mun?'

'Well, it's quite simple really, Jacko,' said the marketing man. 'We have a very good relationship with the local bakery here in Cardiff and they have kindly offered us a terrific deal. There's plenty of value in it and we all know how the Welsh love their sausage rolls.'

Managing to contain another chuckle, Gareth felt he couldn't let the moment pass without comment.

'Of course, the Welsh love their sausage rolls, doesn't everyone?' he said. 'How is this uniquely Welsh? We've got the European Championships coming up – the biggest event in Welsh football for 58 years – and you're offering them a savoury pastry to mark the event? This tournament is going to command huge interest. Surely we can come up with something a bit more relevant?'

'No offence, but you're new to these parts, Gareth,' said Jonah. 'I think you're missing the point. These are Welsh sausages from Welsh pigs reared by Welsh farmers. You put a photograph of Aaron Ramsey biting into one and …voila!'

Editor Lana Desmund interrupted, her Scottish brogue adding a new ingredient to the debate.

'It's not a bad idea, Jonah,' she said. 'It appears, though, our Mr Prince has more ambitious plans in mind.'

It was meant as a question, not a statement. Gareth cleared his throat and tried desperately to shake away the alcoholic fug. Any idea he came up with needed to be vastly superior to the one they were debating or he would be giving Lana more ammunition with which to attack him.

'I was thinking of inflatables,' he said. 'When I first came here there were a lot of those cool, blow-up sheep around. The cameras focus on them at big sporting events so with a recognisable logo or the name of your brand emblazoned on the side, they can be great free publicity. Who doesn't like playing with a balloon?'

He could feel all eyes on him, some of the representatives of the advertising department nodding their heads in agreement. He expanded on the idea. 'I remember the Grimsby supporters taking inflatable fish to an FA Cup game because the town was well known for its fishing. It's the same with the Welsh and sheep … or maybe leeks.'

'Hmmm,' said Jonah. 'Stereotyping. We risk becoming a laughing stock as usual. Aren't there enough accusations bandied around already that we enjoy "romantic" liaisons with farm animals?'

One of the ad reps stood up. 'Too right! The English call us bloody sheepshaggers, mun.'

His moon-cratered face was glowing even more than his bright orange hair. 'I see your point, though, Gareth, and I think it's a terrific idea. If we wanted a compromise, though, what about a free inflatable Welsh sausage roll for every reader?'

Gareth shook his head in despair as some of those around the table nodded their assent.

'Right, we've got the germ of an idea to work with here,' said Lana, attempting to defuse the tension in the room. 'Why don't you pursue the inflatable suggestion, Jonah, see how cheaply we can feasibly do it and maybe we could tie it in with sausage rolls – y'know, get your inflatable plus a free sausage roll? Our marketing budget is negligible, but I may be able to persuade the MD to buy into the idea. We are an award-winning paper now, after all.'

Gareth realised it was diplomacy like this that earned her the big bucks.

'All agreed?' she said, looking around the desk at a sea of nodding heads. 'Now, Jacko, editorial wise—?'

The veteran sports journalist struggled to his feet.

'These two events – The Lions tour and the, ah, European Championships – can be huge for the newspaper, particularly if Wales progress to the later rounds in the football. Gareth and I will be sitting down to discuss the fine tuning. I'm hoping to get one of the legendary Welsh football names to do a column. I realise we need to be mindful of the budget, but with Eurostar it's pretty easy to get people over to France these days and Gareth could stay in one of those, umm, boutique hotels.'

Gareth had his fingers crossed under the table, but the suggestion passed without comment.

'As for the Lions, we have struck a deal with the Beeb to get The Legend out there,' the sports editor continued. 'They'll pay for his flights, hotel room etc and we liaise with him over his articles and column. Win-win. I'm hoping we can find a little bit extra to send our new recruit, Jason, down under, too. We get a far better column out of The Legend when we speak to him face-to-face.'

'Hmmm,' said Lana. 'You mean we need someone out there to stop him going on a bender. You and I both know, Jacko, how trying to get hold of him on the phone is nigh-on impossible, even when he's just down the road. Going to Australia, the scene of his biggest success, is bound to put temptation in his way.'

Gareth felt obliged to mount a defence. 'He's not touched a drop since coming out of hospital,' he said. 'And his family are an extra incentive to keep him from going astray.'

She gave him a hard stare. 'Yes, Mr Prince, we know he's your mate. The trouble is we have been through similar scenarios. People tell me he has changed his ways then he lets us down again. It is going to take more than a couple of weeks off the pop to persuade me this leopard has changed his spots. What's your plan for online, Jacko?'

'Ummm, we'll put all the reports on the website once we've published.'

'No,' said the editor. 'I don't think you understand me. We need a specific online plan which involves more than sticking day-old newspaper reports on the web. We need to react instantly when something happens: I'm thinking team polls, player polls, blogs, Facebook pages, memes, podcasts, the works ...'

'Yes, Lana.'

'So, you've thought about it then? I'm all ears.'

Gareth noticed the old man's face drain of colour. It was blatantly obvious this was the first time Jacko had considered social media. Deciding it was time to repay some favours, Gareth got to his feet.

'I've been looking into this for Jacko,' he said. 'Jason has been developing his online presence over the last couple of months. He'll blog every day from the Lions, answer readers' questions and get a bit of interaction going. A special *Twitter* feed will be set up specifically for Welsh rugby news, and there will also be a *Facebook* page.'

He was pleased to see people nodding their agreement.

'In the case of the football we'll live blog every game, while sending out some of the best behind-the-scenes pictures on *Instagram* and *Snapchat*, particularly those taken by fans. We can invite reader participation, sending in their best fancy-dress pictures and that sort of thing, or a video of them singing their favourite footie anthem. We could have a Euros X-Factor competition.'

'Excellent,' said Lana, nodding keenly. As Gareth sat down Jacko patted him on the knee.

'Thanks,' he whispered. In the past the sports editor had been the biggest victim of Gareth's blagging abilities. This time the younger man had come to his rescue.

As the meeting broke up, Jacko caught up with Gareth as he was buying a cup of coffee in the canteen.

'You know what you said, mun?'

'What about, Jacko? It was a long meeting.'

'You know, the online stuff.'

'What about it?'

'Can we do all that, butt?'

Gareth smiled. 'Most of it will be pretty simple to set up to be honest: *Facebook* pages, *Twitter* feeds, blogs and such. Some of the other things might be a bit more techy but that's why we have an IT department.'

'Lot of use they've been in the past,' said Jacko wearily. 'Still, what you said was great, mun. It's given me an idea. As you're obviously well up on this new techie stuff I'm going to put you in charge of making it happen.'

Gareth swore under his breath. Not for the first time his willingness to help out had landed him in the mire.

HIS mobile burst into 'I'm Forever Blowing Bubbles' as he returned to his desk. The ringtone brought scowls from some of those scattered around the busy newsroom. He had it on full volume and breathed a sigh of relief that it hadn't gone off in conference – Lana wouldn't have been impressed. He put the device to his ear. 'Hello?'

There was silence for a moment, a conversation taking place in the background. Suspecting he was the victim of a cold caller, he was about to hang up when a voice he didn't recognise came on the line.

'Umm, sorry, is that Gary?'

His stomach did a somersault. Very rarely was he called that these days.

'My name's Gareth …Gareth Prince,' he said. 'How can I help you?'

'Oh, sorry, I was after Gary Marshall. I guess I've got a wrong number.'

The caller was putting on his best telephone voice, but Gareth could detect traces of an unfamiliar accent.

'Who is this?' he asked.

'Sorry,' said the caller. 'My name is Detective Chief Inspector Alan Rowbottom.'

A thousand thoughts instantly raced through Gareth's mind: The fire at the Hope, a scowling figure in a wheelchair, his friend Will Shakespeare breaking the speed limit as he drove around the narrow, winding roads on Caerphilly Mountain, Maxi and Anjelica and the fear they might have been involved in an accident. He was so preoccupied he just caught the end of the caller's sentence.

'…Staffordshire Serious Crime Unit. We need to speak to Gary Marshall as a matter of urgency.'

The reporter realised he would learn nothing by delaying the inevitable. 'Well… actually I'm Gary Marshall. I changed my name a while back. How can I help you?'

'I'm afraid it's a rather sensitive matter.' The whispering in the background resumed. 'Where are you?'

'In work … in Cardiff, South Wales.'

'Right, hold on.' More background whispering. 'If we left in the next half hour, I reckon we could be with you by early evening.'

After the police rang off, Gareth leaned back in his chair, sucking on his pen.

Staffordshire? What the hell could concern him in Staffordshire?

16

GARETH opened the door to a tall man in a dark suit accompanied by a young woman, similarly dressed and wearing her hair in a bun.

'Gary Marshall?' The plain-clothed officer seemed nervous, brushing at the thick, brown hair which shone in the reflection of the porch light.

'People call me Gareth these days, but whatever suits you I guess.'

'We spoke on the phone. DCI Rowbottom.'

He held out his hand and Gareth took it.

'It's a bit wet out here and we've had a nightmare drive – M4 was chock-a-block. Is it all right if we come in?'

He flashed his warrant card before introducing his colleague as Detective Constable Dorothy Willetts. Gareth nodded and waved them through.

'Can you tell me what this is about?' he asked.

They wiped their feet on the mat and he pointed them in the direction of the lounge. As the DC went to follow her superior, a child's voice came from upstairs.

'Who's that, Daddy?'

'It's just a couple of police people come to see daddy,' he shouted. 'Why are you out of bed, Max? You've had your story, and it's time for sleep. You've got school in the morning.'

'Are they going to take you to prison?'

DC Willetts intervened. 'Daddy is just helping us with some questions. He won't be long. Now if I was you, I would do as he says.'

'There,' said Gareth. 'You've been told by the police.'

Maxi scurried away, and the policewoman smiled. They listened to the explosion of tiny feet running across the landing above. 'Cute,' she said, pushing through into the lounge. 'What did you say his name was?'

'Max. We call him Maxi.'

Gareth ushered the senior detective into an armchair and indicated his colleague should sit, too, but she preferred to stand. 'Can I make anyone tea?' she offered.

'No thanks,' said Gareth, thinking it an odd situation that she should be offering to make drinks when he was the host. He sank into the comfortable red sofa he and Anjie had bought in a second-hand furniture store on the outskirts of Cardiff. 'I just want to know what this is about.'

'Are you familiar with a Stan Marshall?' asked the DCI, leaning forwards and staring intently into his eyes. Gareth felt the hairs rise on his forearms and fear grip his stomach. It had been years since he'd heard the name.

'My dad,' he said.

'Ahhh, thought as much.'

'I haven't seen him for 15 years,' said Gareth. 'I'm surprised you found me. I changed my name by deed poll some time ago and everyone knows me as Gareth Prince.'

The DCI looked over his shoulder at his colleague. She reached over and handed her boss what appeared to be a notebook in a polythene bag. Gareth felt guilty even though he'd done nothing wrong.

'Take a look at this, but don't take it out of the bag please, sir.' He handed the book over. It was open to the first page. 'Did you write this?'

Gareth realised it was a tattered address book. The phrase *next of kin* was printed on it and the name Gary Marshall was scrawled alongside, together with his current mobile number. He had no idea how his dad had obtained it.

'Not me,' he said. 'Sorry, what is this about?'

'This book was found in the lining of your father's overcoat.'

'He left his coat somewhere? Like I said, I have no idea what he's been doing or where he is so I can't help with that.'

The DCI studied his face.

'What?' asked Gareth. 'You don't believe me?'

He couldn't help feeling it was a long way for these officers to travel in order to find the owner of a coat.

'It's a bit more serious than a lost coat I'm afraid, Mr Marshall,' said the DCI, again studying Gareth's face. 'I'm sorry to inform you that your father, Stan Marshall, is dead.'

Though delivered in a Midlands accent rather than by a cockney copper, the words transported Gareth back to another time, when he'd been taken into custody after fighting between West Ham and Cardiff fans spilled out onto the streets of east London. On that occasion a Welsh supporter had been killed during a street battle and for a short while Gareth had been the prime suspect. Fortunately, he was released after new evidence emerged.

The detective was still speaking.

'The body was found with stab wounds in an alleyway in Stoke two nights ago,' he said. 'As the Senior Investigating Officer, I only thought it right that I should inform you in person ... we have launched a murder inquiry.'

Part II

Reunion

'We coulda been together'

Stan, by Eminem

17

GARETH got off the train just after 2.00 p.m., stepping into glaring sunlight. DC Willetts was waiting for him outside the station.

'Welcome to Stoke-on-Trent,' she said, reaching for his bag. 'Good trip?'

He waved her away.

'I got as far as Newport and they kicked us off because the train had developed a fault,' he said. 'Then we were delayed half an hour outside Swindon because of "Leaves on the line".' He made speech marks in the air. 'That's when I rang you.'

'Are you staying overnight?' she nodded at his bag. 'I can recommend some good—'

'No ... thanks. That's my laptop and some other work-related things. I had some writing to do on the journey. Unfortunately, the WiFi was on the blink. I need to get back to Anjie and Maxi tonight, so if we could get on with it—'

'Fair enough.'

The policewoman led him to an unmarked metallic blue Vauxhall Astra in the station car park.

'Have you been here before, Mr, umm—?'

'Call me Gareth. I'm used to it now.' He looked around briefly. 'A long time ago I came here for a football game. A lot will have changed since then.'

'I suspect some has and some hasn't,' said DC Willetts, opening the passenger door for the reporter. 'We Potteries folk tend to fixate on the past. What was the football game you saw? I'm mad about the Potters, me. Whenever I get time off, I watch the lads. We're doing OK at the moment.'

'I'm a West Ham fan,' said Gareth. 'I travelled up here with a gang of mates in my teens. It was a long time ago. A lot of water has passed under the bridge.'

'Your lot were down here a couple of weeks ago,' she said. 'All leave was cancelled.'

Some things never change, thought Gareth. He looked out of the window as DS Willett manoeuvred the car into the street. A long, red-brick building glided past on the right, peeking out from behind barriers erected to hide the construction work in progress.

'That's Staffordshire University,' said DC Willetts, taking up a running commentary. 'They're always building extensions. You wonder whether it will ever be finished. This is a big student area.'

They passed a row of shops including a large off-licence, fast-food pizza takeaway, newsagent, Internet cafe, launderette and let-tings bureau – everything a student needed to sustain them during their first time away from Mum and Dad. The turquoise wall of a local store was one of the only bright features in an otherwise drab environment. Soon, though, the area opened up, vast expanses of greenery rolling by on both sides of the road.

'Hanley Park,' said the detective constable, making a circular movement with her hands. 'It's a local treasure. In the summer it's a great place to wander around, enjoying the peace and the blooming flowers. There's a picturesque duck pond just through the gates there.'

'Any children?'

'Me? No, it's just me and my boyfriend. Feeding the ducks reminds me of when I was a kid.'

Further up the hill an ornate building boasting a large green dome came into view. The two-storey brick structure stretched for some way, arch windows lining the front and a tall tower butting into the sky at the far end.

'The city's first purpose-built mosque,' explained the DC. 'There's a large Muslim population here, around 10,000. They raised more than £2m to get it built. It wasn't popular with some locals, though. Three years ago, two loonies broke in, ran a gas pipe into the building and started a fire, intending to burn it to the ground. They said they were acting in response to some Islamist who burnt a poppy during the Remembrance Day celebrations. Fortunately, the fire brigade saved the building, but the opening was severely delayed and the bill for damages came to £50,000.'

'Is there a problem here?' asked Gareth.

'Racism?'

He nodded.

'There's tension certainly, but that seems to be par for the course throughout the country,' she said. 'When we lost the pits and most of the pottery industry, the heart of the city was ripped out. Unemployment's high and some of the white population blame their hardship on immigrants, many of whom arrived decades ago to fill a gap in the labour market. Tensions increased after 9/11 and the wars in Afghanistan and Iraq. Stories of British teens joining ISIS in Syria and Iraq don't help, though we've found no evidence of fundamentalist recruitment here.'

'Keeps you busy, I guess, maintaining the peace,' said Gareth.

'We're stuck between a rock and a hard place. Ethnic minorities say we don't do enough to prevent racist attacks and have started up their own 'self-defence' organisations. Some opportunist types have formed gangs and don't always work within the law. The white population think we turn a blind eye to Asian troublemakers, blaming it on political correctness. Not that long ago a Pakistani stabbed his neighbour to death. The victim was a fascist sympathiser who had put his killer through years and years of abuse. The killer was jailed, of course, but both sides attacked us for different reasons. The Muslims said it was our fault he took the law into his own hands because we ignored his complaints. The other lot accused us of letting him off lightly, saying he should be deported, even though he has lived here his entire life. Add into the mix the new influx of asylum seekers and it's pretty volatile.'

'Sounds like it,' admitted Gareth. He was fortunate that in the two areas he'd lived – east London and Wales – different cultures seemed in the large part to co-exist in peace, though there were always a few nut jobs hell-bent on causing trouble.

'We're a sitting duck for right-wing extremists,' said the DC. 'The English Defence League stage regular rallies here and not long ago we had 12 British National Party members on the council. On top of it all we have to contend with this Brexit vote coming in the summer. If what's happening in the world is anything to go by, I reckon it will be a close call.'

'Really?' Until now, Gareth had been convinced the referendum on whether Britain should stay or leave the European Union was a foregone conclusion. The government and all its resources were lined up heavily in favour of the Remain campaign.

'People listen to that UKIP bloke, Farage, and believe a vote for leaving the EU will mean we'll shut our borders to immigrants,' said the DC. 'There are some not-too-bright sparks who think all the Asians who live here will be rounded up and deported – even though most of those under 30 were born here! Ahh, here we are.'

They passed a long, thin building with the police sign on the outside wall. The DC drove into the car park behind it, pulling into a space next to a smattering of similar vehicles.

'Welcome to Hanley,' she said. 'Police headquarters is in Stafford these days and this place isn't as busy as it used to be, but it's a convenient building in which to base a murder inquiry.' She brought the car to a halt. 'The guvnor will be pleased to see you. He was putting off his lunch until your arrival. He'll probably be hangry now!'

Gareth raised his eyebrows.

'Sorry,' said the DC, laughing. 'It's one of those modern expressions, used to describe the bad mood you can get into if you haven't eaten.'

She paused, her expression turning serious. 'Listen, I know this can be a traumatic time for family members – the death of a loved one. It is my job as Family Liaison Officer to help you and your family through as best I can. If you need me, I won't be far away. People call me Dolly, by the way.'

'Thanks, Dolly, but it's fine,' said Gareth. 'Like I said, we fell out. The old bastard was missing for almost half my life. He was a complete stranger to me.'

DCI Rowbottom greeted Gareth with a firm handshake.

'Good to see you again, Mr—'

'Prince is fine. Gareth if you prefer.'

'Great. Before we get onto the identification, I've booked a conference room because there are a few things I want you to see. Our CCTV retrieval team have found some footage of your dad from earlier on the day of his death,' said the DCI. 'We wondered if you might recognise any of the people he was with.'

'It's a long shot,' said Gareth. 'Like I told you before, I haven't seen him in years. He disappeared off the radar. Last thing I knew he was living in Bolton.'

'We know about the Bolton connection,' said Rowbottom. 'Our colleagues in Lancashire are on to it. Mind you, he left there 10 years ago and has been living in a pretty grotty bedsit here ever since. Our dedicated exhibits officers – you'd probably think of them as CSI's from the telly – found very little on their visit, just a mattress on the floor and some cheap bedding.'

'He left a lot of possessions in London, together with his wife and kids,' said Gareth, unable to disguise the bitterness in his voice.

'You really didn't like him, did you?'

Gareth thought about the statement. Then, without warning, the tears formed, memories flashing through his brain like an old news reel: His dad giving him his beloved racing bike for Christmas, his dad on the sidelines at football, his dad being the life and soul at Christmas parties and get-togethers.

Good old Stan Marshall, the joker in the pack.

'I bloody loved him!' he blubbed, the raw emotion surprising him, sweeping away defences it had taken years to build. 'I loved him so bloody much. He was my dad.'

'Sorry,' said the DCI, moving around the desk and patting his shoulder. 'The death of a close relative affects people in different ways. Take your time and I'll get us some tea.' Lifting a phone, he barked instructions into the handset. Gareth delved in his pockets for the tissues Anjie always put there, most of the time without his knowledge. Ripping the packet open, he pulled one out, dabbed at his eyes and blew his nose.

'It's me who should be sorry,' said Gareth. 'I don't know what came over me.'

'It's fine,' said Rowbottom. 'He might not have been the greatest dad, but he was the only one you had. Would you like to have a few moments – I can send Dolly, sorry DC Willetts, in for a chat if you like.'

Gareth shook his head and sat in silence as DCI Rowbottom sifted paperwork. Eventually the door opened and a man in uniform entered, placing a tray containing two China mugs, a sugar bowl and a small milk jug on the desk.

'Thanks, Jim,' said Rowbottom. 'Have a cuppa, Mr Prince, you'll feel a lot better.'

Gareth added a lump of sugar to his tea, poured on milk and stirred. He felt more composed already. It had been a long day, he'd been up early, and he put his unexpected reaction down to tiredness.

On the other side of the desk, the DCI picked up his cup, lifted it to the light and studied the bottom of it. Taking a sip of the brew, he became aware of Gareth's confused expression.

'Force of habit,' he said. 'We Potteries folk always check to see who made our cups and saucers. Ma lady isn't from here and takes the Mickey out of me mercilessly about it. I'm Stoke born and bred and know everything about the place which is why they've assigned me to the case, I suspect. I'll do my best to find those responsible, Mr Prince, believe me. Now let's get down to the conference room.'

Gareth followed the DCI to a room containing rows of tables and chairs, a large TV monitor stretched across the far wall. In front of it a police constable fiddled with a computer on a lectern. Dolly sat silently at the back, ready and waiting in case Gareth broke down again. He had regained his composure, though, and was determined he wouldn't surrender to sentiment.

'This place is mainly used for training and presentations these days,' explained Rowbottom. 'Take a seat, Mr Prince.'

Gareth nodded, and the DCI pressed a button on a remote console. Dolly got up to turn off the lights and blurry images appeared on the screen.

'This is the Coach and Horses. It's not the scene of your father's death but it is another town pub where he was spotted on the day he died. Tell me if you recognise anyone.'

The scene was a busy lunchtime boozer, several people in business suits sitting at tables talking, laughing, joking and tucking into meals. Others in casual gear stood around in groups, sipping from pints and swapping stories. DCI Rowbottom got up and walked forwards, his shadow falling across the screen.

'Here's your father now,' said the DCI, stepping aside and using a stick to indicate a figure pushing through the main doors.

Gareth's mouth dropped open. Though the footage was grainy, the sight of Stan Marshall took his breath away. His face was concealed by an unruly bush of facial hair, his once well-groomed mop now thin and greasy, dripping like an untended leak down the side of his face. His clothes hung off him and had it not been for the familiar donkey jacket, ripped and dirty, Gareth would have thought it a case of mistaken identity. In the 13 years since he last saw the old man, Stan had become a tramp. Watching the figure shuffle to the bar, he felt a twinge of guilt. Was he partly to blame for his dad's sorry appearance?

As the footage rolled on, Stan struck up a conversation with the barman, a thick-set bloke whose shaved head was covered in an ugly purple tattoo which gave the impression he'd walked under a ladder just at the moment a painter dropped his tin.

The barman walked off and returned with a pint of something dark. Stan took a large gulp. *He still drinks Guinness*, thought Gareth, refreshing memories from a past life and fighting back the tears again when he realised he had used the present tense.

As Stan put down the pint and turned away from the bar, Gareth shifted forward in his chair. A young man in a khaki designer airman's jacket and jeans came into view. Under the close-cropped brown hair, the features looked familiar, and the reporter searched for a name to put to the face. As he did so, people in the vicinity of Stan and the young man began moving aside, as if forming a guard of honour, then closed in like the tide returning to a sandy beach.

The person who had created the human wave came into view. Gareth noted solid shoulders, light-coloured close-cropped hair and a familiar glint in the eyes as the figure looked directly into one of the security cameras from his wheelchair.

Barely able to contain his shock, Gareth wanted to charge from the room and shout and swear at the top of his voice. Instead he sat still as stone, his expression unchanged.

He wouldn't give up Arnold bloody Dolan just yet.

BACK in the office, the DCI pulled a plastic evidence bag from his drawer and handed it over. 'These are photocopies,' he said. 'We found the originals lying under the body.'

Gareth took the package. A couple of pieces of ripped card nestled inside. He peered at them, recalling a Saturday long ago when he'd travelled with a group of West Ham fans to Liverpool. In the back of a transit van, Arnie had dished out A5 cards to everyone.

'What are these for?' one of the gang had asked.

'Think of them as our business cards,' was Arnie's reply. 'I want these scouse bastards to know what hit 'em.'

To Gareth, it had all seemed a bit childish.

'You have been visited by the ICF,' the message had said, the initials standing for Inter-City Firm, the name adopted by West Ham's travelling hooligan faction.

'Each time we do one of them, we leave our calling card,' Arnie had explained. 'I want people to respect us like they did in the 70s and 80s, before we went soft.'

He poured the pieces of paper onto the DCI's desk. The evidence in front of Gareth had been some kind of message before it was torn apart, possibly by the victim. Was it a calling card?

'We're thinking DOA, you know, Dead on Arrival?' said Rowbottom, reading Gareth's mind. 'It's a cliché, I know, but if someone likes their cop shows, it might be their warped idea of humour.'

The letters D and O were together on one scrap of card, the A standing alone on the other. He laid them out the way the police officer said and studied them closely.

'What are these do you reckon?' he asked, pointing to some marks in the centre of the O which seemed like they might have been scraped onto the card.

'Just a few smudges, I'm guessing. Your dad's hands were filthy. He'd been scrambling around on the floor.'

'You think he ripped it up?' said Gareth.

'Pretty much. His fingerprints are all over them.'

Gareth lifted the cards again and changed the order. He felt like one of the contestants trying to solve a conundrum in a daytime TV show, but eventually handed them back to the Inspector with a shake of the head.

Internally, his brain was shouting, 'Bingo!'

He didn't need a chemistry degree to work out the equation once he'd switched the letters. A = Arnie DO = Dolan. His former friend had plenty of questions to answer.

18

'THIS place is getting worse!' said Anjie as they pulled into the car park below Alan Minter Towers on the Boxers Estate. There were large potholes in the tarmac and a wrecked Ford Cortina smoked away by the overflowing waste bins. Feral kids were haring around on motorbikes while their hoodie mates stood in the shadows, drinking from cans. It was easy to conclude they were the pyromaniacs responsible for the smouldering wreck. They watched Gareth's Corsa, pointing and whispering to each other.

'Scum,' she said. 'I hope your nice little car doesn't end up like that. Perhaps we should park somewhere more secure.'

She jerked her head in the direction of the hoodies. 'Please tell me we weren't like that.'

'We weren't,' said Gareth. 'We were always the height of fashion – apart from your Arnie, and even he scrubbed up well in his late teens.'

'Poor kid, always wearing Chuck and Sly's hand-me-downs. We weren't poor, but some of Dad's money was, umm, tied up.'

'Buried in Epping Forest, you mean.'

He chuckled, and she punched him on the shoulder. 'Oww!'

'Well, leave my dad out of it!'

'Don't hit Dad, Mummy!' came a little voice from the back.

'Nice to see someone's on my side,' said Gareth. 'Thanks, Maxi.'

'Are we there yet?' he asked.

'Yeah,' said Gareth, ashamed he wasn't taking Max somewhere nicer. These were the boy's roots, though.

Anjie read his mind.

'You've been spoilt,' she said. 'Getting away when you did. You've discovered a better class of poor people. How long has it been since you actually left Barking, five years?'

He nodded. 'This place reminds me of a record my dad used to play – 'Hotel California' by a band called the Eagles. It had a line about being able to check out any time you wanted but never being able to leave. It wasn't about a hotel at all, but a prison. I feel that way about Barking. You never really escape it.' He fell silent for a moment, thinking of his father. 'It's the old man who's checked out now.'

'Oh, love.' She placed her hand gently on his knee.

'It's OK,' he said. 'Couldn't have happened to a nicer person.'

His throat caught on the words and she wondered if he was finally going to shed a tear in front of her. Instead, he took a deep breath, pushed open the door and headed for the boot to retrieve the bags. All the time he kept his eyes on the local hoods. Their presence reminded him of that day he'd escaped a mugging on this very spot, Arnie springing to his rescue. It was the start of a close friendship.

'Let's get in before they decide we might have something worth nicking,' said Anjie, arriving at his side.

Crossing the car park, he was soon tapping a code into a panel by the main doors. The numbers had been the same for years, an open invitation to burglars, though no self-respecting crime lord would break into such a ramshackle shit-hole. Pushing through, he read the hastily scrawled sign on the lift doors.

'Out of order,' he said. 'Sorry, gang, we have to walk.'

Though his tone was cheerful, inside his head a barrage of colourful swear words circulated. 'You carry Max and I'll bring the cases.'

'Why not ring Reg?' said Anjie. 'He'll help.'

'Pool night,' said Gareth, recalling his stepdad's routine.

Taking the bags from her, he held his breath to block out the odour of piss, shit, vomit and marijuana that lingered in the stair-well. If ever he made proper money in the newspaper game or, more likely, won the lottery, his first job would be to persuade his mother to leave this ghetto. It seemed a long time ago that the blocks had received a makeover and been renamed after box-ers synonymous with the east end. Thirty years, he guessed. It was how his old gang had earned their name, the Boxer Boys reflecting the environment in which they grew up.

Three flights of stairs later, he stood in front of the same maroon door he'd barged through millions of times as a kid. When he rang the bell, a shape materialised through the frosted glass.

'The prodigal son returns,' said Reg Philpott, throwing open the door to Gareth's surprise. Thin as a stick and with teeth that deserved to be condemned just as much as the tower blocks, his mum's second husband was dressed in a grungy grey cardigan and black oversized tracksuit bottoms. On his feet, black plimsolls were a gentle jog from falling apart. Pushing his wispy grey hair from his face, Reg patted it down over a rapidly receding hairline. He had aged enormously since the last time Gareth saw him.

'No pool, Reg?'

'Nah,' said the older man. 'I'm getting a bit old for that now, son. Anyway, since the fire the Hope's been closed and they moved the team to another venue. I couldn't be bothered. It's a young man's game. There's always a ruck to be had. All you need is a row over whether someone has two shots remaining or one and the whole place goes up. I wouldn't have missed this anyhow – where is he?'

Anjie walked into the light, lowering Max to the floor. The old man bent down in front of him. ''Ello, soldier,' he said. 'I'm Granddad Reg.'

Max looked puzzled. 'My granddaddy is Pappy Maurice, and he's gone off on a boat around the world, Nan says.'

'You have two grandfathers, Max,' said Anjie, colouring up with embarrassment. 'Grandpa Maurice is my daddy and Granddad Reg is your father's daddy.'

'Oh.'

There's another granddad, too, thought Gareth. He's in the morgue.

There was a yelp and Gareth caught sight of a marauding figure bouncing up the hallway. Before he could mount a suitable defence, the woman smothered him in an embrace then clutched his cheeks so hard his eyes watered.

'My baby, my baby, you're back!' squealed Sheila Philpott, patting at her hair and trying to bring her excitement levels under control. '…And here's the lovely Anjie and, wow, is that my special boy? Remember me, Max?'

The kid ignored the question and turned to his mother. 'I'm hungry, Mum.'

'Sorry, Sheila, we got stuck in traffic,' said Anjie. 'The M25 was horrendous.'

'Always is, not that we get out much these days. Come on in! I've a stew in the oven and I'm sure once Max has had a bite to eat he'll feel more talkative. Gosh, he's grown, love him, and look at that head of black hair.' She looked at Gareth. 'Doesn't take after you love, does he?'

Gareth allowed her the jibe. Though dyed black now, as a kid he'd had a shock of red hair. His mum had helped Anjie organise his makeover before he left London to start afresh. She played the guilt card, ribbing him for not visiting every time they spoke on the phone, but she knew deep down he'd done the right thing, putting distance between himself, Arnie Dolan and the gang.

'Don't stand on ceremony, come in!' she urged. They followed her down the corridor to the front room and as soon as his foot crossed the threshold, Gareth's mind stumbled back in time. It was exactly as he remembered it.

Taking pride of place on the far wall was a life-sized framed poster of guitarist Rick Parfitt of the rock band Status Quo, lording it over souvenirs and pictures of the royal family. Tacky commemorative mugs, plates, cutlery and framed pictures of Wills and

Kate, Harry and their long-dead mother Princess Diana filled every conceivable space.

'Bet you could do with a nice cup of Rosie Lea, Anj, love. Keep our guests company please, Reg.'

'No problem, treacle,' he said.

'I'll help,' said Gareth, following his mother from the room.

As she spooned loose leaf tea from a caddy into a familiar hand-painted teapot with garish purple flowers on the side, he caught up with her. She was dressed in a dull grey house coat and brown slacks, a pair of tatty paisley slippers on her feet. She, too, didn't resemble the woman he remembered, the one who dressed as a rock chick well into her 40s. He wondered if his absence had contributed to her decline. She'd had health problems, including a cancer scare, in the previous decade and he felt guilty knowing he wasn't about to ease the pain.

Putting his hands around her waist as she filled the kettle from the sink, he said, 'I've got something to tell you, Mum.'

'About time—'

'I'm not getting married.'

'Oh, shame.'

'It's about Dad.'

'I know. Reg doesn't look great, but I think—'

'I mean my real dad.'

She fell silent, the water running until the kettle overflowed.

'Mum?'

Snapping back to the present, she put the lid on the kettle, emptied the excess down the sink then plugged it in and flicked the switch.

'I don't want to know anything about that man,' she said. 'We don't talk about him. You know that. He caused us too much misery. I sometimes wish—'

'He's dead, Mum.'

'What?'

'Stan Marshall. My dad. Your ex-husband. He's dead.'

'No,' she said, shaking her head. 'That's a lie. He's up north with some—'

'The Stoke-on-Trent police found him a few days ago.'

'It can't be him,' she said. 'He went to Bolton, not Stoke.'

'He split up with that girl a long time ago, apparently, and ended up in Stoke. I don't know the whys and wherefores, but I had to go and identify the body. The police have done all the DNA and fingerprint tests, checked the dental records … there's no doubt. They found my number in his address book as next of kin.'

'Nah, can't be,' she said.

'I'm sorry, it's true … and there's something else.'

She moved her head a fraction, and he took that as instructions to continue. 'He was stabbed, Mum. Murdered.'

Slowly she took a seat in the crammed kitchen area. He pressed the button on the kettle so that it would boil, then sat down opposite. He could see his mother's eyes watering so grabbed some kitchen roll and handed it over.

'I'm not crying for him,' she spat. 'What's happened just reminds me of everything he put us through.'

'Of course.'

'He was such a bastard,' she said. 'He led me up the garden path, lied and cheated for years. I gave that man everything.'

He nodded, patting her back.

'He saved me in the beginning, it's true,' she said. 'I don't know where I would have ended up if he hadn't been there for me … but that's another story.'

'I'm listening.'

'Not now.'

She blew loudly into the tissue, rolling it into a ball and putting it on the table. Standing, she retrieved another from her housecoat pocket and wiped her eyes.

'I still see him in you.'

He wasn't sure what to make of that. She was throwing her thoughts out scattergun.

'He so wanted you to be a footballer,' she said. 'Up every week-end morning at the crack of dawn, he would take you here, there and everywhere. "Have boots, will travel," he used to say. Then when it came to the crunch, he let you down big time. How could someone get everything so badly wrong? Jesus, he couldn't even die a normal death.'

Rising from the chair having miraculously regained her composure, Sheila then grabbed the kettle and poured hot water into the pot. 'Coming!' she shouted as if nothing had happened. 'Bet you're parched, Anjie love! What can I get for you, Maxi?'

19

'GET that would ya, Bruce?'

Arnie was watching a special report on the local news when the doorbell rang. Footage of the Hope and Anchor fire flashed across the screen as a reporter spoke about a new turf war threatening to tear London apart.

'Remind me what your last slave died from?' said his younger brother.

'A broken neck for answering back,' said Arnie. The interruption was probably due to Jehovah's Witnesses or some other religious wankers wanting him to commit to one myth or another. All they were after was a share of his cash. Like everything else, religion came at a price.

Putting his hand to his pocket he felt reassured by the solid weight of his new taser 'toy'. If they wanted access to the contents of his pocket, perhaps he should let them in, give them a blast and watch them boogie. Once incapacitated, he could ask them why their merciful God had left him to rot in a wheelchair.

'Well, who is it?' he shouted, taking a swig of beer from the can in his hand.

No reply.

Swivelling at the sound of footsteps, he looked up to see the visitor and was forced to do a double-take.

'Fuck my old boots!' he shouted. 'You ain't fuckin' given up on me after all. I thought you wanted nothing to do with an old cripple.'

'Shut up, Arnold!' said Anjie, smiling. 'It's not like you to feel sorry for yourself.'

Moving forwards, she bent and kissed him on the cheek.

'To what do I owe this pleasure?' he asked.

If she detected the sarcasm in his tone, she chose to ignore it. 'Oh, you know, I wanted to see how you were.'

'Oh, come on, Ang! Not a peep for months then you turn up on my doorstep like a bad penny. How did you find me?'

'Mum of course,' she said. 'I popped in on my way around. She wanted to see Max, so I dropped him off then asked about you. She said she'd seen you on the day of Irene Sullivan's funeral. We were there, you know?' She nodded at the TV screen. 'It was just after we left that those nutters lobbed Molotov cocktails through the windows. Gosh, it looks terrible! We had a lucky escape. Poor old Alison Jacks died, you know, and her old man, Richard, is still in intensive care. It could have been worse, though. Do the cops have any idea—?'

'Nah,' said Arnie. 'Sounds to me like Chuck and Sly put someone's nose out of joint again and got more than they bargained for.'

She inclined her head, non-committal, letting her eyes wander over the surroundings.

'This is nice,' she said. 'Bruce has done you proud, fixing you up with a place like this. Canary Wharf. Bit off your beaten track.'

'Yeah, well,' he said. 'Not much for me around the old neighbourhood. I paid an arm and a pair of legs for it though.'

He chuckled then fell silent for a moment, eventually adding reflectively, 'Yeah, it's a dream living the life of a cripple and no mistake.'

'Don't start that!' she said. 'I know you too well, Arnie. You aren't the type to wallow in self-pity and don't try to lay some kind of guilt trip on me. You want help? I'm a nurse. Just say the word and I'll do what I can to organise physio or whatever you need. I know people who might be able to kit this place out with some added extras, exercise machines and the like.'

'And in return?'

'What?'

'What do you want in return? I'm not stupid, Anj.'

She bit her bottom lip.

'There is one thing.'

He gave her the hard stare. Waited.

'Gazza needs to see you.'

Muting the TV, he followed it up by throwing the remote in her direction. She dodged, and it smashed against the wall.

'What was that in aid of?' she said.

'Have you forgotten how I got here? Why would he want to see me other than to gloat at my predicament?'

'You know him better than that,' she said. 'He's not like Chuck and Sly. He was your best friend. That must count for something.'

She looked out of the corner of her eye at Bruce, who gave an imperceptible nod. Carry on.

'It's a family matter ... between brothers,' she said.

She saw his stunned expression, heard him blaspheme under his breath.

'No need for that, of course he told me about it,' she said. 'He's my bloke and the father of my child. I still haven't worked out how his dad and our mum ... it makes me sick, but no matter. He needs to tell you something important.'

'Couldn't call around himself, though, could he? You have to hold his hand and do his dirty work—'

'Not true.'

Arnie knew the new voice as well as his own. He swivelled around. Gareth stood in the doorway, subconsciously nursing the hand that Arnie had put a knife through. 'Hello, Arnie.'

'Oh, here he is!' said Arnie. 'Well, take a good look and then fuck off! Perhaps I should be in a cage, Bruce, not this flat. Then you can turn me into a performing fuckin' squirrel.'

'Hear him out, Arnie,' said Bruce.

'Right,' said Arnie. 'Everyone's ganging up on me as usual. I suppose I ain't got a say in it. What do you want, Gazza? Sorry,

I don't have a clue what your real name is now? Gareth? Don't sound right. Here to finish me off, are you? Where's the Lone Ranger?'

It took a while for Gareth to work out that Arnie meant The Legend. The last time the two men had seen each other, the former rugby player had also been there, dressed as a cowboy.

'I'm here on family business, Arnie,' said Gareth. 'It's got nothing to do with what happened in Cardiff.'

Arnie pressed a button and the wheelchair moved in Gareth's direction.

'Come on then,' said Arnie. 'You wanna talk? Let's talk. We can go in here.'

He indicated a door off the main room.

'Entertain our Anj, Bruce, would ya? Get her somethin' to drink.'

'I'm not sure I should leave you two alone,' said Anjie.

'What am I going to do, bite him?' asked Arnie. He pressed a button on the electric chair and, grabbing a mobile phone from the table, he then disappeared through a swing door. The reporter followed him through and the door banged shut behind them.

'I meant what I told you on the phone,' said Bruce to Anjie. 'They'll be all right. He ain't the same person since the accident.'

'You're sure about that?' asked Anjie.

Bruce didn't reply.

'I THOUGHT we were done,' said Arnie.

'So did I,' admitted Gareth. 'Then something cropped up and I couldn't ignore it. I need to know if it was you, Arnie.'

'I watch plenty of daytime quiz shows,' said Arnie. 'Got bugger all else to do. I don't recall this one though … guess what your fuckin' brother's on about? It's more complicated than *The Chase* or *Pointless*!'

Arnie fiddled with the mobile phone in his hand, his face a blank canvas.

'I'm asking if you killed Dad.'

An expression formed on the ex-gang leader's face that Gareth had never seen before: shock.

'What do you mean?'

'Stan Marshall was found in an alleyway behind a pub. I visited the very spot after identifying the body. He'd been having a cigarette when someone came up behind him and stabbed him in the back and neck.'

'You're joking!' said Arnie.

Here we go, thought Gareth.

'It happened on a Wednesday two weeks ago.'

Arnie nodded slowly.

'The day I saw him—'

'At least you admit it,' said Gareth. 'The police caught you on CCTV in that other pub.'

'Did they record the conversation?'

Gareth shook his head. 'Technology isn't that good.'

Arnie pressed a couple of buttons on his phone.

'He sent me a text shortly after I moved in here, saying Mum had been in touch about my situation,' said Arnie. 'She told him that I knew he was my dad and in the text he said he wanted to apologise for behaving so badly towards me when I was a kid. He intended to make amends, which was the last thing I expected. I agreed to meet him, but only so I could tell him exactly what I thought of him.'

Arnie closed his eyes briefly, the emotion of that meeting still raw. 'He looked in a bad way,' he revealed. 'Of course, I had an axe to grind, but seeing him like that, still dressed in the clothes he used to wear, I honestly felt sorry for him.'

'You don't feel sorry for anyone, Arnie,' said Gareth.

'Not normally, no,' said Arnie. 'But this wasn't the cocky market trader who could sell ice to the Eskimos. His life had gone to the dogs, and he admitted it was his own fault, blaming it on his dick. Said he'd lost the two women he loved most in the world, Sheila and Mum, because of it.'

'How did he end up in Stoke?'

'When things didn't work out in Bolton, he had to try his luck elsewhere,' said Arnie. 'Ended up in this shitty flat, claiming benefits. He said he was working through a few problems, owed people money and such, and intended to repair the damage of the past. I was part of that "damage". So were you.'

Gareth was welling up with emotion again, but kept his feelings under control.

'He felt wretched about what happened to your football career, blamed himself and seemed genuine,' said Arnie. 'He asked if I'd seen you and I told him about our, um, disagreement. Shit, I thought he was going to break down and fuckin' cry! He asked me to write down your number in a book he had with him and I did it without thinking. The way he was talking … it felt like the last confession of a dying man.'

So that was how Stan got my number, thought Gareth.

'You felt nothing but hatred for him the last time we talked,' he said. 'It normally takes something seismic to change your mind.'

'Forget that,' said the man in the wheelchair, fiddling with his phone again. 'I might have felt that way at times but what would be the point in killing him? He was suffering enough as it was. Anyway, think of the practicalities. How am I supposed to sneak up behind someone in this contraption? It's impossible. Listen to it—'

Arnie shifted the chair into gear and the motor whirred.

'On a quiet Wednesday night, down an alleyway? Don't say he wouldn't hear me coming and I don't suppose the access was anything to write home about.'

It was a fair point.

'You've never struggled to find someone to do your bidding,' said Gareth. 'And you still have cash left from the business, even if Chuck and Vickers have shown you the door.'

'Most of that cash went into this place,' said Arnie, holding his hand out to indicate the fixtures and fittings. 'You know, it would have been nice had we met in different circumstances. I got no reason to talk to you. You never visited me in prison, the hospital or the care home. Why not leave all this to the police?'

Gareth thought about it. 'Because they might reach the same conclusion I did when they think about that calling card.'

'Here we go, playing games again,' said Arnie. 'What card?'

'There was something left on the body,' said Gareth. 'The police believe it was all one message originally but having been torn up the only letters they possessed were A and DO on separate pieces of card. Once the police identify you from the CCTV footage, it won't take a big leap to work out all three letters are in your name.'

'Hang on. You think …? You can't read anything into that.'

'No?' said Gareth. 'It reminds me of those cards you printed out for the football. In this case you wanted your victim to know the great Arnie Dolan was responsible. You always liked people to appreciate your handiwork.'

'Fuck off!' said Arnie, moving in Gareth's direction. 'Do you think my head buttons up the back? I'd be doing the Old Bill's work for them! It's ridiculous. Look, this is the text I got from Stan. You might as well read it.'

As Gareth moved forward, his hand held out for the phone, the door swooshed open and Bruce charged in.

'Stop!' he shouted. 'Move away from that ... thing!'

'Eh?' Gareth stepped back automatically.

'Put it down, Arnie,' said Bruce.

'What?'

'You heard … the phone. Put it down.'

'Oh, come on Bruce, you don't think—?'

'Now!'

'Spoil sport.'

Arnie placed the phone on a counter and Bruce quickly snatched it up.

'Oh?'

'Problem, Bruce.'

'It's your iPhone.'

'What were you expecting?' Arnie laughed. 'Worried I was going to text old Gazza to death?'

Gareth looked between the two of them, confused.

'Sorry,' said Bruce, beating a hasty retreat.

'Dunno what's got into him,' said Arnie. 'Anyway, what's your plan, son of Stan? You gonna call the police, tell them how I left my signature on the corpse?'

There was a short silence as Gareth weighed his options. Finally, he made a decision.

'No,' he said. 'I can't do that. I had the chance when I was up there but wanted to come to you first and ask you about it. I needed to look you in the eye to see if I could tell if you were involved. I should have known better. You've had so much practice keeping a poker face, you could fool anyone. Strange as it sounds, though, I believe you. Which begs the question: What now?'

'I'll tell you what I want to do, brother,' said Arnie. 'I want to find Stan Marshall's killer. Like it or not, I'm in the frame, but it's more than that. It took him 30 fuckin' years to acknowledge I exist, then on the day he accepts me some bastard goes and kills him. I can't have that.'

Arnie fished in his pocket, pulled out a cigar and lit it, blowing smoke in the direction of the pristine white ceiling. Gareth coughed, looking at him with surprise.

'Oh, come on!' said Arnie. 'You think I'm going to give up smoking, too? My health's bad enough as it is.'

'It's your body,' said Gareth, bringing his cough under control. He returned to the problem in hand. 'Look, if you're going to do this, you can't do it alone. The police will be looking for you because of the CCTV images. You're a marked man, Arnie. Me on the other hand …'

Arnie thought about it, slowly nodding his head as he reached a decision. 'You're right,' he said. 'It will be a nice little family project. Where do we start?'

20

'YOU'RE a washed-up mess, Jane Sullivan.'

The tousle-haired woman in the faded red bathrobe stared back at her from the mirror, raised the bottle of prosecco and swallowed a mouthful. Sunken eyes ringed with dark smudges, her forehead so inundated with wrinkles it resembled a London tube map.

Downstairs, the doorbell rang.

'Shit!'

Who would be calling at this time of night? It was after 9.30p.m. and the kids were in bed. A small part of her hoped it would be him, but she knew that was unlikely. When he'd walked out of the door after their furious row there seemed little more to say. She'd tried calling him only to get his voicemail and since then they'd communicated solely by text over practical matters. He hadn't even seen the kids and though it hadn't reached the divorce stage yet, she couldn't imagine any other ending. She sounded like a cliché as she repeated the words to herself, but they were true.

It wasn't his fault, it was hers.

After seven years of marriage and having at one stage been deeply in love with him, matters last summer exploded that state of affairs, leaving her in limbo. It was hard to see him as anything other than a weak man now – one who had been unable to keep her safe when the wolf came howling at the door.

The bell rang again.

'Hold your horses, I'm fuckin' coming!' she muttered under her breath as she took another swig from the bottle and stumbled out onto the landing, pausing to listen to the reassuring sound of children snoring.

Then the fear gripped.

Could this caller present a danger to them, the only two people that made her life worth living? After the pub arson attack her mummy alert had been at fever pitch.

'Shit! Shit! Shit!'

Stumbling onto the stairs, Janie descended rapidly, her feet struggling for balance on the deep-pile rouge carpet, the fizzy drink slopping from the rim of the bottle as she made haphazard progress. There was a time when a spillage of that nature would send her scurrying to the kitchen for cleaning materials. What did it matter now? She thought she'd proved herself a good wife only to end up in this mess.

The soddin' bell again.

'OK! OK! I'm coming. Who is it?' The question was asked with trepidation. Where before she'd turned a blind eye to her husband's business, her mother's wake had made her acutely aware of the risks involved. No longer could she kid herself that Pete was like every other hard-working commuter in the street, disappearing off to 'the office' each day.

His was no ordinary job and this might be no ordinary caller. Did a bank manager, mortgage adviser or estate agent create such bad blood that a rival might go after family members with Molotov cocktails? Creeping the final few yards to the door on tiptoe, her hand clung so tightly to the neck of the bottle her knuckles turned white.

'You there, Janie?'

Oh, thank fuck.

A familiar voice.

'It's me. Anj. Your BFF. What sort of treatment is this – leaving me to hang out on your doorstep?'

Slowly, the relief flooded through her though she wasn't sure she wanted her best friend to see her in this state. 'It's late, Anj,' she grumbled. 'I was just off to bed. What do you want?'

'I came to see you, babe – more than four hours on the M4. You're telling me you can't let me in because it's half nine and you need your beauty sleep? What on earth happened to the Jane Vickers I know? You would be just settling in at the bar about now ahead of a night of partying. Have you become a Stepford Wife?'

Ira Levin's *Stepford Wives* was a book Anjie had lent her during their schooldays. Janie wasn't much of a reader but her best friend, the bookworm, tried her best to get her interested. She'd read this one cover to cover in just a few days. In it, women were 'built' to wait on their husband's every need.

The irony made her wince.

Sinking to her haunches she released the bottom latch, almost falling on her backside as she did so. Prosecco bubbled out and made a sticky puddle on the tile. Rising in stages, she slid back the top bolt, turned the Yale lock and pulled the door towards her. Rather than looking into her friend's face, she peered over her shoulder then glanced to either side.

'It's OK, I'm on my own,' said Anjie. 'About time! Ooh, is that prosecco? Grab another glass and I'll give you a hand. Funnily enough …' Anjie's right hand emerged from behind her back and another bottle appeared as if by magic.

'Come in, Anj,' said Janie. Stepping aside, she waved in the general direction of the lounge. 'Take a seat and I'll pour you one.'

Shrugging off her brown bomber jacket with the zips that Janie liked so much, Anjie rested it over the banister. If she noticed the alcohol stain on the fifth stair up, she didn't comment.

'I haven't seen you since the funeral,' said Anjie. 'Terrible what happened at the Hope. You guys were OK though?'

'They got us out pretty quickly,' said Janie, rifling through the kitchen cupboards for a glass. 'Women and children first, you know? It shook the little ones a hell of a lot though. Simon thinks it was a riotous game and keeps going on about it. He wants me to teach him how to make Molotov cocktails! I explained to him I'm not a thug or a gangster, but he thinks mums are capable of anything.'

She sensed she was speaking too quickly but hadn't enjoyed adult company for hours and was glad to exercise her vocal chords. If Anjie noticed her slurring, she gave no indication.

'What about Diane, the little cherub?' her friend asked.

'She has nightmares,' said Janie. 'She talks about men with no faces burning her alive on a bonfire. I'm not sure if I should take her to the doc … hic … doctors.'

At last finding a glass, she filled it with the bubbly liquid and as an after-thought lifted a second one down for herself. There was no point in drinking from the bottle when she had company.

'What's Pete doing?' said Anjie.

'About what?'

'About helping the kids through their ordeal. He's normally a whiz when it comes to calming them down.'

Clutching the two full glasses, Janie thought carefully about her answer as she walked into the living room.

'I've got something to tell you.' She handed over a glass.

Anjie's mouth dropped open. 'Hell, and I've got something to tell you! I can't drink any more after this.'

'Are you driving?'

Anjie shook her head and in the next few seconds Janie read her friend's face and solved the mystery.

'Shit! You're pregnant?'

She put down her glass and raced over to embrace her friend. 'How long?'

'Four months. We had a bit of catching up to do.'

'You can say that again!' agreed Janie. 'Boy or girl?'

'We don't know yet. It's caught us a bit off guard. My head's a mess, as you can tell. What was I thinking, bringing a bottle of bubbly around? I'm not supposed to drink!'

'One glass can't hurt … you know, to wet the baby's head.'

'I don't think they mean literally wet it, Janie.' The two girls laughed, easy in each other's company. 'So, what's your news? You're not pregnant, too?'

'No, mine's not so good, I'm afraid. Pete's gone.'

Anjie couldn't work out if her friend was serious or cracking a bizarre joke.

'What ... left you? But you guys—'

'I know you think you know us, but you don't know anything, Anj,' said Janie. 'You've been so tied up with your reunion, plus moving down to Wales, getting the job transfer, finding Maxi a new school, well, you're out of touch with what's been going on here. I'm pretty sure he isn't coming back, either.'

'Sorry, but ... come on! You guys are the strongest couple I know. If anyone was going to make it, you were. What happened? It must be something drastic.'

Janie grabbed her drink. It was now or never. She'd been holding out on her friend because she didn't want to break her heart; and she knew what Arnie had done would have that effect. Fuck it! There was something in her make-up that just wanted to burst Anjie's bubble, upset her perfect world and bring her back to earth. Why should she be so happy, walking around in blissful ignorance of her rapist brother, no doubt still believing the sun shines out of his arse? Perhaps it was the drink talking, but she'd kept the secret too long.

'Anj, there's something else.'

Just then the phone rang.

21

MITCHELL TIGGS was out of his comfort zone. As he pushed against the crowds moving in the opposite direction through the Westfield Shopping Centre in Stratford, east London, he went over the instructions in his mind.

Pete Vickers had been clear, and Tigger had no reason to question him. Even so, Stratford was further west than Tigger liked to travel. He had a cut-off point at Mile End on the District Line and this was one stop further, deep into the territory of one of the foreign gangs – the Lithuanians – who were building a reputation as merciless thugs. Rivals had been sprayed in the face with acid and run down in the street. There were even rumours someone had been thrown from one of the expensive high-rise tower blocks that had sprouted up in time for the 2012 London Olympics.

Tigger's life revolved around a narrow network of streets. He didn't like crowds because his eyesight wasn't great, and he feared he wouldn't pick out a threat until it was too late. He was old-school, and the hustle and bustle of a shiny, modern indoor mall was the antithesis of his favoured environment. He preferred working in the shadows.

Westfield was a beacon to the 21st century, an unashamed advert for consumerism and greed. Full of shops flaunting brand names and overpriced goods, it stood in glaring contrast to the neglected streets and poverty-trapped population that had grown up around these parts. When London had been awarded the Olympics, opportunistic building firms crawled out of the woodwork to take advantage, evicting locals from their 'condemned' homes and erecting luxurious flats way beyond their price range. The disregard for their basic human rights made them disaffected and angry.

While the shopping centre posers dressed to impress and flaunted their financial wellbeing, Tigger was acutely aware of groups of teenagers loitering with intent, scheming to relieve them of their valuables and cash. Fumbling nervously with the phone in the pocket of his denim jacket, he was sure he'd attracted the attention of a group of hoodies surveying their turf from the entrance to a fast-food restaurant. Jitters trampolined across his stomach as they gave him the eye and whispered to each other, only for a gaggle of teenage girls to arrive and divert their attention.

'Watch it, whitey!' A tall black teen in a baseball cap interrupted Tigger's daydream. Knocked sideways, he almost collided with two women with pushchairs. Thrusting his phone back in his pocket, he gave up on waiting for the GPS to work. He knew roughly where he was going and could ask directions if he got lost.

The farther Tigger sank into the abyss of the mall, the more exposed he felt. He wished he could have bought along a couple of dealers for moral support, but Vickers had insisted he come alone. Hell, he hoped the finger wasn't being pointed at him over the recent trouble. It wouldn't be the first time he'd been mistakenly accused of wrongdoing.

Tigger was as loyal as the day was long and never skimmed off the top, but he knew he had one of those faces people didn't trust. Subconsciously, he dragged dirty, unkempt nails down the scar on his arm, a permanent reminder of how he was perceived by those at the top. That psycho, Arnie Dolan, had plunged a knife into him once, accusing Tigger of ratting him out to the cops. Only Vickers had saved him from further damage, which went a long way to explaining Tigger's loyalty to the man.

It was partly for that reason he was here now. Vickers had told him on the phone that he'd uncovered vital clues to the disappearance and subsequent murder of Tigger's dealers. Unsure who to trust in the gang, Vickers had insisted on meeting his No.1 operative alone and on neutral ground.

Tigger pushed through double doors and into the late spring evening. The street lamps were on, the darkness creeping in. Walking alongside the road which serviced Westfield's car parks, the drug dealer noted a few pedestrian stragglers laden down with shopping but there was no one else to be seen.

After crossing the road, he found himself outside a squat, oblong building called The CopperBox. Life-sized colour posters of basketball players and boxers adorned the front, advertising upcoming events. Taking a right turn as instructed, he ended up in a dimly lit street containing a rank of empty restaurants and bars. Never had he felt more vulnerable, fear seizing his stomach and twisting it as tightly as the knot on a hangman's noose. The rendezvous had to be close. According to Vickers, it was a bar called Player One where visitors could indulge in retro computer games. He seemed to be the only person around.

No.

Wait.

A figure was standing at the far end of the street. Putting his fingers to his eyes, Tigger pulled the skin wide, a mannerism he'd perfected to help him see, negating the need for glasses. Whatever the science behind it, it seemed to work.

Breathing a sigh of relief he realised it was Vickers, and the gang boss appeared to be alone. He hadn't spotted Tigger yet, taking turns to study his watch and take drags from a cigarette. Unusual. Tigger hadn't seen Vickers on the fags since his second kid was born five years earlier.

Opening his mouth, his shout was drowned out by the roar of an engine and a screech of tyres. After that, everything merged into a blur. Tigger leapt into the recesses of a gym building as a large white transit hurtled past him, balancing on two wheels as it navigated the bend. In the front seat he made out two figures wearing balaclavas.

Bank robbery?

With a bang, a clatter and another screech of breaks, the van skidded to a halt. A straitjacket of adrenaline closed around Tigger's chest. Daring to poke his head out from his hidey-hole, the dealer saw back doors spring open. Vickers turned to run but was grabbed by a heavy-set man emerging from the driver's door. As he took a swing at Vickers, people clambered out of the back and plunged into the melee. The Boxer Boy had no chance of escape, a strangled cry perforating the night air as he disappeared from view.

Frozen to the spot, Tigger thumbed his phone nervously, knowing time was of the essence but fearing that if he did or said anything the marauding thugs might detect his presence. He was not the sort to put himself in line for a bravery award and, anyway, who could he call?

Not the cops. That was considered poor form in his line of business. The alternative was to contact one of the Dolan boys, but how quickly would Chuck and Sly respond? They might order him into action – and he could think of no set of circumstances where that scenario would have a happy ending. He decided the best thing to do would be to commit what he saw to memory and relay the information later.

The seething, shape-shifting ball of humanity moved to the back of the van, one balaclava-clad figure after another bringing baseball bats crashing down onto their captive. If that wasn't bad enough, the next image would remain seared on his retinas for a long time. A bloodied Pete Vickers was tossed through the double doors like a carcass being handled at an abattoir. The front door clanged, the driver resumed his place behind the wheel and two hoods followed Pete into the back of the van.

Before the doors slammed shut, one of the balaclava-wearing men took one final look around. Tigger froze. Despite his dodgy eyesight he was convinced the thug looked straight at him before the engine fired into life and the transit vanished around a corner.

22

'Our mum used to call her The Boobs from Bolton,' said Gareth. 'The floozy, I mean.'

'And did she?'

'What?'

'Did she have big boobs?'

'Hell, I don't remember.' Gareth laughed. 'I was in the hospital, drugged up to the eyeballs the only time I met her. I was too busy trying to deck Dad to notice. I just recall her sashaying out, wiggling her arse like a cheap tart.'

'Hard though it is to imagine, I think Mum truly loved him,' said Arnie. 'She stuck with Big Mo, but I think she would have left him for Stan, given the choice. It would have been a huge decision, though, and ripped our family apart. Mo's a difficult habit to break.'

'He was behind bars most of the time, though, wasn't he?' said Gareth. 'She stuck by him through all that so he must have had some redeeming features.'

'I've still got the bruises to prove it,' snarled Arnie. 'When I was a toddler he spent some time on the run, almost 15 months.' Lowering his voice, he cast a glance towards Bruce, who was fiddling about on the computer, a pair of state-of-the-art headphones covering his ears. 'Mum says that was when Anjie and Bruce were conceived. I've no reason to doubt her. I've heard the gossips speculating about who their fathers were, too, but I'm pretty sure Mo was responsible.'

'I'm sorry about the way Mo treated you,' said Gareth. 'I wish I could have done something at the time.'

'It's fine,' said Arnie. 'It taught me to look after myself.'

They fell silent for a moment, both thinking about how their relationship had evolved. Eventually Gareth asked, 'Tell me about your meeting with my ... our dad.'

Arnie picked up a magazine off the table and hurled it in Bruce's direction. It hit him on the shoulder and he almost fell from his stool in shock. Removing the earphones, he looked accusingly in Arnie's direction.

Unfazed, Arnie said, 'Get us another drink, Bruce, this could be a long night.'

Two months earlier

BRUCE DOLAN approached the smokers congregating outside the main entrance to the Coach and Horses, a large, old-fashioned pub opposite the bus station in Hanley, Stoke-on-Trent.

''Scuse, lads,' he said. 'Can you help me get these doors open? My brother's a bit indisposed.'

A sea of curious faces turned in Arnie's direction and he felt like killing his youngest sibling. Arnie hated anyone giving him sympathy and was sure every smoker was thinking, 'Thank fuck that isn't me.'

Barging through in his chair, he was met with a wall of bodies. The lunchtime crowd. Bruce sprinted to catch up.

'Can you see him?'

'I'll just expand my neck like Inspector Gadget or one of them freaks out of *X Men*, shall I?' said Arnie. 'Of course I can't see him. I can't see past these nonces!'

The last two words were shouted so loudly they attracted attention. A few drinkers fixed Bruce with a glare then swiftly moved out of the way when they saw Arnie. Bruce sank to his knees, pretending to fiddle with something on Arnie's chair. 'You'll get us lynched, Arnie!'

'Oh, man up, you woofter,' the older man replied, putting the chair into forward motion so that Bruce had to leap out of the way, stumbling into a dark-haired business-type in pinstripes as he did so. The man turned to confront him, only to rein in his anger when he saw the wheelchair.

'Excuse me, mate, Afghan veteran—'

The man stepped aside and indicated his mates should do likewise.

'Makes me laugh it does,' said Arnie to Bruce as they closed in on the bar. 'The only reason these cunts are so quick to get out of the way is cos they think I'm contagious. Wish I was, sometimes. Hey, could that be … Fuck my old boots!'

Arnie had been interrupted mid-rant by the sight of a figure with straggly grey hair and a full face of beard, leaning over the bar. The only reason he recognised Stan Marshall was through the coat he was wearing, a Leyton Orient football badge pinned to the collar.

Bruce walked forwards and tapped the man on the shoulder. A few words were exchanged before the tramp-like figure looked over, his face creasing into a smile. Pushing away from the bar, he bent down in front of Arnie, arms outstretched as if anticipating a hug.

'Fuck off or I'll deck ya.' Arnie's hand disappeared into his pocket. 'You bloody stink! Christ, I've changed my mind about this. Bruce …!'

'No … wait! Arnold. Sorry. I couldn't help myself, son.' Stan Marshall croaked out the words and Arnie thought there were tears in his eyes, no doubt a result of all the booze and nicotine he'd consumed over the years. Still, it was better than the greeting he might have expected from his 'other' dad, a rabbit punch to the kidneys or a smash around the ear … the words 'keep your guard up' whispered shortly after the assault to legitimise the attack. Still, Mo's 'tough love' had given Arnie the ammunition to survive Wano.

'Forgive me, son,' said Stan. 'Stay won't ya?'

He stood at a reasonable distance now, allowing Arnie his personal space. 'I know I've been a right bastard to you and your family, well, to everyone who cared about me, your mother included. Let's start again, shall we? We can go upstairs for a quiet chat and some lunch.'

'And how do you suppose we get there?' said Arnie. 'I'm not Iron Man. There ain't a jetpack strapped to this thing.'

'There's a lift especially for—'

'Cripples?'

'I was going to say people with pushchairs, the disabled or those who just feel a bit old. I use it myself sometimes, son.' He smiled again. 'We've got a lot to talk about and it really needs to be done somewhere quiet, don't you agree?'

Arnie could feel Bruce looking expectantly at him, just waiting for the order to take him back to the flid mobile and leave this loser behind forever.

'Well, if you really wanna make it up to me you can start by getting me a double vodka and Red Bull,' said Arnie.

Once settled at a table at the back of the upstairs bar, Stan indicated Arnie's wheelchair. 'Did my Gary do that to you?' he asked.

'Leave it out! Gary? Nah, it was some ex-rugby playing geezer … caught me off guard.'

'Right. I can't help feeling I'm to blame, though,' said Stan. 'If I hadn't neglected you, who knows where you might be now?'

Arnie shrugged, but inside he was taken aback. He thought he could detect genuine remorse in Stan's eyes. Hell, those tears were still there.

'Truth is, I'm a coward, son,' said Stan. 'Always was, always will be. Big Mo scared the hell out of me. He did most people on the estate. He had a terrible reputation for violence. Sorry, but I have to say it. And the way he treated your mum—'

Arnie added Red Bull to his vodka and took a large gulp.

'I'd clocked her bruises, see, son,' said Stan. 'First time I saw her. She turned up at the market with a black eye. Even so, I thought she was beautiful and couldn't help falling for her. I was married, though, with a baby on the way – Gary – so it didn't work out. I didn't know your mum was pregnant until years after we split. I always assumed you were Mo's child. Never in my wildest dreams —'

'Mum didn't tell you?'

'I don't think she could,' said Stan. 'She wanted to bring you up without any, uh, complications.'

'That worked out well.'

The old man shrugged.

'So, when did you realise I was your son,' asked Arnie.

'You must have been 11,' said Stan. 'She … your mother … rang me in a panic. Said she'd been careless. I'd written her a letter and she'd put it in the bin. Mo found it when he was looking for a missing betting slip. He went radio rental, beat her black and blue, then came looking for me. After her warning I tried to leg it and was crossing the playground outside the flats when I heard this roar. I turned to see Big Mo charging at me. I was fitter in them days, though, and he was a big unit. I managed to give him the slip but couldn't return home for a while. Luckily for me, the police arrested him for armed robbery a couple of days later and he went back inside. I can't say I was sorry.'

'What stopped you getting in touch once you knew I was your boy?'

'I didn't see the point,' said Stan. 'As far as I knew you thought Big Mo was your dad. Can you imagine what sort of impact that would have made on a teenage boy, knowing his dad wasn't who he'd grown up thinking he was?'

'He used to fuckin' beat me,' said Arnie. 'Abused me every chance he got. That time when mum warned you she'd been careless? That was when I found out. I overheard an almighty row in the kitchen and saw Big Mo throw this note in the bin. When they left the room, I went and retrieved it – your love letter.'

He took another drink before leaning forward and looking the old man in the eye.

'You ain't been exactly truthful have you 'father'?' The last word oozed with sarcasm.

'In what respect?'

'Come on!' Arnie raised his voice. 'You had your own little family to look after. Gary, Lily and your doting wife. Compared to that, I was surplus to requirements. You didn't have the guts to tell them you had a bastard living across the way who was Gary's age. Sheila would have worked out you shagged Mum while she was pregnant, wouldn't she?'

Stan reached across for Arnie's hand.

'What ya doing, you queer?' he exploded, pulling away from the table.

'I just want to make things right, that's all!'

Stan's eyes were pleading, and Arnie found it difficult to keep his emotions in check. Silence descended, both men aware of the strange looks they were attracting from adjoining tables.

Stan broke the web of tension.

'I didn't know he beat you, son,' he said. 'Your mum never told me. When you became friends with our Gary, it seemed even less appropriate to reveal the truth. I had no idea you knew. If I had, things might have been different.'

The anger drained from Arnie's face, his mind assaulted by a jumble of emotions. 'I never thought Mum was the type to have an affair,' he said. 'She always seemed so "proper".'

'Don't hold it against her, son,' said Stan, sighing. 'She wasn't in a normal relationship. She wanted to do the right thing but was having such a tough time. Not only was Mo involved in serious criminal activity he was also seeing a local barmaid on the sly.'

Arnie raised his eyebrows. Big Mo's affair was news to him. Christ, they had all been at it back then!

'There was some sort of trouble with his soldier brother, Clive, and Chuck was having trouble at school,' said Stan. 'Sylvester was a very demanding baby, needing constant attention. Anyone would buckle under that sort of pressure. Your mum had this calmness about her, though, and the first time I set eyes on her I wanted her.'

Arnie scoffed.

'What?'

'Stan the Man, bitten by the love bug?' he said. 'A bloke who's had every floozy from Land's End to John O'Groats? You're killing me here, mate. I'll get the violins out.'

'But can't you see, that's the whole point,' said Stan. 'I actually believe you can have only one true love, Arnold. I didn't love Sheila. We got married too young. I cared about her, yes, but quickly realised it was a mistake. Once she fell pregnant, I was trapped.'

He took a sip of his drink. 'Sure, there were other girls, but they were only to take my mind off the one woman I really wanted. Do you understand? Even leaving London was part of it. I know Gary won't forgive me, too much water has passed under the bridge, but it was something I had to do. Seeing your mother just down the road, or at the market, or in the local pub, and not being able to have her – it was killing me. I also knew I had a son I could never contact. To be honest, your mum was desperate to keep it a secret from you. She feared Big Mo's reaction and wanted to protect both of us.'

Perhaps it was the fact Stan Marshall had always been blessed with the gift of the gab, but his words made a kind of warped sense to Arnie. He wasn't ready to admit it though.

'Come off it!' he said. 'You ran off with a younger model, that's all. It had nothing to do with me or Mum.'

Stan sighed. 'There's more to that story, too, but maybe another time.'

Stan continued to talk, gazing around the room. For a moment, his eyes stalled on the bar area. When he focused back on Arnie, something had changed.

'Let me pay for lunch, it's the least I can do,' he said, pulling grubby notes from a coat pocket. 'I gotta go … things to do, people to see.' He stood. 'I'd like to meet up again, though. I want to know more about my son.'

He held his hand out and Arnie remained still for a few seconds before accepting the olive branch.

'OK,' he said, 'but I don't need your money.' He scooped the notes from the table and thrust them into the old man's pocket. 'I'll be in touch.'

'Sure?'

Arnie nodded.

Then Stan was off, heading for the lift. Hunched inside the old coat with the collar up, his straggly grey hair concealed beneath it.

'Do us a favour, Bruce,' said Arnie. 'Just follow him down, would ya? Make sure he's OK.'

Present Day

'You reckon someone spooked him?' asked Gareth.

'I don't know,' said Arnie. 'But I had a good look at this group of men at the bar. They seemed to be taking more than a casual interest in his departure.'

'Can you remember what they looked like?'

'I can do better than that,' said Arnie. 'I took a photo.'

23

GARETH felt a tingle shoot up his spine as he entered a place he'd only previously seen on CCTV. It was as if his old man's ghost was right there beside him, keen to return to the Coach and Horses, one of his old haunts.

Having taken a few days off work, Gareth had faced the tricky task of explaining his mission to Anjie. Though she wasn't over-joyed about his reunion with her brother, she could understand what they were doing and offered her support, as always. On their way back to Wales from London she'd told him about her strange evening with Janie Vickers and the bizarre anonymous phone call her friend had received claiming Pete had been kidnapped. Gareth had taken it with a pinch of salt, knowing how Janie had been knocked for six by the death of her mother.

His train of thought was interrupted by a woman in jeans and a pink bib weaving in and out of the tables with a noisy vacuum cleaner. At the bar, a man built like a rugby prop stood slicing lemons, a task unsuited to his stumpy, malformed fingers. He had a shaven head adorned by a large purple birthmark. In the CCTV footage he'd seen, Gareth had assumed it was a tattoo. In contrast to the vivid stain, the rest of the barman's skin was so devoid of colour it could have been bleached.

'Help you, marra?' the barman asked. 'We're not open for an-other five minutes.'

Gareth took a moment to decipher the strong dialect before he replied. 'Oh, that's a shame,' he said. 'I've travelled a long way. Should I wait outside?'

The man shrugged. 'I guess it's OK. I've done what I needed to do, so I can bend the rules a bit. What do you sup?'

'What's the local ale?'

'Ah,' said the barman. 'You're not from these parts. Where from, marra? London?'

'Right first time,' said Gareth, lowering his voice. 'I'm up here collecting some of my dad's things. He used to come in here, I'm told. Hey, you might have known him? His name was Stan Marshall. Nasty story really ... He was murdered in an alley outside a pub near here. Stabbed to death.'

Gareth's words were deliberately blunt to catch the barman off guard. He was rewarded with a twitch above the right eyebrow.

'Woah!' he said. 'Seriously? When was this?'

'Two month ago.'

The barman gave him a suspicious look. 'Wait a minute ... That was your dad?'

Gareth nodded.

'Sorry, I didn't mean it like that,' said the barman. 'It's just, you dress a bit posh, like, and he—'

'...looked like a tramp. I know. We lost touch.'

'I served him on the day he died, you know. I had to speak to the cops about it.'

The barman looked around as if someone might be watching.

'Look, let me give you one of our specialist ales on the house. You can drink to his memory. Once you've had one you'll be beggin' for more.'

'Very kind of you.'

The barman pulled a pump and golden liquid flowed into a chunky beer mug, reflecting the light streaming through the windows. Gareth licked his lips.

'What's it mean, by the way?'

'What's that?'

'Marra. Is it a local thing?'

'Oh, sorry. It's so ingrained half the time I don't realise I'm saying it. It's like mate, or pal. You know, short for 'my mate'. It's a typical Stokie greeting.'

'Even if you've never met someone before?' Gareth laughed. 'That's very friendly of you.'

'We're friendly people.'

The bloke who killed my dad wasn't, thought Gareth.

'Get your laughing gear around that, as you cockneys would say. Cheers.'

Gareth raised the pot, swallowed a mouthful and smacked his lips together.

'Wow! Compliments to the chef.'

'You like?'

'Lovely. No wonder Dad came to live here. He liked his ale. What did you tell them – the police?'

'Not much, to be honest,' said the barman. 'I said he was a bit of a local character. I'm sure the brewery wouldn't have been keen on my serving him if they saw the state of him but, well, he never did anyone any harm. Always quiet and polite.'

The barman's jovial expression had been replaced by something more circumspect. 'You say you're his son? You ask questions like a private eye.'

Gareth wondered if he could have been more subtle. Still, there was no dressing it up. He had to gamble to get answers.

'I'm a journalist by profession so asking questions is kind of my business,' he said. 'This has nothing to do with my job, though. I'm on a guilt trip. I lost touch with Dad years ago and never had the chance to build bridges. Now it's too late. To be honest, I'm worried the police will drop the case and he won't get justice. They don't tend to waste resources on murdered tramps.'

'For what it's worth, I'm not a big fan of the police,' said the barman, diverting his attention. 'Bye, Anya!'

'Polish,' he volunteered, indicating the cleaner who was now walking out of the door. 'I suppose she'll be on her way home for good if this Brexit thing goes through.'

'Not likely though, is it?'

'Plenty around here will vote in favour, marra. They think the day after Farage and his buddies win, a giant wall will be erected around the country and there will be one exit door through which anyone who is remotely foreign will be shunted. There's a pro-Brexit march here today, in fact. And I wouldn't be surprised if it all kicks off.'

'You're not a supporter?'

'Well, you wouldn't think it due to my skin "condition" but I'm of Asian descent myself, so I can't say it would do me any favours.'

Before the man could expand on his answer, the door swung open and an advanced party of lunchtime drinkers entered, four well-groomed men in pinstripe suits. He walked off to serve them.

'Speak to you later, marra,' he shouted over his shoulder.

Feeling the phone vibrate in his pocket, Gareth took it out and looked at the screen. A thumbnail picture of Anjie and Max stared back at him. He read the text message. *Call home*, it said.

Climbing down from the bar stool, he then went outside and made the call. Anjie answered on the second ring.

'You OK? The baby—?'

'All fine,' she said. 'Well, apart from a bit of morning sickness. It's not me that's the problem, it's Jane.'

'Jane Vickers?'

'Yes, you know, my best mate?'

'Sorry, my mind's been full of other things. What about her?'

'She's worried about Pete.'

'Well, she booted him out, didn't she?' said Gareth. 'What did she expect?'

'The way she tells it, he walked. Anyway, she's still not heard from him and what with those murdered boys being found on Rainham Marshes and the pub bombing, she's scared there's some truth in this kidnap thing. Have you heard anything?'

'No,' said Gareth. 'He was Arnie's mate more than mine. I haven't spoken to him since the funeral.'

'I just thought you should know,' she said. 'Anyway, with you planning to be away a bit and me being pregnant I thought I'd invite her and the kids down for a couple of weeks in the summer to give her a break. I can take them to Barry Island, or even the Gower coast – they've got some lovely beaches there. It will be nice for Max, too. You know he loves Simon.'

'Sure. When were you thinking?'

'Well, you're at the football in June, aren't you? Maybe then. The weather should be good.'

'Go for it.'

'Thanks … love you, Laszlo,' she said.

'You too, Hanna.'

He hung up, the private joke making him chuckle. When they'd been trying to keep their relationship quiet, they'd given themselves 'code names' from the novel *The English Patient*. It was difficult to break the habit, reminding them as it did of all the traumas their relationship had survived. With a smile on his face, he walked back into the pub.

It was starting to fill out. The barman was serving a pair of youths with shaved heads, bomber jackets, jeans and Doc Marten boots. He figured them for some of the Brexit marchers. As they took their pints away, his new friend muttered something under his breath.

'Problem?' he asked.

'Tossers!' said the barman. 'The local loony bin must be missing a consignment today. How's the pint?'

'Very nice.'

'Sorry to cut you off like that. It was getting busy. Anything else I can help you with?'

'Only if you can tell me more about Dad.'

'I remember him meeting this bloke in a wheelchair and some other lad,' said the barman. 'Things got a bit heated. The other guy – the younger one – had to stand in between them. He managed to calm things down and then they all went upstairs. The police know this.'

'Sure,' said Gareth. 'Was there anyone Dad met regularly in here?'

The barman shook his head. 'Nah,' he said. 'He was a bit of a loner. I sometimes had a chat with him, y'know, on my fag break. We discussed the horses, or football. He liked a bet. He didn't mention London though. Said he'd come down from Manchester. He'd split from a girl and wasn't flavour of the month with her family, who belonged to a rather tasty gang called The Red Moss Crew. Maybe—?'

He fell silent.

'Can I show you a picture?'

The barman nodded.

Gareth pulled out his mobile and showed him the snap Arnie had transferred to him the previous night, five men gathered around a bar area sipping on soft drinks. Bruce was goofing around in the foreground.

'Recognise anyone?' he asked, handing over the phone.

The barman studied the picture. 'Yeah, that's the guy who was with the one in the wheelchair.'

'What about those four or five blokes at the bar?'

The barman peered at the device for another few seconds then thrust it back into Gareth's hand.

'No idea.'

'Are you sure? they were—'

'I said "No". Is there something wrong with your hearing?'

'I just thought—'

'Look, marra, I've tried to help you out, even given you a free pint, and told you all I know about your old chap. Now I have to get on. I'm busy, OK?'

Gareth was surprised by the abrupt change in atmosphere between them. 'Sure,' he said. 'No problem. Thanks anyway.'

The barman grunted and walked off.

Gareth thought about asking questions of some of the others in the bar but realised how random that would be. He had no idea who had been in the pub on the day of Stan Marshall's death. He had a couple of leads, albeit tenuous ones. He and Arnie would have to find out more about this Red Moss Crew for a start. It was time to report back to his brother.

When his mystery visitor disappeared out of the door, the barman walked into the kitchen and grabbed his phone from the counter. Dialling a number, he got through to one of the brothers. He had been prepared to take the stranger at face value, even swallow the tale about his dad, but the man had asked one too many questions and the photo was the clincher. Any cop or spook could have got hold of the information about the dead man. He felt it only right he report the conversation. He was sure he would be rewarded handsomely.

24

SPOTTING the familiar logo of a well-known toy store, Gareth veered off into one of the shopping arcades in Hanley town centre. He had to get Maxi a souvenir and was also hoping to find a coffee shop. With all the travelling plus the myriad questions surrounding his dad's death crowding his mind, a shot or two of espresso would be just what the doctor ordered.

Half an hour later he emerged onto the street, feeling much better for ticking off two items on his mental to-do list. The large box under his arm contained a build-your-own Millennium Falcon spaceship from *Star Wars*, complete with turbo-laser turret, LED cannons and hyperdrive sound effects. He knew he'd made a rod for his own back, anticipating the many hours it would take to put it all together. The stress would be worth it, though, to witness Maxi's face light up when he saw the finished article. No doubt Anjie would chastise Gareth for spoiling the boy but secretly she'd be delighted he was doing his best to make up for lost time with their son.

Turning left onto the high street he became instantly aware of a large gathering of middle-aged men, aggressive-looking teens and hard-faced women. A banner urging '*Vote Brexit and show them the exit*' confirmed his initial impression that this was the march he'd heard about.

'This government hasn't a clue,' a man shouted into a microphone, his message relayed through tinny speakers prone to feedback. 'Neither did the last one! How long have hard-working, normal citizens urged our political parties to protect us from the hordes flooding into our country intent on destroying our traditional way of life? We must regain control of our borders before it's too late, and that means showing the door to interfering Brussels Bureaucrats who think they know what's best for us.

'I say, no more pussyfooting around these ridiculously highly paid do-gooders. Things can change, and they will change. We can't allow people to burn poppies on our streets or impose their Sharia Law on us. No! Let's vote 'Leave' and rid ourselves of this European ball and chain. Join with me now, *Vote for Brexit, show 'em the exit! Vote for Brexit...*'

The chant gained momentum, attracting others to join the group. Banners flying high, the marchers set off, flanked by police officers in high-visibility jackets. From a side street another group emerged, intent on drowning out their opponents with a rousing chorus of, 'Racists, racists, fuck off home! Racists, fuck off home.'

This group contained long-haired hippy types, tough-looking characters in donkey jackets and jeans and a fair smattering of blacks and Asians. Looking at the determined set of their faces, Gareth had no doubt they were hell-bent on confrontation.

Before the two groups came into direct contact, though, a shiver ran down his spine as he sensed he was being watched. Sure enough, looking over his shoulder he saw a third group approaching, Asian men of varying shapes and sizes who seemed focused on him in particular. Their leader, an imposing figure with thick, black hair, seemed vaguely familiar, and it dawned on Gareth he resembled one of the group in Arnie's photograph. Shit! The Coach and Horses' barman must have told this group he'd been asking questions. Hoisting the cumbersome box from the floor, he set off across the street at a canter.

'Hey, watch it!'

The protest came from behind him and the reporter suspected a pedestrian had been brushed aside after impeding the progress of his pursuers. Resisting the temptation to look over his shoulder, Gareth forged on, determined to make his narrow advantage count.

Damn! A large police constable was blocking his path, hand raised.

'Sorry, sir, you can't go any further,' he said.

'But I've got friends in there,' Gareth protested, pointing to the pro-Brexit crowd behind their police escort. The officer shoved him in the chest.

'How do I know you're not out to start trouble?'

A hand came down on the officer's shoulder, the man with the microphone leaning over and whispering in his ear. 'Come on, mate, he's one of us. You can tell. He was just being chased by those bloody Pakis …'

The policeman turned quickly. 'I'll arrest you for inciting racial hatred if you carry on like that, Mr Pilling, sir. Behave and—'

Before the policeman knew what was happening Gareth had ducked under his arm.

'Hey!' he shouted, but it was too late. Eager helpers pulled the new arrival into the bosom of the crowd. Turning, Gareth muttered thanks to a skinhead with the initials SCFC carved into his neck. The bloke was sculpted from rock and Gareth had to chuckle at the irony. The last time he'd been this close to a Stoke City supporter the meeting hadn't been quite as convivial.

Through gaps in the crowd he could make out his pursuers, bobbing and weaving like boxers, trying to identify their quarry. Pulling out his mobile, he tapped a text message to Arnie.

Spot of bother. Locals not happy. Need help.

He tapped out the street name and who he was with so Arnie would be able to track him down. The response came in the form of a laughing emoji and the message:

Joined the fascists eh? Hope for you yet, mate.

Gareth might have seen the funny side if at that moment he hadn't spotted one of the Asian gang pointing directly at him.

'Fuck!'

Moving through the crowd he became aware of a log-jam up ahead, the sounds of battle assaulting his ears. It was like one of those football rucks he'd been caught up in during his teens, the only difference being that those in front were holding their mobile phones above their heads, trying to film the action. Standing on tiptoe, he watched as a large wooden banner crashed down on the thin blue line separating the groups. The pro-Brexit crowd stampeded, sensing a weakness in the police ranks, and all hell broke loose.

Police with batons struck out indiscriminately in an attempt to contain the rioters and the crowd began to fragment, small pockets of fighting erupting everywhere. The protection Gareth was relying on no longer existed.

'Hey, you!'

He turned to see the Asian gang leader pushing his way towards him, a piece of scaffolding in his hand. Gareth desperately sought an escape route, settling on a small lane to his left. He needed a distraction, though, and got it thanks to the Stoke City thug, who stepped in front of him.

'You want some, Paki?' he said, beckoning to the man with the pole. Not waiting to witness the outcome, Gareth hobbled into the lane, his bad leg reminding him once again that he no longer possessed the speed of his teen years. Ducking into a shop doorway, he hoped his pursuer was too preoccupied to notice. He sent Arnie another text.

Emergency sirens fractured the air, reinforcements arriving for the police, ambulances to attend the injured. The noise of battle faded as the warring crowd moved further down the street. Leaving his hidey-hole, Gareth set off swiftly in the opposite direction. When no footsteps followed he started to relax, only for a heavy-set Asian to step out in front of him.

'Shit!' Gareth muttered. The gang had used local knowledge to cut off his escape. Hoping he might be able to blend back into the safety of the crowd, he turned to see the man with the metal pole approaching from the other direction.

He was trapped.

'You've been asking questions about us,' shouted the big man, a scraggly black beard meeting at a point on his chin, brown eyes pinning him with an accusatory glare. Gareth was aware that the longer he delayed his escape, the more gang members were likely to appear. He needed to stall for time so that Arnie and Bruce could find him.

'Who are you, special branch?'

'I was asking about my dad, Stan Marshall, that's all,' Gareth said. 'You were in the same boozer on the day he disappeared. I hoped you might be able to help me.'

The big man looked past him. 'The man thinks we might know about Stan Marshall,' he shouted. 'Says it's his dad.'

The man with the iron bar was closing the gap now, tapping the weapon against the ornamental rings which took up every finger. Gareth's heartbeat matched the 'tick, tick, tick'. He hadn't had a proper fight in ages and didn't fancy his chances against these armed and dangerous men.

'Sure, I knew his dad,' said the man with the pole, stopping 20 yards from Gareth. 'He was a degenerate. A stinkin' tramp. He was into us for two grand. That's a lot of dosh… and he checked out without paying his dues. Rude. You here to settle the debt?'

Gareth wondered whether it was that simple, the old man being killed over a financial dispute. He suspected these people would make an example of anyone who failed to meet their obligations. Gareth saw white teeth interspersed with gold as the man with the pole moved forward menacingly.

'Got it on you, have you, ma mate? Our two grand? Or maybe this is all bull-crap and Stan Marshall ain't nothing to do with you. There's a whiff of the copper about you, ma mate. Maybe you're here to cause us grief cos you suspect we're Islamic terrorists. Why not, in'it? After all, we're Pakis! Don't matter we were born and bred here.'

Gareth sensed his chances of talking his way out of the situation were fading fast. These guys had a massive collective chip on their shoulders.

'I'm telling the truth,' said Gareth. 'My dad left his family in London to come and live here. When I learnt what had happened, I needed to make sense of it for myself. If you say he owes you money, maybe we can sort something out, but I haven't anything like that on me now. I'll need to visit the bank.'

'Sure,' said the first man. 'We're gonna let you walk up to the local NatWest and come back with our money.'

He laughed and stepped forward again.

Penned in from all sides, Gareth knew it was only a matter of time before they jumped him. He had visions of his body lying battered and bloodied in an alleyway far from home.

Just like his father.

''Scuse me, ya bastards. Raspberry comin' through!'

There was a whirring sound and the man with the pole crumpled at the knees, ending up prone across Arnie's lap. The former leader of the Boxer Boys produced a gadget resembling a mobile phone and jabbed it into the fallen man's neck. There was a spark followed by a scream and Arnie flung the incapacitated lump to the floor, the pole clanging against the concrete.

'Anyone else want some?' he demanded, waving the small black object in front of him.

Another man advanced, swinging for Gareth's head. It was a laboured effort, though, and in one movement Gareth ducked and sent a short-hand jab into his attacker's solar plexus. The man fell backwards and another gang member advanced. From his crouching position, Gareth threw the toy box and, unable to slow his momentum, the Asian gangster tripped over it and went sprawling. Seizing the initiative, Gareth aimed two well-placed kicks to the attacker's ribs with his good leg. The three remaining gang members looked uncertain how to react.

'I asked you lot a question!' Arnie said, a demented look on his face. 'Anyone else want to try out my new smart phone?'

Backing away from the psycho in the wheelchair, they reached down and dragged their injured mates away.

'Arnie, let's go!' Bruce appeared at his brother's side. 'I'll get a fuckin' ticket or, worse, the Old Bill will haul us in.'

Gareth saw the white SUV parked at the end of the lane. He started towards it then realised Arnie wasn't following. He was still spoiling for blood.

'Which of you wankers is gonna tell me who killed our old man?' he demanded.

A sea of perplexed faces stared back at him. Gareth saw one of the gang inch forwards, the reflection of a knife glinting in a shop window.

'Watch out, Arnie!' he shouted.

The man in the wheelchair pirouetted acrobatically and threw himself from the seat, ramming the taser into the ribs of the knife man. His victim shrieked, landing on the floor and shaking, foam bubbling from his mouth, his nervous system having been scrambled by the super-charged jolt. The others backed off, hands held high in mock surrender.

'Fuck it, we ain't going to learn anything from these bastards!' said Arnie, sitting on the floor, the taser held out in front of him. 'Let's get out of here.'

Gareth lifted Arnie back into his seat and they edged towards the lane's exit, keeping their eyes fixed on the remaining gang members.

'You'd better drive!' Bruce told Gareth, throwing him the keys. 'As soon as we're loaded up put your foot down and get us out of here!'

Gareth was nervous. 'I—'

'It's automatic so you won't need your damaged leg,' said Bruce. 'Come on!'

Seconds later Arnie and Bruce were installed in the back but, in his anxiety to escape, Gareth put his foot down too quickly and the van kangaroo-hopped away from the kerb. Aware of a figure at the driver's window, Gareth ducked just in time as a scaffolding pole carved through the air, smashing into it and decorating Gareth with flying glass.

He saw the leering face of the gang member with the gold teeth, his hand grasping through the shattered window. Flinging out his elbow, the reporter heard a scream, saw the man fall and floored the accelerator. This time there was a squeal of tyres and the van sped away from the scene.

'Saved your bacon again,' said Arnie with a roar of laughter.

'Yeah,' said Gareth. 'Shame we have to go back. I've left Maxi's present behind.'

25

THE name on the sign sent a feeling of unease coursing through Gareth.

The Sheldon.

He pulled up abruptly at the side of the road. 'This is it,' he said, turning to gauge Arnie's reaction. There was nothing in his brother's expression to suggest he'd been here before, but Arnie was a master at disguising his emotions. 'Dad died just around the corner in that alley with the old street lamp at the end. The area was cordoned off with police tape the last time I was here. The police brought me here after I identified the body, on the way back to the train station.'

He studied the ill-lit, cobbled street. Terraced houses in various states of repair crowded in from both sides, cutting down the light. At the top of the road was a rank of shops.

'What's the plan?' asked Arnie.

'I want to find someone who travelled in the same circles as Dad,' said Gareth.

'An old drunk, you mean.'

Neither man laughed.

'You didn't fancy those boys for it?' Arnie was referring to the Asian gang.

'They had motive,' said Gareth, leaning backwards so those in the rear could hear him. 'He owed them plenty.'

'Doesn't make sense to me,' said Arnie, thinking aloud.

'How so?'

'Plenty of people have owed me money in the past and I've never been squeamish about roughing them up. But kill them? That's just bad for business – in two ways. One, it guarantees you'll never see your money again. Two, a dead body tends to attract the Old Bill's attention which is never a good thing.'

'Maybe it just went wrong,' said Gareth. 'They wanted to scare him, but things got out of hand. They certainly weren't happy to see us, which suggests they had something to hide.'

'Maybe,' said Arnie, but his expression indicated he wasn't convinced. 'Anyway, what are we supposed to do while you're off galivantin'?'

'There's a greasy spoon over the road,' said Gareth. 'Grab some dinner and I'll meet you later.'

'You OK with that, Bruce?' Arnie turned his attention to his younger brother.

'Not really. Look at the place! It's a salmonella factory if ever I saw one.'

'Jeez, you're such a wus!' said Arnie. 'Come on you twat, I'm Hank Marvin.'

'Eh?'

'Oh, get with the programme, Bruce. It's cockney slang. Rhymes with starvin'. Big Mo would despair of you.'

'Who's Hank Marvin?'

'Some old musician bloke, I think.'

'Oh.' Bruce thought about it. 'Can I wait here?' he said. 'I'm sure Gaz will happily wheel me in there.'

'I don't pay Gazza,' said Arnie. 'I pay you. Now do as your older brother tells ya.'

Bruce sighed, eyes fixed on the ceiling.

'OK, OK!' he said. 'Hell, it's just like being a little kid again being ordered around by you two. Fuckin' 'ell! You wouldn't be here if it wasn't for me.'

'I appreciate it, bro, honestly I do,' said Arnie. 'If it wasn't for you I'd have to pay some other little dipstick to ferry me around.'

GARETH pulled the brown beanie hat over his eyebrows and shrugged into a nondescript beige raincoat. He'd been about to enter The Sheldon when Arnie remarked, 'You happy going into that shit-hole like that? They'll think you're minted.'

It was a valid point. Gareth realised he would find it difficult to persuade the locals he was one of them if he was decked out in London designer gear so walked up the road to a charity shop he'd spotted earlier. There, he'd transformed himself from well-paid journalist to down-at-heel loser. Now he was heading for the pub, only for a bookmaker's shop to capture his attention. Thinking of how his dad had got into trouble through gambling, he stepped inside and surveyed the race cards taped to the wall.

'You'm wanna make some brass, you'm better get 'yon tha' Jon-joneil nag.'

Swivelling around, Gareth came face-to-face with a rumpled figure, his grey, matted beard attached to a thin, angular face. A tweed flat cap was perched on top of thinning hair.

'Eh?'

'It int just blather, neither,' said the stranger. 'Jonjoneil. The man. 'E's got a sharp one in t' 3.30. O Ma Gawd.'

Working the words over in his mind, Gareth finally got the gist. Jonjo O'Neill, the successful jockey-turned-racehorse trainer, had a decent chance in the 3.30. The newspaperman looked at the whiteboard above the bookies' window and noticed a horse called O My Lord running at Market Rasen. That had to be it.

'Thanks!' he said.

Gareth shot out a hand and the man grasped it with strong, wiry fingers.

'You ain't from these parts, not seen thee forst.'

'People call me Gaz. I'm from down south. You?'

'Willum,' said the man. 'They calls me Lucky Will. Potteries born 'n bred. Wha' you fiddlin' at?'

Gareth took a guess the man was asking him why he was in Stoke. He had learnt over the years that when fabricating a story, you needed to skate as near to the truth as possible. He'd always been good at telling tales. It was a skill passed down by his market-trader dad.

'Me and my old man fell out a while back and I thought I'd come up here to track him down and make peace,' said Gareth. 'I can't find him, though. I've got a labouring job on that university building site, but we got the afternoon off and I'm visiting some of his old haunts.' He lowered his voice. 'I'm a bit worried, tell you the truth. There's no sign of him. Last time we spoke he mentioned The Sheldon, so I thought I'd take a look.'

'We could go thir for a scrounge round after the races,' said Lucky Will. 'I knowst a few people. Now, if you wanna piece of thit nag, you need to get on sharpish.'

Gareth found a crumpled fiver in his pocket. He didn't want to get out his wallet in case someone saw the credit and store cards inside. Raising his thumb to thank the man for the tip, he walked to the window, grabbed a betting slip and scrawled out his request – £5 to win on O My Lord.

Minutes later he stood among the fired-up punters cheering as Jonjo O'Neill's horse vaulted the last barrier and crossed the line 10 lengths ahead of its nearest rival. Punching the air, Gareth turned to thank his new mate for the tip. Lucky Will smiled, but his joy seemed insincere.

'What's up?' asked Gareth, shaking the man's shoulders. 'We're in the money!'

'You're in the money tha' mean. I was so busy telling you about it, I forgot to load on it me'sel... Bonkers busted, me.'

'S'why he's called Lucky, him,' piped in a bloke standing to Gareth's right. 'What's the word for it? Ironic? He's called Lucky 'cos he finds every bit of bad luck goin!'

26

'PINT of pedi… nectar for the soul. Thank'm.'

'No trouble,' said Gareth, settling onto a stool and raising his glass to his new friend. Lucky Will had been downcast over the missed bet but was cheering up rapidly now Gareth had offered to get the drinks in. Sitting in one of The Sheldon's little nooks, they toasted each other.

'You'm all right, marra,' said Lucky Will.

Gareth took it as a compliment.

'The old fella, what's he look like?'

Gareth brought up a picture on his phone – one he'd copied from his mum's photo album during his brief stay.

'Looks familiar. Reckon I might 'ave seen him about. Wha's like?'

'Eh?'

'As a person, y'know?'

'Well, he speaks with a cockney accent, like me, and enjoys boasting about his Irish roots, even though I'm pretty sure he's never set foot in the country. His dad came to England for work decades ago and the family settled.'

Lucky Will screwed up his face. 'Sorry to interrupt but have you had any snappin', marra? I could eat a man off his horse and the saddle as well!'

'You're hungry?'

'They do a great pie and lobby yer. Unfortunately …' Lucky Will stood up and pulled the lining from his pockets, indicating he didn't have a penny. Gareth realised there would be no more information flowing until food arrived.

'Pie and lobby's a new one on me,' he said.

'It's a speciality of these parts,' said Lucky Will. 'A meaty pie swimmin' in a bowl of veggie soup. Ra'at tasty. You'm should try it, marra. Ma Lady's a dab hand at it, even if she is a scratch-cat.'

He caught the puzzled look on Gareth's face. 'It's owe rite, marra, ma lady – my wife – has a temper on 'er, tha's all.'

'Right,' said Gareth, getting to his feet. 'Two pies and lobby coming up.'

When he returned, Willum had drunk most of his beer and seemed to be taking a nap.

'You OK?' asked Gareth, tapping him on the knee.

The rumpled man shook himself like a manky dog shedding excess water after a downpour.

'Sorry,' he said. 'Ah don't sleep well these days, catch a few winks where and when I can.'

'Better not sleep here, the landlord was looking over.'

'He's owe rite. Got no airs and graces, Norm. Seen all sorts in here. It'll never qualify for Inn of the Year.'

'I guess.'

'Was 'e a bit of a rocker?' Puzzled, Gareth looked back over at the landlord before he realised Lucky Will was referring to his father.

'Now you mention it, yes he was.'

Lucky Will rose and shouted in the direction of the bar. 'Eric!'

A heavy-set man with shoulder-length, greying hair looked over then walked towards them. 'All right, Lucky man?' said the new arrival. 'What can I do for you?'

'Got someone here asking about his old fella,' said Lucky Will, his eyes darting around as if he was imparting a valuable secret. 'Bloke was into his rock, he tells me. I thought "Eric's yer man".' He turned his attention back to Gareth. 'What's the old fella called?'

'Stan,' said Gareth. He stood and shook the new arrival's hand. 'And my name's Gary.'

'Eric,' said the new arrival. 'I suspect Lucky here is putting two and two together and making 45. My brother and I were in a band called Lethal Injection back in the 70s and early 80s. We played Punk rock, put out our most famous single Berlin Party Pogo on pink vinyl.'

Gareth nodded. 'I think Dad has it somewhere. He's into all sorts – AC/DC, Dr Feelgood—'

As he spoke he saw the colour drain from Eric's face. The bloke knew.

'You haven't heard?' said Eric, eyebrows raised in concern. Lucky Will grabbed his shoulder.

'What ya rattling yer chops about?'

'You know, Lucky,' said Eric. 'He means Stan Marshall, the bloke they found in the entry.'

Gareth feigned confusion. 'Sorry … what are you saying?'

'The police haven't been in touch?'

'No,' Gareth lied. 'Like I told Lucky, I hadn't seen Dad for a long time. We'd fallen out. The police wouldn't know where to find me.'

The barman arrived with two steaming bowls of food just as Gareth stumbled back into his seat. Pushing his food away, he looked back at Eric.

'I'll fill you in,' said the musician. 'Smoke?'

He removed a pack of cigarettes from his denim jacket pocket.

'I've given up,' said Gareth.

'Whatever, it's too noisy in here,' said Eric. 'Come outside with me.'

Though wary of being caught in another ambush, Gareth's instinct for bullshit told him the man was genuine. Edging through the tables, he followed Eric out of the front door.

'THEY found your old man down there,' said the musician, indicating with the hand holding the cigarette. 'I was here that night.

Mum and Dad used to own this pub then Dad got sick and Mum couldn't keep it going. I always come back though, even after travelling the world with the band. I know all the locals, and your dad had become one of the fixtures and fittings.'

'He raved about the place,' said Gareth.

'Yeah, I knew him vaguely. He recognised me from the band and we got talking, reminiscing about old gigs we'd been to.'

'Sorry, I don't understand ... how did he die?'

'I won't pussyfoot around it,' said Eric. 'He was stabbed. Cops launched a murder investigation, but it sounds like they're getting nowhere.'

'No!' said Gareth. 'Dad was stabbed? Who would do something like that?'

'You could throw a net in there,' said Eric, indicating to the pub with his chin. 'I guarantee you'd catch at least a couple capable of murder. I remember seeing your dad that night, but he didn't seem in the mood for a natter, and that's a pub in which it's best to gauge a person's mood before you approach them. He seemed preoccupied. I gave him a wave, but he looked straight through me. It was busy, giro day. We still call it that because it was the day people used to pick up their benefit cheques. Nowadays the dole is paid electronically.'

'Was he alone?'

'Your dad?'

Gareth nodded.

'Not at first. A young man bought him a drink and they seemed to be having a row, you know. The boy was waving his finger in Stan's face, angry like. When Stan tried to speak, the guy bawled him out.'

'You mentioned this to the police?'

'I'm not sure what I could say. I'd never seen the bloke before and I would find it difficult to ... Hang on!'

Eric threw his half-finished cigarette into the gutter and marched across the road. Gareth felt a chill pass through him as he followed. When he caught up with the musician, Eric was standing outside the cafe with a phone to his ear.

'What's up?' asked Gareth.

'I'm calling the police,' said Eric. 'See that bloke in the cafe?'

'Which one?'

'Don't make it fuckin' obvious!' hissed Eric.

'Well, who am I supposed to be looking at?'

'The person who was with your dad that night is in there now. He's at that middle table, two rows in. Careful, though. He can't know we're on to him.'

Gareth reached out and took the mobile from the musician, then cancelled the call.

'What the hell?'

Ignoring the protest, he pulled the collar up on his "new" raincoat, walked over and glanced through the cafe window. Returning to Eric, he said, 'I've got him ... the one in the wheelchair.'

Eric shook his head. 'No,' he said. 'I think even I would have noticed if he was in a wheelchair. It's the lad with him. He was talking to Stan the night he was killed ... and he wasn't a happy bunny.'

27

FLASHING blue lights danced across the brickwork of nearby houses, accompanied by shrieking sirens. Local residents poked their heads through curtains and front doors, sensing something big going down.

'You're a strange fella,' said Eric. 'I don't know the reason you didn't want me to call the police, but it looks like they're here anyway. Don't you want them to catch the bloke that killed your dad?'

'Sorry—'

Without time for an explanation, Gareth ran into the cafe. 'Arnie! Bruce! Come on!' he shouted at the two men, who were already heading in his direction.

'What the fuck have you done, Gaz?' said Arnie.

'You think this is me? Seriously? All I've done is chat to a few people. Someone must have recognised you and called the police.'

'But I've never been here before,' said Arnie. 'I swear. Look after this would you, Bruce?'

He held out the taser/phone.

'Not likely!' said Bruce.

'Give it here.' Gareth took it from him.

Arnie was stunned. 'If you get caught with that it could jeopardise your career, everything …'

'The police know me,' said Gareth. 'I doubt they're going to search a professional journalist. They'll probably think it's just a phone. Given your record if you got caught with it they'd lock you up and throw away the key. Come on! We're wasting time.'

Gareth put the object into his pocket as they stepped into the street. A couple of elderly customers cursed them for leaving the door open and letting cold air in. Bruce pulled at Gareth's arm.

'Yeah?'

'Keys!'

Fumbling in his pockets, Gareth pulled out the key fob and, snatching it away, Bruce pressed a button and the van indicators flashed. Rushing across the road, Gareth looked back to see three police cars, lights still spinning, forming a barrier around the entrance to The Sheldon. 'We might be lucky,' he said. 'By the time they've talked to people inside the pub we should be on our way.'

Bruce pulled open the sliding side door and pressed the button to lower the wheelchair hoist.

'Come on, Arnie!' he said.

'Umm, don't think so,' said his brother, nodding in the direction of the van. Bruce and Gareth turned back to see DCI Alan Rowbottom standing in the open doorway.

'What the—?' said Bruce.

'Nice wheels,' said the detective. 'Thought about taking her for a spin then remembered what I was here for … to arrest some scumbags on suspicion of murder.'

He nodded his head and a group of uniformed officers materialised. Arnie reached into his pocket then, remembering he no longer had his weapon, raised his hands in surrender. 'We ain't done nothing!' he protested.

'Double negative there, son,' said Rowbottom. 'If you ain't done nothing, that sure as hell means you've done something!'

DCI Rowbottom paced the floor, his eyes awash with fury.

'You sat in this very police station just over a month ago and watched some CCTV footage with me, after which you denied point-blank that you knew the identity of the man in the wheelchair. Imagine my surprise when I find you, our wheelchair man and A.N other – who, incidentally, is also on that film – trying to make a quick getaway from the very place your father was killed.'

Gareth remained silent, looking around the small interview room. To his left a blinking red light emanated from a half-moon shaped object situated high in the corner between roof and ceiling. The reporter suspected it was some kind of camera. Sat in front of him, another detective silently stared in his direction, no flicker of emotion on his face. At his left shoulder was a recording device, into which the silent detective had inserted two CDs after scrawling something on the labels with a black marker. Two microphones were attached to the device.

'Read the caution, DS Machin,' said Rowbottom.

The detective called Machin held Gareth's gaze, monitoring him for a reaction, then spoke for the first time in a gruff, baritone voice. 'You have the right to remain silent,' he said. 'You do not have to say anything but it may harm defence if you do not mention, when questioned, something you later rely on in court. Anything you do say may be given in evidence. Do you understand?'

Gareth nodded.

'Say it out loud for the recording.'

'Yes.'

'Do you think you need a solicitor, Mr Marshall?' asked Rowbottom.

'I've done nothing wrong,' said Gareth.

'Surely you realise I could charge you with obstructing our investigation and quite possibly a whole lot more. Our wheelchair man, Arnold Dolan, is a convicted killer, a nasty piece of work. I wouldn't put it past him to commit other violent crimes. What I don't understand is why you would conceal his identity from us – you could be aiding and abetting a murderer.'

'He's my brother.'

'What?'

'Arnie Dolan,' said Gareth. 'He's my brother. His mum had an affair with my dad. I only found out last year ...'

The DCI stopped pacing and slumped into the chair next to Machin. 'Right. And how long has Mr Dolan known—'

'Since he was about 12, I believe.'

Rowbottom tapped a book he was holding against the table top. 'Let me get this straight. I have two blokes, roughly the same age, both sons of Stan Marshall and both, for different reasons, with an axe to grind against the old man. Warm? I think I'm close to boiling, actually. I'm told Mr Dolan's weapon of choice is a knife. Bit of a coincidence when you consider that our victim was stabbed in the back and the neck.'

Gareth said nothing.

'Come on!' Rowbottom banged the table again. 'You're an intelligent man, Mr Marshall ...'

'Prince.'

'I'm not playing that game. You're an intelligent man, Mr Marshall, and you can see where the evidence is pointing. Hell, I could throw the book at you.' He waved the thick object in his hand. 'Now tell me what exactly happened, and we can all go home ... or to jail, depending on what you say.'

Clammy sweat pooled on Gareth's forehead. He brushed at it with his hand then dug fingers into his scalp to relieve the ache in his frontal lobe.

'Look,' he said. 'Arnie isn't citizen of the year, granted, but when I saw him on that CCTV footage I felt it only fair to get his side of the story.'

'With the greatest respect, that's our job,' said the DCI.

'I know,' said Gareth. 'But Arnie and I go back a long way. He was my best friend at school. I thought if he was guilty I would be able to tell. I needed to speak to him in person.'

Rowbottom's silence was an invitation for him to continue.

'When we did meet up, he was as angry and upset as I was,' said Gareth. 'He told me Dad had reached out to him and wanted to make amends for treating him so badly in the past. Arnie's trip up here on the day Dad died was supposed to be a new beginning for them both. They planned to meet up again in the future.'

'And they did,' said Rowbottom. 'That night outside The Sheldon. Sadly, I'll never know what the other person involved in this 'bonding' session made of it, will I? On account of he's dead.'

Rowbottom peered down at the desk, letting his point sink in. Then he took the conversation in a new direction.

'So, why are you both here now?' he asked.

Gareth sighed and wiped his brow.

'Arnie asked me to help him find out what happened. He knew he would be vulnerable going around asking questions. You had the CCTV footage, so he thought it was only a matter of time before you pinned the murder on him. He felt he had to be proactive and find the killer because, like you said, he has a record and knew it would count against him. He couldn't do it alone because people might recognise him from the CCTV. On the other hand, I was free to go where I pleased. I admit I had my suspicions Arnie might have been responsible but thought the longer I spent in his company the more likely he was to let something slip if he was guilty. In that event, I would have passed any information straight over to you.'

'Very public spirited of you,' said the DCI. 'How are the detective exams going, by the way?'

Gareth's failure to reply prompted another outburst.

'It's bloody typical of you newspaper boys to think you can do our job better than we can,' said Rowbottom. 'And all it's done is land you in the doodah. I could charge you quite easily with what we have at the moment, let alone adding this into the mix.'

Machin passed the senior detective a polythene bag and he put it on the table between them. Gareth's show of bravado died as he recognised the taser/phone.

'This yours, Mr Marshall?'

Gareth thought quickly.

'It's part of an investigation at work, one of the devices football hooligans are expected to smuggle into grounds at the European Championships this summer,' he said.

'Really?' Rowbottom wasn't convinced. 'Strange, because we have some bloke lying in hospital with the kind of injuries you associate with this weapon. He was attacked during today's Brexit march. Know anything about that?'

Gareth shook his head.

'Play it your way,' said Rowbottom. 'But I have to warn you this is not only an illegal device, but it's ranked right up there alongside the sawn-off shotgun in section five of the Firearms Act 1968. To make it clearer, anyone owning one can expect a pretty stiff jail sentence. Unfortunately, devices like this are readily available on the dark web these days and it's a right ball-ache trying to clamp down on them, so when we do catch people we like to make an example of them.'

His eyes honed in on Gareth's. 'I wonder what the fine, upstanding people at the *Sunday Tribune Despatch* would make of their chief football writer being dragged through the courts on a dangerous weapon charge. Think on that one while I talk to your mates.'

Standing, he picked up the package and the book. Gareth read the cover. It was *A Clash of Kings*, one of the novels from George RR Martin's *Game of Thrones* series. The DCI obviously enjoyed a bit of drama. Gareth almost laughed before the hardened features of editor Lana Desmund's face sprang to mind. She certainly wouldn't be smiling when she got to hear about this.

'I'VE spoken to your friend, Gary,' said DCI Rowbottom. 'He tells me you're brothers.'

Arnie stared back at him through emotionless blue eyes.

'I'm thinking that maybe you combined your resources against a common enemy. I mean, he's the clever one, capable of making all the necessary background arrangements and you, well, you're the practical one who could carry out the plan. I'm thinking—'

'Don't think,' said Arnie, 'the ticking gives me a headache.'

The DCI leapt across the table, his face inches from Arnie's. Realising he'd struck a nerve, a smile crept across the former gang leader's face. Rowbottom brought himself under control and slipped back into his seat.

'This is the way I see it,' he said. 'You drove up here, met the old man, followed him from the Coach and Horses to The Sheldon, then did away with him in the alley using one of those knives with which I hear you're so adept.'

'That's right,' said Arnie. 'But, first of all, I sped along the cobbles without being heard, hauled myself out of the wheelchair, whipped my useless legs into action despite the fact doctors have told me I'll never walk again, and plunged the knife in without toppling over. Stan Marshall was in excess of 6ft and I'm … oh, hang on … crippled for life. I'd do your sums again if I were you.'

'Perhaps that brother of yours helped – not Gareth, the other one, what's his name? Bruce? Or maybe you had something on you with which to incapacitate your victim before you killed him, something like, I don't know, a stun gun that looks like a mobile phone?'

Arnie's face was a blank mask.

'Know of anyone with access to one of those gadgets?' the DCI probed. 'That would solve a problem. You debilitate him first then plunge the knife in. Now, if you'll excuse me I've got a case to make out to the Crown Prosecution Service.'

He began to rise from his chair.

'Why would I come back here?'

Surprised at the response, Rowbottom sat back down.

'Sorry?'

'If I'm a murderer why would I return to the very spot the killing took place?' said Arnie.

'You tell me,' said Rowbottom. 'Perhaps you left behind a vital clue and were trying to recover the evidence.'

'Or perhaps I can't trust you lot to score in a brothel,' said Arnie. 'It's been well over a month and you're none the wiser. It explains why you're clutching at straws like this. You know it and I know it. The press will know it, too, once I get out. Have you looked into his debts?'

'Stan? We know he didn't have much, certainly,' said Rowbottom.

Arnie nodded slowly, savouring the moment.

'The bloke owed more than two grand to a local gang,' he said. 'Muslim bastards. He borrowed the money to gamble and couldn't pay it back. Perhaps you should look closer to home before picking on outsiders – it's your mess, after all. How did you find me, anyway?'

'Simple detective work,' said the inspector. 'Your picture has been in the local paper in relation to the crime, and we did a TV reconstruction with a man in a wheelchair recently which helped to jog memories. The owner of the cafe recognised you straight away and gave us a call. And it was easy to establish which vehicle you were in … the one that had been specially adapted for a wheelchair. Simple detective work. See, we can do our job. It would have been better for you if you had just left us to it.'

28

'BLOODY HELL, Gareth, mun, lucky you used your phone call to ring our Jase.'

Former world rally champion Will Shakespeare moved in for a man hug. 'I got here as quick as I could and brought Mr Albrighton with me.'

The old man alongside Will was wearing a black suit two sizes too big for his emaciated body. Looking Gareth up and down, he held out a withered hand, the veins protruding prominently. Gareth shook it.

'Hello, Mr Prince. Big fan of yours. Read that newspaper article you wrote about The Legend. Excellent.'

'Mr Albrighton's a top lawyer,' explained Will. 'He represented me when I was done for speeding on the hard shoulder a few years back. Got me off on a technicality, saying I was desperate to use the loo after being caught short because of a traffic accident on the M25. The magistrates sympathised, fortunately. I'd have lost my licence without Alby here.'

The elderly lawyer patted him on the back. 'You deserved to get away with it, you're one of the world's greatest drivers.'

Gareth was reluctant to disband the mutual admiration society but wanted to leave the building before the police pinned something else on him.

'We OK to go? I need to get back to the family. How's Anjie?'

'In complete ignorance, mun,' said Will. 'Didn't tell her a dicky bird.'

'Cheers,' said Gareth. 'I guess I'll have to let her know eventually. It's probably best coming from the horse's mouth that her boyfriend and two of her brothers were arrested. I wouldn't want her to have any nasty shocks in her condition.'

'Two brothers?' Albrighton looked confused. 'The way I understand it they are only holding one other person.'

He pulled a creased piece of paper from his pocket and read the words on it. 'Arnold Dolan?'

'They let Bruce go?'

'If you say so.'

'Well, if he isn't here, we need to find him!'

'Right-o,' said Will.

GARETH struck lucky in the first place he looked. He found Bruce Dolan in the bar of the Dolphin, the cheap hotel where they'd spent the previous night. He was on his third pint, judging by the empty glasses on the table.

'Care to tell us what's going on?' asked Gareth, looming over the youngest Dolan.

'They had nothing on me, Gaz,' said Bruce. 'I pleaded innocence, explaining I was only around to drive Arnie where he wanted to go and that I was his primary carer. I'm just hanging around until he needs me. I feel like getting pissed after the day I've had. Are you heading—?'

He didn't have time to finish the sentence. Gareth grabbed him by the lapels of his jacket and hauled him out of his seat, glasses rolling off the table and crashing to the floor. Some of the other customers looked up briefly but soon returned to their drinks and private conversations. They had learnt over the years it was better to mind your own business if you wanted to remain in one piece.

'Owww, that hurts!' Bruce moaned as Gareth dragged him into the spacious car park and threw him across the gravel. He came to rest against a red Corsa in which two people were sitting. 'Who are they?' stuttered Bruce.

'Friends,' said Gareth. 'You're lucky I've got company. It stops me doing something I might later regret.'

'But I ain't done nothing,' said Bruce. 'The cops said.'

'Yeah well, the cops know naff all!' stormed Gareth. 'They didn't talk to the same people I did. In particular, they didn't talk to the one person who saw you with Dad in The Sheldon on the night he was stabbed to death.'

Gareth grabbed Bruce again, throwing him head first against a hubcap.

'Oww, my dose!' he shouted, putting his hand to his face. 'No need for dat.'

'You'll survive,' said Gareth. 'Unlike my old man ...'

'What you on about? I din' do anything!'

Blood dripped onto the younger man's smart clothes and Gareth suspected his nose was broken. He wasn't normally an aggressive man but felt the only way to the truth was to scare his victim.

'I want to know why you were with my old man the night he died, and I won't be happy until you start talking,' said Gareth, lifting his captor to his feet, then jerking his knee up between Bruce's legs.

'Aaah!' The youngest Dolan flopped forwards, raising his hands just in time to protect his damaged face from impact with the gravel. Gareth knelt down in front of him.

'Story time,' said Gareth. 'And you'd better make it a good one. Let's go to your room for some peace and quiet.'

29

Two Months Earlier

BRUCE DOLAN caught up with Stan Marshall outside the Coach and Horses, tugging him back by the sleeve of his scruffy coat.

'What do you want, son?' Stan asked, turning to face him.

'I need a chat … in private.'

'Without your brother, you mean?'

'Yeah.'

'Well, tell me what it's about and I'll see if I can fit you into my busy schedule.'

'I haven't the time now, Arnie needs me back. Where will you be later? I assure you it will be worth your while.'

Stan looked into the younger man's hazel eyes. Bruce was the spit of his mother, Beryl, and a ripple of remorse passed through him.

'Well, if you fancy buying me a pint down The Sheldon this evening …'

'Where's that?'

'You've got a satnavthingamajig?'

'Yeah.'

'You should find it OK.'

Stan strode away, leaving Bruce to rejoin Arnie in the upstairs bar.

'All OK?' his elder brother asked.

'Sweet,' said Bruce.

Arnie glanced towards the bar. There had been a group of men standing there but it had thinned out, one or two leaving while Bruce was outside. He wasn't sure they'd even had a drink, and he got the impression Arnie had been keeping tabs on them.

'No one followed him?' asked Arnie. 'You're sure?'

'Who do you think he is – an international gun runner? He's a tramp, Arnie. I can't see anyone but you having any interest in him.'

'Shut it!'

Bruce stepped back, surprised by the ferocity of the outburst.

'Sorry,' said Arnie.

'It's OK. I expect you're feeling a bit raw after your first proper conversation with your old man.'

'Ah, fuck him,' said Arnie. 'Like you say, he's just a tramp. Still, strike a pose, bro, I want to get a picture to mark the "momentous" occasion.'

'Eh?'

'You know, I should have a record of the place where I first met my real dad. Smile, would ya?'

'Seems a bit pointless if he ain't going to be in it,' said Bruce. 'Hey!'

Arnie had taken the picture.

'Bloody hell, I wasn't ready,' said Bruce.

'Who do you think you are, Barking's next top model?'

'Give over,' said Bruce. 'Another drink?'

'Nah, you're all right. I'm off out tonight.'

'Don't you mean we're off out?'

'Sorry, Brucie, I've got a few things to do and I don't need you hangin' around like a lost puppy,' said Arnie. 'If things go well I won't see you until the morning. I don't need the van either, so you can have a drive around, perhaps see a gay porno or pick up a rent boy.'

'Fuck off, Arnie.' Bruce was only acting hurt, though. His brother had just made that evening's rendezvous much easier.

BRUCE was taken aback by the gloomy surroundings and put the lack of lighting down to the feral youth of the area, who obviously took great pleasure in using the streetlamps as targets in their regular stone-throwing sessions. A gang of them loitered on the pavement as he left the van, watching two of their number perform figure eights on their bikes in the street. It reminded Bruce of when he was a kid back on the Boxer's, sitting with his brother Arnie and friend Gary, teenagers banding together for their own protection.

Stepping through the door of The Sheldon, Bruce searched for his 'date'. The clientele was a mixed bag of ageing hippies, grubby OAPs, teen delinquents and Hell's Angel wannabes (bike surplus to requirements). He suspected there were even a few nonces, fresh out of prison and onto the Sex Offenders' Register. The only women in residence were two ageing, tattooed crones hogging the dartboard. He might have mistaken them for men had it not been for the ample breasts on display.

Spotting Stan Marshall at the end of the bar, he wondered in which category he should place the old man. He appeared to be the only tramp.

'Found it OK then?' said Stan.

'Not straight forwards,' admitted Bruce. 'The satnav took me all around the houses before depositing me here. These streets are a maze.'

'That's why I like it. It's a little bolthole from the world's problems, like a smaller version of the Hope. I miss that pub, and this is a decent substitute.'

'The Hope's shut at the moment,' said Bruce. 'There was a nasty fire. Some cunts threw Molotov cocktails through the windows. We were all there for Janie's mum's funeral. Not everyone got out alive.'

Bruce could see the old man was shocked by the revelation.

'Did you know Irene Sullivan?' said Bruce.

'Oh, not that well.'

'It was her wake. You probably knew Janie though. She was Irene's daughter. Used to hang around with our Anjie and your Gary, not to mention the rest of the gang.'

'Rings a bell,' said Stan. 'Arnold's girl, wasn't she? Did she have a kid when she was a teenager or something?'

'Nah, you must have the wrong person,' said Bruce. 'Janie married Pete Vickers and they've got two sprogs now: Simon and Diane. She was never really Arnie's girl. It was very much an on-off relationship, more off than on.'

Bruce brought the drinks and Stan led the way through the early evening crowd, pint of Guinness in hand.

'You were telling me about the Hope,' he said once they'd settled. 'Someone died?'

'Two of the older locals, Alison Jacks and Ray Brendal, who used to collect glasses.'

'I knew them both,' said Stan, reflecting on old times.

'Chuck's old mate, John Fallon, was touch and go for a while, too' said Bruce. 'We used to call him Fancy Man. This beam fell across him and broke two of his ribs, one of them piercing a lung. Fortunately, the paramedics did a great job. They reckon the attack was gang-related, an open challenge to the Boxer Boys.'

'Your brother's little mob. They still going strong? I warned Gary not to get involved. Fortunately, his football kept him busy.'

'You know what doesn't make sense to me?' said Bruce, changing the subject. 'You had a family, a wife, two kids doing you proud and yet you fucked off with some tart. I don't buy this business about you seeing my mum every day and being tortured by the fact you couldn't have her. You had plenty to keep you in London.'

'Look,' said Stan. 'I owe your brother some answers, but I don't give two fucks about what you think! If you don't believe me? Tough!'

Bruce lurched across the table and grabbed Stan's wrist, anger burning in his eyes.

'I know your game, mate,' he said through gritted teeth. 'I saw you coming a mile off. Our Arnie is brilliant at reading people, but where you're concerned he's got blinkers on. It's clear as day to me. You're a chiseller, mate, always were and always will be. You used to con people on that market stall and you're still conning them now. The difference is you're washed up, got no friends, no family and no money, so you're looking for a way back. You get in touch with my brother because you see him as a nice easy target. All you have to do is break out the violins and pour on the sob story, knowing he'll put his hand in his pocket and help you out.'

'That's not true,' said Stan. 'I really—'

'Bullshit!' Bruce slammed the table and beer splashed from his glass. He lowered his voice to a growl. 'Scrounging off our Arnie while he's at his most vulnerable – you make me puke! It would have worked, too, if he didn't have me looking out for him. He looked after me as a kid and I'm returning the favour. For 20 years you've been the itch he couldn't scratch, but he'd learnt to put you out of his mind. Now you charge in like the conquering hero expecting it all to be sweetness and light.'

Bruce leaned forwards, his nose almost touching the other man's, spittle forming on his lips.

'He's all confused, and you've made the doubt that's been eating away at him worse than ever. If he's a bad apple it's you who planted the tree. At least it helped him learn to stand on his own two feet though, you refusing to acknowledge he existed. By appearing in his life like this, you've pulled the rug away and left him flat on his back. He needs to forget all about you, Stan the fuckin' man.'

'It's not up to you,' said Stan, recovering quickly from the brutality of the younger man's words. 'Arnold's had his share of knocks, true, but I can see he's got the Marshall determination. Look at how Gary recovered after his football world collapsed, going on to become a sports journalist. Arnold can do likewise. I'm sure he's capable of great things despite the wheelchair, and I aim to help.'

Bruce released a humourless laugh.

'You? Help him? What the hell can you do? The best help you can give him is to stay as far away as possible.'

Scrabbling around in his coat pocket, he retrieved an envelope and slammed it down in front of the other man. 'There,' he said.

Stan stared.

'What's this?'

'Take a look.'

Confused, the old man pulled the envelope towards him, opened the flap and peered inside.

'How much?' he asked.

'Three grand,' said Bruce. 'Three grand to walk away forever. You want his money? Well, there it is, and you don't have to put on this guilt-ridden charade to get it. Disappear and it's yours. It will be enough to cover your debts and when I have proof you've done as I asked, I'll forward you another five. The deal is you don't give Arnie a clue where you've gone, or why.'

Stan puffed out his cheeks and began to push the envelope back in Bruce's direction.

'Ten,' he said.

'What?'

'You want me to set up somewhere else? I need rent, food, all sorts. Ten grand.'

The younger man put his hand out and pulled the envelope back.

'We're negotiating, are we?' he said. 'OK. Good. I'll tell you what, you get yourself set up somewhere a long way from here, give me a call, prove to me you've done it and I'll give you that ten grand – three now, another two once I have the proof and five more in six months' time. All you have to do is stay away from Arnie, no contact whatsoever … in fact, don't even get in touch with our mum. The whole sordid mess is over, right now.'

Bruce thrust the envelope back in his direction and Stan took it. Then the younger man delivered what he believed to be the clincher.

'You know our dad still despises you, don't you?'

'So? Banged up, isn't he?'

'Yeah, but he talks about you every day and I believe he's coming out soon. The way I understand it he has a long list of scores to settle and you're right at the top.'

The older man leaned back, contemplating the news.

'That's not all,' said Bruce. 'Remember our Chuck?'

Stan's mouth dropped open and his eyes widened. Bruce knew he had his opponent on the back foot.

'Of course, I remember Chuck,' the old man said. 'It was through him I met your mother. She came to the market to get him some boxing boots.'

'Yeah? Well how about we forget the history lesson,' snapped Bruce. 'Chuck ain't a kid any more, learning how to look after himself. He's a big boy and is more than capable of fighting his corner. On his last trip to the island ...'

'What island?'

'The Isle of Wight, where Dad's locked up.'

'Oh.'

'...On that trip I understand Big Mo gave him one instruction: To find you. Now, if I were you I'd be very, very worried. I can only imagine what delights Chuck would have in store if he tracked you down.'

Seeing Stan tuck the envelope away inside his coat, Bruce got to his feet. 'That's all I've got to say for now. If you know what's good for you, you'll take that money and board the first train out of here ... or preferably, the one that's going the farthest. I'll speak to you again in a few months' time. Here's my number ...'

He took a pen from his inside pocket and scrawled his name and phone number on a beer mat, then headed for the exit. At the doorway he looked back. The old man was still seated, the envelope out of sight.

Satisfied, Bruce headed back to the van.

Present Day

'SO, you didn't kill him, you simply bought him off?' said Gareth.

Bruce nodded furiously.

'It was Arnie's money,' he said. 'He gave me control of some of his accounts so that I could sort the flat, adapt it for the wheelchair, etc. It was easy to fiddle about with things and 'lose' three grand. He's not been on the ball with money since the accident.'

'You didn't trust my dad one bit.'

'Can you blame me after all he's done to fuck you and your family over?'

Gareth ignored the question. 'He was never a scrounger or a charity case,' he said. 'Making money was a game to him, all about the selling. We weren't that well off, but we scraped by. I wonder what happened to the trainers he used to sell. There was a lot of stock left when he quit London. I always assumed he took it with him.'

Bruce shrugged.

'Maybe he sold out.'

Gareth didn't buy it. That wasn't the shrewd market operator he knew of old. He stood up.

'I don't know what you're doing now, Bruce, but I'm heading back to Wales,' he said. 'I can't do any more here and hanging around is inviting them to arrest me again.'

'You believe me, don't you?' said Bruce.

'I'm not sure. Where's the money?'

'The killer must have taken it. The old man definitely had it when I left him.'

Gareth got up and headed for the door. A thought striking him, he then turned around.

'The beer mat. Did you write your name on it?' he asked.

'Of course.'

'What did you write?'

'I don't recall – Bruce, I think.'

'Not Dolan?' Gareth realised that if the pieces of card found with the body were laid out in a particular order they could just as easily spell Dolan as Arnie Dolan. DO space A space.

'I never saw him that night, you know,' said Bruce, interrupting his thoughts.

The reporter turned back. 'Who?'

'Arnie,' said Bruce. 'I hope he's got a rock-solid alibi.'

Gareth nodded and pointed to the younger man's nose.

'You would have saved yourself a lot of trouble if you'd mentioned this meeting with Stan in the first place.'

'And risk Arnie's wrath?' said Bruce. 'If this is how you've reacted, imagine what he would have done. He actually thought the sun shone out of that old man's ass.'

'Well, I hope you've told me everything,' said Gareth. 'If I find out you've held out on me, that injury's going to feel like a splinter compared with what's in store.'

BRUCE lay back on the bed. It felt like fire ants were dancing in his belly. There was one thing he'd left out, but he wanted to tell Arnie first. Just before he drove away from The Sheldon that night he thought he recognised an SUV parked on the other side of the road. Taking a closer look, the West Ham United sticker in the back window made him even more suspicious.

It looked remarkably like one of the vans the Boxer Boys used in their operations. And the last person he'd seen driving one of those was elder brother Chuck on his return from his visit to Big Mo.

At the time he'd thought about going back into the pub and warning Stan Marshall but feared his intervention would bring down trouble on his own head. Climbing back into his van he'd driven off, wondering if he'd just sentenced an old man to death.

30

WHEN Gareth entered the newspaper conference room on Tuesday morning he felt refreshed, having spent a relaxing few days at home with his family after the traumas of the Stoke trip. He had been surprised but surprisingly pleased to learn that Arnie had been released without charge but realised the chances of tracking down Stan Marshall's killer were fading fast. In the meantime, he had to knuckle down to some serious work.

Beside him, Jacko looked more dishevelled than ever, dressed in a loose-fitting grey sweatshirt and paint-stained jogging pants. Silver flecks of stubble sprouted from his chin and he seemed to be accompanied by a strange, musty smell. Gareth wondered if the pressure was getting too much for the ageing sports editor. In the past, Jacko would have concerned himself exclusively with domestic rugby and the Six Nations. With Welsh sport expanding at a rate of knots and international football grabbing its share of the limelight things were different and the newspaper business was changing, too, with everything being adapted for the digital generation. Was Jacko struggling to cope?

Gareth turned his attention to the cardboard box in the centre of the oval table. Opposite him, marketing man Jonah Quinn was looking particularly smug.

'A-ha!' said Lana Desmund, joining the gathered ensemble. 'It looks like the inflatables have arrived … right, Jonah?'

The marketing man brushed a stray black hair back into his slick, gelled mop and stood.

'Indeed, boss,' he said. 'After a bit of wheelin' and dealin', like, I reckon you'll be pretty happy with the outcome.'

'Well, don't stand on ceremony,' said the editor. 'Rip it open!'

Her enthusiasm produced a chuckle from the gathering. Jonah reached forward, tearing through the tape with scissors and pulling back the flaps. Reaching inside, he grabbed some flattened samples then tossed them out like a casino croupier dealing cards.

'Right. You lot have got plenty of hot air so start blowin'!' he said. 'Let's see what we've got for our money.'

Gareth grappled with his inflatable, twisting it until he found a small plastic hole in which to blow. Next to him he heard Jacko wheezing into his sample, the effort producing a bronchial rattle. *Poor old bloke might drop dead any moment*, thought Gareth, then immediately cursed himself for his flippancy.

As the reporter blew he sensed something wasn't right. When people began standing their fully inflated sheep on the table he knew immediately what was troubling him. The letters STD were printed on the side of each sheep. Ignoring the little voice inside his head which warned against confrontation, he asked, 'What's this Jonah?'

'Well.' Jonah drew out the word in his lilting Welsh accent. 'The sheep had to be closely associated with our brand, butt, like you suggested. It's basic marketing. I made sure the initials of the paper were printed on the sheep, so no one was in any doubt about who produced them. With the help of a mate in the printing game, it was achieved with the minimum of fuss and at a bargain price.'

'And did your friend point out what the initials stood for?' asked Gareth.

'You're havin' a laugh aren't you, mun?' said Jonah. 'It's *Sunday Tribune Despatch*, isn't it. Our paper!'

An eerie silence descended, the others intrigued by the game of verbal ping-pong.

'What about the more universal meaning, though?' said Gareth. 'Sexually … Transmitted … Disease.'

Someone at the far end groaned and Gareth glanced over to see one of the young ad reps blushing. Others occupied themselves doodling, twiddling pens or picking at fluff from their clothes. No one was prepared to look Gareth or his marketing adversary in the eye.

Like a boxer on the ropes, Jonah came out swinging. 'Oh, come on! People will know it refers to the paper.'

'Well, I sure as hell wouldn't feel comfortable waving it about,' said Gareth. 'It's like an advert for chlamydia! Surely *Trib* would have been better?'

'I was being charged by the letter, mun.' Jonah was flustered. 'It would have cost me another … oh, I don't know, I can't work it out now.'

Losing his grip on the sheep he was holding there was a squeaking sound, and it flew off around the room.

'Fuck!' he said.

'Um, Jonah? Sorry to interrupt—'

News Editor Monica Matthews was the first brave soul to join the conversation. Jonah tried valiantly to compose himself.

'Yes, Monica, love?'

'Can you tell me what the purpose of this hole is?'

She was holding the sheep at the front and pointing towards its backside where an opening was plainly visible.

'Ahh,' said Jonah, his face turning the same shade as his red Welsh rugby tie.

'Oh … my … God!' The full story unrolled in front of Gareth like a carpet. 'You got these sheep from that bleedin' sex shop that's having a closing down sale! No wonder they were cheap. Didn't it at any stage occur to you their design might be questionable for our purposes? I understand you lot are accustomed to being called sheepshaggers but, Christ on a bike, we can't have readers waving around sex toys advertising sexually transmitted diseases. What sort of alternative universe is this?'

'I've ordered them now,' Jonah protested. 'I've paid a grand for 5,000.'

'That's enough you two!' Lana's voice rose above the bickering. 'A grand you say, Jonah? Well, it's a pretty big balls-up and no mistake. Still, can we salvage the situation? Perhaps we could fill this, umm, orifice with something.'

'I think that's the general idea,' Gareth said.

'OK, Mr Prince, we've heard enough from you,' said Lana. 'Let's brainstorm the problem and see what we can come up with. Maybe the art desk can get us out of this hole.'

A snigger burst forth from one end of the table, cut short abruptly when the culprit saw the furious expression on the editor's face.

'What about a suggestion box?' Jacko asked, holding his hand in the air like an eager schoolkid. 'You know, throw it open to the whole staff, like. Call it: "Best use for your inflatable sheep".'

'OK,' said the editor. 'That's the sort of thing I mean … Let's discuss it again when we have a better idea in which direction we're heading.'

31

ARNIE had always despised the new pub chains, preferring to do his business in backstreet boozers. Since he'd been in a wheelchair, though, he could appreciate the merits of the modern pub, even if they resembled a school classroom with their tables laid out neatly in rows. The electronic doors were a godsend, opening as you approached, and there was plenty of room in which to manoeuvre. Casting his eyes around, he spotted a couple of familiar faces and moved in their direction.

'Well, well … if it ain't Arnie bleedin' Dolan,' said a tall man in a leather jacket, black hair cascading down to his shoulders. 'Ain't seen you since Wano.'

'Bloody hell, Miggsy, you look like Jesus f'ing Christ,' said Arnie. 'You got religion or something?'

'Same old Dolan. Always with the lip,' said the man called Miggsy, smiling. 'I had my hair short for ten bloody years in the nick. As soon as I got out, I made a vow I'd grow it. Suits me, don't you think?'

He twirled his head from side to side.

'You'd make a fuckin' brilliant brass, and no mistake,' said Arnie, chuckling. 'And look at you.'

He focused his eyes on the other man at the table, who wore an expensive suit. 'You look like one of them Jehovah's Witnesses, Cams. Where's the bike?'

'Important to keep up appearances,' said the other man, brushing his hand across neatly sculpted blond hair. 'I'm a businessman now, making a nice wedge.'

'Bet Her Majesty's tax collectors ain't seen any of it,' said Arnie. 'They can go whistle.'

The man stood and offered his hand. Arnie squeezed and pulled him close. Jordan Cameron was well over 6ft and built to last, square shoulders sitting on top of a muscle-bound torso, the elasticity of the suit material being tested to the limit by his physique.

'I heard the news, Arnold,' he said in a rough north-east England accent. 'Travels fast among the old network. Sorry and all that. You OK?'

'Dealing with it,' he said, tapping his wheelchair. 'D'you like the motor? There's some state-of-the-art stuff around these days.'

'You need anything sorting?' asked the other man, who Arnie knew as Carl 'Miggsy' Morgan. 'We always had your back on the inside, then the moment you get out this happens. Rival gang was it? We'd be happy to spend a few days in the Smoke, take care of business for you.'

The man spoke with a gravelly Mancunian accent and Arnie knew him as an enforcer for one of the top drug gangs in the north-west.

'It's all sorted,' said Arnie. 'I'm here because there's something else I need to talk to you about.'

'You mentioned The Red Moss Crew on the phone,' said Miggsy. 'They're big in Bolton, but small fry in the grand scheme of things. I put a bit of business their way now and again. Can't see why they would be a bother to you. What's this about?'

'Someone close to me got done in,' said Arnie. 'Knifed. Red Moss was mentioned.'

'Bad news,' said Miggsy. 'I've got someone you can talk to. Name's Frank Belstead. He's Red Moss, but on the level I reckon. Follow me ...'

Miggsy stood and Cams followed suit.

'You need a hand, Arnold?' asked Cams.

'No, I'm fine. We're not doing it here?'

'Not bloody likely,' said Cams. 'You never know who's watching or listening. There's a feud going on between us and another lot from across the city. You heard about that cop killing?'

'Sure,' said Arnie.

'Poor old Noddy was collateral damage,' said Miggsy. 'Wrong place, wrong time. One of my top boys was the target, ended up with a bullet in his shoulder. Copper was in the way as the shooter made his getaway. That's how it goes, sometimes.'

'It's getting heated,' admitted Cams. 'We're biding our time before we strike back. The trouble is we have to be tooled up all the time.'

Moving his jacket aside, Arnie saw the gun in the man's inside pocket.

'Can't be too careful,' agreed Arnie.

'REMEMBER him? I could hardly forget the fucker.'

Frank Belstead, a wiry character with thinning hair and a high forehead, was smaller than the other two men. Dressed in black designer tracksuit and gleaming white trainers carrying the name of a popular brand, he leaned back in his chair.

'How so?'

'He lived among us for more than three years. Met our Cyn in some nightclub in the Dam.'

'Amsterdam?'

Belstead nodded. 'Full of patter and charm apparently.'

Another notch on the Stan Marshall bedpost, thought Arnie.

'He hadn't counted on us – Cyn's family,' said Belstead. 'We looked into his background, found out he had a cosy married life down south. Two kids. We paid him a little visit. Told him to shit or get off the pot. We thought that would be the end of it.'

'It wasn't, though.'

'Nah. He gave us the sob story about how he couldn't desert his kids then one day everything changed. He turned up out of the blue and said he'd made a big decision and wanted Cyn.'

'You were surprised?'

'I thought it was just a fling for both of 'em and I guess I was proved right in the end.'

'How so?' asked Arnie.

'Well, at first he seemed totally committed,' said Belstead. 'Moved his business up here, gave us a cut of the profits and moved in with Cyn. He was a lot older than her, though, and eventually she got bored. She wanted to resume her single life, go pubbing and clubbing with her mates before she got too old.'

'He objected?'

'No. It was when she told him she was pregnant he really did his nut. Said kids had caused him enough headaches and accused her of tricking him. The next minute he was gone ... out of her life. We couldn't leave it like that, of course. Family pride.'

Arnie sensed he was getting to the bottom of things.

'You killed him,' he said in a matter-of-fact manner, watching the man's eyes for tell-tale signs of guilt.

'Hell, no!' said Belstead. 'Just because he did a flit and upset the little slag? To be honest, we weren't even sure he was the father. She had another couple of blokes on the go, according to the rumour mill.'

'Well he's dead,' said Arnie.

Silence fell on the room as the Bolton gangster tried to establish if Arnie was joking. When he saw the eyes were devoid of humour, he said, 'Really, how?'

'He was stabbed six weeks ago in an alley in Stoke-on-Trent. You're telling me you knew nothing about it?' Arnie's hand went to his pocket and produced a knife, waving it in front of the other man. Suddenly Belstead realised this was more than a friendly chat. 'Hang on! Who the fuck—?'

'Stan Marshall was my dad,' said Arnie, waving the blade under the other man's nose. From behind, Cams stepped forwards and grabbed the Red Moss gangster's arms. 'I reckon you were so angry with him leaving your beloved sister with a baby on the way that you eventually hunted him down.'

'You... you're the footballer? He said you had a nasty injury. Raced down to London when he heard.'

Arnie ignored the question.

'So you went to Stoke and, what? He refused to go back to her?'

'No... no,' said Belstead, his eyes widening as the blade touched his throat. 'Come on, man, if we wanted to do something it wouldn't have taken us ten years. I presume he only died recently?'

Belstead watched his accuser's eyes, hoping his message was getting through. He was pleading for his life.

'Couple of months ago,' said Arnie.

'Jeez man, give us some credit. If we'd wanted to track him down we would've been a bit quicker than that! Cyn shacked up with someone else soon enough and forgot all about him. By then, though, our mum had got involved. She plays merry hell if she thinks someone's upset her little treasure.'

'So Cyn was upset?'

'Well, to be honest, we were more upset than her because it hurt our mum. Also, he'd been doing a tidy bit of business around the markets and we were getting a nice little taste. Now that had gone, damaging our revenue stream.'

'So he couldn't just walk away,' said Arnie. 'It would make Red Moss look bad.'

Belstead looked into the cold eyes of the man with the knife and knew he had to choose his words carefully. He'd mixed with bad men all his life and Arnold Dolan had the eyes of a killer.

'All right, yes, I went to see him,' said Belstead. 'It was a few months after he left, and he was lodging in a flat just outside Manchester. I told him we had to save face with the family. Mum was upset, Cyn was unhappy, we were losing out. He had made us look silly and needed to offer us a sweetener to make it all go away.'

'Interesting,' said Arnie. 'I'd love to know how he managed that. When he died he didn't have a penny to his name.'

Belstead said nothing, just lifted his foot in Arnie's direction. The man in the wheelchair moved forwards, the knife shaking in his hand.

'No! Look!' Belstead realised his move had been interpreted as aggressive. 'Trainers!' he squealed.

'What?'

'The compensation,' said Belstead, his eyes pleading with the man in front of him. 'Stan Marshall handed us the keys to his lock-up and gave us all his merchandise!'

32

'NO news then?' Anjie stepped back and let Janie into the hallway.

'Not a sausage,' said Janie. 'Only what I told you at the time. Chuck said someone had seen Pete being bundled into a van. That was more than a month ago now.'

They were disturbed by the sound of laughter, Janie's two kids bouncing up the path pulling small suitcase behind them. Maxi stood between them, a beaming smile on his face.

'Come on, you lot,' said Anjie. 'Let's get you inside and Maxi can show you where you're sleeping.'

Looking over their shoulders she gave Gareth an almost imperceptible nod, letting him know that things were OK. He slammed the boot shut, grappled with three heavy cases and started up the path. Janie never did travel light.

'WHY did you and Pete split anyway?'

Anjie sat in her favourite chair overlooking the back garden, a white towel wrapped around her head. She was wearing a pink onesie.

'It started to go wrong when I couldn't sleep,' said Janie. Feet tucked beneath her on the sofa, she wore an oriental bathrobe and cradled a glass of red wine. 'Everything was getting on top of me and Pete seemed to carry on regardless. We hadn't 'slept' together for months. Part of it was down to me, I guess, giving off the wrong signals but I felt he no longer wanted me.'

She didn't reveal that Arnie was at the root of the problem, having decided to conceal the rape from her friend. She cringed when she thought about how she almost blurted out the sordid details during their last meeting. It showed how jumbled her mind had been.

'What about you?' asked Janie, changing the subject.

'To be honest, Max and I haven't seen much of Gazza since he found out his dad was murdered …'

'Murdered?'

Anjie saw the colour drain from Janie's face.

'You said Gareth had lost his dad but—'

'You didn't know?'

'No idea. Really. I thought it was natural causes.'

'He wasn't that old, though. Mid-50s?'

'Yes, but he lived a life of Riley, didn't he? Booze, fags—'

'Women,' said Anjie. She smiled. 'I guess he had a good innings.'

Janie nodded, but the pained expression remained on her face.

'Mummy!'

'Shit, that's Diane.'

'Mummy, I've had a bad dream.'

'Told you! Every soddin' night since the Hope. I'm praying it will go away in time. Coming!' She turned back to Anjie. 'Let me deal with this. I might put her in my bed. That sometimes does the trick. I'll talk to her for a bit, maybe read her a story … and when I come back, I'll tell you about that trip to the docs and everything that led to our break up.'

'Fancy a top-up?' said Anjie.

'Does a one-legged duck swim in circles?'

It was another classic Jane response and brought a chuckle from her best mate. Underneath her cool veneer, though, Anjie sensed there was a whole untold drama playing out.

'SO, I went to see my GP,' said Janie, back on the sofa with another glass of wine after the 15-minute interruption. 'To be truthful, I was fed up with Pete's constant nagging.'

She laughed, but there wasn't much humour in it.

'It sounds like he was desperate,' said Anjie, sipping water from a tumbler.

'I suppose,' said Janie. 'I wasn't easy to live with. There were all these thoughts going around in my head and I had no respite at night. Sometimes I would just go downstairs and watch some mundane documentary on the 24-hour news channel, you know? I don't think I could have gone on much longer as I was. I was at breaking point. I was angry with the world and taking it out on Pete.'

'He's a diamond,' said Anjie. 'I'm sure he understood.'

'You think, Anj? You don't realise what I put him through.'

'He's mentally tough, though, I'm sure—'

'Yeah, but I started flying off the handle at the slightest thing. Honestly, I battered him, and he would just take it, damn him, sit there and wait for my temper to blow out. He put his fist through the conservatory window once rather than fight back against me. Silly sod.'

'I had no idea things had got so bad,' said Anjie.

'Why should you? Remember, you were busy with the move, sorting a new job and everything. We barely spoke, and it's not the kind of conversation you have on the phone, a domestic violence confession.'

'I'm sure it wasn't like that, Janie. That's not you.'

'In all fairness, you've no idea what I'm capable of,' said Janie. 'Anyway, a couple of days after Mum's death he went out 'on business', telling me he would be back at three. As a result, I booked Di into the hairdressers. He was late home, and I went mental, punching and kicking him and then – shit I don't know what possessed me – I stabbed him in the arm with a pair of dressmakers' scissors. There was blood everywhere. It snapped me out of it. The kids heard a scream and came down and saw their dad bleeding all over the front room. He made up some story about falling and bashing his arm – I don't know whether they believed him – and

I came to my senses and bandaged him up. Later that night we had a heart-to-heart. He told me I should see a doctor. I was obviously suffering from acute depression or something and needed expert help. So that's what I did.'

'Any good?' asked Anjie. 'In my experience they write out a prescription for antibiotics or recommend painkillers then let you get on with it.'

'To be fair, she was OK,' said Janie. 'She said the problem went deeper and wanted me to talk to a friend of hers. The next thing I know I'm bawling my eyes out in the office of the local quack.'

'Psychiatrist?'

'Psy… something or other … psychologist, psychiatrist … psychotherapist I think he called himself. Anyway, this bloke certainly knew how to get me talking. I told him everything: Dad dying, various 'boyfriends' popping in and out of Mum's life, my stepfather – all the way up to Pete. I explained how the Sergeant Major treated parenthood like a military operation, all the stuff that went on with other blokes in my late teens and eventually my marriage.'

'Phew! Some session.'

'It took three visits to get the full story from me and then he arrived at a devastating conclusion.'

Anjie leaned forwards, intrigued. 'Yeah?'

'He told me that men had let me down all my life: My real dad, the Sergeant Major, Arnie and others. I had developed a pathological hatred of them and was taking it out on Pete. He said I needed him as an ally and had to sit down and talk it through with him.'

'And?'

'That's what I did,' said Janie, sighing and taking another sip of her drink. 'I took him through everything; my home life, my relationships … I laid myself out bare to him and admitted things I had never told him before.'

'What happened?'

'He lost it with me,' said Janie. 'Couldn't handle it. That visit to the shrink was the end of us.'

'Nah, he dotes on you. He'll be back. He just needs time.'

Janie looked at her best friend, a tear sprouting from her left eye.

'I've not seen him since,' she said.

33

JW OWENS studied the departure board again.

'Sydney – two-hour delay'.

Wiping sweat from his brow, he tried to focus on the newspaper article he was reading. It was no use. 'I need a smoke, butt.'

'Another? You had one 10 minutes ago!' said Gareth.

The Legend's expression invited no argument. Gareth guessed that the former rugby star was restless. He had never been good at sitting around twiddling his thumbs and it wasn't as if the two of them could while away the time in one of the airport bars. JW had been off the booze since learning about the brain tumour that threatened his life.

Making their way out through the long-haul terminal's revolving doors, The Legend watched the swathes of humanity coming and going, lugging suitcases from taxis and fighting over trolleys. He peered into the gloomy British sky.

'Wonder what the weather's like over there?' said Gareth, reading his mind.

'It's rarely bad, though they do get their share of thunder and lightning, plus the odd cyclone,' said The Legend. 'I remember playing in Canberra once when they had to abandon the game; a bolt of lightning struck the floodlights and we ran for cover. Never seen anything like it, mun, hailstones the size of golf balls …'

Retrieving a rusted tin from his pocket he took out his cigarette papers and a machine resembling a miniature printing press.

Winding the paper into it, he added tobacco and turned the wheel. A perfectly formed cigarette popped out of the end.

'Got a light, mun?'

'You know I don't smoke,' said Gareth. 'What happened to that lighter you bought earlier?'

The Legend fiddled in his pockets and removed a disposable pink object he had bought from a nearby garage. Gareth noted his hands were shaking and put it down to the after-effects of his battle against illness. Otherwise, he looked good: his shoes shone, his crisp white shirt was free of blemishes and his old Lions blazer and tie were in such good condition they belied their 40-odd years.

'Sorry you won't have company on the flight,' said Gareth. 'The bloke from the Beeb's wife went into labour. Young Jason will meet you at the airport in Sydney, though, so you should be OK. There's a refuelling stop in Dubai and you may be joined by one of the TV producers there.'

The Legend flinched and ducked, dropping burning ash onto his hand as a passenger jet dropped low over their heads.

'Shit, mun, that's a big bugger!' he exclaimed, sucking on the wound as his face turned a sickly yellow, the sweat plastering his fringe to his forehead. It looked as if he'd been rubbing waxy product into his hair, just like in his younger days.

'You OK, John Wayne? You look a bit off colour,' coaxed Gareth gently.

The Legend smiled, recalling one of the many jokes he had played on Gareth a short time into their relationship. He had told the reporter his initials – JW – stood for John Wayne like the film star when his full name was really John Wallace Owens. It was gentle humour like that which had cemented their friendship.

'I know it's a long flight but think of the rewards,' said Gareth. 'It will be like *I'm a Celebrity*, with the added bonus you don't have to chew on kangaroo testicles or swim with crocodiles. You seem like a man for a challenge, and there couldn't be a better reward on offer – seeing your lovely daughter and wonderful grandson.'

The Legend patted his jacket pocket. Inside, there was a picture of beautiful blonde Ellie and little tinker John enjoying a day at the beach.

'It will be fantastic to see them again,' he admitted, applying the lighter to the remainder of his cigarette.

'Come on,' said Gareth. 'We don't want you checking in late and missing your flight. I've got plans for the rest of the day and will have to leave you in a minute.'

The Legend nodded, threw the remainder of the cigarette to the floor and pulled up the collar of his blazer to combat a chill breeze. As he did so, he failed to notice the picture of the smiling woman and child fall to the floor and tumble away in the direction of the car park.

'LOVE-A-DUCK, it's the great JW Owens! Look, Cyril! Well, well, well. What an absolute pleasure, sir.'

A hand was thrust in his face as The Legend grappled with the Rubiks Cube-like puzzle of the airplane's seat belt. He took his mind off the conundrum long enough to accept the shake.

'Josh, Joshua Morgan from Talyceiriog – just down the road from you, boy!' said his fellow passenger, cheeks puffed out in a red, well-rounded face. His stomach protruded unashamedly from a tight-fitting Welsh rugby jersey. 'This is my best mate, Cyril. We've been going abroad with the rugby since, well, since your trip to Oz with the Lions all those years ago. I doubt you recall it, but you gave me your autograph …'

The words were a jumble to JW Owens, though he did catch the reference to his village in west Wales. He thought it funny that the man considered him a neighbour when he had left the family home and moved to the big city decades ago. He supposed it was a Welsh thing. People tended to connect you with your birthplace rather than your current abode.

A small queue had formed behind the fan, others straining to see what the fuss was about.

'Hey, Mavis, that's a famous rugby player, look you,' said one delightfully tuneful Welsh voice.

'Aye, JW it is!' said another.

'Oh, it's him,' a third one chimed in. 'Great player, granted, but I don't think much of his punditry. He was right critical of my boy. I'm gonna give him a piece of my mind.'

The man lurched forward, barging past some of those ahead of him in the queue. They turned to protest but had second thoughts when they got a proper look at him. The bloke was built like a boxer and had a flattened nose to match.

As he leaned in, his rancid, beery breath invaded the former rugby star's nostrils. He'd obviously spent the flight delay in one of the airport bars. In fact, The Legend had a feeling many of those crowded around him had enjoyed a few drinks more than was normal before a long-haul flight.

'My son's Joseph Webster, ring any bells?'

The Legend held his breath. The name was familiar to him. Webster was a young rugby player rising through the Welsh ranks. Before he was able to acknowledge the fact, his interrogator poked him aggressively in the chest with a podgy finger.

'You said my boy had a slower turning circle than a fully-laden oil tanker in a basin of porridge,' the man said. 'What gives you the right—?'

'He's got every bloody right, mun. He's The Legend,' chimed in the man previously introduced to him as Cyril. Affronted by the fact his big moment had been so rudely interrupted, Cyril grabbed JW's accuser by the throat. 'You start on him and you'll have to go through me,' he said.

Cyril had the stature of a rugby prop forward who had seen better days. Short and squat with misshapen ears, many of his muscles had turned to flab. What he had retained from his playing days was the confrontational spirit of a front-row bruiser. It was the irresistible force meeting the immoveable object. Joseph Webster's father now considered it a matter of family pride that he didn't back down. Thrusting out his hand, the angry dad grabbed hold of Cyril by his tender parts.

'Shit! Get your hands off my bollocks!' cried the victim.

The two protagonists lurched into JW's personal space and he feared he would be squashed under their combined weight.

'Excuse me, excuse me!' A woman's voice, polite but firm, rose above the jeering of the jostling crowd. The next thing JW noticed was a slim, petite woman with auburn hair attempting to insert herself between the two scrapping giants.

'Cut it out please or I will have you both removed from the air-craft,' she said. 'I realise you are overcome with excitement at the fact we have a genuine celebrity on our flight today, but there will be plenty of time to say "Hello" to Mr Owens once we're in the air. Now, we're already two-and-a-half hours behind schedule and don't wish to delay your holidays any further so please could you all take your seats ASAP.'

Despite some seriously grumpy posturing, both men eventually backed down, encouraged to do so by other members of their re-spective entourages. Once they had returned to their seats, the stewardess lent in to speak to JW.

'I'm so sorry about that, Mr Owens,' she said. 'My name's Mel and I'll be one of your flight attendants today. If you need anything during our journey to Sydney just holler and I'll see what we can do. OK?'

He nodded distractedly, fiddling with the seat belt as he did so. 'While you're here, lovely, there is just one small thing … Can you reach up and get my jacket from the locker. There's a photograph in the inside pocket which I could really do with right now.'

34

FROM Gatwick, Gareth travelled east on the M25. Having gone as far as he could in investigating his father's death, he'd found himself roped into the case of the missing husband. When he'd collected Janie and her kids from Cardiff Station the previous evening she'd begged him to help find Pete Vickers.

About to reject her plea due to his busy schedule, he noticed the tears forming. It was a shocking sight, simply because in all the time he'd known this hard-headed, independent girl at school, he'd never seen her cry. At that moment she seemed close to break down and he found it impossible to refuse her request.

Anjie wasn't quite so reticent. 'You're no detective, love,' she told him when he explained what he intended to do. 'A couple of lads associated with that gang ended up dumped in marshes, shot and mutilated. If that isn't enough, the local pub was burnt to the ground. It's all kicking off around there and, whoever you think you are, you're not that Liam Neeson and you don't have a "particular set of skills".'

He had sniggered at her reference to the scene from one of their favourite films, *Taken*, but she insisted it was no laughing matter. Patting her belly, she'd said, 'You're a family man now, and your family would quite like you back in one piece.'

After that she'd kissed him in a way that made him want to take things further. Unfortunately, he had to be up early to deliver The Legend to the airport and Janie was waiting for Anjie downstairs, ruling love-making out of the equation.

Because of the usual lane closures and minor accidents on the notorious orbital motorway around London, he didn't arrive in Barking until early evening. Driving through the familiar east London streets, he thought about where his search should begin. The Hope had always been fertile ground for estate gossip, so he was delighted to see a sign outside the pub announcing, 'Grand reopening party tonight'. It gave him the perfect excuse to meet up with old acquaintances and ask his questions.

GARETH put his pound on the new pool table and whispered to the player bending over to play a shot, 'Get this one out of the way and we can have a match for old times' sake.'

'For fuck's sake, mate, I was down on my—' The player stopped mid-sentence and span around, his eyes widening in disbelief. 'Fuck me!' he said, a smile breaking across his face.

'All right, Tigger?'

'As I live and breathe if it ain't Gazza fuckin' Marshall. How are you, Gaz?' He patted Gareth affectionately on the arm. 'Good to see ya. Bloody hell, I ain't seen you in here since—'

'I was at the funeral.'

'Sure, sure,' said Mitchell Tiggs. 'I wasn't. Vickers didn't really like having me around, God rest his … bad for business he said. Anyway, what brings you to these parts?'

'Catching up with the folks, you know? Just thought I'd pop my head around the door and see if any of the old characters were here. It's an amazing turnout and they've done it up nice … considering.'

'Yeah, one of them big breweries got involved. We're going up-market, I hear. Even got red baize on the pool table! It's all about serving posh meals and "attracting a better class of clientele".' He stuck his nose in the air and pressed a finger against it. 'I don't suppose my sort will be welcome here long. They know what a money spinner this place could be if it was spruced up.'

The two of them surveyed the decor.

'The fire was the perfect excuse,' said Tigger. 'Hell, you should see the loos! They've got seats on the toilets and some of those fancy hand dryers.'

'Someone will have nicked 'em by last orders,' said Gareth. The two men laughed and for a moment it felt like Gareth had never been away.

Mitchell Tiggs turned and played his shot, the yellow striped ball disappearing down the pocket. He walked around the table, applying blue chalk to the tip of his cue as he identified his next target.

'You used to be pretty handy with a cue, Gaz,' said Tigger.

'You're not on about that Chelsea set-to?' asked Gareth, laughing again.

'Nah, though that was impressive, too. You know, the pool team. We missed you when you disappeared from the scene. One minute you were here, the next … gone. Still, I know why you done it.'

He played a long pot up the table, the blue stripe rattling in the jaws. Stepping away, he waved for his opponent to carry on.

'Sorry about that business in Cardiff,' he said. 'I didn't want anything to do with it. I'm a doper not a fighter. I just got dragged along. It's hard to say "no" to Arnie.'

Gareth nodded, the smile fixed firmly to his face.

'I've got scars to prove it!' said Tigger as his opponent missed a long pot. Returning to the table, he potted another stripe, leaving the white ball well placed to plant the black in the middle pocket.

'By the way, fair play knocking up Anjie Dolan,' he said, turning back to Gareth. The reporter wasn't keen on the terminology but could make excuses for Tigger. He hadn't changed from those days when he hung around the local youth club selling weed.

'She and Max are living with me down in Wales now,' said Gareth. 'There's another kid on the way.'

'Wow! Wedding bells?'

'We're just getting used to being together, y'know? Janie Vickers and her kids are staying with us at the moment.'

'Oh?' A note of concern entered Tigger's voice. 'How is she? Bad business that with Pete.'

'She looks rough,' said Gareth. 'She's lost weight.'

'No bad thing.'

Gareth let it ride. He never really thought of Janie as fat, and he thought the scrawny, pitiful example of humanity leaning over the pool table was hardly well-placed to body-shame anyone.

'What do you know about it?' Gareth asked. 'Vickers, I mean.'

'I was there,' said Tigger. 'I saw these geezers bundle him into a van. They were wearing masks, like the blokes that did this place. Mind you—'

Gareth waited patiently, encouraging Tigger to fill the void.

'Well, let's put it this way, I reckon he was about to leave her anyway,' said Tigger. 'She was giving him a bad time at home and had done ever since that business with Arnie. What a cunt! Fancy doing the dirty with your best friend's piece.'

He slammed the black into the pocket and shook the hand of his opponent.

'You make it sound like Janie played a part,' said Gareth. 'It was rape, mate. That's why Arnie became persona non grata with the rest of the gang.'

'Personal what?'

'You know ... why he got booted out. Last I heard Chuck and Vickers had taken over the business. Wonder how that's working out now Pete's disappeared. Can't imagine Chuck doing all those hard sums.'

'Shhhh!' said Tigger, sniggering. 'He's over there.'

Gareth turned to see Chuck and Sly pushing their way to the bar which now took up the centre of the pub, though you still had a clear view of who was coming and going from the pool table.

'Fancy that game for old time's sake?' said Gareth, racking the balls as he watched Chuck and Sly grab their beers and head in the direction of the window seats on the other side of the bar. He breathed out slowly, relief flooding through him. He knew he would have to face them at some stage but wasn't ready yet.

'Challenger breaks,' said Tigger.

Gareth took a cue from the wall, chalked it and slammed the white into the pack. Balls spread everywhere, a spot and stripe going into different pockets to give him a choice of balls to play. After a moment to survey the table, he smashed a stripe into the bottom pocket.

'Ooooh, bloody Ada, look what the cat's dragged in, Shar!'

There was a guffawing sound behind him and Gareth looked over his shoulder. Two women in their late 20s stood there, dressed as if they were heading for a night in the West End. All bright red lipstick, big hair and spray tans, they might have been stars in a burlesque show.

'Gary soddin' Marshall,' said the one named Shar. 'As I live and breathe. We thought it was you. Nice to see you can still fill a hole!'

The loud cackles resumed.

'Well, the evening's looking up,' said Tigger. 'You look beautiful, girls.'

'Fuck off, you lech,' said the other girl. 'We see plenty of you. Unlike your oppo here …'

Gareth was struggling to remember their names. He knew they'd been school pals of Anjie and Janie but didn't know them that well. He seemed to remember Arnie having a night with one of them at some stage.

'You remember Shaz and Fenella, don't ya, Gaz?'

It was Tigger to the rescue. Gareth put down his cue.

'Nice to see you again, girls!' he said, leaning in to kiss them on the cheek, his mind turning out recollections like a tumble dryer. They had been Janie's bridesmaids at the wedding and probably knew more about the marriage than anyone.

'I hear you're with Anj now, Gaz,' said Fenella, her blonde hair done in a retro style, sitting on top of her head like a Walnut Whip. He recalled it used to be called a 'beehive'. 'I always thought you two would make a nice couple. You have a son, too?'

News travels fast, he thought. His curious expression registered with the other girl, whose long dark hair curled over her shoulders before falling halfway down her back. 'Oh, don't look so surprised,' she said. 'Janie keeps us up to date with all the news. Living with the Taffies now, ain't ya? How's that going for you?'

'Good,' he said. He missed a pot, leaving Tigger with some easy options.

'Ooh, we put you off,' said the girl known as Shaz. 'Soorrry!'

'Hey, Tigg, I'm going to get the girls a drink,' said Gareth. 'You want anything?'

'Pint of cooking lager is fine, Gaz,' he said. 'Can't afford to get too pissed, need to keep my wits about me with what's been going on.'

'Terrible business with Pete,' said Fenella. 'Janie must be worried sick.'

'She's staying with us,' said Gareth. 'She and the kids needed a break.'

'I can understand that,' said Sharon. 'I thought she'd done the hard bit, too.'

Gareth looked at her, perplexed.

'You know, kicking him out. They weren't getting on well, even before their heart-to-heart.'

Gareth indicated to a table in the corner. 'Why not sit there and we can have a proper chat,' he said. 'What are you two drinking?'

WHEN he returned, Tigger offered him his cue. 'Your shot,' he said, but Gareth's mind was elsewhere.

'Look, I concede,' he said. 'You were beating me fair and square, Tiggs, and my mind just isn't on it. Sorry!'

Tigger nodded over at the girls. 'I can see that,' he said, winking. 'Thought you were a happily married man.'

'Not married yet, mate,' he said. 'But it's not about that …' He decided not to elaborate.

Tigger chuckled. 'Nah,' he said. 'Course it's not. Let me hit a few balls and I'll join you in a minute.'

Gareth walked closer to him, a £20 note in his fist. 'Do us a favour, Tiggs,' he said. 'I need some privacy with these two. Why not go and buy some of your mates around the corner a drink?'

He thrust the money into the drug dealer's hand.

'You sneaky dog!' Tigger whispered, grasping the note. 'You're after a bloody threesome, ain't ya! Well don't let me get in the way. I'll carry on here and leave you to it. Some of the old pool team boys are coming over now.'

He took his drink from the tray and walked back to the table.

'Right, girls,' said Gareth. 'I think I've got this right: A sex on the beach and a slow, comfortable screw against the wall. It's my pleasure.'

'Oh, it will be,' said Fenella, a wicked grin on her face. They all burst out laughing.

35

'WE had a right laugh back in the day, didn't we, eh, Fee? It was me, you, Janie and Anj against the world!' said Sharon. She was rolling around on her seat, her drink held high, the cocktail sloshing around and threatening to breach the rim of the glass. The more drinks Gareth plied them with, the louder the two girls became. They weren't the most discreet people when sober, so he was hoping they would let their guard down further.

'I thought Janie settled down after the wedding?' said Gareth.

'Oh, she did,' said Fenella. 'She couldn't get any worse, mind. She was wild beforehand eh, Shazza?'

'Janie? Hell, we could tell you some stories.' Sharon lowered her voice. 'I don't think Pete knew the half of it. She went with Arnold, Phil Miller from the football team—'

'Yeah, OK, Shazz,' said Fenella. 'Don't give away all her secrets. Remember who we're talking to …' She made a jerky head movement in Gareth's direction, then put a finger to her lips to indicate her friend should shut up.

'Oh shit! Sorry.'

'Don't stop on my account,' Gareth said, wondering just what juicy secrets Sharon was about to spill.

'You would say that, you're the press!' Sharon squealed.

Fenella winked at her.

Gareth felt he was missing out on a private joke.

On the other side of the bar, he caught a glimpse of Chuck standing amid a group of people, swigging from a bottle and occasionally looking in his direction, a stony expression on his face.

'Hey, Gaz, I think it's time I was going.'

Gareth looked up to find Tigger standing over him. 'Nice to see you again and all, but Chuck will expect me to be working, not gossiping.'

Grabbing his coat, the dealer headed for the rear exit. Gareth told the girls he would be back soon and slipped out after him. 'Hey, Tiggs!' he hissed as the other man started walking away. He turned back, putting a lighter to a suspicious looking roll-up.

'What?'

'You said you were there when Vickers disappeared. What happened, mate?'

Tigger took a long drag, savouring the taste of the chemicals passing through his body. Gareth detected the sweet, unmistakeable smell of skunk.

'Look, it was just as I told you, real quick,' he said. 'Vickers asked me to meet him in Stratford. When I got there, I saw him being bundled into a van. They really gave him a good kick-in and I had to keep my head down or I might have been next. Once they had him on board, they drove off.'

'What sort of van?'

Tigger thought about the question. 'Well, strange you should ask that,' he said. 'Something has been nagging at me – I swear I'd seen it before. My memory's useless, though. I think there was an advert for some kind of electrical company down the side and St George Cross flags on the wing mirrors. Typical white van man stuff.'

'No worries. If you remember anything else …'

'I'll let you know,' said Tigger, walking off in the direction of the Boxers' Estate.

GARETH watched him go then turned, bouncing off a sturdy figure blocking his way. Somehow, he managed to retain his balance.

'Well, well, if it ain't my old mate, Gazza,' said Chuck Dolan. 'What brings you around this way? Looking for that bastard brother of yours?'

'Actually, I'm trying to find Pete Vickers. Seen him, Chuck?'

'What would you want with him?'

Chuck took a step back, studying Gareth's face intently.

'Janie tells me he's gone missing and I'm helping her track him down.'

'Oh, that's nice,' said Chuck. 'Return of the conquering hero, eh? Brought your cape, have you? Gonna save the day as always? Well, I'm using all the resources at our disposal to find him and I ain't had any luck. He's either been kidnapped or doesn't want to be found. I ain't surprised. I heard Janie was making his life a misery. Whatever the reason for his disappearing act, the fucker's left me in the lurch.'

Gareth wasn't surprised at Chuck's concern. Without the financial brains of the operation the Boxer Boys were impotent.

'Have we got a problem, Chuck?' asked Gareth. 'I don't recall upsetting you but—'

'My problem, Mr Big-time newspaper reporter, is I don't trust you as far as I can throw you. What is it they say? The apple doesn't fall far from the tree? Your old man was a sneaky, conniving git. He conned our mum with his silky-smooth talk and then slept with her behind our dad's back. Big Mo ain't been the same since he found out and we've all had to suffer for it.'

His eyes glazed over, memories flooding in. 'I remember Arnie being born. I was only eight, but I was aware he represented a fresh start for our family. My dad was in jail awaiting trial and his brother had been killed just along the way here …' He nodded towards an ill-lit alleyway which wound from the pub to the centre of the estate.

'I didn't know,' said Gareth.

Chuck was silent for a minute, his vacant stare making Gareth feel uneasy.

'Dad's brother's – the one who died – his middle name was Arnold, you know,' he said, breaking the spell. 'Clive Arnold Dolan, a war hero. He fought for his country in the Falklands but came back a broken man. Such a waste! Naming Arnie after him was the greatest tribute our dad could pay him. When he learnt Arnie wasn't his it tore him apart.'

'I'm not my dad,' said Gareth. 'That's unfair.'

'Yeah?' Chuck's stare took on a mean intensity, and the reporter sensed he was in real danger. 'You fucked my sister, put her in the club, ran away and changed your soddin' name, for Christ's sake,' said Chuck. 'To my mind that's exactly the sort of thing Stan the Man would have done.'

He stepped forwards so their noses were practically touching. Gareth could smell the stale beer on his breath. Though both men were roughly the same height, their body shapes differed massively. Whereas Chuck was wide shouldered, muscle bound and solid, Gareth was flabby and out of condition, his injured leg contributing to his lack of fitness. Recently, he'd started going to the gym again, but it was going to take a lot more than two introductory sessions with a personal trainer to get him back in fighting shape.

'It wasn't like that, Chuck,' he said. 'Anjie and I have been in love since we were teens.'

'In love? You bloody left her holding the baby!' stormed Chuck. 'Exactly like that scum father of yours did to our mum. You and Arnie were made for each other, two brothers born of a scheming, cheating—'

Gareth felt his knuckles tightening, the words cutting deep. His father might not have been perfect, but his death was still fresh, and Chuck was jumping on the grave. Had this block of human granite taken his hatred for Stan Marshall one step further and killed him?

A screech of tyres in the car park caused Chuck to glance over his shoulder. Gareth briefly considered the flight option, only for the oldest Dolan brother to steal the initiative from him. An iron fist crashed into the reporter's jaw, the left hook delivered with the perfect timing of a trained boxer. It took less than a second for the message to transmit from Gareth's brain to his knees and, as they buckled, he saw the grim satisfaction etched on his assailant's face. A voice in his head told him he had to put distance between himself and Chuck Dolan or he was in serious trouble. His mind was scrambled, his vision blurred, his brain incapable of transmitting the message to his legs.

Chuck's face leered down at him, hate and anger writ large in every crease and blemish. It was the image of a man determined to finish off what he'd started. As Gareth shut his eyes there was an indecipherable cry, a mixture of pain and fury, then … nothing.

'LIE him down here, right? That's it. Give him some water. Come on, stand back people, please, can you? Bloody hell, it ain't no sideshow on Southend pier. The bloke needs air.'

Gareth slowly opened an eye, focusing on the voice. As his vision cleared he saw Sly Dolan holding a cup of water to his lips.

'Wha… What happened?'

'I should ask you the same thing, Gazza,' said Sly. 'Chuck said he was nipping out for something and would be back in a few minutes. When he didn't return after half an hour I thought I'd better look for him, what with all the trouble we've been having. I found you spark out in the car park, but no sign of our Chuck at all. Did you come across him on your travels?'

Gareth put his hand to his chin and grimaced. He thought his jaw might be dislocated, even broken.

'I haven't a clue what happened, to be honest,' he said, wishing to keep his altercation secret. 'I must have tripped and bumped my head. You sure Chuck hasn't gone to another boozer?'

'I tried to ring him from the car park and heard his ringtone,' said Sly. 'His phone was a few yards from where you were lying. I'm worried, mate, truly. First, we lose two of Tigger's boys, then Vickers, now Chuck. The whole thing is falling apart.'

Gareth pushed himself into a sitting position. His chin pulsated as if he'd been hit with a rock. He tried to loosen it with mouth exercises, but the pain was intense.

'You're in a bad way,' said Sly. 'Sorry, mate. I know Chuck didn't have much time for you because of who your dad was, but I never had a problem with you. In some ways, I felt sorry for your father. I remember him when I was a young kid. He was pretty good with me even if he was doing the dirty deed with Mum.'

'Thanks, Sly, appreciate it,' Gareth mumbled.

'You gonna be OK?' asked Sly. 'I've got to make some calls, strike while the iron's hot. If this other gang has got hold of Chuck, then I can't waste any time. Damn, it's getting crazy around here. I'm starting to wonder if it's time to get out of the game.'

GARETH lay on the bed in his old room having turned down the offer of a hospital check-up. The pain in his jaw was easing slowly and he wasn't sure if that was down to the alcohol or the fact the damage wasn't as bad as he first feared.

Looking around, he studied the old football and music posters of his childhood, opening his mind to a flood of memories. There was a signed picture of the West Ham striker, Tony Cottee, who he and Arnie had met at an open day at Upton Park, while on the far wall was a poster advertising a live gig by Blur, one of his favourite bands when he was growing up.

He'd seen them perform live once and remembered each of the gang had been ordered by Arnie to sneak a small bottle of alcohol into the venue. Most of the Boxer Boys had raided their parents' drink cabinets and devised their own awful concoctions but Vickers somehow got his hands on an expensive bottle of brandy. Unfortunately, it dropped out of his sleeve and smashed on the floor at the entrance, splattering a bouncer's trousers. The large, shaven-headed figure had grabbed young Vickers by the ear and read him the riot act, making him the butt of their jokes for some time to come. It was typical Pete Vickers, thought Gareth. He had to go one better and buy the real stuff, having never been prepared to 'slum it' like the rest of them. If he was alive, Gareth wondered what condition he was being kept in.

The feeling of encouragement he'd felt when speaking to Tigger had dissolved after the car park incident. Gareth had a flashback, Chuck standing over him, having delivered the knockout blow, looking set to finish what he started when ... what? Where had the eldest Dolan boy gone? It was like some friendly spirit had been looking out for Gareth and intervened at his moment of need.

More likely it was a rival gang, though, which begged the question ... why hadn't they taken him, too? Unless, of course, they knew exactly who he was and had left him behind deliberately, not wishing to bring unwanted attention on themselves with the kidnap of a journalist.

His recollection of the night's events were interrupted by the familiar first bars of *I'm Forever Blowing Bubbles*. He reached over to the bedside cabinet, retrieved his phone and peered at the display.

Strange.

It was Will Shakespeare.

'What's wrong, Will?'

'Oh, uh, nothing ... I mean, well, Anjie's OK so don't worry. I just had a call from our Jase in Sydney, though.'

'How's he getting on?'

'Fine,' said Will. 'It's not him I'm worried about, mun. He went to the airport to pick up The Legend—'

Gareth glanced at the time again. Of course. It was approaching midday in Australia. JW Owens was due to arrive in Australia about now.

'Don't tell me, he got pissed on the bloody plane.'

'No. That is ... he might have done, I suppose.'

'Don't you know?' said Gareth incredulously. 'Look Will, you aren't making sense. I know he's your mate, but you aren't helping him by being coy. Spit it out. Is he or isn't he all right?'

'Well, that's the strange thing, see,' said Will. 'Jase got to the airport on time and everything and the plane landed safely. The problem is that JW wasn't on it.'

36

THE constantly dripping tap was playing on Chuck Dolan's nerves. He had been listening for clues to his whereabouts and all he could hear was the plink, plink, plink of water on concrete.

Strapped to a chair, wrists and ankles bound in unbreakable plastic cuffs, he felt sore and angry. He had considered rocking the chair until it fell over and smashed on impact only to discover it was bolted to the floor. He wasn't sure if he had the energy for an escape bid, anyway, suspecting he'd been dosed up with drugs to rob him of his natural fighting spirit. In an hour's time when the effects started to wear off, he would make another concerted effort to free himself.

'Bastards!' he shouted in an effort to release the tension that gripped his body. His mind replayed the incident in the car park, searching for clues as to who his abductors might be and where he was imprisoned. It was hard to believe that a few hours earlier he'd been enjoying a few pints at the reopening of the Hope, happy in the company of his brother Sylvester and their mates. That was until he noticed Gary Marshall and an invisible switch flicked inside his head. Oblivious to the jokes and banter continuing around him, he'd felt his muscles tighten and his jaw set firm.

He'd never liked Arnie's old school pal. From the moment his brother had met Gazza, Chuck felt that he and Sly had been demoted to second-class citizens in Arnie's eyes. With the Marshall boy's backing, Arnie had become more opinionated and self-possessed, flaunting an air of superiority around the Boxers'. Then, when the shit hit the fan, Gazza was nowhere to be seen, as if he'd lit the blue touchpaper to Arnie's ambition then retired to a safe distance.

That Hackney business was a typical example. Chuck and Sly had risked their lives marching onto the territory of another gang while Gazza was off playing football with Arnie's blessing. The two older Dolan boys were not only lucky to get out of the Ottaman Club alive that night but also forced to spend a year in exile with their granddad, Billy, in Marbella. Arnold and his little pal, meanwhile, carried on without a care in the world.

Secretly, Chuck had been glad Gazza injured himself so badly his football career came to a premature end. He needed to be brought crashing down to earth and no one had ever suspected Chuck's contribution to his downfall. The oldest Dolan, fearing that Gazza and Arnie's reunion had stolen his thunder on a trip to Brighton that had been organised to celebrate his birthday, had slipped a hallucinogen into Gazza's drink earlier that night. When the promising footballer, gripped by paranoia, had thrown himself from a nightclub balcony, the boy's family blamed Arnie for encouraging him to take speed earlier that evening.

While Arnie had accompanied his friend to hospital in the ambulance, Chuck had rounded off his special night by serenading the rest of the party with Jimmy Cliff's 'The Bigger They Come, The Harder They Fall' on a pub karaoke.

Chuck thought that would be the end of Arnie's dealings with his 'best friend'. He couldn't see Gazza's family ever forgiving Arnie for leading him astray and believed his gang boss brother was unlikely to want a washed-up cripple as an ally.

On both counts he was wrong. A couple of years later the Marshall bastard was once again Arnie's sole concern when he accompanied the gang to a football match between West Ham and Cardiff. When it all kicked off afterwards, Gazza managed to wriggle out of trouble while Arnie took the rap, eventually being sent down for helping his mate. By contrast, the Marshall boy walked away scot free. It was as if he was coated in Teflon, nothing ever sticking to him.

At least Arnie wizened up behind bars and when he pursued Gazza to Cardiff, believing him to be the one who had ratted him out to police, Chuck gleefully went along for the ride. Even then, the slippery sod managed to get off the hook while Arnie ended up in a wheelchair.

Chuck had known Arnie's big secret – that he was the illegitimate son of Gary's old man – for some time. His own father, Big Mo, had even tried to have Arnie killed in prison. Though he was not particularly happy about that, when Chuck learnt Arnie had raped Janie Vickers it was the final straw in their relationship and Chuck saw no option but to disown his brother.

All the old wounds and buried feelings had burst to the surface the previous night when Chuck had clapped eyes on Gazza in the Hope and, on the spur of the moment, he had decided it was time to dish out a cold dose of karma.

The left hook he'd thrown to spark out Gazza would have made his old boxing teacher proud. Then, just as he was about to finish the job, a thunderous pain erupted in the back of his head and darkness descended.

CHUCK woke to the clanking of chains and for a brief moment thought he was being released. Raising his head, he tried to see below the blindfold, but it was wrapped too tightly around his face. He sensed someone beside him and turned, directing a flow of spit in that person's direction.

'Nasty habit,' said his captor.

Fuck.

The voice was instantly recognisable, and suddenly things seemed a whole lot worse.

'Let the dog see the rabbit.'

The blindfold was ripped off and Chuck squeezed his eyes shut against the intense glare. Hearing a whirring noise, he felt a powerful slap connect with his cheek.

'Look at me, you cunt!' the voice growled.

Chuck lowered his head and turned in his captor's direction. He saw pitch-black pupils floating in a sea of cobalt blue.

'Hello, Arnie,' he said.

Part III

Revelations

'This is my cassette I'm sending you, I hope you hear it'

Stan, by Eminem

37

'YOU had us all so worried, JW!' Gareth leaned forward on the bar stool and tried to make eye contact with the old man. 'The last time I saw you everything was hunky dory and we were at the terminal waiting for your flight. What on earth happened?'

The Legend looked up from his empty glass, the double vodka having been dispatched with one gulp. His eyes were red and his face blotchy, his clothes no different from the ones he had been wearing three days earlier. Rather than immaculate, they were now dishevelled and stained.

'I couldn't fly, mun,' he mumbled.

'I can see that,' said Gareth. 'Why though? Was it your health? Did the pains in your head return?'

'Nothing like that,' said The Legend. 'I wanted to tell you on the night of the awards, but the words wouldn't come out.'

'Well, now is your chance. Have you had your passport revoked or something, or did you hit the booze after I left?'

JW Owens looked mournfully into his empty glass. Gareth beckoned for the barman to refill it. He knew he shouldn't be indulging the ex-rugby star's bad habits but thought it was the best way to get to the gist of the story.

'I'm scared to death of planes,' he said finally. 'I haven't been near one in 30 years. If God meant us to whizz around in the sky he'd have given us damn wings!'

'But you used to fly everywhere with Wales, the Lions—'

'Exactly, Gareth, mun,' said The Legend. 'How do you think I developed the soddin' phobia? It was on those bloody trips. They used to put us in these flying death traps with a couple of propellers for internal flights... scared the crap out of me. One time we overshot the runway in the middle of nowhere, bounced along some scrubland in the Bush. I thought I was a goner. Honest. Now I'm a nervous wreck whenever I see one in the sky.'

'You're one of the bravest men to ever take the rugby field, though,' said Gareth. 'You can't be afraid of flying! You know you're more statistically likely to crash in a taxi than—'

'Hey, I know some great taxi drivers,' he protested. 'And if you do end up in a shunt, it's hardly the same as falling 30,000ft from the sky. That's a completely different story. I've read about pilots going on the booze for days before a flight and then relying on the automatic pilot to get you safely to your destination. Sure, planes are supposed to be safer in this day and age but tell that to the families on that plane in Malaysia that disappeared without trace.'

Gareth nodded. The old man had a point.

'I wish you'd said something at the airport,' he said.

'I thought I might be able to conquer the fear but what with the delay and then a bit of a palaver when I first boarded the flight, things just got too much,' replied The Legend. 'These two guys were fighting, mun, and one had real hatred in his eyes as he tried to get to me. I'm not used to that sort of thing and found it quite scary. As a rugby player I've had nothing but praise and I guess I never expected a Welsh rugby fan to turn on me over something I'd written. Anyway, talking of fighting, what happened to you?'

Gareth had almost forgotten his facial wounds. He had a nasty bruise on his chin and cuts on the side of his face from the impact with the gravel in the pub car park. He touched it and pondered his answer. 'I was playing around with Maxi and he accidentally hit me with one of his big toy cars. Hurt like hell,' he lied. 'Forget me, though. You were on a plane ready for take-off, how did you get from there to here?'

The Legend drained the glass and stared off into the distance. 'The last straw was when I searched for the photo of Ellie and my lovely grandson – just to calm my nerves – and found that it was no longer in my blazer. I flipped then, accusing the flight attendants of all sorts of things. When I realised it was gone forever, I demanded to be let off the plane.'

'It was too late, though, surely?' said Gareth.

'Never too late, butt,' said The Legend. 'I created a right fuss, referring to my ongoing medical condition. They couldn't remove me quickly enough. They must have feared I'd sue the airline if something went wrong. The other passengers were getting edgy, too. By the time my luggage was removed from the hold and the whole ordeal was over, I was shattered. I just needed a few days away from everything to get my head straight, so I jumped in a taxi and asked the driver to take me to the nearest budget hotel. Now here we are. How did you find me?'

'Quinten Tucker-Green,' said Gareth. 'It was a piece of pure luck. He just happened to be staying here overnight before flying out to Oz this afternoon. As he was waiting for his taxi to the airport he saw you propping up the bar and gave me a call.'

'Quinten? Really? Why didn't he say "Hello"?'

'He didn't have time. He guessed you probably weren't in the best state, so urged me to hurry. I got here as soon as I could. Now I need you to sober up sharpish. I'm heading for Paris and you're coming with me.'

'Oh, no, butt,' said the rugby legend, his face bleached of colour. 'No way am I getting on a plane again!'

'No need,' said Gareth. 'We're getting the Eurostar from St Pancras and we've only got just over two hours to make it. You're OK with trains, aren't you?'

GARETH checked the two of them into a cheap budget hotel on an industrial estate north of Paris. It wasn't the most salubrious of surroundings, everything in the room being made from some kind of durable plastic: bunk beds, a shower and a toilet. Fortunately, among the grim-looking storage units in the vicinity there was a fast-food outlet which enabled them to refuel on burger and chips.

The reporter knew he had to act quickly. He told the old man he had squared things away with the office and the BBC. When asked how he'd managed it, the reporter explained that Jason Shake-speare had found another ex-Welsh rugby star in Australia to cover The Legend's BBC commitments, while Jacko had understood why the mission had to be aborted for health reasons.

For good measure, Gareth had arranged for The Legend's daughter Ellie to contact him via his laptop that night, so they could have a Skype conversation. It was this that finally restored some colour to The Legend's cheeks.

Now, as they sat munching their burgers, Gareth told The Legend about his investigation into his father's killer. JW listened with rapt attention, asking questions here and there, alarmed when he learnt his nemesis Arnie Dolan was involved.

'You still speak to the bastard who killed my son?' he asked Gareth as he perched on the bottom bunk and took a bite from his cheese burger. 'I hope you haven't forgotten he tried to kill you, too.'

'I know,' said Gareth, 'but I reckon he's paid for that. He's going to spend the rest of his life in a wheelchair.'

'He deserves it.'

'Maybe, but I've known him a long time. He's not all bad. In different circumstances you two might have got on.'

'Can't see it myself,' said The Legend.

They sat in silence for a while, eating their food. When they had finished Gareth collected the wrappers and put them back in the carrier bag.

'So why are we here, Gar?' said The Legend. 'The Euros don't start for a few days, do they?'

'No, but I've managed to persuade Jacko to let me travel out and do some background articles,' said Gareth. 'The Wales players are spending a few days in Paris before heading to Bordeaux for their first match.'

'Oh, right. And where do I fit in?'

'I told Jacko you would do your rugby column and blog from here. That's the joy of social media, it doesn't matter if you're on the doorstep or thousands of miles away. We'll find a quiet cafe somewhere and you can tell me your thoughts about the first Test. Jason sent me the team news and we can watch his latest vlog for other ideas.'

'Vlog? I thought they were called blogs.'

'Ah, this is like a blog, but on video,' said Gareth. 'The wonders of new technology, eh? All he has to do is film himself talking about the match on his smartphone, maybe get a few fans involved, and voila!'

'I see you've been practising your French,' said JW Owens, chuckling. Gareth was delighted the old man was showing signs of recovery. He figured it had been worth telling a couple of white lies to see him back on top form. In truth, he had no idea how the Trib's editor was going to react to the fact JW Owens was 9,000 miles from where he was supposed to be. Gareth was hoping that Jacko would protect them once more from the full force of her wrath. Then it would be up to them to produce a series of strong, hard-hitting columns to 'save' the situation. It would be tough, but it could be done. They had done it before.

'I bet you're shattered,' he said, noting the blood vessels threading through the old man's eyes. 'I've got to nip out for a bit JW, so I'll leave you to your Skype call.' He went silent for a moment, weighing things up in his mind.

'By the way, I think I should apologise,' he said finally. 'When you told me you weren't happy about the Australia trip I should have asked more questions. Why didn't you say straight away you had a fear of flying?'

'You said it yourself, Gareth,' said JW. 'I guess I didn't want to admit that I was scared of anything, least of all zooming about 33,000ft above the ground at a speed of 275mph.'

'Putting it that way, it does sound pretty terrifying,' said Gareth, laughing. 'Still, I blame myself for being so wrapped up in the fact we'd been given a second chance on the newspaper. I didn't twig there was a problem. No hard feelings?'

He held out his hand but JW pulled him close and wrapped him in a bear hug. 'You've made up for it, son,' he said. 'I reckon you've saved my bacon again.'

Not quite, thought Gareth, picturing a seething Lana in his mind's eye.

'So, this trip of yours. Work is it?'

The question roused Gareth from his private reflections.

'Umm, yeah, I promised to meet someone for a story. Will you be OK on your own?'

'Sure,' said The Legend. 'You know me. Reliable as the day is long.'

He winked, and Gareth smiled at the joke before switching his mind to the real task ahead – his continuing hunt for Peter Vickers.

38

FIERCE morning sunlight greeted Gareth Prince and JW Owens as they clambered from the train in Bordeaux. The reporter's mission in Paris had proved fruitless, the tip-off amounting to nothing, the people he was looking for having moved on. Pete Vickers was still a missing person.

'Nice this, butt,' said The Legend, shielding his eyes with one hand as he lifted his bag with the other. The two men walked towards the station exit. 'I prefer the rugby, of course, but above all things I'm a Welshman, and to be here for the football team's first appearance in a major championship for almost 60 years is an immense honour, I can tell you. Look at all the red shirts, mun! It's fantastic. There's even a bloke with one of them inflatable sheep. What does it say on the side? Sid? Didn't know there was a Sid in the team. Must be a new fella. And what's that sticking out of its backside? Looks like a Welsh flag. Very inventive.'

Yeah, thought Gareth, cringing. The *Sunday Tribune Despatch's* marketing department had been up to its old tricks again, coming up with 'creative' ways to use their sex toys. His face reddening, he hoped no one would recognise him and ask about this marketing disaster. Joining the queue for a cab, he hid his embarrassment behind a newspaper.

'Don't get too excited, JW,' he said after handing their luggage to the driver and clambering into the taxi. 'You're supposed to be in Australia so you need to keep a low profile. Fortunately, Jacko has smoothed things over with Lana, insisting you had to pull out of the flight for health reasons and luckily the Beeb haven't been chasing her for a refund.'

'I doubt they'll be kicking up too much fuss, mun,' said The Legend. 'Spend money like water, that lot. Have you seen how many people they send to these big events? Researchers, reporters, make-up artists, radio producers, cameramen, gofers and whatnot are probably all on this latest jolly, and there will be a similar entourage in Oz. I've saved them a bit of cash, to be fair.'

'I'm sure they're very grateful,' said Gareth. 'Meanwhile, as they live the life of Riley, I've got to scrimp and save to find us bargain hotel rooms. I'll have to be a bit creative with the expenses. Now, let's find somewhere showing the rugby. There's a sports bar not far from here – I just hope it's open.'

NOT ONLY was it open, but Gareth and JW had to force their way into Le Coq sports bar on the outskirts of Bordeaux. They were amazed to find the out-of-the-way establishment rammed to the rafters at nine on a Saturday morning, red-shirted sports fans knocking back bottles of the local booze and singing with gusto. There was some friendly banter between those in the Wales football shirt and others in rugby jerseys who had jumped on the Euro 2016 bandwagon.

'You lot are just glory hunters!' one bloke shouted to a group of rugby boys at the other end of the bar.

'At least we've had some glory!' came the reply, the joker raising good-natured belly laughs and high-fives from his mates. 'Three Grand Slams in ten years and we've been at every World Cup since it started, mun. You lot only qualified in 1958 because there was a war going on and Israel had to drop out.'

'Yeah, well, it's easy to do well in a "minority sport",' said the other man, his pals cheering his riposte. 'Good supporters you are, watching your beloved rugby boys on TV in a French bar instead of being there in person.'

'We're not the only ones,' said the rugby fan. 'Look! It's the great JW Owens. Legend!'

Spontaneous applause erupted among the rugby fans, quickly taken up by the football supporters. Before long, a song was ringing out among followers of both sports, the words adapted to the tune of the Christmas song 'Winter Wonderland'.

'There's only one JW Owens, one JW Owens, walking along, singing a song, walking in an Owens' Wonderland…'

JW lapped it up. Rather than keep his head down he stood in the middle of the two groups and waved his arms around like a conductor. The singing grew louder, and Gareth noticed plenty of inflatable sheep as he surveyed the packed bar. Many had flags sticking out of their bottoms and had found homes in vases, jugs, beer tankards and as part of the bar's ornamental decor.

'Hey, mun!'

As if by magic the Trib's marketing man, Jonah Quinn, appeared, a beaming smile on his face. He was bedecked in every souvenir imaginable: Wales rugby shirt, Wales football hat, one of those scarves which combined the colours of both teams and a pair of tracksuit bottoms emblazoned with a fire-breathing dragon. The sheep in his hand was attached to a thick stick like a novelty lollipop.

'See, Gareth butt, I told you, didn't I? The sheep have been a massive success. They've been selling like Welsh cakes. Got a little van outside and been giving the sheep away with the weekend's edition of the paper and a sausage roll. Hey, what happened to your face, someone take objection to your column?'

Gareth was about to trot out his well-rehearsed lie when the Trib man became distracted.

'Hey, you bought The Legend along," said Jonah. 'Awesome! I thought he was heading to Australia, mun. I suppose there was a change of plan. We minions don't get told about these things. Luckily, I bought my camera, so we can get him posing with a sheep. It would be good—'

'Jonah Quinn!' The Legend leapt forwards and gave the marketing man a hug. 'I ain't seen you for ages, mun. I remember watching you playing for Nantyglo fourths up at Cwmtawe in a Felinfoel Bitter Trophy third qualifying round match a few years back. Pretty good little centre you were. Still playing?'

'Uh no,' said Jonah, his face a darker shade of crimson than his shirt. 'You saw me, mun, wow, I don't believe it! The Legend not only watched me play rugby but remembers my name, the exact game I was playing in and even my position. That's something to tell the grandkids.'

JW put his arm around Jonah, placing him in a strong neck hold and giving the marketing man no chance of escape.

'Listen, you know my great mucker Gareth Prince, don't you?' said The Legend. 'Gareth is chief football writer on the paper. Gar, this is Jonah Quinn, a pretty decent rugby player when he's not coming up with marketing ideas for the Trib.'

Gareth was stunned. The Legend may have been nursing a brain tumour for 25 years or more, but he had a photographic memory for Welsh names and faces. He didn't want to burst the ex-rugby star's bubble by telling him they'd already met.

'Look, we're on a bit of a secret mission, see,' said The Legend, squeezing his prisoner harder. 'I don't want it to get out that I'm here because I really should be in Oz. If you could keep it shut, I'd be much obliged.'

He motioned a zip closing in front of his mouth.

Jonah Quinn looked around at the hundreds of Welshmen singing and dancing, arms around each other, claiming to be in an 'Owens' Wonderland'. Then he nodded.

'Sure, your secret is safe with me.'

Behind them, Gareth stifled a chuckle.

THE Welsh rugby fans were delighted to give The Legend pride of place at a table nearest the screen. He produced his famous pocket-book to scribble down notes and, despite the temptation, stuck to orange juice throughout the game. At the end he politely declined as fans clamoured to have their picture taken with him and buy him a drink.

They were heading for the exit when a news item caught Gareth's attention on one of the smaller screens. 'Woah!' he said, putting his hand out to halt his colleague.

'I thought you were in a hurry, butt,' said The Legend, his eyes darting to the screen. 'Shiiiit, mun, looks like those English nutters are causing trouble again... bloody hooligans. Love to get them on the rugby field.'

'Leave it, JW!' Gareth snapped, instantly regretting his reaction as he recalled The Legend had lost a son to football hooliganism. He needed to concentrate though. He had spotted something on the screen and wanted to make sure it wasn't a trick of the camera. A group of black-shirted men armed with tables, chairs, bottles and other ammunition were running into a bar, sending customers scattering. Those unable to get away were subjected to a barrage of fists and feet. The subtitles underneath said there had been overnight trouble in Marseille between Russian and English supporters ahead of their Euro 2016 match that evening. Gareth watched French police arrive at the big square in Marseille's old port before using water cannons and batons to disperse the two factions.

Switching again, the images settled on a group of England fans, identifiable by their clothing, tattoos and plethora of St George Cross flags. They'd gathered in an alleyway ready to make a stand against the Russians who, from what Gareth could gather, had been the instigators of the trouble. A shout of 'Engerlund, Engerlund' broke out and bricks and bottles flew from their ranks, followed by heavier items including chairs and tables. Those in the front had covered their faces, not just to conceal their identities but to combat the effects of tear gas.

'Fuckin' hell!' said Gareth.

'Very nasty,' agreed The Legend.

Gareth ignored him. The camera focused in on one England fan decked out in designer T-shirt and jeans. He wore a scarf across the bottom half of his face which wouldn't have looked out of place in the window of an Italian designer store in London's West End. As he invited Russian fans to fight, Gareth looked on amazed. Despite the effort that had gone into the disguise the figure was instantly recognisable to Gareth, who had spent the best part of his teenage years in the company of the man on screen.

'Pete bloody Vickers,' he muttered. 'Found you, you bastard!'

39

GARETH'S arrival in Marseille was greeted by a huge police presence, armoured cars patrolling the streets, water cannons at the ready. Unsure of the best way to approach his task, he guessed most of the Three Lions fans would be heading back to the old port area for pre-match beers. His first priority, though, was to get to the media centre and watch Wales' opening match in Euro 2016. He had a laptop in his bag but not much time.

When he'd told The Legend he had to go to Marseille the former rugby star was speechless. He couldn't understand why Gareth would be heading into the eye of a storm when Wales, the team he was supposed to be reporting on, were about to play Slovenia in their biggest match for more than half a century. It wasn't easy to explain his dilemma, but he knew he would need The Legend's help to carry out his plan. Having listened carefully, the former rugby star had agreed to go along with the deception, knowing he owed Gareth a big favour for supporting him over the flight debacle. 'No drinking, though,' Gareth had warned before he left The Legend in the bar of their hotel and jumped on a train to the Mediterranean port.

Checking his mobile phone, he was glad to see that the cover-up was in operation. Logging into Twitter, he checked his recent updates and saw a video of Wales' fans singing a Tom Jones classic outside a bar in Bordeaux. The video had been uploaded by @PrinceTrib with a tagline below reading:

On the way to match, everyone in good voice. #Walesstrong

Anyone following Wales' progress on social media would think he'd posted the video. More importantly, Jacko and Lana would have no reason to think he was anywhere other than Bordeaux.

The Legend's job was to upload regular tweets and videos to the feed, keeping them as simple as possible. He had been given a series of hashtags to use. If people began asking questions, Gareth was able to log on and answer them, which meant he needed to monitor the feed at regular intervals.

Earlier, in the hotel, part one of their mission had gone to plan with The Legend supplying a rugby column for Sunday's paper – the Lions having unfortunately lost 26-13 having led at half-time – and a blog about the challenges ahead, which had instantly been uploaded online. Under the tagline @LegendTrib they'd got Jason, in Sydney, to video a group of Welsh fans singing outside the Opera House. What better way to show that their star columnist was at the heart of matters, rather than thousands of miles closer to home? He even recorded a brief message against a nondescript background, a rugby scarf around his neck which had been borrowed from one of the lads in Le Coq.

The Legend was so impressed by his ability to interact with 'his' public he was now fixated with social media. Throughout the afternoon he uploaded a constant stream of smiling Welsh faces from the stadium in Bordeaux.

Even though things appeared to be going well, Gareth felt a knot forming in his stomach. He wasn't sure if it was due to acute anxiety or because he hadn't eaten that day. There were so many phases of his plan that could go wrong, many of them entirely out of his control.

'GREAT report, butt. I can see why you consider football your forte. Top effort and nice quotes, too. What a win, eh? The Bale goal was special but Hal Robson-Kanu? Who would have thought he had that sort of goal in him? It was like watching Cruyff play. Bloody hell, mun, has it kicked off there, too? What are those sirens?'

'There's been a bit of a traffic pile-up,' Gareth lied. 'Nothing to worry about.'

'Good,' said Jacko. 'Well, I don't mean good for the people in the bloody accident, of course, but I'm glad our lot haven't got involved in any fisticuffs. Not like those bloody English... sorry, butt, I keep forgetting.'

'You're all right, Jacko,' said Gareth, looking around the concourse outside the Stade Velodrome where each wail of a siren signalled another outbreak of trouble. He was struggling to hear what his boss was saying. 'Nothing I haven't been saying myself.'

Gareth had found the media centre in Marseille to be a godsend, big screens showing the Wales match everywhere. The instant the game was over he'd taken down quotes from the after-match interviews before inserting them into his already written match report and pushing the button on his laptop to send it winging back to Cardiff.

Half an hour later The Legend, having attended the managers' press conference with Gareth's recording device, had played him their comments over the phone, enabling him to write a back-page story. Finally, he'd filed a comment piece which he had written before a ball was kicked, then adjusted to suit the result. It was all about Wales' next big task, taking on the old enemy England with a place in the second round now up for grabs.

'Sorry?'

He was so wrapped up in his own thoughts Gareth had forgotten he was on the phone.

'I was wondering if you'd bumped into Lana yet,' said Jacko.

'She's here?'

'Oh yeah, she's got another corporate jolly in Bordeaux. All right for some, eh? She was going to track you down and take you to dinner as a reward for your sterling efforts.'

Damn! Suddenly the perfect plan didn't seem so perfect. He would have to tell The Legend to stay out of sight then come up with a good excuse for snubbing the editor. He prayed she hadn't got access to the press box or asked too many questions of his colleagues. Rubbing at the side of his head to alleviate a throbbing pain, he abruptly cut the call. Across the concourse, Pete Vickers stood on the periphery of a large group of England supporters chanting their new favourite Brexit-inspired anthem: *'We all voted Yes, We all voted yes, Fuck off Europe, we all voted yes'.*

Shit!

The phone rang again.

'You there, Gareth? What's that? Sounds like—'

'Sorry, Jacko. Terrible line…'

He scratched his nails over the phone's microphone then hit the off button. Running over, he forgot the fans were on tenterhooks following the earlier violence. A big skinhead stepped forwards, a cartoon of a snarling bulldog adorning his T-shirt. Raising his fists, he demanded, 'You want some!'

'I'm English!' shouted Gareth.

'Come and join us then mate, lot of them Russki bastards about. Strength in numbers, eh?'

Bobbing around on his toes to scan the crowd, Gareth was alarmed when he realised he could no longer see Vickers. There were some big lads in the way, as tall as they were wide. Then he spotted the Boxer Boy sprinting in the opposite direction to the ground, looking over his shoulder, his eyes fixed on Gareth.

Handicapped by his bad leg, Gareth gave chase as the England fans watched in bewilderment. A voice rang out from behind him.

'Boys, boys, it must be kicking off again!'

Gareth felt tendrils of pain shoot up his leg. He hadn't put his old injury through such strenuous exercise in a long while. He watched other England fans race past him, the roar rising as they sought out the latest battle.

40

ONCE again, chaos reigned on the streets of Marseille. His body dripping with sweat from the humidity, Gareth – still dressed in his work clothes of white short-sleeved shirt and chinos – was marooned, staring into the abyss. His journalistic mind was churning out clichés: hell on earth, carnage, mindless barbarism.

Blue flashing lights lit up the jet-black evening sky, the football stadium sitting in a beacon of light behind him, the jarring, ear-mangling sounds of battle in front: police sirens, smashing glass, cries of anger and hatred, shrieks of pain and futility. Whatever was going on, he couldn't afford to be caught up in it, but something forced him forwards, a macabre desire to see what was at the end of this tunnel of terror.

Hobbling in the direction of the loudest and most terrifying sounds he turned down a side street, his eyes taking in scenes of mind-numbing destruction. Broken chairs and tables littered the cobbles outside a small cafe-bar, a sea of glass glittering under the street lights. Various pieces of masonry lay around on the floor, weapons recently discarded, and as he continued walking he passed the odd straggler heading in the opposite direction.

One fan, his head wrapped in the ripped-off sleeve of a shirt he'd once worn, looked at him suspiciously. The bloke had a tattoo of a lion on his arm and was weaving from side to side, blood smearing his sunburnt torso. Gareth knew it was time to act the part or attract further unwanted attention.

'Where's the action, mate?' he demanded, reverting to the street slang of the terraces.

'Just up there,' said the injured fan. 'It's mental, mate. Fuckin' Russians. It's a game to them. They took my Rochdale flag, bastards! They rip them off you then turn them upside down and have their pictures taken with them. It's to show they done the business. They're cowards, though. They've been attacking bars where lads are just having a laugh and a drink. It's coordinated, without warning. One smashed me with a bottle just as I came out of t'bog.'

He hobbled off in the direction of the ground. Gareth doubted those manning the security barriers at the stadium would let him through, given the state he was in.

'Hey, bro!' A black fan with a strong Midlands accent walked up to him. 'You don't wanna go up there. The Russkies are giving us a right pasting. The cops are just watching, filming on their phones. When it's all over they'll wade in and arrest the victims, no doubt. They're scared to get involved. It's the worst I've come across and I've been in some battles with England over the years.'

Gareth picked up his pace, hoping he would be able to knock sense into Pete Vickers before it was too late. Eventually the street spilled out into a wide concourse, shops, hotels and restaurants on either side. The loudest noise came from his left and he saw a few policemen, batons at the ready and guns at their belts. Slowing to a walk, he hoped they might think he was an ordinary tourist caught up in the mayhem.

To the right he heard a rumble and looked up to see a procession of vehicles approaching the area. They were sturdy, grey machines which would look more at home in a war zone. On the back were large cannons, capable of discharging powerful blasts of water. He had to move quickly.

Senses honed, he looked around and caught sight of three or four figures behind a fountain. They seemed to be jumping up and down, launching high kicks as if in some bizarre episode of Hooligans Come Dancing. They were big blokes, their faces covered with plain scarves, giving no indication which team they might support.

Manoeuvring to get a better look, his eyes locked on the victim of their wrath and he knew he had to act, bending and lifting a discarded metal pole then hefting it in his hands. It was a bit too unwieldy for his purposes really, but it would have to do. He needed to take the attackers by surprise.

To his left a barrier of police held back other fans and on-lookers intent on recording the drama on their smart phones. For a brief moment he felt like an actor on a film set, the hero arriving to save the day. Then it dawned on him. He wasn't even supposed to be here. If someone posted this to *YouTube*, by tomorrow morning his face would be plastered all over the world, making it impossible to maintain his innocence to Jacko and Lana.

Looking around the floor again, he spotted a curly red, white and blue wig and placed the discarded piece of fancy dress on his head without hesitation. He might look like Coco the Clown going into battle, but it was better than nothing. A pair of cheap, cracked sunglasses lying on the floor a few yards further forward added to the comedy effect.

He heard a whistle and saw French riot police in headgear, wielding batons and advancing from the far side of the square. Drawing a breath, he ran forwards, wig flapping, the bar thrust out in front of him like some ancient knight in a jousting tournament. The limp must have made him look absurd, like a comedian mimicking a galloping horse.

'Come on then you bastards!' he shouted, doubting the Russians would understand a word.

As the others delivered kicks to their victim, who was now sprawled against the fountain, one man moved menacingly towards Gareth, shaking his limbs like a wild animal embarking on a strange mating ritual. Suddenly he charged, head down, taking aim at Gareth's midriff. At the last moment, the reporter stepped aside and brought the bar crashing down on his attacker's back.

Unable to stall his momentum the Russian smashed head first into the paving slabs and Gareth limped on, no time to admire his handiwork.

'Come on fuckers! It's Hammers time,' he shouted, remembering a call from his younger days when the Boxer Boys were cornered by Chelsea fans on the Kings Road. It hadn't ended well, but at least he earned his stripes in that battle, his peers looking at him in a different light from then on.

Suddenly, he realised he was in big trouble. The others had turned to face him, but at least he'd drawn their attention away from their victim. Spreading out in different directions, the Russians seemed well organised, as if trained to carry out this sort of coordinated attack. They encircled their prey like a pack of wild animals in one of the nature programmes Maxi loved to watch. England might wear three lions on their shirt but in this case his opponents were the predators.

'Hold on, geez, we're coming!'

The shout came from the other side of the square and distracted the Russians, who for once seemed unsure what their next move should be. Advancing towards them were 20 or 30 youths in T-shirts, shorts and trainers. They were armed to the teeth and desperate to get involved. More shrill whistles added to the cacophony of sound as the riot police closed in and before he knew it, something the size of a large stone plopped down in front of him, wisps of smoke appearing to cloud his vision. In no time, tears were streaming down his face and he began to cough and splutter.

Tear gas.

He had to get away but had one more thing to do. Bringing the pole crashing down on the first person that appeared in his vision, he hoped it was one of the Russians. A clang rang out as he dropped the weapon to the floor and turned his attention to the fountain. Holding the wig firmly to his face in a farcical attempt to nullify the effects of the gas, he tripped over the body he was trying to find and nearly fell head long into the fountain.

Steadying himself, he bent down and attempted to lift the injured man.

Jeez, he was heavy. A dead weight. He trembled as he tried to get a grip of the body then felt a hand on his shoulder.

Police or Russians it didn't matter. He was done for.

41

'YOU'RE a bloody hero, geezer. Now let us take the strain. They'll be singing your praises at every England away game from now on. What's your name?'

Gareth felt relief as the familiar cockney tones washed over him. A balding, heavy-set man stood in front of him, a Millwall Lion tattooed on his arm. *Bloody hell*, he thought. Escape from the Russians and the next thing you're faced with is a fan of West Ham's sworn enemy. They might both support England, but in other circumstances…

'Gary,' he replied, 'Gary, um, Bale.'

'You're kidding! Like the footballer? Gareth Bale? Fuckin' 'ell, you ain't a taff are you?'

The irony was not lost on Gareth. He felt a grin form on his lips, despite the bizarre circumstances, and decided some cockney slang would ease the tension. 'Nah, mate … sheepshagger? You're having a giraffe!'

'Good man.' The Millwall fan slapped Gareth on the back and he nearly fell to the ground. 'I'm Tommy. They call me Tommy Tank Top from back in the day. Let's put him on here, shall we?'

Through his streaming eyes, Gareth saw a large wooden board at his feet. It advertised a particular brand of luxury Italian coffee and had been liberated from outside a nearby restaurant, Tommy Tank Top and his mates deciding it would make a decent stretcher. Leaning forwards Gareth then grabbed the unconscious figure under the arms while Tommy and another man lifted his legs.

'Come on then, boys, grab a corner each and let's get this fucker to an ambulance,' said Tommy as two more helpers arrived. 'Shit, he took a right shoe-in. I don't know what he was thinking, running into danger like that. We'd already taken a bit of a pummelling and gone away to regroup. Must have a death wish…'

When they reached the edge of the square, blue flashing lights weaved funky patterns on the surrounding buildings.

'Put him down here and leave him for the medics,' ordered Tommy. They did as they were told. He turned to Gareth. 'Cheers, mate, we'd better get to the match … you comin'?'

An awkward moment. He didn't know how the bloke would react if he replied in the negative, but he'd experienced enough drama for one day.

'I'm gonna stay thanks, Tommy,' he said, holding out his hand to shake. 'I've done my leg in somehow. Want a doctor to check it over.'

The other man accepted the handshake with a firm grip.

'Like I said, you're a real hero, Gary Bale,' said Tommy. 'I'm looking forward to telling my grandkids about the bloke with the iron pole who took on four Russians to rescue a fellow Brit. The way you took out that first guy … They'll call ya, hell, yeah, the Matador of Marseille!'

It was all he needed, thought Gareth, an undeserved nickname hanging around his neck. He watched the stretcher bearers disappear into the distance, swallowed up by the mists of battle. Feeling a tug on his sleeve he looked down. A hand was grasping him, mumbled sounds coming from the prone figure on the makeshift stretcher.

'Gazza, I'm … so … sorry,' muttered Pete Vickers through a face camouflaged by drying blood.

'WHAT the hell are you playing at, Gareth, mun? This week of all weeks you should be contactable. I really don't know what gets into you sometimes. You're like that bloody maniac you used to keep an eye on for me. It was your job to pass on good habits to JW Owens, not for him to give you his bad habits. Christ on a bike, it's like getting a bleedin' audience with the Pope, having a proper conversation with you.'

Gareth stood outside the emergency department of the hospital in Marseille where his friend had been taken. He was still trying to piece together the sequence of events that had left Vickers needing an operation to repair a number of injuries, the most serious being a fractured skull. Now he had to find the right words to appease his boss, who still believed he was in Bordeaux sampling local wines.

'Sorry, boss, dropped my phone,' said Gareth. 'Didn't think I would be able to get it working again but fortunately there was a late-night shop—'

'Never mind that,' said Jacko. 'Lana's been asking after you, butt. Said if you could get yourself to a restaurant near the Opera House called Le Chat Noir, then she would buy you dinner. It's a proper five-star Michelin jobby and was going to be her treat. You buggered up there, mun. She'll be tucked up in bed now.'

'It's OK,' said Gareth. 'I had McDonalds.'

A siren wailed in the distance and Gareth wondered what the latest port of call for the city's overstrained emergency services would be. He had spent some time in a communal TV room watching England draw 1-1 with Russia, Roy Hodgson's men conceding an equaliser in injury time.

Afterwards, news reports showed Russian hooligans clambering over barricades to get at England fans, many of them innocent parents with children. Some youngsters had risked a sheer drop over a wall to reach safety.

'You there?' interrupted Jacko. 'You've gone quiet again, Gar. Is that a work phone? You are bloody careless, mun, I'm not sure if —'

Gareth saw the doctor approaching and put his hand over the mouthpiece. 'Sorry … crrr, crrr … you're breaking up,' he said and promptly cut the call.

'Monsieur! Monsieur!' The doctor was waving at him. 'We have done as much as we can and hope he will make a full recovery. Do you know his next of kin?'

'Sorry,' said Gareth, untruthfully. 'Look, can I talk to him? I'll find out what I can for you.'

'He is resting now,' said the doctor. 'You are quite welcome to take a seat in one of our waiting rooms. I realise it's not a bed, but … are you OK? You look a bit worse for wear yourself.'

The doctor pointed at his face.

'Oh,' Gareth said, touching it. He could still feel the filmy residue of the tears brought on by the gas attack. 'I was unlucky. Wrong place, wrong time. Tear gas.'

'Disgraceful!' said the doctor. 'I apologise, but what can I say? There are a lot of innocent victims who have been caught up in the trouble. Still, I suppose serious breaches of the law warrant such measures. Now, I must go … please, make yourself comfortable.'

JANIE Vickers was just getting another glass of wine from the kitchen when she heard a yelp from the front room. For a moment she thought her friend had gone into premature labour and rushed in to find out what the fuss was about. Anjie was sitting with her feet up on the sofa, watching television, the children having gone to bed some time ago after wearing themselves out on a trip to Barry Island funfair.

'What is it?' asked Jane. 'You OK? Your waters haven't broken, have they?'

'Look!' said Anjie, pointing at the screen. The TV was tuned to a late-night news channel and Jane saw the tickertape running below. It announced another night of violence in Marseille.

'Surely you aren't surprised?' said Janie, taking a large swallow of her wine. It wasn't the best – supermarket label – but it was cheap and did the trick. She was starting to feel a buzz. 'They're louts … the lot of 'em.'

'Look at the picture!' said Anjie.

Janie moved closer to the TV, trying to make out what she was seeing. It wasn't easy, the camera work erratic as it followed the progress of some idiot wearing a red, white and blue wig and carrying a metal pipe in his hands. 'What's your point?' said Janie, laughing. 'Want him to do your roof extension?'

'It's Gary.'

'What?'

'It's my Gary … Gareth … hell, you know, it's him! Look!'

'Oh, come on!' said Janie. 'It's nothing like him. That bloke's probably about a foot shorter and your old man wouldn't be seen dead in something as daft as that. Anyway, his fighting days are over. He's not as fit as when he was playing football and he's got that limp. You said he was working in Bordeaux anyway, not Marseille.'

'But look, Janie – the way he moves. It's my fuckin' Gary, I tell you. I would recognise him anywhere.'

'Well if you say so, love, but I think you're probably knackered,' said Janie. 'You've been on the go with the kids all day and it can't be easy when you're six months pregnant.'

'Listen, lady!' said Anjie stroppily. 'I know my bloke when I see him, and that's him. I would pick him out of any identity parade anywhere even if he is dressed like something straight out of a Harry Enfield Scousers video.'

Janie fell silent, worried for her friend's sanity.

'Let's see what they're saying.' Anjie picked up the remote and raised the volume.

'The terrible scenes of violence and destruction continued in Marseille tonight as hooligans fought running battles for a third night in the old port. English fans clashed with Russian ultras before, during and after the match at the Stade Velodrome. Some French and Tunisian gangs were also involved in a place which has become a no-go area for law-abiding tourists. Amateur video shot in one of the squares shows this one hooligan, blatantly sporting England colours, charging at a group of other fans. He strikes one on the back with this pole, a signal for another horde of England fans to invade the square. Police using—'

Anjie froze the screen. A badly cut and bruised face stared back at them, full of anger and alarm.

'Shit!' said Janie as she stared at a man she'd last seen just a few days ago in that very room, saying goodbye before setting off on his 'business trip' to France the following morning.

42

PETE VICKERS lay on the bed, his head wrapped in bandages, plastic tubes dripping fluids and painkillers into his body. It was two days since the trouble and, with the doctors stating they were pleased with his progress, Gareth at last had a chance to have a serious talk with his friend. He knew he had to move on soon, with England meeting Wales in Lens later in the week, but so far he'd managed to keep the charade going, filing reports from the Marseille press centre thanks to information passed on by The Legend.

The thing that troubled him most was the frosty reception he'd got from Anjie. She'd let out a derisory snort of laughter when he told her over the phone he was still in Bordeaux. When he asked what was wrong, she wouldn't elaborate, just saying, 'We'll talk when you get home.'

She knew, he thought. But how?

'What are you doing here, Gaz?'

The patient's mumbled words brought Gareth back to the present.

'I could ask you the same thing,' replied the reporter.

'It … it's complicated.'

'I saved your life, mate,' said Gareth. 'The least I deserve is an explanation.'

Vickers grimaced as he shifted to a more comfortable position. 'I had a chance to come to the Euros with a group of blokes I know, so I took it.'

'Really?' said Gareth. 'See, everyone else thinks you've been kidnapped. Tigger saw you being shoved into a van by some geezers in balaclavas with baseball bats. People are convinced you're the latest victim of this gang war. Your wife and kids are worried sick.'

Gareth thought he saw tears forming in his friend's eyes.

'Are they OK?' asked Vickers.

'Apart from the fact they miss their dad ... and Janie misses her husband.'

'I doubt that,' said Vickers. 'She thinks I'm a waste of space ...'

'I'm sure that's not the case,' said Gareth. 'You've given your family a lovely home, spoilt them rotten. Why would she send me to find you if she didn't care about you?'

'She sent you?' Vickers was clearly surprised. 'I guess she did it for the kids.'

They sat quietly for a moment, the normal sounds of hospital life going on around them, the bleeping of monitors, clatter of breakfast utensils being stored away and squeaking wheels of a passing trolley. It was still early, but the hospital was in full swing.

'Look,' said Gareth. 'We need to get you better and get you home. OK?'

Vickers bit his lip, looking at the ceiling. 'I'm not sure I want to go back,' he said.

Gareth scratched his head. 'Why not? Is it this gang war? I know you were in the pub when it was firebombed, but plenty of people have got your back.'

'Not that.'

'What then? Even if you and Janie aren't together at the moment, you've always got the Boxer Boys. What was this elaborate 'kidnap' charade for?'

Vickers took a deep breath and held his hand out, pointing to a pitcher of water. 'Give us a drink,' he said. 'I'll try to explain.'

Gareth poured the water into a plastic beaker and passed it to the patient.

'I wasn't thinking straight,' said Vickers. 'I felt like I was having a breakdown and needed to get away and clear my head without others knowing where I was.'

'Because of your marriage?'

'Partly.' His mind seemed to be drifting. 'Don't you ever feel like escaping?'

He looked at Gareth, only to see the smirk on the other man's face. It lightened the mood and he let out a small chuckle. 'Course you do,' said Vickers. 'You're the undisputed master at it, aren't you, Gazza? Or is it Gareth? You remind me of that character on TV my dad used to love, Reggie Perrin.'

'I had strong reasons,' said Gareth. 'What are yours?'

'Well, I guess it started with Arnie and … you know.'

'The rape.'

'Yeah. Janie lost faith in me, didn't believe I was capable of protecting her. We stopped talking and sex was off the agenda, of course.'

'She needed time.'

'And I gave it to her,' said Vickers. 'But things escalated when her mum became ill. She turned into this different person – someone I didn't know. She would fly into these rages and nine times out of 10 I was the target. When people talk about domestic abuse, it's always men on women but I tell you, she battered me.'

Gareth found it impossible to hide his surprise. 'Really?'

'Sounds ridiculous, doesn't it?' Vickers let out a mirthless chuckle. '*East London gangster is battered husband*'. How would that play out in the papers? She knew I wouldn't raise a fist in response though maybe that was what she wanted. She would just let rip and fire into me. It was only after her mum's funeral that we sat down and talked it through. It was all very emotional. She wasn't sure she wanted to be with me anymore. I told her she was under a lot of stress – what do they call it? Post-Traumatic Stress Disorder. Someone at the squash club said it isn't just soldiers who suffer from it and that if a person has had a particularly gruesome experience, it can trigger all kinds of things.'

He sighed, his mind drifting. 'After our chat she saw a psychotherapist. Look, I'm tired, can we——?'

'Get to the point and I'll leave you alone,' said Gareth.

Vickers looked to the ceiling, tears filling his eyes. 'OK,' he said. 'She returned from one of her sessions and said she had things to tell me. She blurted out a load of stories about her past I didn't know, and I admit I didn't react well. It was a whole side of her I didn't know about, but others did. I remembered hearing two of her friends at the wedding gossiping about her past, and it made me feel foolish. I wondered if I really knew my wife at all. The upshot was, we had a flaring row, and I walked out. I haven't been home since.'

Gareth shook his head.

'This isn't making sense,' he said. 'Sure you were upset, but to run away completely and not contact your kids for two months? That's not you, Pete.'

Vickers' face reddened, and Gareth realised he might have gone too far.

'Well you would know, Gar, eh? Christ, how long was it you went without seeing Maxi? You're the last person who can lay a guilt trip on me. I'd had enough of everything, right? This bloke Barry at the squash club mentioned he was running a trip to the Euros a while ago. He's a twat to be honest, but he agreed to help me out when I said I needed an escape. He knew about the trouble at home and also had an inkling about my "work" so together we came up with this 'kidnap' plan. He had the van, and I got the reliable witness.'

'Tigger,' said Gareth. 'I guess he was already pretty freaked out about his two dealers being snatched.'

'Plus the fact he's normally off his face. I didn't expect him to act the hero or ask too many questions.'

'He alerted me to what had really gone on though he probably didn't realise it,' said Gareth. 'He described the van pretty well and I made some inquiries locally and heard that one of your fellow squash club members drove something that fitted the bill. When I was told he'd gone to France, I tracked him down to Paris but must have just missed you. When I got to the campsite where you were supposed to be staying there was no sign. I thought I'd come to a dead end until I saw you on the news.'

'You really should be a detective not a journo,' said Vickers. 'Does Janie know you've found me?'

'Not yet,' said Gareth, 'I think it's up to you to tell her. I've a feeling I'm in enough trouble as it is.'

43

GARETH opened the door with a degree of trepidation. He had no idea what reaction he was going to get but was guessing it wouldn't be a hero's welcome.

He had travelled back on the Eurostar immediately after the Wales-England game in Lens, his sports editor calling in a euphoric mood just before he boarded the train.

'Bloody hell, mun, it was so close!' Jacko had gushed. 'We nearly had those English, only for them to score a spawny last-minute winner. Bloody Sturridge. Comes on as a sub and scuffs one into the net. Oh well. Great job you've done there, anyway … no doubt about it, butt. The whole kit and caboodle. Marvellous. Sorry I had a go at you the other day, you know, about the phone cutting out. I know what it's like reporting from abroad. In my day—'

Gareth proceeded to get another lesson in old-school journalism as Jacko ranted on about having to use public phone booths and filing stories to copy-taker typists. 'God help you if the line broke down, pardon my French,' he'd said. 'Anyway, I think the whole thing has been excellent; the live blog, the tweets—'

'You're starting to sound like you know what you're talking about, Jacko,' Gareth had said, chuckling. 'Are we likely to see your presence online soon?'

'Eh?' Jacko had pondered the question. 'What do you mean, mun, I'm already on Twitter, got a knob and everything. Even got 60 followers. How about that?'

'Knob?' For a moment Gareth had been completely mystified. Then he'd worked it out. 'Ahhhhh, you mean handle.'

'That's the fella.'

Gareth had smiled at the thought of the old dog learning new tricks. The sports editor was in a better mood than he'd been for some time, and all because Wales had put up a good fight before losing 2-1 to the old enemy. It was a pity Gareth had to burst his bubble.

'Actually, I've got a problem, Jacko,' Gareth had said, interrupting the older man's flow. 'I need some time at home to arrange my dad's funeral.'

'It's family, so you have to do what you have to do,' said Jacko without hesitation. 'It's lucky that this next game is on a weekday, really, because it means we don't have to cover it live. The daily reporter will do something for the website I'm sure and we'll muddle through. Could you—?'

'Write a preview? Already done some stuff for Sunday, Jacko, so you're sorted.'

'Thanks. As soon as you've looked after your bit of business perhaps you can get back out there in time to follow our brilliant boys all the way to the final. Where's your sidekick, by the way? We haven't heard hide nor hair from The Legend.'

Gareth had explained that the former rugby star was staying out in France to 'help with some promotions'. The truth was that he and Jonah Quinn had become inseparable in Gareth's absence. JW had phoned the previous night to say that Jonah had a twin room booked in Toulouse – where the Russia game was taking place – and had invited him to share. Gareth was happy enough with the arrangement, having far more pressing things to worry about. It was handy to have a close ally on the ground, too.

Dropping his bags on the mat, he shouted from the hallway, 'I'm home!'

For a moment there was silence before Anjie said, 'We're in the lounge watching a bit of TV. Come and join us!'

He pushed open the door.

'We've put it on pause because we thought you couldn't miss this. It's right up your street.'

Looking at the screen he realised immediately he'd been ambushed. Frozen in the centre of the picture, a figure in a red, white and blue curly wig was wielding a piece of masonry. Anjie pushed the play button, and the person hobbled at speed in the direction of a fountain where a fight was taking place. Gareth knew he could brazen it out or tell the truth but, while he was an expert at blagging, he couldn't pull the wool over his girlfriend's eyes. They had been through too much together.

'You've seen it then,' he said in a resigned tone. 'That explains why—'

'Why I wasn't the loving girlfriend on the phone?' Angie didn't hold back. 'God, Gary, what the fuck do you think you were you doing?' Jumping to her feet, she pointed in the direction of the stairs. 'You've got a little boy who needs his father and you're running around the streets of a foreign city, getting involved in fights like you're a teenager again. This is a bit more serious, though, isn't it? The papers have been full of how these Russians are supposedly highly trained, former policemen, soldiers and the like. You're hardly SAS. It seems to me I'm lucky to have you back in one piece.'

She moved closer, pointing to his face where his injuries were still visible from the incident with Chuck in the car park. 'From the look of you, it seems you got off lightly. I hear a couple of fans were taken to hospital with serious injuries. One of them is fighting for his life ...'

Behind Gary, the door opened.

'Maybe I can explain.'

Pete Vickers walked into the room to be greeted by open mouths, the two women stunned by the appearance of a man they thought they might never see again.

'Jeez, Pete, what happened?' said Janie, slowly getting to her feet. A bandage was wrapped around his head like a turban and his arm was in a sling. His face was puffy and bruised, stitches evident on his chin and forehead. 'Was it that Hackney gang?'

She moved towards him, her arms out. For a moment he wasn't sure what to do. Tentatively he walked towards her, disappearing into her embrace. As she squeezed, Gareth saw him wince from the impact.

'You silly bastard!' she said, her voice full of emotion, the tone loving rather than admonishing.

'I'm sorry,' he murmured.

'You should be!' she said. 'Do you know what we've been going through? I had to come to Anjie's I was so distraught. I was dreading having to break it to the kids that they'd lost their dad.'

She wasn't yet prepared to acknowledge how much he meant to her personally. Gently removing her arms from around him, she stepped backwards.

'If you want the truth, there was no kidnap,' he blurted. 'I faked my own disappearance because everything was getting too much. I thought I might be going insane.'

Anjie stood behind her friend, putting a hand to her back as she realised Janie was about to burst into tears. Even though they'd split up, it was clear the woman was hugely relieved her husband hadn't fallen into the clutches of a murderous gang.

'We'll let you two have some peace,' she said, indicating to Gareth they should leave the room. 'You need time to yourselves.'

44

'BRUCE, you gotta... help me... geez.' Chuck Dolan mumbled through broken teeth and swollen lips. 'He's lost it. He's gonna kill me, I tell you. I know nothin' about that... bastard dad of his! You're my own flesh n' blood, you gotta see... this ain't right, mate.'

Face transformed after countless hours of punishment in his dank prison, Chuck's crazed eyes stared out through a skeletal head. How long had he been here – One week? Two? For most of that time he'd been left alone with his thoughts; minutes turning to hours turning to days. At times he prayed to hear the rattle of the heavy chain on the door, knowing that visitors had arrived, even though it probably meant more torture and pain. At least when it was over they tended to clean him up.

For most of the time he was denied toilet privileges, soiling himself when resistance proved too painful. The smell was horrendous, and Chuck wasn't stupid. Arnie was exacting revenge for the humiliating treatment he'd received in the nursing home.

When Arnie did turn up, he asked the same questions over and over, only to get the same answers. His response was to arrange a variety of exquisitely painful punishments, convinced of Chuck's guilt. The bastard couldn't prove anything though and, for a long time, Chuck believed that somewhere in Arnie's warped mind there was a slither of compassion that might prevent him killing his brother.

Now he wasn't sure.

Christ, if he'd known he was going to suffer this indignity he would have gone the whole hog and bumped off Stan Marshall. It would have pleased his father and at least justified the treatment he was getting.

Chuck discovered early during his captivity that the best way to deal with it was to imagine he was an elite soldier having been captured by the enemy. After all, everything Arnie did was intended to mess with his head. His captors told him it was night time and turned off the lights to let him sleep, only to wake him abruptly at the height of his dreams. They then flooded the room with spotlights that seared into his retinas, bringing on excruciating headaches. When there didn't appear to be anyone around he tried to grab an impromptu nap but found it impossible, white noise and heavy beats being channelled in through hidden speakers.

Having been allowed to stew for the first two or three days, he could still remember being stunned when Arnie showed up. He also recalled that first torture, the one that set the tone. He had taken the piss when Arnie began babbling on about giving him the 'Sir Alex Ferguson' treatment. Shortly afterwards his two brothers left to be replaced by a burly, masked guy with a hairdryer.

'Wash, trim and blow dry please, son, not too much off the top,' Chuck had quipped, not fully aware of the pain he was about to suffer. His torturer had plugged the dryer into a socket on a nearby table then applied the heated end of it to the tender area beneath Chuck's armpits. He had screamed, almost passing out as a smell of burning hair and flesh filled his nostrils. He had been determined not to show weakness, though, knowing Arnie was watching somewhere.

When Arnie had re-entered the room demanding answers, the man with the hairdryer had whipped away Chuck's gag and applied his tool of torture to other tender areas: his cheeks, the bottom of his feet and his inner thighs. Arnie's questions had come thick and fast, but Chuck couldn't get a word out through his screams.

'What did you do to Stan Marshall, Chuck?'

'Why did you kill the old man?'

'Was it on daddy's orders?'

Eventually he lost consciousness, but that was just the start.

Waterboarding was next, a favourite technique used on terror suspects. A flannel had been placed over Chuck's face and water poured over him, making it impossible to breathe without inhaling and making him think he was about to drown. After that came the pliers, applied studiously to finger and toenails.

Today had been dedicated to live electricity, a particularly painful experience even though it had been a short, sharp session, and now Bruce was back to check on him. Could Chuck read signs of guilt in those eyes? The youngest Dolan had never been involved in the nasty excesses of the family business and Chuck suspected he was more squeamish than he let on.

'Sorry, Chuck,' his youngest brother said, kneeling to apply lotion to his wounds. 'I had to tell him.'

'Wh …what?' said Chuck, fighting against the pain.

'I heard you talking to Sly the day you came back from the island,' said Bruce. 'You thought I was out, but I was upstairs looking through some old photo albums with Mum. I came down to make us a cup of tea and was about to join you in the lounge when I heard you say, "The old man's like a broken record. He wants me to sort out this Stan Marshall, good and proper. I can't ignore him this time. I reckon it's his dying wish".'

'That's your proof?' mumbled Chuck. 'That's why I'm being tortured like this? Dad's been saying that for… years! I might have said it, but I was only reacting to the shock of seeing him in such a state. He's dying, Bruce. He's a shadow of the man he once was.'

'There's the van, too.'

'S...sorry? You're babblin', s...son. What van?'

'The van I saw in Stoke on the night Stan Marshall was murdered. It was one of yours, Chuck, parked up outside the pub he visited shortly before he was killed.'

'You were there?' Chuck shook his head, astounded by the new information. 'You're saying … you were at the scene, on the night in question, and you're pointing the finger at me? If you and Arnie were there on the night then I'm amazed—'

'Arnie wasn't there.'

'Where was he then?'

'I…uh… dunno. I took him to meet his dad at lunchtime then dropped him back at the hotel.'

'Right. So how do you know this isn't some trick he's pulled so he would have an alibi? He might be setting me up to cover his own tracks. Bloody hell, Bruce, are you really that stupid? He's using you, kid. Those vans are company vans. Any one of our mob has access to them. Have you thought it could have been driven by someone still loyal to Arnie? What was the date? Tell me and I'll look it up in the logs … see who signed one out.'

Sensing his youngest brother wilting under the pressure, Chuck played the family card.

'Look what he's done to me, Bruce,' said Chuck. 'Then ask yourself, 'Is it right he's torturing one of your brothers when there's such flimsy evidence on offer?'

EVERYTHING was a blur to Bruce. He had acted in good faith but as he saw the physical and mental deterioration of his eldest brother, he began to question everything he thought he knew. He had been sure Chuck's intention was to frame Arnie for the murder and the idea had made him incredibly angry, but what if he'd got it the wrong way round? What if Arnie was framing Chuck?

Bruce had always considered Arnie a flawed genius and knew he was quite capable of pulling off the deception. Perhaps this was another example of his powers of manipulation. He imagined Arnie still had some contacts within the Boxer Boys ranks willing to do his bidding for a price. What if one of them had taken the van, driven to Stoke, picked up Arnie and taken him to kill Stan Marshall? Arnie could have sneaked up behind his father, stunned him with the taser then stabbed him to death.

Realising time wasn't on Chuck's side, Bruce rushed back to the flat and looked up one of the cuttings Arnie had kept about the murder. Checking the date on the paper – March 31 – he counted back one. He had to find out what Chuck was doing on March 30 and he had to do it quickly. His big brother's life was at stake.

45

THE riot began at just after 1.00 a.m. A local greengrocer's window was put through and the owner had to run for his life as the culprits set the place ablaze. Soon the street was heaving with people and a mass brawl broke out. Eye witnesses reported a vast array of weapons being put to use, road signs, scaffolding poles, car jacks … one even said a bloke had emerged from his house waving a coffee table above his head. Sounds of shattered glass mingled with cries of hatred to turn a quiet suburban area into a war zone. At the end of it one body lay dead in a back alley, blood draining into the cobbles.

Detective Sergeant Adam Machin looked down at the lifeless figure in front of him and wondered what was happening to this peaceful, friendly city. The Potteries had always been a place where everyone was in the same boat – poor, working class and trying to make ends meet – but got on with it with a smile on their faces. Now it seemed destined to become murder capital of the Midlands, division and hatred everywhere.

Two weeks earlier, a young man in his 20s, believed to be a recruit of the far-right group Britain First, had been stabbed to death by person or persons unknown. Now it seemed the fascists had taken their revenge, the Asian in front of DS Machin having been sent to meet his maker with a sharp blow to the back of the head from a heavy implement.

'Do we have a name?' he asked a detective constable from the Homicide Action Team, who had been first on the scene when the body was discovered.

'It's Amir Masood, sir.'

'THE Amir Masood?'

'Sir.'

'Love-a-duck!' DS Machin whispered, stifling his reaction in case it might be interpreted as racist. There was no getting away from the facts, though. Amir Masood was a scumbag of the highest order. He was a local gangster, pimp and money lender. There were plenty of rumours about how far the Masood tentacles spread.

'One of our witnesses says Amir's name was shouted before it kicked off,' said the DC.

'You think he was the target all along?' Machin was surprised. Even though the Masood family were notorious, they were considered pretty much untouchable. People had tried in the past to muscle in on their turf and always come off second best.

'Apparently some bloke was shouting his daughter's name, demanding they bring her out,' said the DC. 'Sounds like she was one of these 'groomed' kids you hear about, y'know the ones from broken homes that are lured into prostitution. We've heard the stories: Rochdale, Rotherham ...'

Machin nodded. The gang's legitimate businesses, which included a taxi firm, car sales unit and fast-food outlets, provided the ideal set up for luring young girls with the promise of free food, drink, cigarettes and lifts. In other well-known cases the drink had been spiked with drugs and rendered the victims incapable of resistance. They were then exploited by the gang's 'client list'.

Amir Masood was the banker, the man who dealt with all the family money, so would be a legitimate target for anyone aggrieved at the exploitation of a child.

'CCTV?'

The DC, a conscientious young copper with a mop of curly blond hair, didn't need to refer to his notes. 'The corner shop, but it's only directed inwards for the purpose of catching shoplifters,' he said. 'The CCTV boys are going through it now. When I asked the shopkeeper, he went very coy. We can expect a wall of silence.

It's a big Muslim area. Even with Amir Masood gone, the locals won't raise their heads above the parapet.'

'Have we spoken to the family?'

'Yes, sir. They're not saying much, just demanding justice.'

'Anyone been to Masood's office?'

'Not yet. I doubt they will give us permission.'

'Shit!' Machin looked at his watch. 'We're still in the golden hour, but time is running out. I'd love to get a look at their books, but we'll need a good reason for a search warrant.'

'We may have found one,' said the DC, aware the first hour after the body was found was the most important in solving a murder. He produced a polythene bag from behind his back and Machin could clearly see a small, black notebook inside it. He raised an eyebrow.

'We found it on the body, sir,' said the younger man with enthusiasm. 'There's a list of names in it with amounts of money pencilled next to them. One name in particular will interest you – it was crossed out.'

THE exhibits officer in the white paper suit stepped from the mobile home and removed his mask.

'Anything?' asked DS Machin, standing outside the portable office of the Masood family, tucked away in the corner of a second-hand car lot. As soon as the DC had handed over Amir Masood's black book, Machin had phoned DCI Rowbottom and urged he contact a friendly judge to authorise a warrant.

The forensics man raised a hand. He was holding a sturdy brown boot by its laces. He pointed to a stain on the toe cap. 'I reckon I know what this is,' he said.

'Whip it down the lab,' said Machin. 'If the blood on it is a match for Stan Marshall we may have solved one murder while investigating another.'

'I think you'll find this interesting, too,' said one of the other members of the forensic team, appearing in the doorway with a brown, padded envelope.

'WE believe we've found him … your dad's killer.'

Gareth recognised DCI Rowbottom's voice.

'Seriously? Who?'

Gareth held his breath, expecting to recognise the name.

'A nasty little gangster called Amir Masood. His nickname's Big Daddy. Heard of him?'

'Only the wrestler,' said Gareth. 'My dad used to rave about him.'

As he spoke, though, his mind replayed a confrontation with a gang of Asians in a shopping arcade. Had Masood been one of them? Was it that simple?

'Unfortunately, we can't ask Mr Masood,' said Rowbottom. 'He's dead.'

'What?' Gareth saw another picture in his mind, his brother Arnie swearing revenge through gritted teeth.

Don't get mad, get even.

He realised the DCI was still talking.

'There was a riot. We found his body in an alleyway shortly after we got there.'

Gareth pictured another dark lane, a grimy passageway meandering between a down-at-heel public house and some derelict buildings, decorated with crime scene tape and bloodstains on the ground.

'What goes around comes around,' he said. 'How do you know it's him?'

'This Daddy character was a loan shark and a pretty vicious one,' said Rowbottom. 'He had names pencilled into a book of those who owed him money. Your dad was into him for more than two grand. We found his name with a line through it.'

Gareth thought the evidence flimsy.

'That's not the clincher, though,' said Rowbottom. 'There was a boot in the office, Masood's size, and it had a bloodstain on it which matched your father's blood type. It's at the lab now. Also, we found an envelope in a drawer in Masood's office with your old man's fingerprints all over it and fibres from his coat attached. May be pure coincidence but it all seems to stack up.'

Gareth nodded. He had never told anyone about Bruce's £3,000 bribe, but he knew it had been handed over in a padded envelope.

'As a result of all this, we got the landlord of The Sheldon out of bed and asked him if he could recall Big Daddy being in the pub on the night your old man was killed,' said the detective. 'At first he said "no", but later he admitted that, yes, he'd appeared briefly at around the time your dad disappeared. Not only that, but Masood had actually approached the bar to ask about your dad's whereabouts. Scouring the CCTV footage of the Coach and Horses earlier that day, we again spotted Masood, watching your dad in conversation with Arnold Dolan.'

As soon as the call was over, Gareth tried Arnie's number, but got no reply. Damn! He was about to try again when his 'I'm Forever Blowing Bubbles' ringtone started up.

'Arnie?' he said.

'No, it's Bruce,' said the flustered voice on the other end of the line. 'Gareth, you've gotta do something – he's gonna kill him!'

'I don't—'

'Arnie's got our Chuck,' said Bruce. 'He's holding him as a prisoner and torturing him. He grabbed him nearly three weeks ago in the Hope car park and thinks he killed your dad.'

'Arnie took him?'

'Yeah. He wants him to confess to your old man's murder, but Chuck denies it. I thought Arnie would have let him go by now.'

'Shit!' said Gareth. 'You've got to stop him. They've found the killer. It had nothing to do with Chuck. It was one of that gang that jumped us in Stoke.'

'That's great news, but Arnie's off his nut. We have to stop him.'
'We?'

'Nothing I say will make any difference,' said Bruce. 'There's only one person in the world he really listens to… and that's you.'

Gareth sighed. 'Where's Chuck?'

Bruce gave him the address.

46

BRUCE pulled a bulky bunch of keys from his pocket and searched through for the right one. 'We haven't got much time,' he said, pulling back the bolt and pushing his way inside. Gareth followed.

There was a quiet, continuous hum, a solitary light bulb illuminating the desolate passageway.

'Down here,' said Bruce and for the briefest moment it crossed Gareth's mind he might be walking into a trap. It wasn't that long ago he was at the top of Arnie Dolan's hit list. He looked at the scar on his hand to remind himself of their violent encounter. The gangster, who wasn't then in a wheelchair, thought Gareth had ratted him out to police and left him to rot in jail. Arnie was altogether a fitter and more dangerous rival at that time, but anyone who wrote him off because of his recent injuries did so at their peril.

Gareth asked himself the question: Why had he come? He owed Chuck Dolan nothing. The last time they'd come into contact, Gareth finished up sprawled across a pub car park, nursing an array of ugly cuts and bruises.

'In here… quick!' said Bruce. 'Arnie could be back any minute.'

'What? You mean he isn't here? Why the hell do you need me then, Bruce?'

'I just… you know, if he came back I thought you would be able to talk to him, persuade him we're doing the right thing. After all, you know all about the cops finding the killer.'

'Yes, but—'

Gareth hesitated for a moment but realised he had come this far so might as well continue. He followed Bruce into a room bathed in harsh white light. Squinting, he could see a figure hunched over at the far end of the room. A few more steps and the smell hit him, knocking him back like an uppercut from a heavyweight champion. He put his hand to his nose and retched. The stench was so strong it lodged in the back of his throat, a mixture of raw sewage and body odour with an underlying whiff of damp and decay.

Willing himself forward, he found Chuck strapped to a chair and stripped to bloodstained boxer shorts, his feet and arms shackled with plastic ties. His torso was a canvas of welts and scars, caked blood like brown sauce streaking his pale flesh. On hearing their footsteps, he raised his head slowly, peering into the gloom through one half-shut eye. His nose was swollen and clearly broken, rivers of solidified blood trailing from his nostrils to his chin.

'What the fuck did you do, Arnie?' The question was rhetorical, but Bruce chose to answer.

'What didn't he do? You know how creative he can be. He'd read about this gang who used a hairdryer as an instrument of torture and liked the idea. He set it to maximum heat and applied it to areas of Chuck's body, hence those savage burn marks. He put a special 'tool kit' together... knives, pliers, a screwdriver, too. That's before he started administering the shock treatments.'

'Shit!'

Gareth risked another look at Chuck. He couldn't tell if the prisoner was conscious. 'He did all this to his own brother?'

Bruce nodded. 'He had help, of course. His movements are a bit restricted. But he watched it all. Insisted on it.'

'You couldn't stop him?' The younger man gave Gareth a meaningful look. 'I guess not.'

Bending to get a closer look at the damage, he almost fell backwards when a swollen lid popped open and an eye latched onto his.

'Sh… should have guessed,' Chuck mumbled.

'He's here to help, Chuck,' said Bruce.

'And… why would he… do that?'

'Because whatever I think of you, Chuck, this is barbaric,' said Gareth. 'You may not like me and I'm not that keen on you, but nothing justifies this. Cut the ties, Bruce.'

'You sure, Gar? He's dangerous.'

'Dangerous?' Gareth raised his voice. 'You think he's capable of anything in his position? He needs a hospital. The bloke has had enough.'

There was silence, followed by a scraping sound, an ill-fitting metal door fighting with concrete.

'He got what he fuckin' deserves.'

Gareth froze and turned. Arnie was crossing the room in his wheelchair, a man either side of him. Behind them, another figure lurked in the shadows.

'No one deserves this, Doles, whatever your problem with them,' Gareth said. 'He's your brother.'

There was a humming sound as Arnie moved forwards and stopped inches from him.

'Yeah?' he said, waving a finger menacingly in Gareth's direction. 'Well, that's why I'm me and you're you, ain't it, Gaz? You were never strong enough for this shit. You were happy to be "in the gang" but when things got rough, the dirty work was left down to me. You saved your skin, and I went to jail.'

Gareth maintained eye contact, aware of the tension. Bruce was right, though. In the past, when Arnie was at his destructive worst, the reporter had always found the words to reach him. Maybe it was the brotherly bond they shared, though none of the Dolans bar Anjelica perhaps had that same influence over Arnie.

'Arnie, you went to prison because you killed a man,' said Gareth. 'I know you were helping me and I'm grateful, but you can't continue to pin everything that goes wrong in your life on me.'

'Pot calling kettle … It's you who blames everything on me!' said Arnie. 'You told me I wrecked your life.'

'I was wrong. I know that now. Stan Marshall was to blame as with everything else.'

Arnie nodded, considering the idea. Pushing the lever forwards on the armrest, the wheelchair advanced. Gareth stepped out of the way.

'This cunt went out of his way to damage me, mentally and physically,' he said, spitting the words out angrily as he switched focus to the man tied to the chair. 'What you see here is how I react when someone treats me like a mug. Fuck! Most people look up to their older brother and rely on him to have their back. You wouldn't expect your big bro to sign your death warrant when you're in prison or walk away from you when you're crippled for life. That's what he's done, and worse. Look at the big gangster now though.' He waved his hand up and down in front of Chuck. 'He's just a pukey, piss-stained, shit-eating bastard. He's nothing… ain't that right, Chuck?'

Gripping the prisoner under the chin, he lifted his head, so their eyes were level. 'Nothing,' he spat. 'The fact he killed our dad was just the final—'

'He didn't.'

For a moment silence engulfed them.

'You're just saying that because for some reason you want to save his sorry ass.'

'No… I'm telling you, it wasn't Chuck,' said Gareth. 'The police called me. It was that Asian gang in Stoke-on-Trent you suspected all along.'

Arnie thought about it. 'Nah. What about the transit van eh? Explain that.'

'I don't know anything about a van,' said Gareth. 'All I know is the police have evidence this Asian guy lent our old man a great deal of money and wanted it back. Eyewitness accounts put him in the right place at the right time, and there was an envelope found in his possession with our dad's fingerprints all over it. There was also about a grand of cash in one of the drawers – that had Dad's fingerprints on it, too, and a shoe with dad's blood on it.'

Concentrating on Chuck, neither Arnie nor Gareth noticed Bruce's hand spring to his mouth.

'The evidence is overwhelming,' said Gareth. 'It makes more sense cash would be at the bottom of it all. And what about Chuck's alibi?'

Arnie looked confused.

'You didn't ask him?' Gareth shook his head, incredulous. 'At the exact time our old man was being stabbed Chuck was with Janie Vickers, consoling her after Pete walked out. Janie told Anj all about it when she was staying with us. I looked into it and the dates match. Face facts, Arnie, Chuck couldn't have done it.'

'Oh, come off it!' Arnie objected. 'He could have found a way. Don't underestimate him.'

There was a grunt from behind him and Gareth turned to see Chuck leaning forwards, staring intently at Arnie through his one good eye. He looked furious. 'Don't… underestimate me?' he spluttered. 'You've underestimated me my whole… fuckin'… life. Older brothers normally get respect, but you gave me nothin'. Why don't we settle this now, Arnie, just you and me?'

Arnie stared back at him.

'It would be my pleasure,' he said.

'Stop!'

The gruff, deep-voiced interruption came from the back of the storage facility. Arnie backed away, allowing Chuck a sight of the new arrival. His face registered surprise and confusion.

'Mr Durak?'

A thick-set man with black, curly hair moved forwards to stand between Arnie's two bodyguards. 'You are surprised, Chuck?'

'Thank God,' said Chuck. 'Get me out of here, would ya?'

'Ahhhh,' said Durak. 'I'm afraid I can't do that… the reason being, you're here because of me and this is my facility. Arnold here got in touch with me a while ago to explain you'd kicked him out of your little gang. It sounded like something from a kids' TV show, no?'

The man moved further into the room. He exuded power and looked totally out of place in the surroundings, his clothes pristine, a knee-length Cashmere coat falling over a slim fit pair of black trousers. On his feet were expensive-looking Italian loafers. His booming Mediterranean voice resonated off the walls.

'I'm not happy with you, Chuck. You talk about respect but no one on your side had the decency to show me any and inform me of the new arrangements.'

'Sorry, Mr Durak, but—'

'Shut it! I warned you boys at the very beginning if you screwed with me it would end badly for you. In all my dealings with Arnold I was happy with our relationship. He proved time and again that he knew what he was doing – even during that unfortunate vacation at Her Majesty's Pleasure – and he kept his mouth shut. Our working relationship was extremely lucrative and based on trust. Call me old fashioned, Chuck, but I don't like change for change's sake – particularly when it's forced on me.'

Gareth saw the flash of understanding illuminate Chuck's eyes.

'Oh God, it was you…' said the prisoner.

Durak stepped closer and Arnie moved aside. Bending down, the Turkish drug lord drew level with Chuck, staring into his one good eye. Patting him delicately on the head like a pet dog, he said, 'The kidnappings? The pub fire? All that stuff?' he shrugged. 'I don't know what you're talking about.'

He smiled.

'Consider it a test, Chuck,' he continued. 'I wanted to see how long it would take for you to come to me when those poor little street dealers got themselves kidnapped. You failed. I didn't hear a dicky bird. You carried on as if nothing had happened. To be honest, I was so upset I was going to pull the plug on your entire operation before Arnold here persuaded me that would be premature.'

'People died,' said Chuck.

Durak shrugged. 'Collateral damage. You know that. People died in that nightclub fire when some careless bastard threw a grenade. All businesses have their casualties, the drug business more than most. Even after the pub burnt down, though, you didn't come to me and explain your problems. I found that immensely disrespectful.'

Gareth wondered where the conversation was heading. He had never played any part in the illicit affairs of the Boxer Boys, but he'd heard from Arnie how they had strong backing. This big man was obviously the head honcho.

'What would you like me to do then, Arnold?' said Durak. 'My boys can take out this… trash… for you and when everything dies down we can have a chat about where we go from here. I don't want to steal your thunder. You may feel this is a score you have to settle yourself.'

Before Arnie could answer, a faint, high-pitched sound filled the air, sirens rising and falling somewhere in the vicinity. Without a word, Durak got to his feet and walked back to his men. There was a quick discussion and one of them pulled a mobile phone from his pocket. Punching in some numbers, he had a whispered conversation then cut the line and said something to his boss.

'Arnold, I'm afraid we must go,' said the Turkish crime boss. 'Someone, it appears, has been indiscrete.'

His eyes locked on Gareth and Bruce. Neither man flinched.

'There is no time to waste.'

'What about him?' asked Arnie.

'Do what you wish, but my people tell me we have five minutes at most.'

Arnie turned back to the man tied to the chair. 'I swear to God, Chuck, you've got a guardian angel looking over you. All the things you've done yet you get away with it every time.'

Listening to Arnie's words, Gareth almost laughed. If this was getting away with it, he hoped he never had Chuck's luck.

'You two, come on!' Arnie's words snapped Gareth out of his reflections. He turned and followed Arnie to the exit, Bruce alongside him.

'What will happen to him?' asked Gareth. 'Shouldn't we——?'

'You want to hang around for the Old Bill and explain what's gone on here?'

Arnie trapped Gareth in a steely glare. The reporter shook his head.

'Thought not,' he said. 'Get the flid mobile, Brucie.'

'You ain't worried, Arnie?' said Bruce. 'You know, about Chuck telling the filth?'

'Nah,' said Arnie, leading the way through the corridor towards the exit. 'We Dolans may be a lot of things but we ain't grasses. Chuck won't rat out his family, but at times I wonder about you, Gazza. It's strange how those sirens turned up right on cue.'

47

CHUCK Dolan's abduction only made a few column inches in the *Barking and Dagenham Post*. According to police, an unnamed man had been taken to hospital with serious wounds having been kidnapped and subjected to torture. The man, from Barking, claimed to have lost his memory and had no recollection of his captors. The officers in charge of the investigation believed it to be the latest move in an escalating gang war.

Gareth put the paper down, finished his coffee and ate the last slice of toast. 'Right, Janie, what have you got in store for me?' he asked.

Depositing cup and plate in the dishwater, Janie Vickers then turned to her guest.

'It's great of Anj to volunteer your services,' she said, chuckling. 'I imagine helping us pack was exactly the way you wanted to spend your Sunday. I can't tell you how much I appreciate it. Do you think you could start in the loft? Some stuff up there I would really like to keep, you know, baby pictures, wedding cards and the like, but others—' She made a throwing motion with her hand.

'Sure,' said Gareth. 'Where's Pete? I thought he would be here too. I wanted to see how the old boy was recovering.'

'He's taken the kids out for a couple of hours so I could organise things here,' she said. 'Otherwise it would be 'mummy this, mummy that' every five seconds and I'd get nothing done. Plus, it's Simon's birthday tomorrow so they deserve a treat. I realise it's a bit of a cheek asking you to do the donkey work when my own husband isn't here to help, but since that France business he's been as useful as a chocolate tea pot, what with one arm in plaster, not to mention the cracked ribs and assorted aches and pains. The doctors have insisted he does no heavy lifting, so he would be more a hindrance than a help, and I don't imagine you want a foreman telling you what to do.'

'No,' said Gareth. 'One foreman is enough.'

'Hey, you cheeky bar steward!' She slapped his arm, laughing. Gareth was glad to see her in a better mood than she'd been for ages. 'Come on then, coffee break's over and it's time you got off your lazy arse and got started. Follow me.'

She led him into the hallway and up the stairs. When they reached the landing, Janie moved a chair into position below a hatch, then clambered up and opened it. A ladder slid down.

'It's all yours,' she said. 'Anything too heavy, give us a shout and I'll help you. Maybe go through the lighter things first. I know with your leg it won't be easy negotiating the steps, so you don't want to be up and down every five minutes.'

'Do I check what's in the boxes?'

'Have a look by all means. I don't want to be hauling old Christmas decorations around if they're no good to man or beast – you know, broken baubles, faulty lights…' She smiled.

'Leave it to me.'

She started back down the stairs.

'Oh, and, Janie…' he said.

She turned and looked back at him.

'I'm glad you're giving it another go,' he said. 'Pete's a good lad and I know he loves you and the kids very much. I can understand how it felt for you at the time, the Arnie business, but in a way, Pete is as much a victim as you.'

She nodded.

'That's what my shrink said. Sometimes you get so wrapped up in your own lives, you're reluctant to take advice from others, but I'm so glad I did. We're going to see a marriage guidance counsellor next. The one thing I realised was that to make it work we have to move. This is where it happened, and it's with me every time I enter that bloody kitchen. I guess I could have decorated top to bottom, but no end of cleaning can take the stain away.'

She touched herself above the heart. 'The truth is we both need to move on. At one stage I thought that meant divorce but when you bought him back from France and I saw the state he was in, the old feelings came back. He was an idiot and I don't know what he was playing at, but I know I love him.'

BORN with an inquisitive nature that made him so suited to journalism, Gareth was thoroughly enjoying his trip down memory lane. He felt like a spy going through the Vickers' private things, particularly when he lingered over certain pictures longer than necessary. All their teen years had been linked so closely together he couldn't resist. Armed with a robust pair of scissors, some packing tape, a roll of black bin liners and a green marker pen, he quickly established a routine, cutting open a box, checking inside, removing anything disposable and placing it in one of the bin bags, then repackaging and sealing the box, before scrawling the contents on the outside, not a complete inventory but just a reminder of what it contained.

He picked up a photograph of young Simon Vickers in a toddlers' West Ham kit, riding his first two-wheeler bike with the aid of stabilisers. Pete was behind him, willing him on like a cheerleader, looking much younger than he did these days, his hair black, his stomach more generously padded than it was now. It made him smile. Placing it in the box he picked up another photograph from the pile and tears pricked his eyes.

In this one a smiling Janie had been captured with her arm around Anjie who, head down, was giving her full attention to a small baby wrapped in a blanket. Maxi. Where had the years gone? His boy, no larger than a child's doll in the picture, was always raiding the larder for biscuits and chocolate these days with the excuse they were 'Just to tide me over until lunchtime, Mum'. Max had probably spent the morning playing games on his computer or scoring goals in the back garden. Gareth suddenly felt old.

He put the picture to one side, making a mental note to ask Janie whether he could take it home with him or, at the very least, make a copy of it. Putting all the things worth keeping back into the box, he sealed it then scrawled 'Simon, youngster, pics and stuff' on it with the marker pen. Now there were just a couple of regular-size cardboard boxes left.

Pulling one of them towards him, he noticed there was something already written on the side. It said simply 'Jane school days' in an unfamiliar, extremely precise hand. He tore through the lid, his stomach giving a rumble to remind him lunch couldn't be far away. He didn't want to have to clamber back up in the afternoon with a belly full of roast beef, Yorkshire pudding, parsnips and potatoes so vowed to finish up before Janie called him down.

Reaching inside, the first thing he removed was a white shoe-box. It was the kind of box Gareth had been surrounded by as a youngster, his dad regularly bringing samples back from his market stall. There was no branding, and nothing written on it to indicate its contents. Opening it, he was confronted with a mish-mash of things: letters, poems and a *Now That's What I Call Music 43* cassette tape. He chuckled, reading through a list of vaguely familiar songs on the back of the box. Then, keen for other reminders of the music they'd listened to back in the 90s, he opened it. Removing the tape, he twisted it over and over in his fingers. It wasn't what he was expecting. Rather than a pre-recorded tape it just had the words 'Mix tape for a special lady' scrawled on it in biro. Gareth's stomach flipped, but this time it had nothing to do with hunger.

Remembering something he'd seen in one of the earlier boxes he shifted his weight, crying out as a wave of cramp swept through the calf of his bad leg. He rubbed it ferociously and pressed his foot firmly to the floor until the moment passed. Continuing his mission, he grabbed the previously sealed box and ripped it open to remove a portable tape player. He had already checked it worked by pressing the play button and watching the spindles turn. Now, all fingers and thumbs, he inserted the tape and reached back into the earlier box for headphones.

Slotting them into the side of the player he put two small black buds in his ears and pressed the arrow button. Within seconds he was rocked by thrashing, frenetic guitar chords, a pounding beat assaulting his ears. Before long, a wailing harmonica joined in to move the beat along.

Tapping his foot to a tune familiar to him, he reached back into the shoebox and came out with a creased piece of A4 paper. On it were printed the words: 'My darling, adorable, sexy, Jane. I made this tape especially for you. The songs might not be your scene, but they were selected as a symbol of my love and devotion to you. I hope you like it. We should be together.'

There was no signature, but there didn't need to be. As the unmistakeable voice of Lee Brilleaux, lead singer of 70s and 80s rock band Dr Feelgood, burst in, Gareth sat back against a pillar, his mind whirring, tears rolling down his cheeks.

'Baby Jane, what a fool I've been—'

You and me both, Lee, thought Gareth, as the pieces of a complicated jigsaw began falling into place, the picture becoming frighteningly clear.

48

THROUGH lunch, Gareth found it hard to keep it together, but did his best for the sake of the kids. They were thrilled to see their Uncle Gary and kept asking him questions.

'How is Maxi?'

'When are you coming to live back here?'

'Do they have Yorkshire puddings in Wales?'

He kept his answers brief then returned to the loft after lunch. Taking a break in late afternoon, he excused himself with a migraine and retired to the spare room where he was staying. Lying there, his mind in turmoil, he listened to the family going through the normal Sunday night routines. After watching a popular TV talent show, Janie marched the kids upstairs for baths before Vickers read them a bedtime story. Simon and Diane popped their heads around his door to say goodnight before lights out and when he thought they were settled for the night, he made his way downstairs.

He found Janie curled up in her favourite recliner, a glass of red wine in her hand, while Vickers emerged from the kitchen, one arm in a sling and the other carrying a six-pack of lager.

'Ah, thought I heard movement!' he said. 'I was worried we'd killed you off. I bought some beers for the hired help.'

Smiling, he handed Gareth a can and deposited the others on top of a Sunday newspaper resting on the coffee table. The front-page headline read: 'Cameron to quit over Brexit defeat'.

Shit.

Gareth was beginning to think the world had gone mad.

'Mental, eh?' said Vickers, cracking open his own can. 'We voted leave, didn't we, babe? Hopefully now some of these bloody Lithuanians, Albanians and the like trying to muscle in on our business will be shown the door. What d'you reckon?'

'I'm disappointed,' said Gareth. 'I think it's a mistake. It seems obvious to me some Tories who supported the Leave campaign were just doing it to enhance their own careers.'

When Gareth had heard the decision on Friday morning he'd felt numb, having convinced himself the country wouldn't risk the giant leap into the unknown. It came as a surprise that so many of his friends were fervent in their belief that Britain should go it alone. He had expected Prime Minister Cameron and his sidekick, the Chancellor George Osborne, to make a better case for keeping the status quo.

Status Quo.

The two words took him back. In his mind's eye he saw the life-sized poster of Rick Parfitt, Quo's guitarist, on the living room wall at his parents' place. When he'd lived there as a kid, the flat was always full of rock music.

'Sorry I couldn't help you with the packing,' said Vickers, interrupting his train of thought and raising a can in a mock toast. 'We've a lot to thank you for, what with the France business and now this.'

Gareth took a swig of cold lager, hoping the alcohol would give him Dutch courage. Pete and Jane were observing him with affection. It made what he had to say even tougher.

'You're quiet, mate,' said Vickers. 'Still suffering, eh? I bet you needed that pint to wash down some of the dust in that loft. Jane and I were only saying at tea time, "What can we ever do to repay Gazza for what he's done for us"?'

They looked at him expectantly.

'You can tell me exactly how my dad died,' he said.

Vickers froze with his drink halfway to his lips. Janie spluttered on a mouth full of wine. Gareth reached inside his pocket and removed the cassette tape.

'Sorry?' Vickers peered out at him from beneath a furrowed brow, gripping his can so tightly in his fist Gareth thought he might squash it.

'Too late for sorry now,' said Gareth. 'I think you know that. It's time you told me what happened, Janie … between you and Dad.'

Resting his arm on the shelf above the artificial coal fire, he absent-mindedly picked up the envelope lying there as he waited for a response. It was addressed to Simon, to be opened the following day, on his eighth birthday. Another piece of the jigsaw snapped into place.

'You're tired, mate. I don't know—'

'Stop!'

Gareth's shout exploded across the room and for a moment he feared waking the kids. Lowering his voice, he spoke through gritted teeth, 'It's time to stop all the lying. I've figured it out. You nearly got away scot free thanks to the police finding that dead loan shark rather conveniently, but what I've learnt today changes everything.'

He threw the cassette into Janie's lap. Pete leaned across, retrieved it and read the label.

'*Now That's What I Call Music 43*. I guess having this is a bit of a crime. It will have all those bloody 90s boy bands on it.'

'Look inside,' said Gareth.

He opened it.

'Oh … a mixed tape.'

Janie snatched it from him and stared at the writing on it, her mouth open. 'But how …? I threw this away ages ago!'

'You must have put it in the wrong box,' said Gareth. 'I always used to get my tapes muddled up when I was a kid.'

'This shouldn't even be in our loft. How did it get there?'

Vickers looked sheepish. 'I think I know,' he said.

Both of them directed their attention towards him.

'The Sergeant Major marched around here just after your mum died. I forgot to tell you. He said he'd found some stuff that belonged to you when clearing out at home. He handed me a couple of boxes. I thought nothing of it, just shoved them up in the loft and left them there.'

'There was a piece of paper lower down the box,' said Gareth. 'It was a note to your wife … from my dad. He was her married lover when we were at school, Pete. But you know that because she told you, didn't she? In fact, that's the reason you left home.'

Gareth felt a crushing pain as he watched the tears roll down Janie's cheeks. He gained no satisfaction from his revelation. He wished he didn't have to put her through this, but the time for brushing dirt under the carpet was long gone.

Moving across, Pete cradled his wife's head in his hands. 'You fucker!' he said, turning an angry glare on Gareth. 'How dare you —?'

'How dare I? I dare because I've been put through the ringer for the last couple of months. I was even in custody for a while, as was Arnie …'

'Yeah?' said Vickers, 'Well, fuck Arnie. He should be behind bars for what he did to my wife. Our nightmares are all of his making: yours, mine and Jane's. Are you doing his bidding again, just like in the good old days, Gazz?'

'This isn't about Arnie,' said Gareth, his voice level. 'It's about your wife and my dad. I need to know the full story, Jane. I think I deserve it. He left me, my sister and my mum in the lurch, ripped the heart out of our family. It almost ruined my life. Don't I deserve the truth?'

Pete Vickers stood, a menacing look on his face, but Janie put out a hand and grabbed his arm. 'Don't!' she said. 'He's right. You know most of it anyway, Pete … Please stay by my side while I fill in the gaps.'

He gave her a squeeze in agreement and she turned and waved the tape in Gareth's direction. 'Have you heard it?'

He nodded. 'And I read the note. I recognised the handwriting, of course. When I put the tape on it was clear from the first song it was a gift from Dad to you.'

'Baby Jane.'

'Yeah,' he said. 'The Feelgoods were his favourite band. He always played their music loud around the house and I recognised it instantly. Then there was 'Lady Jane' by The Rolling Stones and 'Sweet Jane' by the Velvet Underground. You see a theme developing?'

Tears streamed down Janie Vickers' face.

'The last song was a real giveaway, though,' said Gareth. 'It wasn't Dad's type of music at all, but it told me everything I needed to know.'

Vickers stared at him, struggling to grasp what he was being told. 'What song?' he muttered.

'*Stan*, by Eminem,' said Gareth. 'I was 17 when that came out. It was my favourite song, and I used to play it in the car on the way back from football. I remember Dad asking me who it was then chuckling, saying it was nice of Eminem to name a song after him.'

He paused, remembering his dad nodding along to the tune as Gareth explained the story of how a stalker fan, Stan, drove off a bridge and killed himself and his girlfriend because the famous rap star had failed to respond to his fan mail.

'Maybe you should fill in the blanks, Janie,' he said.

Jane Vickers knocked back the rest of her wine and topped up the glass. Wiping her face, she looked in his direction, rivers of mascara cascading down her cheeks. She looked like she was wearing a Hallowe'en mask from an X-rated horror film. Finally, she spoke.

'It began on the night of your sixteenth birthday party—'

49

May 26, 1999

JANIE SULLIVAN lay among the crumpled coats, trying to work out what had just happened. Had she lost her virginity? If so her 'first time' hardly lived up to its billing.

She hadn't expected angels to appear amid a fanfare of trumpets, but somehow she thought it would have been more memorable. After all, it could only happen once – there was no going back – and she'd allowed herself to be brainwashed into expecting it would be special.

One of her pals had spoken about seeing stars while another claimed to have felt the earth move. The more poetic females, those who had been going steady for at least six months, described the closeness of the act, skin touching skin and hands carefully caressing flesh, goose bumps appearing all over their bodies. The act was a union, a shared moment, a physical demonstration of love between two people. She'd been envious of them for having something so cool.

Janie realised she was still pretty much fully clothed though one of her boobs was poking out of her blouse. It reminded her of the rough, undisciplined hands which had pawed at her in such a way that a button had sprung off and pinged against the dressing-table mirror.

A chill passed through her as she thought of Paul, her step-dad, sitting at home waiting for her arrival, watching the clock and building up a head of steam. The Sergeant Major would confine her to barracks for a year if he knew the reason for her tardiness, and if he caught sight of the missing button she could expect a full-scale military inquisition. How could she explain it away?

Shuddering, she realised it wasn't her nerves playing games but a draught coming from the door. She pulled her blouse around her, a pointless exercise in the circumstances, and thought about Arnie Dolan, the boy who had left her lying here, listless and confused.

Of course, she'd wanted him. She'd put out enough signals. For God's sake, she'd been bending her best friend Anjelica's ear for months about how much she fancied her brother. She could hardly lie there now and regret the fact he'd responded to those wanton messages. She'd let him know she was available, and he'd taken advantage of an open target for his teenage lust. He had been less subtle than she expected, but why should he be anything different. Everyone knew Arnie was a rough diamond who, at the age of 16, was leader of the coolest gang around.

He scared the shit out of some of the boys she knew, so she could hardly expect him to be a caring and attentive lover. He had working man's hands – moulded from fixing chains on bicycles, scrapping in the street and wrestling with that mad dog of his. He was not the sort to spend his spare time reading books and bathing in essential oils. Those hands weren't made for caressing and, anyway, what did she want: a man or a child?

To be fair, the initial contact had been exciting, waves of exhilaration and trepidation combining to flood her nervous system. Grabbing her from behind he'd pulled her towards him and she'd smelt alcohol, cigars and something uniquely Arnie. He was desperate, ravenous and when his lips sank onto her neck and his tongue circled her flesh, her toes curled so much she thought they might snap. Then she was on the bed, him on top, with other people's coats, hats and scarves tangled around them. His stiff fingers probed and prodded and her efforts to prize him off just made him desperate.

A groan of pain had caught in her throat when the fingers were replaced by something altogether wider, longer and more inflexible, a solid mass of muscle she feared might rip her open. It withdrew almost immediately, but the moment of relief didn't last long. When the next thrust came, it had gone so carelessly deep that it practically pushed tears from her eyes. At the time she thought she was suffocating, unable to scream, his tongue squirming in her mouth like a restless snake.

At that moment she abandoned all forms of resistance, shut her eyes and removed herself from the situation. In fairness, it didn't last much longer. With a long groan he removed his face from hers, smirked, rolled over and stood in one movement before pulling up his flies and heading for the door. As a warm dribble rolled down the inside of her thigh, she thought about saying something, anything, but the words wouldn't come. Then he was gone, leaving her alone with her thoughts and his cum.

Suddenly the door burst open, and she rolled over to hide her shame. A couple of teenage girls she vaguely knew walked in, laughing and joking. When they saw her they muttered apologies, grabbed their coats and left. She heard their excited chatter outside, her name mentioned in the conversation.

Sitting up, she looked around for her puffer jacket, reached for it and pulled it over her shoulders. The clock on the wall said 11.20 p.m. and her thoughts went to her stepdad again, imagining him standing furious and menacing at the front door.

'All OK in here?'

The voice made her physically jump. She hadn't heard him enter. This time the intruder was a grown man. Clambering to her feet she brushed at her skirt, which had twisted and risen up her thighs. It hadn't been very long to begin with but now she felt terribly over-exposed.

'Sorry,' she said. 'I was just, umm, getting my coat.'

'Oh, right. Do I know you?'

'Ummmm, no. I'm Gary's mate, well a friend of a friend really … you know Anjie?'

'Of course, I know her and her crazy brother. He's Gary's best mate.'

She fell silent, the mention of Arnie stealing the words from her mouth.

'Anyway, don't let me keep you.' The man started for the door then turned back. 'I'm Gary's dad, Stan, by the way. And you are?'

'Janie, Janie Sullivan.'

'Ahhhh!' A light of recognition flashed on behind his eyes. 'You're Irene's girl, aren't you? I can see it now. The apple doesn't fall far from the tree. Good-looking lady, your mum. She was a target for all the boys back in the day... oh, sorry, inappropriate.'

'It's fine,' said Janie.

'All I'm saying is that you look the spit of her and that's no bad thing. The boys will be queuing... what's wrong?'

'Nothing.'

Janie had tried to stifle a sniffle to no avail. She didn't know why the waterworks had come on but it was embarrassing in front of someone else's father. Pausing briefly to straighten her skirt, she took off at a run. 'Sorry!' she shouted, pushing past him. 'I'm late.'

The master bedroom was elevated at the back of the flat, and she had to descend four or five steps to reach the passageway. The two girls she'd seen earlier were whispering and pointing in her direction and one of the boys they were with shouted, 'Hey look, it's the slag who was bouncing on Dolan's dick. Any chance of sloppy seconds, love?'

He rubbed his crotch as she brushed past him, intending to run from the flat. Before she could do so someone grabbed the boy by the collar, grappled him to the door and threw him out.

'Get out and stay out if you can't treat girls with respect,' Stan Marshall shouted after him.

'Fuckin' 'ell, keep your hair on, mate. My jacket's still inside,' the boy said from the walkway.

Stan fixed the other members of the group with an icy glare. 'Please get your coats and leave quietly,' he said. 'The party's over.'

'Jeez, mate, who died and made you king?' whispered one of the girls.

'OUT!' he shouted, reaching across and grabbing her by a pigtail, then dragging her towards the door.

'Hey! Hey! You old perv, get your hands off me.'

'Get out and don't come back,' he shouted.

Janie also went to leave but Stan gently grabbed her elbow. 'No, love,' he whispered. 'Wait around a bit.'

'But my dad—'

'I don't trust this lot,' he said. 'I think they've been on the bloody alcopops. Don't worry, I'll give you a lift and explain to your dad what happened, that some girls tried to pick a fight with you and that I didn't want you to walk home alone. He'll understand.'

'You don't know—'

'Paul? I do a bit, and I know your mum. I'm sure between us we can ease his worries.' He smiled at her. 'I'll go and make sure the wife is OK. I promised her a cup of tea. Would you like one?'

Janie shook her head.

'Right, you wait in the front room and I'll tell her what's been happening.'

She nodded, walking back down the corridor until she was outside the lounge. Peering around the doorway she saw Gary sat on the sofa, deep in conversation with Anjie, who was holding the book she'd bought him for his birthday, something about football by a bloke called Nick Hornby. There was no sign of Arnie and his crew, thank God, and she guessed he'd left after the bedroom incident.

Gary and Anjie seemed to be getting on so well she felt it would be rude to interrupt. She stood there watching them for a while, feeling a pang of jealousy they had such a good rapport. By contrast, Arnie had said just a few words to her – something about fancying her – before they had sex. It didn't seem right.

A hand fell on her shoulder and she jumped.

'Gosh, sorry!' said Stan Marshall, coat in hand. 'If you'd care to join me I think we'll take the Rolls tonight.'

PERCHED high in the passenger seat of Stan Marshall's dilapi-
dated old blue van, Janie felt she could relax.

As Stan turned the key in the ignition, the only response was a
rat-tat-tat sound, the engine failing to catch.

'Sorry, she's a bit temperamental... like the wife!' he said, smiling. 'You like music? Course you do, you're young. What are you
into? Not this rap crap, I hope!'

'A bit,' she said. 'I like the Backstreet Boys, All Saints, that song
from Titanic by Celine Dion...'

'Hold up, girl! I'm talking music that gets you going... not this
mass produced, soppy commercial garbage that puts you to sleep.
Do you like any rock bands?'

She thought about it. 'Oasis are OK.'

'Oasis? Oh man. I've got my work cut out here.' He turned the
ignition again and the van rumbled into life. 'Listen to this.'

Reaching into the glove compartment he pulled out a tape.

'You don't have any discs?' she asked.

'CDs? I've a few at home but I've only got the tape deck in the
van. If I converted to a CD player I would have to buy all my
favourite albums again. I'm going to hang on until either my tape
decks give up the ghost or I become a very rich man.' He laughed.
'This band are called Dr Feelgood, and that's what they do, make
you feel good. Sit back and enjoy it and we'll be home in no time.'

Within moments the noise of the van engine was drowned out
by jangling guitars as a growling vocalist began singing about 'Milk
and Alcohol'.

'First impressions?' he asked.

She shrugged her shoulders.

'I can see I'm going to have my work cut out with you. I think
I'll make you my special project.'

'My dad wouldn't let me have music like this in the house,' she
said. 'He would say it was too loud.'

'Then he doesn't know what he's talking about,' said Stan. 'Bit
of a grump, is he?'

'He's not my real dad.'

'No,' said Stan. 'I realise that. Irene met him a few years back, didn't she? I suppose that was difficult for you, a new man adopting the father role after it had been you and Mum for so long.'

'He's strict and treats me like a little girl,' she said.

'How old are you?'

'I'll be 15 in January.'

'Blimey! Back in the old days you would be married by now and popping out kids – in some countries that still applies.'

'Arranged marriages? I don't think I'd like that.'

'Me neither,' he said. 'Mind you, sometimes I feel I'm in one.'

She didn't respond, not knowing what to say.

'Don't worry, I did the arranging,' he said. 'Sheila was a runaway. I met her outside a tube station and felt sorry for her. We hit it off and, next thing, we were married.'

'You've been together a long time, though.'

'Nineteen years,' said Stan. 'Can't believe my boy was 16 today. I remember when he was a babe in arms.'

He fell silent for a minute, reflecting.

'Excuse me, Mr Marshall, you missed my turn!' said Jane.

'Did I? Oh shit, sorry. We were having such a good conversation …' He pulled the van to a halt. 'Listen, Janie, you're really easy to talk to and I've enjoyed our little chat. It sounds like things aren't easy for you at home so I'd like to help. Sometimes you need advice from an old head, but someone independent of the family. Let me give you my number, no pressure, just in case of emergencies. Friends?' He stuck out his hand, and she took it, smiling. 'If you want to discuss home problems or anything really – like the best place to buy Dr Feelgood albums – I'll be there for you. And if I'm not around leave a message.'

Leaning over he reached into the glove box, his hand grazing her knee. A tingle passed through her and she blushed. Shit! What was that about? Yes, he was nice and kind and seemed to be able to dial into her worries and inhibitions. He also had a sense of fun, but that was all. Having an adult like him guiding her life might be a good thing right now.

He placed the card in her hand and sat back in his seat. Looking down, she noted that it was handwritten, a single number with no name or indication of whom it might be from.

'Our little secret,' he said.

STAN MARSHALL was as good as his word. He had taken the blame for Janie's late return on his shoulders, saying that as a parent he felt responsible for ensuring she got home safely. Her stepfather had been suspicious, asking why she couldn't call ahead if what Stan said was right.

Thinking on his feet, Stan blamed a faulty telephone at home, claiming an engineer was due to fix it the next day.

That night it wasn't her fumbling first attempt at sex that interrupted her sleeping thoughts, or even the fear of pregnancy... it was the gentle touch of an older man's fingers making contact with her thigh.

His parting words as he left her on the doorstep were, 'Sweet dreams'.

She slept like a baby.

50

Present Day

'OK, he gets the picture, love. You don't have to say any more.'

Pete Vickers knelt at the side of his wife's chair and put his good arm around her. The tears were forming again, and she was stumbling over her words. Even so, she wriggled from his embrace.

'No,' she said. 'He deserves to know what a proper rat bag his father really was.'

'I assume you phoned the number?' said Gareth.

'Not for a while,' she said. 'When I eventually did, it was in response to the Sergeant Major's personal campaign to "protect" me.' She said the last words with a sneer. 'You guys have known me a long time and could never describe me as an academic. Unfortunately, my loving stepfather had trouble working that one out.'

July 1999

JANIE'S knees were shaking as she handed over the envelope to Paul Sullivan. The relief that had come with the end of the school term was countered by the fact she knew her report wouldn't be full of A-pluses and complimentary comments.

It didn't help that her ability to concentrate on her end-of-term exams had been compromised by fellow pupils intent on making her life a misery. The incident with Arnie at Gary Marshall's sixteenth birthday party had spread through the playground like wildfire and she'd acquired the tag 'Slag No.1'. Meanwhile, the boy responsible was roaming around like a Lord. Though he'd quit school, she caught sight of him in the street, the younger kids his willing servants. Arnie hadn't spoken to her since that night, but she had a feeling he'd been talking up his 'conquest' behind her back. Bastard.

Janie's stepdad ripped open the envelope and read the report in silence as she stood in front of him, hands gripping each other so hard her knuckles were turning white. She could see from his eyes he wasn't impressed. When he finished the letter, he placed it carefully back in the envelope without a word. Janie just wanted him to get on with it, tear her off a strip and send her to her room.

The silence was torture.

Beckoning her into the dining room, he pointed to a seat at the table. She suddenly felt an overwhelming desire to pee. Getting up again, she was about to ask permission to visit the toilet when he shouted in her face.

'Where do you think you're going, young lady?' The words were so full of venom, spittle formed at the corners of his mouth. 'Sit down!'

She crossed her legs, willing the feeling to go away. He lowered his muscular frame into the seat opposite and thrust the envelope in her direction. 'I want you to read this and tell me what you think,' he said.

Opening it, she saw a few C grades, mainly for things like domestic science and needlecraft, but the majority were D's. Alongside them were unfavourable remarks from her teachers. 'Struggles to pay attention in class', 'Prone to let her mind wander', 'If only she had as much interest in maths as she does in boys', 'Needs to listen more and talk less' … and so on and so on.

Paul Sullivan leaned forwards, his face a few inches from hers, the animosity radiating off him like heat from tarmac on a scorching summer's day. For a moment she was tongue-tied but knew she couldn't delay. He would expect some response, anything, or would mistake her silence for insolence.

'Not very good,' she said.

'Damn right it's not very good!' he stormed, raising a huge, hairy hand. She thought he was going to strike her but instead he pinched finger and thumb together in front of her face, his hand shaking. 'Your mother and I have sacrificed everything to help you get on,' he said through gritted, stained teeth. 'We knew you might find it hard – what with your real father not being about – so we compensated for that and made your life a bit easier. What do we get in return? A big, fat zero! I feel for your mother. She loves you to bits and doesn't see what I see – a sullen, ignorant, selfish young lady who likes nothing more than to throw our love back in our faces. Well, it's stopping here and now. All the treats, the nice clothes, the nights out with friends, the expensive hair-do's, the… hell, I'll show you, shall I?'

He sprang from the table and went over to an antique Welsh dresser standing against the back wall. Opening a small drawer, he pulled out an envelope and stomped back to the table, almost tipping over his chair in his keenness to punish his step-daughter. Janie was wide-eyed, unsure of what she could say or do. When she saw what he pulled from the envelope her heart sank. 'No, Dad, please … you can't!'

Too late. He held the flimsy piece of paper in his hand and ripped through it once, twice, three times, hurling it in the air like confetti. Her Backstreet Boys ticket, the one for the gig at Wembley Arena she and Anjie had been looking forward to for ages. They were going with Anjie's mum later in the summer holidays, a special treat she'd begged for on her knees. She couldn't believe he could be so callous.

'Now maybe you'll understand what disappointment really feels like… the kind of disappointment your mother and I feel every time you let us down.'

With that he casually walked from the room, leaving her to scrabble under the table in a desperate attempt to find all the pieces of the ticket in the vain hope she could stick them back together again.

That night she rang Stan and told him all about it.

JANIE waited nervously on the bench in Southend shopping centre, scanning the faces. She was dressed smartly in a two-piece trouser suit which her mother had bought her from one of the local charity shops. As soon as she'd mentioned a summer job, Irene had been thrilled, telling her stepfather, 'See? She can do it if she really puts her mind to it.'

He had grunted a response as he packed clothes neatly into a suitcase for a weekend reunion with some of his army mates up north. 'She's still under curfew,' he said. 'She mustn't be late.'

'Oh, you and your curfews!' her mother had said, but that was the total sum of her protest. Sometimes Janie wished Irene would join her in presenting a united front against the bully, but she seemed just grateful a man had stuck by her side while others had walked away.

Having taken an overland train from Barking to Southend Central, she was sitting on the bench listening to tunes on her Walkman when the hand fell on her shoulder. Whipping her head around, she saw Stan, a big grin plastered across his face.

'You nearly gave me a fuckin' heart attack,' she said, immediately regretting her choice of words. His expression changed, but rather than registering shock he broke into infectious laughter and soon she was laughing, too. From being wound up like a spring, he'd managed to put her at ease within seconds.

'Come on, I've a surprise for you,' he said.

Leading her through the shopping centre they ended up at a record store and, once inside, he marched her across to the section reserved for rock CDs. She'd vaguely heard of some of the bands but many she didn't know at all.

'Consider this the start of your education,' he said, grabbing a couple of CDs and marching off to the counter. She watched him speak to one of the assistants and the next moment power chords were blaring out of the speakers.

'I'm sure you'll like this one,' he said, and she stopped searching through the racks to listen.

'Who is it?' she asked.

'You don't know?'

'Sorry,' she said, 'I'm not an expert on old man music.'

He punched her playfully on the arm.

'Hey!'

'Well, don't be so cheeky, you! I'll give you old man music. These are one of the giants of rock and they'll outlast your little boy bands. It's a song called 'Back in Black' by a band named AC/DC.'

She shrugged. 'Not bad if you like that sort of thing.'

'Look, it's don't-give-a-shit music … just the kind you need in your life. You can let your hair down to it and lose your inhibitions. I'm gonna buy you the album.'

Before she could protest he marched off, returning moments later with a CD which he handed to her, the smile glued to his face.

'I can't take this,' she said. 'How do I explain—?'

'You say you bought it with your first week's wages.'

'But I haven't got a job.'

'Well, we know that, but your parents don't. We'll work something out. One of my mates down the market has a music stall and is crying out for someone to help at weekends and during the hols. He'll give you some work but, even if you don't fancy it, I don't mind paying you for the odd shift.'

'You want me to work for you?'

'Not exactly,' he said. 'Let's say I'll pay you for your company.'

'You're kidding?'

'It won't be much, just enough so you have an excuse to leave that bloody house. I hate seeing you upset. Kids your age have enough to deal with without having pressures at home.'

'If you're giving me money the least I can do is earn it,' she said.

'Well, if that's how you feel you can help me tidy up the warehouse. I've got to pop over there this afternoon.'

'Deal!' she said, sticking out her hand. 'As long as you get me back in time for curfew.'

Accepting the shake, he said, 'Curfew? That's not very rock n roll.'

IT was more like an extended garage space than a warehouse, sitting behind a row of houses in Dagenham. Unhooking the padlock, he opened the small door, stepped inside and turned on the light. Entering at his invitation, she took one look at the Aladdin's cave of boxes, plastic carrier bags and bits of furniture and laughed.

'Not quite what was advertised in the brochure,' she said.

'What do you mean?' he complained. 'There's thousands of pounds worth of stock here – and don't go telling any of your mates. I don't want to attract tea leaves.'

'Are you saying my mates are untrustworthy?'

'You forget I know most of them,' he said. 'People like that Arnold Dolan and Mitchell Tiggs, I wouldn't trust them to put their shoes on the right feet in the morning.'

'You're funny,' she said, laughing.

He offered her a seat on a sofa that had seen better days. She sat down, and he joined her, studying her closely. Strange. It was as if he was peering into her soul – her hopes, insecurities and fears laid out in front of him.

'How am I funny?' he said. 'You mean funny weird? I make you laugh, how?' It was a line he'd borrowed from one of his favourite films, *Goodfellas*. He doubted she'd seen it.

'Not weird. Not like that. You've got a great sense of humour, unlike those immature rat bags at school.'

He smiled. 'I'm glad I amuse you,' he said. 'Now, let's put some music on.'

'You've got a stereo in here?'

'You bet!' he said. 'I can't do without my fix.'

Walking to a table by the back wall, he then removed a vinyl record from its sleeve and popped it on the turntable which rested there. She heard the crackle of a needle hitting vinyl before a soft lilting melody filled the air.

'Come on,' he said. 'Dance. I'm dedicating this one to you.'

He put out his hand and stood. Caught up in the moment, she grabbed hold and joined him. She felt his fingers, gentle against her back, his digits barely making an impression. The goosebumps were back, and it wasn't even cold. She could smell his breath, minty from the chewing gum he regularly popped in his mouth, and the musk of an aftershave she didn't recognise. Before long they were waltzing around the room.

She didn't know quite what she was supposed to be doing, but it was more tender and exciting than a smooch at the end of the youth club disco, when some libido-swollen, acne-infected youth tried to cop a feel as you swayed in one place.

'Who is this?' she whispered.

'You're kidding,' he said. 'You don't recognise the magnificent Mick Jagger? It's "Lady Jane" by the Rolling Stones.'

'I'm not a lady,' she said.

'Well, you're not a girl either. You're too bright and mature for that.'

'Thanks.' She was genuinely pleased. She'd always felt more grown up than other girls in her class, perhaps because she'd been forced to learn so many of life's lessons at an early age. She also didn't have the kind of parents who bowed at her feet and catered to her every whim.

His stubble tickled her cheek and she was surprised how much she enjoyed the intimacy. She thought she would be repelled getting up close and personal with an adult male, but it provoked stirrings inside she'd never experienced before. Was this what it should be like? She clung tighter to him, the nails she'd battled so hard to grow digging into his back.

'I really like you,' he whispered.

'The boys say I'm fat.'

'That's ridiculous!' he muttered into her ear, making her tingle. 'You have the perfect figure. Men love a girl with curves. They're real women.'

'You think I'm a real woman?'

He nodded, his face inches from hers, and before she knew it they were sharing a long, slow, sensual kiss that seemed to go on forever. Just as she committed herself to it totally, he pulled away.

'I can't do this,' he said.

'Oh God!' She put her hand to her mouth. 'I'm so sorry. You're married. What was I thinking?'

She went to grab her handbag and coat from the sofa, her face colouring with shame.

'No!' he grabbed her by the forearms, his touch just firm enough to halt her progress. His inquisitive eyes sought hers and looked so deeply into her it was in that brief moment she knew what love was.

'It's not that,' he said. 'My wife and I haven't been close for years. We don't even sleep with each other. You're the first girl who has made an impression on me for … hell, I can't even think. When I say I can't do this, it's because of you. You need someone your own age: young and exciting, like, I don't know, that Dolan boy. I know you like him…'

She felt tears gathering and wasn't sure if she was upset or relieved. 'No!' she cried. 'You're wrong! Those boys are all horrible. Arnie used me. You're the only man I know who has treated me like a real person. I love it. I love—'

His eyes searched her, trying to work out whether she would be receptive to what he had to say next. He finally made a decision.

'You must understand,' he said. 'I have needs and wants, sexual drives … if I get any closer to you I will struggle to contain them. I'll want to touch you, to take our relationship further, as far as it can go. It would be wrong—'

'I'm not a virgin, you know,' she said. 'I want what you want. You're so kind and gentle and I know you would be patient with me. You can teach me.'

'Well, I—'

She kissed him again and led him to the sofa. Once it was done, there was no turning back.

51

Present Day

'IT lasted nearly a year,' she said. 'He got me weekend work on a fashion stall at the market with one of his mates. Do you remember?'

Gareth and Vickers both nodded. 'You were always the best dressed girl around,' said her husband. 'The others were jealous.'

'I got paid in clothes as well as money,' she said. 'I really enjoyed it and it meant I could see your dad whenever I wanted. If we needed to sneak off somewhere, I would ring Mum and tell her I had agreed to work late or that I was helping with stock taking. I know it sounds bad, but I was young and in love. I didn't think I was doing anything wrong.'

'You weren't,' said Vickers. 'He was. It's called grooming these days. You were 14 when you met him. It makes me sick.'

He was sat on the floor at her feet and, leaning forwards, Janie kissed his forehead.

'I'm sorry,' she said. 'This is awful for you … both of you.'

'Hell, imagine if those on the Boxers had found out,' said Vickers. 'You know what they do to nonces.'

'I hate that word,' she said.

'It's true, though, isn't it? I'm sorry, Gaz, but your old man was a fuckin' nonce, pure and simple.'

'I get it!' Gareth shouted. 'Now for fuck's sake shut up, Pete. I'm a victim here, too. Look at the way he walked out on us.'

'I might be to blame for that, too,' said Janie.

They fell silent, staring at her.

'I got pregnant.'

Bang.

'What?' Gareth cut through the suspense in the room.

'Your dad put a bun in the oven,' she said. 'He was scared shitless the Sergeant Major would turn over every rock to find out who was responsible, so he packed up and left like the coward he was. I know about that other girl up north, but I reckon she was a smokescreen. I told him I was pregnant on the day before you had that big football match. Mum thought I was going to Anjie's after school, but he picked me up and drove us to a quiet cafe near Fairlop Water.'

June 2000

'WHAT do you fancy? Coke? Milkshake?'

Janie felt the knot tighten in her stomach.

'You.'

'Apart from that.'

'Nothing … thanks.'

'You're sure?'

She nodded.

'OK, take a seat and I'll get myself a cup of tea. I've a couple of surprises for you!' he grinned.

And I've got one hell of a surprise for you, she thought.

Moments later he joined her at the table. He took a swig of his tea. 'I can't be long. I'm picking Gary up from football practice.'

'Sure.'

'You seem a bit … distant,' he said.

'I've got something—'

'Look, I reckon this will cheer you up.' He put his hand in his pocket and came out with something wrapped in a piece of white A4 paper.

'What is it?'

'Take a look.'

She opened it carefully. Read the words he had written on the sheet, the message signed simply S with a dozen kisses next to it.

'It's a mix tape,' he said. 'A bit naff I know, but I've put it together for you with love and care. Each song has the word Jane in the title, except the last. That's a newer song but I think you'll guess why it's there. Go on, open it.'

'I can't play it now, so what's the point?'

'Trust me.'

She levered open the case to find a card inside. Opening it, she discovered two tickets for a Backstreet Boys concert at Wembley in London that October. She'd heard the band were heading to the UK for a second tour and was wondering if there was a way she could get to see them.

'Wow!' she said. 'How do I get there?'

'I'll make the ultimate sacrifice and take you myself.' He grinned. 'Nothing's too much for my girl.'

'Even if she's seven months pregnant at the time?'

Silence. It seemed to stretch for minutes, his eyes interrogating her across the table without a word being exchanged.

Eventually he spoke. 'Whose is it?'

She was stunned. 'Yours, of course! I haven't been with anyone else …'

'There was that party.'

'You really mean that?' She was incredulous. 'You've had two kids yourself. You know how it works!'

'Shhhhhh! Keep your voice down!'

She lowered it slightly though frustration was building inside her. It wasn't supposed to be like this.

'That party was over a year ago. We've been seeing each other since then. It's your baby, love.'

She watched the blood drain from his face and realised she was being hard on him. It was bound to be a shock. She'd had more time to get used to the idea.

'Look,' she said, putting her hand over his. 'Is it really that bad? I'm 15 now and I'll be 16 by the time the baby is born. All we have to do is hold off for a bit then you come in and ride to my rescue. Don't you see? It's the perfect chance to leave your wife, be with me, and start a family. We could move away.'

'They'll crucify me,' he said, looking off into space. 'Paul – your dad – will kill me, for Christ's sake. You stupid girl, you've done this on purpose! I thought you were on the pill. You said it was OK that I didn't wear a condom.'

'That's because you didn't like them!' she protested. 'I didn't insist you wore one because you were always talking about how much you hated going to bed "wearing your wellies", remember?'

'But when you said it was OK, I assumed—'

She felt the tears pressing against the back of her eyelids. He grabbed her hand and put something in it, closing her fingers around it.

'Get rid of it,' he said. 'For both our sakes.'

His hand released hers and she heard his chair scrape against the tile floor. She watched his retreating back through a filter of tears, the familiar donkey jacket swaying as he disappeared out of the door and out of her life.

'HE left me stranded and I didn't know what to do,' she said. 'He'd given me £50, obviously towards an abortion, then legged it. I was distraught. I thought he loved me. I had kept the relationship secret for his sake which, at the time, added to the fun and excitement. By walking out like that, with barely a glance back, he tore my world apart.'

'What did you do?' asked Gareth. 'How did you get home?'

'I rang Anjie, of course,' she said. 'Told her I was in a bind and that some bloke had dumped me. She got Chuck to pick me up. I was in such a state I honestly didn't know what to do. I thought about taking Mum's anti-depression tablets and ending it all but couldn't go through with it. I wanted to be hurtful, though, and when she found me with them I told her that it was pressure from the Sergeant Major that had pushed me to it. She was cold to him for weeks after that, but it made my life a bit easier.'

'What about the baby?' asked Gareth.

'I had the abortion and Anjie came with me. She's the only one who ever knew. I said the father was some knob head we met on a night out and I hadn't been careful enough. She understood. I'd given the impression I'd been with all sorts of blokes so people didn't twig the truth. The real father fled, of course, moving on to his next innocent victim.'

Gareth's mind was awash with conflicting emotions. He hadn't realised how close he'd come to having another sibling, something which would have caused the family more pain and shame. He felt fury towards his father and anger towards Janie, though he knew deep down he wasn't being fair. She'd been a vulnerable child, not much older than Gareth's own sister, and his dad had taken advantage. He wondered what other disgraceful acts Stan Marshall might have committed during his lifetime.

Through it all his over-riding emotion was fear. Was he capable of similar despicable acts? He had his father's genes.

'I didn't kill him,' she said.

Gareth shook his head.

'No,' he said. 'You didn't.'

He picked up the birthday card from the mantelpiece.

'This is your writing, isn't it, Pete?'

'Yeah,' agreed Vickers.

'It's a real giveaway,' said Gareth.

The couple stared at him, waiting for an explanation.

52

GARETH took a swig of his beer and sat on the chair Vickers had vacated. He had known these people since his early teens but was seeing them in a completely different light.

When they originally got together, friends called them the odd couple. Janie Sullivan was loud, bubbly and vivacious, a young girl who dressed in all the modern fashions and craved to be the centre of attention. Pete Vickers was the opposite, serious and reserved, studious and quietly clever, the least likely gang member you would ever come across. It had its advantages. Pete was able to stay below the radar while the more high-profile Boxer Boys like Arnold and Chuck hogged the limelight.

Many questioned whether Vickers would be 'exciting' enough for the whirlwind that was Janie Sullivan. It was only very close friends like Anjelica Dolan who thought them a match made in heaven. She knew Janie had hidden insecurities and needed a calming influence in her life.

'When I tracked you down, I couldn't work out why you would run away to France without letting anyone know, including your kids,' said Gareth. 'None of it made sense, particularly the fake kidnapping. Then again, I hadn't thought of you as a murderer on the run.'

Janie stroked her husband's head and he looked up at her. 'I was worried to death,' said Janie. 'I thought you'd been snatched by that rival gang and feared your body would be found mutilated and dumped, just like those drug dealers.'

'The mix tape told me a lot, but this made everything clear,' said Gareth, holding up the birthday card, Simon's name scrawled on the envelope. 'There was a message left on Dad's body. He had tried to rip it up but some of the letters were found nearby. There was an A on once piece of paper and a D and O on another. I guess the rest had blown away. When the police showed it to me at first I thought it was Arnie's doing, then I realised it could be any of the Dolans. There was one thing the police and I had dismissed as irrelevant though. In the middle of the O there were some marks. The police thought they were just smudges, but I reckoned they resembled an emoji character, two eyes and a mouth turned down in an unhappy, angry expression. It seemed preposterous but then I saw this envelope. Like to decorate your O's don't you, Pete? It's become a habit when you're signing cards or writing messages.'

He held up the envelope. Inside the O of the name Simon was a smiling Emoji.

'No!' Vickers shot to his feet. 'I couldn't ... I didn't ... what the fuck?'

'Old habits die hard,' said Gareth. 'Bruce told me the other day he saw one of the Boxer Boys' vans close to Dad's murder scene. I knew Big Mo had ordered Chuck to settle an old score with Stan and suspected that was what had happened. Then I realised it was impossible.'

Vickers raised his eyebrows. 'Why?'

'Ask your wife.'

'Shit!' Janie put her hand to her mouth. 'Chuck couldn't have been there because he was here! He came looking for you the day after you stormed out. He hadn't heard anything from you and was worried because of all the kidnappings. He saw the state of me and called his Mrs, who came around too. They were as good as gold. She kept an ear out for the kids while he calmed me down. It was the evening after our clear-the-air talk, Pete, when I told you about Stan.'

'Right,' said Gareth. 'I guess that didn't go down well.'

'No,' she agreed, stroking her husband's head again. 'Before he left me he kept muttering words like nonce and pervert under his breath. You really did it? Killed him?'

Vickers buried his head in his hands and said nothing.

'You called Dad a nonce and a pervert,' said Gareth. 'What about a paedo?'

'That, too,' muttered Vickers.

'That was the word you wrote on the card we found on my dad's body, wasn't it, Pete?' said Gareth. 'It wasn't Dead or Alive, or Arnie Dolan, or just Dolan. It was a clear, unequivocal message to tell my dad you knew what he'd done.'

Peter Vickers didn't answer. He stared off into space as if trying to capture a memory just out of reach.

'I was looking at it the wrong way, all along,' said Gareth. 'I already had it in my mind that Arnie was involved, but it was far simpler than that. You wanted the old man to know what he was being punished for so scrawled out a crude PAEDO message and left it on him. He couldn't accept it, of course, and tried to destroy it completely but didn't have the strength. The P and the E disappeared but the other letters stuck under his coat. I think it's time you told us all about that night, Pete, don't you?'

53

March 30, 2016

THE marriage had been a sham and now it was over.

On the four-hour journey – M25, M1, M42 and M6 – all Vickers could do as he stared at the traffic ahead was go over his wife's sordid words in his head.

Vickers had been under no illusions when he married Janie Sullivan. Stories abounded about the good-time girl from the Boxers' Estate who lived for the moment and refused to hide her light under a bushel. In fact, it was her open personality that attracted him in the first place, when he was 15 and she two years younger. She had a way of making a bloke feel special and a seductive gaze he just couldn't resist. She was easy going, cheeky and gave the impression she was up for anything. He envied her.

Vickers had no idea how to speak to girls at that age and had lost count of the number of times he wasted the opportunity to progress their friendship further. When he finally felt capable of taking the plunge she became off limits because she was seeing his mate, Arnie. He remembered clearly the moment Tigger turned to him at Gazza's sixteenth birthday party and said, 'Bloody hell, Pete, I just seen Arnie giving that Sullivan bird a right seeing to and she's loving it. She's moaning like one of them girls in those *Scream* films, ha ha.'

Vickers had left the party immediately, his heart broken, a sick, hollow feeling in his stomach. After that, he gave her a wide berth, taking ridiculous detours just to avoid bumping into her at school or on the street. Arnie, in the meantime, just treated it as another notch on his bedpost.

It wasn't until he was 18 that Vickers connected with her again. Kids on the estate graduated from youth club to the Hope and Anchor as a rite of passage and it was difficult to avoid people when all the young adults in the area congregated in the same places. Janie and Anjie often tagged along with the Boxer Boys and Vickers still felt pangs of rejection when the girl he adored disappeared into the night with Arnie, despite his tendency to spread his attention fairly among his harem of female admirers.

It was the night before Arnie was arrested that Vickers and Janie finally got together. The rest of the lads had gone to the West End high on adrenaline after their clash with Cardiff fans outside Upton Park, but he'd taken a beating and was licking his wounds. After Anjie disappeared for the night claiming to have something important to do, Janie spent the rest of the evening in his company and they snogged on the way home. Later, with Arnie heading for a long stint in jail, Vickers seized his chance and whisked Janie down the aisle.

The next few years were bliss until Arnie was released and paradise destroyed. Vickers stupidly offered his best friend a sofa to crash on for a few days and Arnie repaid him by raping Janie in the kitchen one morning. When he learnt the full story, Vickers cut all ties with Arnie but couldn't erase the nagging feeling his wife had sent out the wrong signals.

For Janie it was a different story. She blamed her husband, feeling that a stronger man would never have let it happen. He was the one who had invited Arnold Dolan into their home, so it was he who should feel responsible.

Robbed of her chance to punish the real culprit when Arnie was confined to a wheelchair, she took her simmering animosity out on her husband. The first physical manifestation of that rage was a simple slap to the face because he forgot to bring home something she needed for dinner, and more alarming and sustained assaults followed. She threw a kettle at him, stabbed him in the knee with nail scissors, broke a wine bottle over his head and punched and kicked him when he arrived home late having forgotten he'd promised to babysit.

It was only when her mum died that Janie re-evaluated her actions. In a tender, drunken moment they made love for the first time in months and she whispered to him how sorry she was for the way she'd acted. When she told him of her fear that she was having a nervous breakdown he begged her to see the doctor. Taking up his advice, she was then referred to a psychotherapist.

The previous night, over a bottle of wine, she'd told him all about those sessions and confessed to some of the mistakes she made during her younger days. She talked about her treatment by the Sergeant Major, losing her virginity to Arnie – which she now viewed as rape, too – and finally her relationship with Stan Marshall.

Though he'd tried to hide his shock and disgust, he lost the battle when he heard about the pregnancy. Unable to handle the fact she'd kept such a massive secret from him, he lost the plot.

Spending the night on the sofa, Vickers had then hastily packed an overnight bag and dropped the kids at school that morning before going to a local cafe to gather his thoughts. Recognising the waitress as an on-off girlfriend of Arnold Dolan's youngest brother, Bruce, he'd overheard her conversation with a friend as he waited for his coffee.

'Bloody Bruce is at his brother's beck and call,' the girl was saying. 'He was supposed to take me out last night, then texted to say he was taking that cripple to Stoke-on-bloody-Trent. Something about visiting his long-lost dad.'

Vickers was perplexed. Arnie hated his dad and, anyway, wasn't Big Mo Dolan incarcerated on the Isle of Wight, not locked up in Stoke. Then the tumblers clicked. It was Arnie's biological father they were going to see, Stan bloody Marshall, the source of the flaming row which had torn him and Janie apart. He made a decision instantly. He would follow the trail of the Dolan boys and they would lead him straight to Stan the Nonce. He had no idea what he would do when he found himself eye to eye with the man, but at least he had a mission.

Now, after what seemed an eternity, his eyes locked on the signpost for the Potteries. Even though it was late spring a chill had seeped into the cab of the Transit van he was driving. He always thought Stoke was in the Midlands, but the biting wind suggested he was much further north.

Following the signs, he passed the Britannia Stadium where Stoke City played their home games, jolting memories of an away day with Gary and Arnie. With no idea where he was heading, he exited the carriageway and stopped at a garage for directions to the city centre.

'Not much in Stoke, duck,' the girl on the till told him. 'You'll want to go Uppanly.'

'Where's Uppanly?' he asked, and for a moment she looked confused. Then she roared with laughter.

'Oh, sorry, Duck, tha's not from 'round here,' she said. 'I mean you need to go up to Hanley. It's one of the towns. Look, I'll show you on thit map …'

After a 10-minute drive he reached his destination and searched in the back of the van for something warm to keep out the chill. He found an old, black hoodie he guessed belonged to one of the street dealers and pulled it on. It was on the tight side, but it would do. He raised the hood. Beginning his search, Vickers figured local pubs were his best option, suspecting that if Arnie was meeting his old man for the first time, they would both need a drink to calm their nerves.

Drawing a blank in the first three pubs, he struck lucky at the Coach and Horses by the bus station. He was just about to cross the road and enter when the double doors opened and a man in a wheelchair came out. Vickers watched as Arnie headed down a side road, his brother Bruce following.

Dawning on him that they probably had a disabled sticker which enabled them to park anywhere, Vickers set off on a lung-bursting dash back to his own vehicle, retrieving the van and heading in the direction of the pub again. He was lucky. Just as he pulled up outside, a people carrier emerged from the side street with Bruce at the wheel. Ducking down to avoid being recognised, Vickers then pushed himself upright and eased out into the traffic, tracking them for two miles.

Eventually the Dolan boys pulled up in the car park of a down-at-heel boozer called The Blue Dolphin Hotel. Parking opposite, he decided to wait them out and see where it led him. As minutes turned to an hour, the adrenaline of the chase began leaving his system. It had been a long drive following a night spent on the sofa and he could feel the weight of his eyelids pressing down. Desperately in need of something to keep him alert, Vickers reached into the glove compartment and was delighted to find a small bottle. Holding it up to the light he saw a couple of small, white tablets.

Speed.

Just the job.

He emptied one into his hand, knocked it back and washed it down with water he'd bought from the service station. Then he settled down again to wait, listening to tunes on the radio for company.

After a short while his phone buzzed, and he picked it up, viewing the caller ID. It was Janie, but he didn't want to talk to her so let it pass to voicemail. Then, just after 5.30p.m., Arnie's SUV emerged from the car park and turned right. Without hesitation, he followed.

Now fully wired, he felt he was closing in on the moment when he would come face-to-face with the man who had sexually abused his wife when she was a gullible 14-year-old. Anticipation turned to annoyance, though, when the van stopped outside a dodgy looking back street boozer and only Bruce emerged.

Shit, shit, shit!

Where was Arnie? This couldn't be right. It was the older Dolan who was meeting his father, not his gofer. He slammed the van into reverse and was about to head back to the Blue Dolphin when a voice in his brain told him to check inside the pub first. Pulling the hood over his head with trembling hands, he followed Bruce into the pub. The sign above the door announced he was entering The Sheldon and that it offered a variety of local ales, not that Vickers had any intention of drinking.

Even at 6.00 p.m. in the evening the place was teeming. There was a queue at the dartboard in the corner and old men were hunched over dominoes at another table. Where the fuck was Bruce, though, and why was he here without his brother? The impression Vickers had formed was that these days Bruce couldn't take a dump without Arnold's permission.

There! The youngest Dolan was sitting opposite some tramp at a table in the corner. They were deep in conversation and Vickers shifted position to try to get a better view. No sooner had he done so than the tramp raised his head and a close study of the face told the watcher he'd found his quarry.

It was incredible. Although the hair and beard had grown massively out of control, certain mannerisms were pure Stan Marshall. Hell, he even wore the old donkey jacket from the days when he worked at Walthamstow Market.

In other circumstances, Vickers might have felt this harmless down-and-out had suffered enough. Recalling the previous night, though, he began clenching and unclenching his fists, the anger rising. This den of filth and flotsam was the ideal place for an old nonce to hide. Here he could see out his days safe in the knowledge his past would never raise its ugly head.

Surprise, surprise.

Vickers wanted to storm up to the old man, grab him by the throat and beat the living crap out of him. But a small voice in his brain told him such rash actions rarely paid off and he would do better to return to the van and clear his thoughts.

Blood boiling, he pushed his way out of the pub before either man spotted him. Back in the van he reached into the glove compartment for the remaining pill … and his hand touched something else. Perplexed, he lifted it out. It was a knife, at least 6-inches long. He was going to put it back, but something stopped him. Concealing it in the pocket of the hoodie, he began the waiting game again.

54

HE let the phone vibrate on the dashboard a few times before reaching for it and checking his voicemail.

'Hey, Vickers, where are you, geezer?'

It was his partner-in-crime, Chuck Dolan.

'We need a proper chat, mate. We're no nearer to tracking down those ratbags who firebombed the boozer and that bastard Turk will want to see his cut in a few days. I can't put him off much longer. You're the money man. I need to know exactly where we stand in case there's another war coming our way. I can't do it on my own, mate. If I don't hear from you soon, I'll pop over tonight.'

Vickers muttered 'shit!' and deleted the call. Automatically his phone moved on to play an earlier message.

'Pete, it's me.'

His heart pounded, and his breath caught in his throat.

Janie.

'I don't know where you are or what you're planning to do but I just wanted to say I'm so, so sorry. I never meant to hurt you and if I kept things from you it was to spare you pain. I feel a fool for dropping this bombshell on you. To be honest, for years I'd wiped Stan clean from my mind. I was disgusted and ashamed of myself, to be honest, especially over the abortion.'

The voice went quiet and he heard the faint sound of sobbing. Janie had shed tears of joy when the kids were born but never had he heard her give vent to such undiluted misery. It winded him like a punch to the gut.

'I think about our Diane (sob) and what I would do to anyone (sob) who took advantage of her in the way Stan used me. It makes me (sniff) sick to the stomach.'

He had a vision then of Janie, the bubbly young girl he'd known at 13 with her whole life ahead of her, smiling cheekily at him and offering him a sherbet dip. The picture in his head morphed instantly into the hardened, aggressive and slightly insensitive woman he'd met in the Hope five or six years later, her main aim in life to enjoy herself and damn the consequences. How could such a sweet, caring person be transformed into someone capable of delivering a physical battering to the man she was supposed to love?

Stan Marshall had done that. He was responsible for stealing the light from her soul, aided by Arnold Dolan and the Sergeant Major. But mostly it was Stan the Man. He had turned her from a trusting child into a devil-may-care young woman in barely more than a year. Since then her issues had grown and festered, being released suddenly in a frenzy of fists, feet and, on occasion, teeth. He could still feel the pain she had caused him. No, not her. Him. Stan. His evil having made a home deep inside her, like a parasite. Pete hadn't realised it at the time, but it was probably this more than anything that had provoked him to make this journey to Stoke.

'How can I blame you for walking out?' Janie's voice broke into his private thoughts. 'If it had been the other way around (sniff) I probably would have done the same. All I can say is if I had my time again I would be open and up front with you ...'

If she had her time again.

If she had her time again Vickers would want to protect her and keep her out of the hands of predators like Marshall. His hand went to his face to wipe his own tears away.

'Please come home, Pete,' Janie said, her throat catching on the words. 'Simon and Di need their dad but, more than that, I need you. You are my rock (sniff, sniff), my lover and my best friend and although I haven't shown it much of late, I have never loved you more. If there is *any* chance we can work it out, please let me know.'

'End of message', said the electronic voice.

He was so choked up he could barely see, his body an empty husk, insides torn to pieces by emotions he struggled to understand. He had always been susceptible to a sob story, but this was his own and he had no idea how it would end. He needed to focus on something, anything.

Putting his hand into the window pocket he pulled out a pen and some packaging from the sandwiches he'd bought during the journey. Ripping the discarded cardboard into a square, he carved the letters into it, his anger spilling from the pen. Going over it again and again, the tears continued to flow as he released his pent-up anger.

P...A...E...D...O

He didn't even realise it when he added the two dots and the curved line to the O, the emoji for a miserable face. He was running on muscle memory.

Pausing, he stared at the ceiling through the misted curtain of his vision. Shit! For a short time, he'd forgotten what he was doing here, outside this scummy shit-hole in the backwaters of the Potteries. Wiping at his eyes, he looked across the road ... and froze. Bruce Dolan was standing at the kerb looking directly at him!

Now, instead of turning towards his own vehicle, the youngest Dolan headed in his direction. Damn, this was the worst scenario he could imagine. There was no way he could handle an interrogation, and he really didn't want Arnie alerted to his presence. Thankfully, he was still wearing the hoodie.

Vickers ducked down, opened the door gently and slid out onto the pavement. Hearing the footsteps getting closer, he realised Bruce was just the other side of the van. Crouching, Vickers moved away from the vehicle, using other parked cars as cover.

Risking a peak over his shoulder, he saw Bruce peering into the cab, a baffled expression on his face. The Dolan kid had his hand resting above his eyebrows to filter out the glare of the streetlights. Moving along the van, he was looking for clues as to why it would be parked there.

As Bruce disappeared around the back of the vehicle, Vickers saw his chance, darting across the road into an alleyway.

It was the perfect hiding place.

PEERING out from the lane, Vickers watched Bruce scratch his head, walk back along the pavement and return to his SUV. A minute later the engine rumbled into life and the youngest Dolan drove slowly away, once again peering into the parked van as he left.

Hearing a noise behind him Vickers span around. Nothing. He retreated further into the alley to investigate and, as his vision cleared, he made out a figure walking away from him beyond the hazy glow of a streetlamp. Though the person had a stoop, Vickers sensed he was tall and wiry and, edging closer, he recognised the coat and long, scruffy hair. It was as if fate had taken a hand.

A dark alley in a location far from home.

A person who deserved to pay for their sins.

Adrenaline coursing through his body, Vickers was unsure whether it was natural or caused by the speed kicking in. The figure had stopped in a particularly poorly lit area and instinctively Vickers tightened his grip on the handle of the knife in his pocket. A flare of light and the smell of burning tobacco alerted him to the fact the old man was having a cigarette.

Seizing his chance Vickers rushed forwards, wrapping his hand around the nonce's mouth. Shocked, his victim dropped the cigarette as Vickers bent the body backwards, pulling it down onto the blade. He felt the warmth of sticky fluid embalm his hand and quickly withdrew the weapon before plunging it into the side of the neck. Blood spurted backwards at speed, Vickers unable to avoid the spray hitting him in the face.

Retrieving the weapon, he moved around to look his victim in the eye. There was no glimmer of recognition and, feeling total contempt for the old man, Vickers shoved him hard on the forehead, sending him toppling backwards onto the cobbles.

Walking away down the lane, Vickers stopped briefly to spit into a tissue and rub blood from his face, the way his mum used to clean him when he got mucky as a kid. As he did so, he heard it. To the normal ear it would pass as just a faint gurgle, but his senses were so finely tuned at that moment, he was able to pick out the words.

'No, please! Don't go … I'm hurt!' pleaded his victim. 'Look … tell me, what am I supposed to have done?'

Suddenly, like fog lifting, Vickers knew what he had to do. It was important the old man understood exactly why he was being punished. As his lifeblood drained away he would be able to reflect on his crimes. Marching back to the prostrate figure, Vickers pulled the card from his pocket. Feeling pure hatred for the figure in front of him, he coughed up a clump of spit and let it fall onto the other man's cheek, feeling a sadistic pleasure in watching him squirm.

'You know what you've done!' he growled. 'But just in case you need a reminder …'

Reaching down, he pressed the card into his victim's hand.

WHAT Pete Vickers didn't know was that someone else came across Stan Marshall's body five minutes after he'd fled the scene. A well-built figure in designer clothes knelt down beside the tramp, the only sound that of expensive jewellery jangling as he reached out a hand and searched for a pulse. Turning the cold, lifeless face towards him, Amir Masood muttered, 'So this is how you get out of paying your bills, Stanley.'

Standing, he connected with a careless kick at the corpse … and froze. His boot had struck something heavy. Bending again, he brushed some scraps of wastepaper from the dead man and pushed his hand into a coat pocket. There it was, in the lining. A package. He retrieved it, opened the flap and looked inside.

'OK,' he said, slapping the cold skin of the dead man's face. 'We're all square now. Be seeing you around … or not, as the case may be.'

Concealing the envelope in one of his overcoat pockets, Masood followed the same route as Pete Vickers, heading home to count his unexpected windfall.

55

Present Day

'WHAT now?' asked Janie. 'Do we sit and wait for the police?'

Gareth sank to his haunches in front of her. 'Look, Janie, I owe you an apology. He was my dad and I had no idea any of this was going on. Yes, after he left me I started to learn about the affairs and the cheating, but I swear I didn't have a clue—'

'It's not your fault,' she said.

'I know but saying it doesn't make me feel any less responsible. I can't do anything to make it right now, but I can keep your secret. I don't condone murder and at the end of the day he was my father. But he never acknowledged the wrongs he did and he's in no position to make up for it now. Well, maybe I can. The police already have a prime suspect – a loan shark to whom Stan owed money. He's dead, so it's not as if he'll rot away in jail for a crime he didn't commit. And the last thing my family needs is Dad's messy past being laid out in front of a jury. If we keep our nerve, I reckon this is one secret that will never see the light of day.'

They sat in silence for a moment, thinking over the implications.

'There will always be rumours, of course,' said Gareth, a thought jarring him back into action. 'Your friends, Fenella and Sharon, seem to have a good idea what went on. They almost told me as much the day the Hope reopened.'

'They saw me with Stan once,' said Janie. 'It was embarrassing. We had just had lunch in the market and were on our way back to the stalls. He pulled me down a lane for a kiss. When we emerged those two mares were there, sniggering away. They didn't know the full story but, even so, I had to swear them to secrecy.'

'Skeletons in the cupboard,' said Vickers, his mind revisiting the day of Irene Sullivan's funeral. 'That's what they were talking about when I escaped for a cigarette on the day of your mum's funeral. With all the drama surrounding the fire I'd forgotten all about it.'

'When did you decide to kill him, Pete?' asked Gareth.

'It wasn't like that,' said Vickers. 'The idea was to get him to confess then march him along to the police, but my anger took over. After I'd killed him the guilt weighed so heavily on me that, when I went to Marseille, part of me wanted to end it all. I never expected to see Janie and the kids again and. I think that's why I took such stupid risks in fighting those Russians. I was having a breakdown.'

'Well, you've got another chance now so don't mess up,' said Gareth. 'It's been a long day and if you don't mind I think I need to go home. I'm missing Anjie and Maxi like crazy so I'll take a rain check on the overnight stop.'

'Sure,' said Vickers, raising his can and looking at the ceiling. Gareth knew he was thinking about his kids lying asleep upstairs, blissfully ignorant of the drama that had been unfolding.

Gareth put down his beer can and headed for the spare room to pack, leaving Pete and Janie to rebuild their shattered life.

56

GARETH was in a good mood as he took the elevator up to the editorial floor. He was popping into the office to make sure the sports desk was ready to handle the big Wales football match before resuming his period of compassionate leave.

It had been great to get back to his family after days spent on the road. Anjie was delighted he was in one piece and even happier when she heard that Janie and Pete Vickers were making a go of it. As promised, he kept the truth about his father's murder a secret.

When Anjie had opened the door to him she looked radiant. Pregnancy suited her, despite the odd bout of morning sickness and the fact she struggled to find clothes that didn't cramp her style. He had been expecting a real rollicking for the Marseille business but as she squeezed him to her all she said was, 'How on earth am I supposed to keep you out of trouble?'

Anjie's latest scan had provided more good news. Their child was healthy, and the vital signs were good. Maxi insisted he took the small scan picture of his sibling to school for show and tell. For the briefest moment, Gareth found himself wondering what size Janie's child had been when it was aborted.

Other than that, he was happy for everything to return to normal. In the last few months he'd solved a murder, repaired a marriage and organised coverage of two big sporting events. There was just one hurdle to overcome before he could draw a line under this chapter of his life: the funeral of his father.

Walking out onto the Tribune office floor, he was surprised to find all the department work spaces empty. Where was Jacko and the sports production team? Checking his mobile phone, he realised it had just gone 10.15 a.m. A normal working day on the Trib began at nine thirty.

The first human movement he saw was his friend Monica making a bee-line for him.

'Hi, Mon,' he said.

The news editor gave him a stern look. 'You haven't been up to your old tricks have you, mate?' she asked. 'Lana isn't happy.'

A sick feeling encroaching on his stomach, he wondered if somehow his flying visit to Marseille had come to light. Anjie had recognised him from the TV footage so maybe others had, too.

'What do you mean?' he asked.

'She has a face like thunder,' said Monica. 'Been like it for a couple of days. She's called your entire sports team in this morning for an impromptu conference.'

'I spoke to Jacko the other day,' said Gareth. 'He thought everything was going brilliantly.'

'That's the other thing,' said Monica. 'No Jacko. He's been acting pretty strangely ever since that awards' night when he got drunk and we had to send him home. Maybe—'

She mimed a pushing movement with her elbow.

'No,' he said. 'She wouldn't ditch him just like that. He's part of the furniture. It would cost the company a fortune and the union would cause a right stink. It wouldn't play well with the local TV stations, either.'

'Maybe he turned up drunk. That would be gross misconduct and instant dismissal, right?'

Gareth was forced to interrupt the chat when he caught sight of the editor's secretary waving her hands frantically in his direction. 'I've been summoned,' he said. 'Better go. I'll fill you in later.'

'Promises, promises,' she said with a cheeky smile.

'AH, Mr Prince,' said Lana as he walked into the glass-fronted office. He had been here many times before in his first year on the newspaper, normally to receive a rebuke of some description. 'Thanks for popping in. I know you have some family matters to attend to so I won't keep you.'

He tried to detect a note of sarcasm in her voice but his Lana radar was way off this morning. He took a seat next to the chief sports sub-editor. Two other production journalists and a young reporter were also in attendance.

'I'm afraid to say I have some bad news,' she said. 'Not being one to beat about the bush I'll give it to you straight. Jacko's ill. For the last month or so, he has been having various tests and yesterday he was told by a specialist at the Heath Hospital he has kidney cancer. It is curable, as far as we know, but will require an operation and an extended leave of absence, so I'm afraid he won't be back any time soon.'

There was a sharp intake of breath. Gareth exhaled, making an 'urgh!' sound as if he'd been punched in the gut. The news was worse than he could possibly have imagined. He couldn't blag his way out of this situation. Peter Jackson had fought his corner on countless occasions, bringing him to Wales contrary to the advice of many, including Lana. The old man had become a friend and Gareth owed him big time.

'Does The Leg ... does JW know?' he asked.

'Yes,' said Lana. 'I spoke to him this morning. Obviously, he's as upset as we all are. More so, I suspect, because the two of them go way back. In the early days I'm sure JW did a lot for Jacko's career and more recently it's been vice versa.'

Her gaze passed slowly over the anxious, blood-drained faces.

'Obviously, we will do the usual, send a card and flowers. I've spoken to his wife and told her that if there is anything she needs ... Well, I'm sure each of you will want to get in touch with the family yourselves. I can't pretend Jacko has taken it well. It's hit him hard. You may have noticed a change in his personality recently. He's not been the jokey, chatty Jacko we know and love, and I can't say I'm surprised.'

Andy Garvin, the chief sports sub-editor, asked the question lurking at the back of all their minds.

'What now? With the desk, I mean. I guess we can bumble on without him but—'

'There will be no bumbling,' said Lana, standing with her arms pressed firmly on the desk. 'I've had to think on my feet and make some quick decisions. Jacko is not a young man, he's in his early 60s. He's due to retire in a couple of years anyway and he has indicated to me that he doubts he would want to come back to work in a full-time capacity once his treatment is completed.

'During our chat, he informed me of everything that has been going on over the last few weeks and I know he backs the temporary solution I've come up with. In football parlance, I'm appointing a caretaker manager, and Jacko and I are convinced there is only one man for the role.'

Her eyes fell on Gareth. 'We might not always be on the same page, Mr Prince – and I must admit there have been times when I quite honestly wanted to throw you to the wolves – but your work over the last few weeks, with Wales involved in two major sporting events on opposite sides of the globe, has been nothing short of outstanding.'

Gareth almost choked on the compliment. He didn't expect praise at the best of times, but it was pretty much unprecedented coming from Lana Desmund.

'We are moving into a new era, people,' she said. 'Newsrooms are having to change and adapt to cope with it. These days our competition isn't coming from other papers, it's coming from the Internet, whether it's information about a top sports personality or the car and home advertising market. Papers have always relied on the revenue from homes supplements or car showroom features to pay the wages of their staff, but these days everyone has their own website on which to advertise their goods. Instant access to the net has turned newspapers into a different beast.'

She stared off into the newsroom, watching people scurrying about their business. 'Jacko was from the old school,' she continued. 'He was a brilliant sports journalist and a man of his time. We have all heard his stories and marvelled at the way he performed in a tough environment when he had far less technology at his fingertips than we have now.

'But as you sports people often say, "It's horses for courses", and the reason I have decided Gareth is the man to take up the mantle is that all the things we have managed to do digitally during this exceedingly busy period for Welsh sport is down to him. Whereas we would have concentrated totally on the paper before, we now have to satisfy an instant audience through *Facebook*, *Twitter* and *Instagram*, *YouTube* videos, podcasts, blogs … you name it, they all add another string to our bow and get our brand out there. During this Euro campaign and, of course, the rugby tour down under we have utilised these new tools highly effectively, and for that I believe we have Mr Prince to thank.'

She saw a couple of sceptical looks in the room. 'You're wondering how we know it's been effective? Because of the interactive communication we have with readers and the number of clicks we get to our website.'

Gareth looked around the table, questioning whether he had the support of the other staff. It was difficult to read. Web journalism wasn't popular with those brought up in a different era, and he could sympathise in many ways. Quite often these days the extra effort needed for story gathering and research was sacrificed for an instant response to someone else's breaking news. If there were any objectors, though, they were keeping their power dry.

'Would you care to say anything, Mr Prince?'

Jolted back into the present, Gareth nodded his head slowly.

'Like a sports team, we're only as good as our weakest link,' he told the small gathering. 'I believe we have an exceptionally strong team and can thrive and grow while still sticking to the principles Jacko held dear. I, for one, hope that at some time we welcome him back and he will appreciate that we have kept things ticking over for him in the right way. Meanwhile, thank you, Lana, for the opportunity. I will do my utmost not to let you down.'

'I know you will, Mr Prince,' said the editor. 'It's not making too much of a deal of it to say all our careers may depend on how you perform.'

No pressure then, he thought, resuming his seat.

EPILOGUE

EVEN though the weather was pleasantly warm, Gareth still felt a shiver run through him as the casket disappeared behind the curtain. Putting his arm out, he hugged his sister, Lily, and allowed her to sob on his shoulder. She and her husband, Mac, had travelled down from Inverness to the Potteries the previous day while Gareth and Anjie had driven up from Wales early that morning, leaving Max in the care of their reliable friend Will Shakespeare.

Gareth hadn't explained to Lily the significance of Arnie Dolan being there – she had enough on her plate coping with the death of her father. To point out she had another brother would not only be hard to put into words, he feared it might turn a sombre occasion into a farce. He was happy for the moment to let Lily believe Gareth's best mate was there to provide him with moral support.

After the ceremony they retired to a pub around the corner from the crematorium where Lily told him how she'd tried to persuade their mother and stepdad to attend.

'Whatever you say, Dad and Mum were married for a long time and had much in common, namely us two,' she told him. 'Reg was also one of Dad's best mates. I don't think he was totally against the idea, but she wouldn't budge. Some of the things Dad put her through were impossible to forgive, I guess.'

She was barely skimming the surface, thought Gareth. For the first time he wondered whether his mother ever had an inkling of Stan Marshall's relationship with an underage girl barely a year older than Lily.

As for Arnie, he seemed different somehow, more at peace with himself. The former gang leader was quiet and circumspect throughout the day and it was only when they sat alone in a corner of the pub later that he confided in his brother and former best friend.

'What I did to Chuck was wrong,' he said.

Gareth raised his eyebrows. This was a stunning admission from a man who rarely acknowledged his mistakes. For a moment Gareth wondered whether the former leader of the Boxer Boys was beginning to crack up.

'He always had it in for me, but I can just imagine how I might feel if I found out my younger brother had a different dad,' Arnie said, letting his gaze drift to Bruce, who was chatting with the barman. 'Chuck was always No.1 son, loyal to Big Mo, and I can understand that. He dedicated himself to protecting the old traditions Big Mo and his mob led their lives by, and one of those was that if your father asks you to do something, you do it without question. He's his father's son, all right.'

Gareth let the irony pass.

'There's no point in being too hard on yourself, Arnie,' he said. 'Chuck was a bastard to us both.'

'I know, but the Dolans have been through enough, especially Mum,' said Arnie. 'Big Mo's dying and when that old bastard goes we can all finally move on. How do you think Mum would feel if she knew two of her sons were out to destroy each other? It would kill her.'

Gareth wondered what was going on inside that complex mind. He was about to leave Arnie to his own devices when the man in the wheelchair rediscovered his train of thought.

'She wanted to come to the funeral, you know.'

Gareth frowned.

'Your mum?'

'Yeah. I think she loved Stan more than anyone … even Big Mo. I guess I'll never know the full story, but I suppose she turned to him when Mo was in and out of jail. She needed someone reliable rather than a man who always let her down.'

Reliable. It was the last label Gareth would give his father. Paedophile, pervert, sex addict, lousy, cheating, untrustworthy… all of those would have been a better choice, not that he had used them in the eulogy.

'Big Mo used to hit Mum, you know,' said Arnie. 'If Stan gave her respite from that, then for that reason alone I'm grateful to him.'

Gareth preferred to keep his own counsel, fearing that if he joined in the conversation, he might reveal too much. What were the merits of popping Arnie's bubble when he was at last discovering his human side? Let him keep that vision of his father. Try to warp it and Arnie would be freefalling towards self-destruction again.

'So, what's happened with Chuck?' he asked.

'He spent some time in hospital, no surprise, and he's back at home with Mum now,' said Arnie. 'He could have gone to his own place, but she insisted. She doesn't know what happened, of course, just assumes he was another victim of gang warfare. Of course, it's a war that never existed… as you discovered in that warehouse.'

'It can't be over yet, though,' said Gareth. 'Chuck isn't going to let sleeping dogs lie.'

'True,' said Arnie. 'Except, I think I've figured out a way we can come to an agreement without any more blood being spilt.'

'Oh? You gonna make him an offer he can't refuse?'

Gareth smirked at his use of the phrase from the Mafia film *The Godfather*. He watched as the dimples showed on Arnie's face, a smile playing on his lips.

'You could say that,' he agreed. 'I've had a word with Durak.'

'That Turkish mobster bloke?'

'Yeah,' said Arnie. 'You have to understand, he was the starting point for me, the bloke who took the Boxer Boys to a higher level. He supported me through prison and was right behind me when I was released. When Vickers and Chuck decided they were going to take over just like that, I reached out to him for help. He said he trusted me and thought if they could do that to me, what would be stopping them from screwing him over, too. He was unhappy he hadn't been told about the new arrangements.'

Arnie took a sip of his pint. 'He visited me in Devon and when he heard Chuck had paid someone to drug me he decided it was time to shake them up. He snatched those dealers off the street and ordered the firebombing of the Hope. He also helped me kidnap Chuck,' he explained, letting the facts sink in.

Arnie sprang forwards, remembering something. 'The two bodies they couldn't identify – the ones found in Rainham Marshes – they weren't Tigger's men, you know. They were fresh corpses from a local cemetery, fingerprints and teeth removed so they couldn't be identified. Mr Durak had the real dealers transferred to Glasgow, where he also has interests. He gave them money and somewhere to stay, then set them to work. They were under strict instructions not to tell a soul where they were – including their families. If they did—'

He drew a finger sharply across his throat.

'Good to know,' said Gareth. 'I guess they were scumbags – selling drugs to kids – but no one deserves to be chopped up and left in marshlands.'

'I spoke to Mr Durak after the warehouse business with Chuck,' said Arnie, continuing his tale. 'I told him I wanted out of the game and that he could do far worse than make Chuck and Vickers his permanent business partners. He thought that boat had sailed, but I persuaded him. It was still too raw for me to approach Chuck directly, so I went to Sly and discussed the deal. I told him that provided he, Chuck and the rest of the gang let me get on with my life then I wouldn't interfere with their business. I said it was all cleared with Durak and the supply line would continue. I asked him to tell Chuck there were no hard feelings. It's business after all… right?'

Gareth shrugged his shoulders. He had never been involved in that sort of business and never would be.

Arnie looked at his phone. 'Shit! We gotta be somewhere,' he announced. 'I need you and Anj to come and meet someone. I've booked a table in an Indian restaurant down the road.'

'Oh, I don't know, Arnie,' said Gareth. 'It's been a long day.'

'Sure,' said Arnie. 'But I need Anjie back in my life, mate. She's flesh and blood, y'know? Until now, she's always been there for me.'

He peered out of the window for a moment before snapping back to reality. 'Truth is, I've got a girl as well now and I'm serious about her. I want you and Anj to meet her.'

AFTER a few moments of persuasion from Gareth, Anjie agreed to her brother's request. Despite the rift between them, Anjie couldn't help being curious about any woman who had stolen her brother's heart. As they studied the menu, Arnie wheeled around and headed back towards the entrance. Neither of them could re-member him being so nervous.

'Must be someone special,' said Anjie.

'I think she's a miracle worker,' said Gareth.

'How so?'

'He's talking about giving up the gang stuff and all his dodgy escapades… and it's down to her, apparently.'

'Could be just another fad?'

'I guess. There's been something different about him, though, ever since the police discharged him from being a suspect for Dad's murder.'

'Hmm,' she said. 'I don't suppose it looked too good for him. So what happened?'

'They put him in a cell all day, sweated him and tried to extract a confession. They were convinced they had their man and just needed someone to come forward and place him at the scene. Instead, Arnie produced a mystery witness from nowhere who was able to prove categorically he'd been somewhere else at the time the murder took place.'

'And who—?'

Her words were cut short as Arnie returned to the table.

'Ladies and gentleman,' her brother said, a wide smile on his face. 'I'd like to introduce you to Miss Abigail Winstone.'

As he moved aside, a beautiful woman stepped into their line of vision. Her hair was in tight ringlets and cascaded down the side of a beaming black face.

'Lovely to meet you all,' said the care assistant. 'I can see you're a bit shocked. Please don't be. Arnold here is planning to revive the slave trade and has chosen me as his first recruit. One of my jobs was to wipe his arse in rehab.'

There was a stunned silence.

Then Arnie produced a sound Gareth and Anjie had heard only on rare occasions. It began as a chuckle and turned into a full-blooded, throaty roar. The girl stood with her hands on his shoulders, her booming laugh echoing through the restaurant, prompting the other guests to turn, searching for the cause of the disruption.

'That's what I love about this woman,' said Arnie, reaching his arm out and wrapping it around her waist. 'She doesn't stand on ceremony. If she's got something to say, she f'ing well says it.'

Still wondering whether it was an elaborate joke at her expense, Anjie got slowly to her feet and leaned across the table, giving the woman a peck on the cheek.

'Nice to meet anyone capable of taming my brother,' she said.

Gareth, unsure what to do next, held out his hand for Arnie to shake. Whatever he thought about the man, he couldn't doubt Arnie Dolan's ability to shock. In almost a lifetime together, though, this development trumped all others. Arnie had never hidden his racist views from anyone. It was almost as if aliens had abducted the real Arnold Dolan and left this imposter in his place.

'I didn't tell you at the time, Gareth, but Abigail and I had a wonderful evening up in Stoke-on-Trent. She was doing a nursing course at one of the local colleges and we spent the night at a hotel near Trentham Gardens. It took some persuasion for the filth to believe me, but Abigail turned up at the cop shop with all the receipts and after a quick check with the hotel staff they had to let me go. After all, it was hard for them to confuse me with anyone else thanks to the Bader-bus, wasn't it? You should have seen that Detective Chief Inspector Rowbottom's face, mate! He wasn't happy.'

The story was told in a light-hearted, warm manner which was completely out of character for Arnie. Gareth loved it. If this was the new version of Arnie Dolan, it was going to take a hell of a long time to get used to his reformed brother.

Gareth thought it just might be worth the effort.

THE END

About the Author

NICK RIPPINGTON is the award-winning author of gritty UK gangland thrillers. His debut novel Crossing The Whitewash received an honourable mention in the 2016 Writers' Digest eBook awards with judges describing it as "Evocative, unique, unfailingly precise and often humorous". The second novel in the Boxer Boys series, Spark Out, is a prequel which won a Chill With A Book award with readers describing it as a "Fantastic Read", "Compelling" and with an "unexpected twist". A former Welsh Sports Editor of the News of the World, Nick started writing the series after being made redundant with two days notice after Rupert Murdoch closed down Europe's biggest-selling tabloid six years ago. He lives in London with wife Liz and has two children – Jemma and Olivia.

Read more at www.theripperfile.com
Other Books by Nick Rippington:
Crossing The Whitewash
Spark Out

www.ingramcontent.com/pod-product-compliance
Lightning Source LLC
Chambersburg PA
CBHW051113120726
47905CB00005B/1256